Also by Haley Harrigan:

Secrets of Southern Girls

HER YOUNGER SELF

HALEY HARRIGAN

Silver Wren BOOKS

For the good girls who grew up and rebelled, trading expectation for authenticity and seizing control of their own damned smiles.

PART ONE

CHAPTER 1

T his bathtub could swallow her whole.

Claudia is steeped in bubbles and hot water, trying—and failing—to relax. An unopened paperback sits on the floor next to the tub, some spicy romance she's been struggling to get through. She considers picking it up, her fingers wet against the spine, and skipping to the good parts. It's not like she has to worry about Beau walking in on her. He's probably sprawled out on the sofa in the living room, scrolling through photos of anonymous bikini-clad women on one of those apps that market to "nice guys" by tossing in a few jokes, dog pics, and inspirational stories to break up all that flesh.

She gets it. Really, she does. Sometimes it's easier to take care of things on your own.

It's hard to believe now, but there was a time when Beau used to sit on the linoleum floor of the bathroom in their first rental house and talk to her while she soaked in the tub. He would pick up the book she was reading (it wasn't always steamy romance—but sometimes it *was*) and read aloud from it, or he'd bring in magazines and read articles he thought she would like. It was calming to have him there with her, freshly showered and leaning against the bathroom cabinet in his worn sweatpants with no shirt on, the curls of his auburn hair still damp against his forehead and his silver-rimmed glasses perched on his nose. It was all new then, their marriage. This life. Claudia would sit back in the tiny bathtub and watch his mouth as he read. *I married him*, she would think to herself. *I am a wife.* It was what she'd wanted. And still it felt surreal, like she'd stumbled into someone else's narrative.

Beau doesn't read to her these days, though Claudia can't remember when it stopped. Now he looks forward to her nightly bathtime ritual for a different reason; he knows it's time he'll have to himself, away from her. Sometimes late in the evenings, when they've been sharing the same space for too long, he'll look at her and ask *isn't it time for your bath?*

A burst of sound in the small room makes her jump. Her phone's ringtone is turned up too loud. Water splashes over the sides of the soaker tub and onto the cover of the book as the phone dances around on the ceramic tile, chiming and vibrating and begging for attention. A photo of Graham, her assistant, flashes onto her screen. She sighs. It's Sunday night. She's been trying to avoid work business on weekends, but Graham and Liza both know that. So if one of them is calling, it had better be important. Claudia reaches for the towel on the floor and attempts to wipe the suds from her hands. Her fingers are moist and wrinkled when she reaches for the phone, and it almost slips from her grasp.

"Hey," she says, after a clumsy recovery.

"Hey Claudia. Listen, I think you need to get over to the property. Like, nowish."

Graham is naturally dramatic, so she doesn't automatically react. Things happen all the time. A few months ago, a drunk college kid kicked an elevator door off track, which put the elevator out of service entirely. Thankfully there are three elevators in the building or Claudia never would have heard the end of it from the other residents. At a luxury apartment community built exclusively for college students, this kind of thing isn't exactly uncommon.

"Hello to you too. What's going on?" *I will not get stressed about this, I will not get stressed about this.* She repeats the mantra in her head, over and over. She takes her job too seriously. It's entirely possible for her to get worked up over the smallest details, but she's trying to do better. The whole "no work business on weekends" thing is part of that. Beau says he can look at her and see that her mind is still at The Prestige at Ellen Point, even when she's at home sitting next to him. Not that he has any room to talk. When he's at home, Beau keeps his phone practically glued to his hand. He may save the risqué photos for private moments, but he'll answer work emails, check sports scores, and read news articles right in the middle of dinner.

"Graham, what's up?" she asks again. She tries not to sound as impatient as she feels.

"I don't know. I think...I think someone *died*."

"Wait, what?"

"There are cops here, and an ambulance outside. I came home early from a concert and ended up on the elevator with the police. They were talking to each other about calling the coroner. I asked what was going on, but they wouldn't say. They looked at me like I was mining for gossip or something."

"Someone died?" Claudia is frozen in the sweltering bath water, fixated on the faucet, shiny and silver. She and Beau have talked about a bathroom remodel, but they've yet to actually do it. Beau is very handy, when he's working on other people's houses.

Graham is talking, but it's not sinking in. Someone in the building she manages is dead.

"Who?" she interrupts. "Do you know who?"

"No. But...the cops got off on the sixth floor."

"I'm on my way," Claudia says. "Give me ten minutes."

She drops the phone against the tile and grabs her towel from its plush heap on the floor. The drain makes a slow swooshing sound as water circles down and when she opens the bathroom door, steam billows out into the bedroom, hovers, disperses into nothing. She pulls open three dresser drawers before finding a pair of wadded-up blue jeans. She thought she'd be putting on pajamas next, crawling into bed with her book. Instead, she's struggling into jeans, pulling on one of Beau's Ellen Point University long-sleeved t-shirts, and sliding her feet into tennis shoes so she can drive over to The Prestige.

She rushes out of the bedroom and down the hallway to find Beau lounging on the sofa.

"I'm leaving," she says quickly, grabbing her purse from a hook by the door. "Work. Someone...died. I've got to go."

Beau's eyes jump up from the phone. "Wait, what?"

She's already halfway out the front door. "Graham called. He thinks someone died in the building. I've got to go."

"Shit," Beau says, sitting up. "I'll come with you. Just let me get some shoes on."

"No, it's fine." It's not, but she can't wait. "I'll be fine. I've got to go." And then she leaves before he can argue.

"Claudia!" He calls out as she's closing the door, but she doesn't turn back.

She can't worry about her preoccupied husband right now. She's got to go find out which of her residents is dead.

CHAPTER 2

S he should have waited for Beau. He knows how much she cares about these residents, and he'll be worried sick about her. It was stupid rushing out like that, and now her foot is trembling and it's difficult to keep it steady on the gas pedal as she turns onto the steep lane that leads to The Prestige. She's in no shape to drive.

Claudia thinks of the students who live on the sixth floor. She knows them all, and some of them she's friendly with. She thinks of Lily, the sweet law student with long dark hair and the addiction to reality TV. And DJ, the philosophy grad student who can't keep his apartment tidy. Claudia schedules his cleaning service every week. She thinks of Amy and Carlos, the only married students in the building. They eloped as juniors, and even though Amy's parents pointedly DO NOT APPROVE, they still foot the bill for the rent. *I won't have my daughter living in squalor because she rushed into marriage,* Amy's father told Claudia over the phone before they moved in. She thinks of Taylor, the undergrad English student who cried at Claudia's desk last week because her mother signed her up for a weight-loss meal subscription service without telling her. She found out she was "changing her eating habits" when the first box of food arrived in the mail.

There are others too. So many. Their faces flash through Claudia's mind.

Please don't let it be Lily, she finds herself hoping. *Please not Carlos, not Amy.* She's not willing to part with any of them, not like this. Usually her residents leave the building when they graduate, from undergrad or grad school (or law school or med school) and then they move on and become successful adults in some other city—Atlanta or Knoxville or Chattanooga, or farther away sometimes. New York or L.A, even Europe. Nothing is out of reach for these kids.

She can't help it; she starts to barter in her mind. If she *had* to choose, she would sacrifice DJ over Lily. Lily over Amy or Carlos. Taylor over Lily. She's a terrible person, thinking like this, trying to determine whose life is more valuable. Like it's even up to her.

It occurs to her (and she should have thought of it sooner) that the person who died could be a guest, and not a resident of the building at all. She clings to this selfish hope. *Let it be someone else entirely.*

Claudia should have accepted the offer from Margo, her boss at the corporate office, to live on-site at The Prestige at a discounted rate. Then she would *be* there already. But she'd wanted more privacy, and then Beau had come along and there was no way he would have given up their little slice of Southern mountain suburbia for a building made for college students. Residents would have been knocking on her door at all hours of the night, and the whole "no work business on weekends" idea would have been shot all to hell. It wouldn't have been a smart move, not really. And she only lives ten minutes away, if anything should happen.

But something *is* happening, and ten minutes away is too far.

The Prestige at Ellen Point is a sparkling gem in the small but prestigious college town nestled in the foothills of the Blue Ridge Mountains. The building is tall and elegant, with warm light from the oversized sconces bathing the sidewalk. It's the only place like it in town and it's where everyone wants to live, though not everyone can afford it. It wouldn't even occur to you to think that someone might be dead inside right now, if not for the three police cars parked at the curb. Claudia remembers Graham mentioning an ambulance, but she doesn't see one. This gives her hope; maybe the resident (or guest) isn't dead at all, just injured or ill and the ambulance has taken that person away to the hospital to be put back together somehow.

She fumbles with her garage remote, presses it, waits four hundred years for the ornate iron gate to slide open. Finally she pulls through, circling the levels until she pulls into her reserved space. She steps onto the nearest elevator and it takes her to the main lobby, where Graham is pacing back and forth. The night security guard is behind the lobby desk. "Ma'am," he says, nodding his head. "I would've called, but Graham here beat me to it."

"They tell you anything?" she asks him.

"Only that they were headed up to the sixth floor." She doesn't know why she bothered asking. The guard doesn't exactly run a tight ship; he's a happy, bumbling guy, there more for show than staunch security detail. Last weekend, a troublemaking resident riding an electric skateboard had stolen a NO PARKING sign and led the guard through the parking garage on the world's slowest foot chase.

Claudia's best friends, Ingrid and Ruby, had laughed so hard when she'd relayed the story during their weekly coffee date that Ruby spit her matcha latte across the table.

The resident made off with the sign, though the security camera footage later implicated him in the heist. It doesn't surprise Claudia one bit that the real police didn't brief the guard on this situation.

"It looks like they went to 607," Graham says.

Claudia's stomach sinks. Paxton Gale. She hadn't thought to bargain for him. As if that's a thing that matters.

"I'm going up," she says.

Graham nods. "I'll come too."

9

Claudia grabs a handful of her business cards from an artfully arranged table near the elevator. With her messy hair and wrinkled clothes, it may take some convincing to prove that she's the person in charge here. Graham is dressed casually too, but more presentable than she is in a pair of relaxed khakis and a white t-shirt with a logo for an indie band Claudia has never heard of. They step into the elevator together, and he clasps and unclasps his hands as they ride up, his smart watch illuminated on his wrist. He's obviously nervous. She forgets, sometimes, how young he is, only twenty-three, in a graduate program for Real Estate Management. One day he'll have her job, or a job *like* hers but better. His brown eyes are on her, and it occurs to her that she should probably say something to show him she has the situation under control. Something comforting, at least. But all she can do is stare at the closed stainless steel elevator doors and think about what's going to happen when they open.

She wants someone to comfort *her*.

"Floor. Six," the automated female elevator voice says, and they step out into the sixth-floor hallway with its fancy chandeliers and hotel-style carpet. The walls are painted light, inoffensive gray, and in between each apartment door is an ornate faux column, Greek in architectural style and protruding from the wall. It's meant to make every apartment feel like it has its own private entryway. Silver-framed black-and-white photos line the walls between the columns, not of the town of Ellen Point but of exotic locales, beaches and snowcapped Swiss peaks and Parisian cafes. The Prestige at EP isn't selling "local"; it's selling grandeur, adventure, luxury.

Two policemen stand in the hallway talking quietly with two crying young women. Across from them, a thick strand of yellow "Caution" tape blocks the doorway to apartment 607. Claudia recognizes one of the women as Amberly Vance, who lives on the eighth floor. The other young woman doesn't live here in the building, but Claudia recalls seeing her around the property with Amberly. A shaggy golden puppy lies at their feet, bored with the whole thing. The puppy belongs to Paxton Gale. Paxton, who Claudia doesn't see anywhere. Paxton, Amberly's sometimes-boyfriend. Amberly's face is tear-streaked and red. Her friend stares down at the floor.

A third policeman steps out of Paxton's apartment, removing and then reattaching the tape. "Excuse me," Claudia says. "I'm the manager of the building." When he looks skeptical, she holds out her business card. The officer takes it, inspects it like there's more there than her name and title. "I'm Claudia Aldridge. Can you tell me what's going on?"

He finally shrugs. "Well, the kid is deceased."

She'd known to expect it, but hearing it aloud is still a shock. She'd been clinging to some small hope that there was a different explanation, some non-fatal event: a fight or an accident or literally *anything* else. Her chest feels tight, suddenly. "Kid?" she asks. "Do you mean Paxton Gale?"

The cop motions back to the door of unit 607. "Is that the occupant of this apartment?"

She nods. He hasn't even bothered to commit Paxton's name to memory.

"Paxton Gale," she repeats. She thinks again of how she hadn't mentally bargained for him. That's not the reason he's dead. "What happened?" Explanations pop into her head at random as she rubs her hand against her collarbones. It's probably alcohol-related (in a college town, when young people die, alcohol is usually involved). Or a terrible accident, or something unfair but natural.

"Suicide," the cop—Officer Stewart, according to his name tag, though he hasn't introduced himself—says, in his matter-of-fact manner. He seems completely unaffected by the word, though it nearly knocks Claudia off her feet. It should have been her first guess.

"How?" Claudia asks. She draws a deep breath, even though it feels like there isn't enough room for it in her lungs. "I mean, can you share that information?"

"Asphyxiation." She doesn't know what that means, but she doesn't push for more details.

"How do you know it was suicide?" she asks instead. "Are you sure? Could it have been something else?"

Officer Stewart shakes his head. "Trust me. We're sure. If you saw it, you'd understand. He even left letters for his loved ones. There's nothing else it could be, ma'am."

"Oh," she says. "Oh."

There are goodbye notes, somewhere.

"How well did you know him?"

"I know all of my residents," she says automatically, but as she says it she realizes she doesn't know Paxton as well as most of the others. Not even as well as she knows Amberly. She thinks of him, his dark hair and ripped jeans. That beat-up black leather jacket. He wasn't usually in the mood to chat when he ambled through the lobby, though he'd sheepishly stopped in on two previous occasions shortly after he moved in to request that maintenance unlock his door because he'd locked himself out.

One of the cops waves a hand to Officer Stewart. "Excuse me," he says, and steps over to the young women and the other officers.

Claudia stands there, useless, staring at Paxton's door while Graham does his best to eavesdrop on the conversation happening down the hall. The door to the apartment isn't closed all the way; light sneaks out where it's cracked open. Graham doesn't notice when Claudia steps toward the door, places her hand against it, pushes. No one sees her duck beneath the "Caution" tape and slip inside.

Paxton's apartment smells vaguely of cigar smoke, a scent that reminds Claudia of her stepfather and the expensive cigars he enjoys after dinner. The entry table is stacked with junk mail, dog treats, car keys, but it's the letters she's looking for. She doesn't touch anything, but she doesn't leave either, even though she knows she should. Surely they've moved Paxton by now. An ambulance was here and now it's not, so they must have taken him.

Or not.

Definitely not.

She should go, she knows she shouldn't be here, but she's frozen in Paxton's living room. She sees one bare foot, then another. Blue jeans. No shirt. She steps back, but her eyes betray her and take in the scene before she can stop them. He's right there, suspended from what looks like a leather belt. He's facing away from her (small mercies) and though she's never seen someone hanging from a light fixture before, the whole scene feels familiar and there's nothing around *her* neck but it still feels like she can't breathe.

"Claudia!" Graham calls from the door to the apartment, but he doesn't come inside. Smart. It's Officer Stewart who comes barreling through the door and down the hallway. "Miss, you shouldn't be in here." Miss, even though she's wearing her wedding rings. How did women end up with these titles that are less about them and more about their relation to others? She's never considered the indignity of it before. Officer Stewart takes her arm, and she allows him to steer her out of the apartment. "He's here," she stammers. "I didn't know he'd still be here." It's her own fault she saw him. She wanted to know. Wanted to know what he did to himself, and wanted to know what he wrote in those letters he left behind.

For one deranged instant, she thinks of how lucky his loved ones are to have some kind of explanation. Even if it's flimsy, even if it's senseless.

Killian hadn't left any notes. Not for Claudia, not for anybody. When he was gone, it was like he'd never existed at all.

CHAPTER 3

"**O**h my God," Graham says. "You went in there. Why did you go in there? Are you okay? What did you see?"

On a different day, Claudia would have laughed at his rapid-fire questions. Now she just stares.

"Claudia?"

"You don't want to know," she says, finally.

"Do you need to leave?" he asks. "Sit down or something, at least. Let's find you somewhere to sit." The sleeves of Beau's t-shirt are pushed up around her elbows and she feels Graham's hand against her arm. She'd never admit it to anyone, but there are days, days that aren't today, when Graham passes her a file or does any number of perfectly professional things that require their hands to meet and a little thrill passes through her. Times when the contact seems intentional, harmlessly flirtatious. There are only eight years between them, after all.

Claudia's ravenous yearning for touch can be traced directly back to Killian. He was the one who taught her (without even meaning to) that the *right* touch could narrow the world down to its smallest and most perfect essence. It could be as intimate as a lover's caress or as mundane as a handshake. Claudia and her husband go days, now, without intentionally touching one another, and sometimes she tells herself she doesn't even need to be connected that way. But the lie of it is right there, in her craving.

Paxton Gale won't feel casual handshakes or soft caresses anymore. He won't feel anything at all.

"No, I'm okay." Funny how people just *say* that sometimes.

The cops seem mostly unconcerned that she's walked in on an active crime scene. If that's what this is considered.

"Ma'am." An officer she hasn't met yet approaches.

"Yes?"

"Stewart says you're the manager here. Is there somewhere we could go to finish talking with these young ladies? Somewhere that's not so out in the open?"

Claudia nods. The lobby won't be private enough. "The lounge," she suggests instead. "Twelfth floor. It's labeled." It's hard to miss. The lavish resident lounge and rooftop pool take up the entire top level of the building. Claudia went to college in an artsy city in Texas, and back then the height of luxury was a block of four-bedroom flats with shared bathrooms and laminate countertops. She'd visited classmates there on occasion. Her own place had been even less impressive, a run-down duplex with thirty-year-old shag carpet and a landlord who refused to replace it. But sure, give *these* kid/adult hybrids an infinity pool and hardwood floors. They don't even know how different it could be. "Were they..." she gestures toward Amberly and her friend. "Were they involved somehow, Officer..." she looks to his name tag, "Grundy?"

"*Sergeant* Grundy," he corrects her. "The deceased's girlfriend is the one who called us. "He wasn't answering his phone. She found a spare key under his mat and let herself in." Claudia would bet anything that Paxton had started keeping the spare hidden for himself, after the previous lockouts.

So Amberly saw it too. Poor girl.

"The coroner should be here soon. Could you show him a good place to park, you know, where he can get on and off an elevator easily?"

Claudia nods. The pressure in her chest won't ease up.

She presses the button to call the nearest elevator, and the doors open without making her wait. Graham steps in behind her.

"I'm meeting the coroner," she says. It's so clean and shiny in here that she can see her reflection in the stainless steel and glass.

"I know."

The elevator takes them to the lobby, and the security guard looks up from behind the desk.

"Paxton Gale," Claudia says. "I don't know if you knew him."

"No ma'am."

There's a knock on the glass of the lobby door, and she looks up to see another man in uniform. He could be a cop too, except the name tag looks different. His smile feels inappropriate for the circumstances.

"Hi," Claudia says as she opens the door. "I'm Claudia Aldridge, the Property Manager." She holds out her hand and he shakes it. Too late, she realizes she doesn't want to be shaking the coroner's hand. She thinks about where he'll be putting his hands next, with part of her essence still right there in his palm.

"Buddy Pritchard," he says, pointing to his name tag. "County Coroner. So, where's our guy, and what's the best way to get him out?"

She stares at him until Graham elbows her gently. "He's on the sixth floor. And taking the elevator to the parking garage would be best for um, getting him out of the building. Right, Claudia?"

"Right." Logistics.

"Okey dokey. Where should I pull the van?"

"To the bottom level of the parking garage," she says. She reaches in her pocket and pulls out her own garage remote. "Use this. If you want to drive the van around, I'll meet you down there."

"I can't believe this is happening," Graham says, on their way down to the parking garage. His hands are stuffed into his pockets now. His dark hair, normally tamed with product and styled into a low ponytail or a manbun, is loose around his shoulders and tousled like he's been running his hands through it. Graham is friendlier with the residents than she is; he gets the *real* versions of them. When Claudia sees the college girls and boys in the lobby during the week, they're shiny and clean with fresh smiles and mostly-innocent faces. Her imagination isn't colorful enough, anymore, to guess at their late-night adventures. Graham is the one who gives her the details.

She holds open the elevator door while the coroner unloads his supplies from the van. She and Graham both step back to allow room for the stretcher.

"Nice place," Buddy Pritchard says. Claudia doesn't respond.

They come to an unexpected stop on the third-floor parking garage level. When the doors open, Lily the law student stands on the other side. She starts to smile, but then she sees the stretcher.

"I...uh, I'll grab the next one," Lily says finally, and Claudia nods.

On the sixth floor the coroner exits the elevator, stretcher in tow. Sergeant Grundy and Officer Stewart are gone, presumably upstairs with the young women, but the coroner stops to chat with the remaining officer, the only one Claudia has yet to meet. The two of them shake hands, share a laugh.

"Is there anything else I can do here?" Claudia interrupts. She can't take it, watching them laugh like this, like it's just another evening, like there's not a real person in that apartment.

The officer shakes his head. He's young, probably not much older than Paxton Gale. "It's a closed investigation," he says. "We'll finish up here tonight."

"Just like that?"

"Just like that."

"Do you have contact information already? For his family?"

"Yes, ma'am. Got it from the vehicle registration. We're already making contact."

She hears the creak of a door opening, and a young couple steps out of an apartment down the hall. Janie and Paul. Janie catches sight of Claudia with the cop and practically runs over. She's too nosy not to ask questions.

"What's going on, y'all?" Janie's loud whisper echoes in the hallway. Graham and Claudia create a barricade with their bodies between the couple and the police officer; Claudia steers them back toward Janie's apartment despite Janie's best efforts to take it all in. Claudia's instinct is to tell her it's none of her damned business. It's not. But Janie's father is an overprotective millionaire hotel owner in Louisiana. If Claudia doesn't handle this right, she'll be hearing from him about this incident. He'll be jumping to conclusions about his daughter's safety, or lack thereof.

"It's bad," Claudia admits. She realizes it's the wrong thing to say when Janie's eyes widen. She's scared her. Great. "Something happened to a resident. Nothing you should be personally concerned about," Claudia stresses, "but you really should go back inside, so the police can do their jobs. If you'll excuse me, I need to..." Get out of here, is what she's thinking. She doesn't want to be here when the coroner rolls out that body, and she doesn't want Janie to be here either.

"Okay...but I actually think I have a package? In the mail room? Since you're here now and all, could you get that for me, maybe?" There's a secure mail room in the lobby, where resident packages are locked away at the end of the day. Janie looks at Claudia expectantly, as if she genuinely thinks Claudia will stop in the midst of a serious afterhours issue to go retrieve Janie's monthly makeup subscription box.

Claudia stares at her in disbelief.

"It's...not a good time," Graham finally says. "We'll be happy to get it for you tomorrow." Graham is more polite than Claudia. Then again, he hasn't just walked in on a dead body.

Janie looks, for a moment, like she wants to press, but then Paul interrupts. "That's cool, right Janie? We'll uh, we'll see you guys later." Finally, Janie shrugs and follows him back to her apartment. The nerve of these kids. Claudia presses the button for the elevator.

"I'm going to the lounge," she says to Graham. "Check on Amberly, and her friend. Do you know her, the other girl?" Graham shakes his head and follows after her again, much to her irritation. It's like he thinks she knows what she's doing.

"Are you okay, really?" he asks her. "What you saw..."

"Does Liza know what's going on?" Claudia asks, ignoring his question. Liza is the new part-time leasing consultant, an undergrad who doesn't live in the building yet. There's a six-month trial period, and Liza has a few more months to go.

"No," Graham says. "I didn't call her. I didn't know if you'd want me to."

"Yeah, it's a lot. I'll tell her in person." She rests a hand against the cool metal of the elevator, turning her head away from Graham so he doesn't see the way she gasps for air.

On the twelfth floor, Claudia pushes open the ornate wood and glass lounge doors.

The young women are sitting alone at one of the dark wooden tables, the police officers nowhere to be seen. Amberly and her friend look up at the sound of the door opening. Red eyes, splotchy faces, the puppy on a leash at their feet. Dogs aren't allowed in the lounge, but Claudia doesn't mention it. She wants to help these women somehow—it's what she came up here to do—but now she feels like an intruder, interrupting their grief. Still, she's in charge of this building. She can't leave without speaking to them.

"Hi. I'm so sorry to bother you." Amberly's eyes are like glass, shiny and green. She doesn't speak, so Claudia turns to the girl beside her. "I'm Claudia, the manager here. I...I mean, can I get you anything? Some water? Can I call someone for y'all?"

"Water would be nice," she mumbles. Claudia nods, and Graham retrieves two bottles of water from the stocked drink fridge.

"I don't think we've met," Claudia says to Amberly's friend. "What's your name?"

Amberly answers for her. "This is Lou."

"Mary Louise," the girl says, with a sniffle. Ah, a Mary. There are dozens of them around here. When Ellen Point sorority girls grow up and have Southern baby girls of their own, they grant those girls double names that begin with *Mary*. Mary Christine, Mary Claire, Mary James. It's a charm, an offering made to some ambiguous higher being (Virgin Mary or otherwise) in exchange for the promise that those girls will follow in their mama's footsteps. Have the same good fortune. Claudia would bet money that Lou's mother is an Ellen Point grad.

Nice to meet you, is what Claudia would normally say, but it's not right for this situation. "Hi," she says instead. Lou nods.

"Were you and Paxton together for a while?" Claudia asks Amberly, even though she knows the answer. According to Graham, Paxton and Amberly have been on and off since they met at a resident party at the beginning of the summer. The puppy wanders away and lifts his leg on one corner of the pool table. No one but Claudia seems to notice.

"A few months. But, we loved each other." Amberly rubs her face, pushes her blond hair behind her ears.

"Did you know, then?" Claudia blurts, and Amberly looks confused by the question.

"Know what? That he loved me? Of course I knew."

But that's not what Claudia means. She wants to know if Paxton told Amberly about the doubt and darkness creeping in. Did Amberly write it off as part of his personality, the way Claudia had with Killian? Did Amberly even know Paxton well enough to see this coming? Does she see it now, everything unwinding, inevitably, to this point? To this exact fatal moment, where the person she cared about is dead.

Graham sets the water bottles, weeping condensation, on the table in front of them.

"I'm sorry," Claudia says, finally. "I'm so sorry for your loss. If you think of anything I can do to help, please let me know." She passes them each a business card, and then she gets the hell out of there.

CHAPTER 4

Claudia has had enough of these elevators for one night. She feels off-balance, like she might tilt right over. She and Graham ride back down to the lobby, and the whole time she prays the elevator doesn't stop on the sixth floor, that they don't find themselves stuck with the coroner again, this time with Paxton's body in tow.

Mercifully, they make it to their destination without any stops. The gas fireplace in the empty lobby creates a warm ambiance at odds with how she feels. The security guard is away from the desk, likely off making his rounds.

"There's nothing else we can do here," Claudia says. "You should go. Get up to your apartment. Thank you...for letting me know this was happening. For everything."

"Yeah, of course. You sure you're good?" She nods, but he seems reluctant to leave her there. Finally, he presses the elevator button. "Okay. Well, goodnight, then," he says, as he steps inside. She hopes he goes straight home to his apartment, locks the doors, insulates himself against anything else he could possibly see tonight.

Claudia sinks into one of the leather armchairs, gripping the arms and taking measured breaths to calm herself. She looks around the fancy lobby, the marble tile floor covered with sumptuous patterned rugs, the soft leather chairs with dark wooden side tables, the huge fireplace that's the feature of one wall. A flat-screen TV hangs above it. The gas fireplace lacks the smell of a real fire, but the fragrance of summer mountain air and smoldering logs fills the space nonetheless, thank to the scented wall plug-in hidden in a corner.

She wonders if suicide makes the local news these days, if she should expect a write-up in tomorrow's paper about a death at The Prestige at EP. She hopes not. When Killian died, mentioning suicide was taboo, unless you were troubled and famous. His parents never even admitted he died that way. According to them, he had an undiagnosed heart condition.

But that was a lie. Claudia should know.

Killian's parents cleared out his apartment a few days after the funeral, and aside from the pictures Claudia had of the two of them, there was hardly anything left of him at all. Not for her.

But maybe things aren't like that now. It's been years.

Claudia had abandoned her phone on the lobby desk, and she sees that she's got four missed calls and seven text messages from Beau.

> Did you make it safely?

> Who was it?

> What happened?

> What's going on there?

> Are you okay?

> Check in with me please.

> Claudia, seriously.

She puts her phone in her pocket and heads to the parking garage. She has to force herself to go. Her residents don't need her, but she feels like she should stay close just in case. In case of what? She shakes her head.

Once she's in the car, she sends Beau a message.

> I'm okay. On my way home. I'll see you soon.

The sky is dark and foggy, and downtown Ellen Point is quiet on a Sunday night, recovering from the weekend like so many of the Ellen Point University students. The parties are always the biggest at the start of the school year. The mountains loom like shadows over the town.

Her house is exactly the way she left it, which is comforting and also not.

"Claudia." Beau rushes to her the second she's through the door, wrapping his arms around her, drawing her close. Here's the intimacy she's been craving. "Jesus, please never leave here like that again. Are you okay?"

She nods. "His name is Paxton Gale."

"Was he...?"

"Dead. Yes. Suicide." She doesn't tell him about *seeing* Paxton. She can't get out the words to describe what she saw.

Beau shakes his head, pulls her even closer. "How terrible. What can I do? What can I get you?"

"Nothing. Thank you." She feels guilty now for her earlier thoughts, for the way she'd felt bitter towards Beau only hours ago for nothing at all. He's a good man, and he's here for her when it counts.

She opens the refrigerator door for a bottle of water, and when she does, a piece of paper flutters free from a magnet and sails to the floor. It's an invitation, the paper creamy and embossed with silver, to the upcoming engagement party for Ingrid Wyatt, one of Claudia's closest friends. Ingrid is President of Wyatt McIntyre Birch Real Estate Group, the largest commercial and residential real estate and development company in the region. She's also Beau's boss. Claudia picks up the invitation and tucks it back under the magnet. She imagines how Ingrid would have handled the situation tonight. Ingrid is more comfortable in a position of power than Claudia has ever been, but then again, Ingrid has had far more practice. It's late, but she pulls her phone from her jeans pocket and sends a group text to Ingrid and Ruby.

> Anyone up for coffee in the morning? It's been a night.

She needs her friends, but she's never been good at saying so.

She sets the phone on the counter without waiting for a response and goes to the bedroom to change. She swaps the jeans for sleep shorts, but she leaves on Beau's big long-sleeved t-shirt. Usually he'd object to her wearing his clothes (the bit of time in their relationship where he thought she was adorable in his oversized shirts has long past), but tonight he doesn't say a word. He's on the sofa watching ESPN when she comes back into the living room. A glass of wine is waiting for her on the coffee table.

"I'm so sorry, honey," he says.

"Me too." She sits beside him, tucking her feet underneath her. "It's like, when I knew it was Paxton Gale, I was kind of *relieved*," she admits. She doesn't look at Beau. "I mean, of all my sixth-floor residents, I knew him the least. That's messed up, isn't it?"

"It's not. It's natural." That's what he's supposed to say though, because he's her husband.

"It's messed up."

He rubs her shoulder. "It's going to be okay."

"Yeah, I know," she lies.

"Want to watch something?"

"I think I just want to go to bed."

"Sure. Okay with you if I stay up, or...do you need me?"

"No, it's okay. I'm okay. Goodnight." Beau kisses her forehead and she climbs from the sofa, wineglass in hand, bottled water forgotten on the coffee table.

On the way to the bedroom, she grabs her laptop from the desk in their joint office. In bed, with her back propped against two pillows, she opens her computer. While it's booting, she looks around the room, from the giant portrait on the wall of Beau and her on the beach on their wedding day to the *Home is Wherever I'm With You* throw pillow tossed on the floor to the cushy armchair in the corner that doubles as her clothes hamper. Her eyes land on the stupid book she was reading earlier, discarded on top of the dresser. She thinks back to how she thought this night was going to go. Funny how quickly things can shift.

When her computer is up and running, she searches for the folder. It's hidden amongst her documents and it's labeled PHIL. Beau knows she keeps all of her essays from college, and her philosophy papers bore him so much he'd never think to open this folder, if he was using her computer to begin with. When she double-clicks the folder though, photos (not essays) pop up onto the screen. It's been years since she's done this and she shouldn't do it now, but Paxton's death has cracked open the shuttered place in her heart where Killian lives, and suddenly it feels like just yesterday that he left her.

She clicks through the photos slowly, one by one. In her mind, he's shiny and sparkling as a gemstone, so much that sometimes she suspects her memories have exaggerated his brilliance. But no, the photos are proof. The two of them at the Victorians & Vampires party, Killian breathtaking in head-to-toe steampunk (he was usually the buttoned-up one) and Claudia in a snug black top with a black and silver tutu skirt (she'd worn her own clothes). She studies the angles of his jawline, the softness in his eyes. She clicks again and there they are outside of Mocha Margaret's at sunset, Killian's arm wrapped around her, Claudia's blue hair vibrant against the pink and orange sky. It's been a long time since she wore her hair like that. Click. There she is alone, in a photo he had taken of her. She's looking out the window, and she's wearing the olive-green military jacket she'd lucked out on at Goodwill. He loved her in that jacket. The last photo in the batch is a selfie of Killian that he'd sent her a few weeks before his death. He's staring into the camera with a thoughtful expression on his face. *Something to remember me by*, the text had read and she'd had some flippant reply, and she's spent the years since wondering if the text was a joke or another warning sign that she'd missed. As if she could ever forget him. She remembers it all now, every detail. They'd met in Texas, when she was a college student working part-time as a barista at a little coffee shop called Mocha Margaret's, and Killian was a beautiful, indecisive customer. She teased him about taking forever to make up his mind, he commented on her jacket. And then his fingers brushed against hers when he handed over his debit card and the entire world shrank, reduced to a bubble that held only the two of them. His eyes were dark blue, like a stormy sky, and her one singular thought was that she had to have him. She didn't know a thing about him then other than how it felt when his skin met hers, and still she hauled herself up and halfway over the counter to kiss him right on the mouth. She'll never forget the stunned expression on his face and the wild, uncertain beat of time that passed before those soft lips curved into a surprised grin.

It's hard to imagine she'd ever been so careless.

She clicks through the photos again. If Killian was alive, these are the kinds of nostalgia-tinged pictures she might post on Facebook or Instagram now, with a cheeky #TBT caption. If she and Killian were even still close. She certainly isn't the same girl she was back then, but then again, he's the reason for that.

Claudia isn't asleep when Beau comes to bed, but she pretends to be. She doesn't want to talk. She's sure he doesn't intend to wake her, but his efforts to keep quiet are half-hearted. He sleeps so peacefully at night that he assumes everyone else does too. She hears him, though. Showering, brushing his teeth. She sees the light from the bathroom behind her eyelids when he opens the door, hears his dirty clothes dropping into the actual hamper. The blue-white glow of his phone once he settles into bed, watching sports highlights with the volume down low but not low enough.

It's hard not to think of the dead college student. Less than twenty-four hours ago, Paxton Gale was alive. If she'd gotten to know him better, would she have recognized the signs this time? She thinks of Paxton's mother, who she's never even met, getting a call from the police department tonight and her heart thuds in her chest.

Her thoughts of Paxton and his family get all twisted up with her memories of Killian and how everything went so wrong, and she's wide awake long after Beau's phone has gone dark and he's snoring softly beside her.

CHAPTER 5

C laudia wakes up to two text messages.

One from Ingrid:

> Rough night for me too. Gilded Mug at 8:00?

And one from Ruby:

> Sounds good to me

Claudia nods and types out a quick reply.

> See you there

Beau is leaned over the kitchen island, drinking coffee and sending emails in his gray slacks and dress shirt, when she kisses him goodbye. "You're early," he comments. "You all good?"

"I've got a coffee date with the ladies."

"Isn't that usually on Thursdays?"

"Monday, too, this week."

"Ah," he says, and understanding dawns on his face. "Well, put in a good word with Ingrid for me." He smiles. He's trying to keep things light for her after last night, but they both know he doesn't need a "good word." Beau is the Head of Construction at WMB, and he's known as one of Ingrid's professional confidantes. They'd worked together before

Claudia had ever arrived on the scene; in fact, Ingrid is the one who introduced Beau and Claudia in the first place.

Like most college towns, there's a coffee shop on practically every corner in Ellen Point (no excuse for anyone to walk around without a caffeine buzz). Mocha Margaret's is probably still there in Texas, too, though Claudia never set foot in the place after Killian died. It was cursed for her after she lost him, rife with the imagined ghosts of the two of them flirting and making out in the back and studying and sipping lattes like they had all the time in the world.

The Gilded Mug here in Ellen Point caters to local professionals and graduate students, which is a refreshing change from the undergraduates flooding the Starbucks down the street. The Gilded Mug is a good central hub for grown-up Claudia and her grown-up friends. Claudia even meets Beau there during the work week on occasion. Beau appreciates good coffee. It was one of the small things they'd bonded over, in the beginning.

Claudia pulls into a parking spot next to Ingrid's Lexus. Ingrid is on the phone—work call, no doubt—but she ends it when she sees Claudia.

"You wouldn't believe these subcontractors I'm working with," Ingrid says by way of greeting. "Three weeks behind schedule already and now they tell me there's another delay? Unbelievable." Ingrid looks polished and pulled together, even before the caffeine. Her blond hair is pulled back in a sleek low bun and her makeup is flawless. She and Claudia are dressed similarly in business attire—a dark skirt suit for Claudia and a wide legged pant suit for Ingrid, but the look is more natural on Ingrid. Claudia can't shake the feeling, especially today, that other people (people like Ingrid) have adulthood figured out, while she herself is playing dress-up in someone else's clothes.

"What are you going to do about it?"

"Send Beau over to lay eyes on the situation, see if we can get back-up. Or pull these guys altogether and get another team in." Ingrid pushes open the door to The Gilded Mug and Claudia follows her in. "Anyway, how are you?"

"I've been better," Claudia admits. She starts to launch into the horror of what she'd experienced at The Prestige last night, but they're in a line three people deep and she decides to wait until they're seated.

Ruby breezes in behind them, a giant purse slung over her shoulder. "Excuse me," she says to one of the other patrons, when her bag bumps him in the shoulder. "Excuse me, ooh, sorry. Morning, ladies," she says, with a big smile.

"Good morning," Claudia says.

Ruby Duvall is the free spirit of their group. She's also a few years younger than Claudia and Ingrid. Ruby would probably rather go naked than wear a business suit, but she doesn't hold her friends' wardrobe choices against them. Her own closet is filled with bright tunics and scarves and long skirts. Ruby is the one most likely to think something and just *say* it; she adds a lightness to Ingrid and Claudia's varying levels of intensity. She owns a local event planning company, which puts her in a position to work with Ingrid often in a professional capacity, and a personal one too.

The three women have a lot in common, but the most obvious is their single-minded ambition. It's what brought them together in the first place. Here in the South, other women their age have settled into family life, with a baby or even two (one of which may have a double-name that begins with *Mary*). Those women may have careers too, even thriving ones, but if they do, it's because they've achieved a level of balance that Claudia can't even fathom. Ruby, Ingrid, and Claudia share a different vision for success, and it's one that doesn't include motherhood.

Claudia and Ingrid get their drinks (latte with extra shot for Claudia, regular coffee with cream and sugar for Ingrid, and Matcha latte for Ruby) and take a seat on the patio at a wrought-iron four-seater table.

"I may have to leave soon," Ingrid says. "My father took a fall yesterday morning right before breakfast and he's in the hospital. I'm meeting Harley there when he gets into town."

"What?" Ruby says. "What happened? Sweetie, why didn't you call us?"

Ingrid looks down. She doesn't like talking about her father's health. "There was nothing you could do. He'll be okay. Concussion. They wanted to keep him overnight for observation, given his existing issues. He should have been using his walker, or his cane at the very least, but he's so damned stubborn." The morning sunlight is almost blinding, but it's not unbearably hot yet. It will be. Summer days in Ellen Point start out mild and turn harsh and humid before—sometimes—cooling down again in the evenings.

"He'll be okay, though?" Claudia asks.

Ingrid nods. "He will. For now, at least."

Ruby squeezes Ingrid's hand. "Call us next time, okay? Even if there's nothing we can do."

"Okay," she says. "Actually, there's something else I want to talk with you two about." Her face brightens, eyes sparkling and lips curving into a small smile. "This may come as a bit of a surprise, but—"

Her phone rings. "I'm sorry," she says, "Let me grab this." She picks up her phone. "Hey. You're there? Yes. I'm down the street. I'll be back there in five." She ends the call and tucks her phone into her purse. "So much for a coffee break. I'm going to have to run," she says apologetically. "Harley is just getting to the hospital and we need to speak to the doctor about my father's care plan."

"So strange to hear you talking about Harley again," Claudia says. Ingrid's brother Harley had been out of touch for years before reappearing earlier this year. It had been quite a shock.

"I know, it's...different. Anyway, I do have something to tell you both, so can we plan to get together again soon? Keep our Thursday coffee date, or get drinks after work one day, maybe?"

"Just let us know when," Ruby says.

"Tell your dad we're thinking of him," Claudia says.

Ingrid smiles. "I will. Don't forget about the Golden Hour Gathering this weekend. Ruby doesn't have a choice, but I expect you to be there too, Claudia."

"Wouldn't miss it."

"Okay, good to see you both, even though we got cut short." She gives a little wave and rushes out, her heels click-clacking against the concrete.

"So," Claudia says, taking a sip of her latte.

"So," says Ruby.

"Something horrible happened last night." Claudia looks down at her cup as she says it.

"Oh, shit," Ruby says. "For you too? What happened?"

It's harder to say out loud than Claudia had expected. "It's...a...well, one of my residents *died*."

"*What?*" Ruby says, her mouth falling open. Claudia relays the events of the night before.

"Oh, shit," Ruby says, again. She leans over and wraps Claudia in a sandalwood-scented hug. "Oh my goodness, sweetie, let me grab some napkins," she says, and it's only when she returns with napkins in her hand that Claudia realizes the napkins were for her, that she's crying. In public. She grabs a napkin and dabs roughly at her eyes. Her mascara is probably all over her face.

"Jesus Ruby, I'm sorry. I didn't mean to fall apart like this." Claudia sniffs and tries to pull herself together.

Ruby offers a sympathetic smile. Her long light brown hair falls into her face and she pushes it away, one curly strand stuck to her magenta lipstick. "That's okay. Sounds like some heavy stuff. That poor boy. And poor you. I can't believe you actually *saw* him."

"Me neither. I was stupid to rush in there. I wish I hadn't." The mental image of Paxton in his living room is hard to shake.

"So...what happens next?"

Claudia sips her latte and blinks back the tears this time. No more of that. "I wish I knew," she says.

***

What happens next is nothing. The world keeps spinning. The Prestige looks as elegant as it did last night, and last week, and all the times before, back when people *weren't* dying here.

The three-man maintenance team is waiting in Claudia's office, where she fills them in on the resident death. And then they all silently agree to go on as if it was a normal day, the guys picking up their work orders from the weekend and going about their business while Claudia tidies up the lobby.

There's a key and a business card sitting on a side table. The business card is flipped over to the blank side, with "607 – spare" scrawled in messy handwriting. Claudia picks up the business card, turns it over. Sergeant Grundy's card. She takes the silver key next. It's cool in her palm. This must be the spare that Amberly used to get into the apartment. Claudia *has* keys to every unit in the building, and it would be all too easy for her to pull a key for Paxton's apartment if she wanted access. Still, she slips this one in her pocket.

She thinks of those letters Paxton left behind for his loved ones. There's a chance they are still in the apartment. Not on the entry table—she'd checked there last night. But somewhere else. The police could have taken them...or not. Maybe they'd left those notes there for Paxton's family, for when they come to clean out the apartment.

It would be an invasion of Paxton's privacy to enter his apartment again, but she's desperate to know the contents of those letters, desperate to understand why someone would do what he did. What Killian did. The elevator is empty, so Claudia doesn't have to feel guilty about the key in her pocket. No one's eyes are on her. Her mother told her once that if the idea of people knowing what you're doing makes you feel ashamed, then you shouldn't be doing it in the first place. Whatever "it" happens to be. Her mother has always been pious that way. Claudia had gone four states away for college and had rebelled the second she was there, dying her hair violent red the first week of freshman year. Then pink, and later blue. Not that her mother ever saw any of it. They'd fallen out of touch for almost the entirety of Claudia's college years. They'd never been terribly close to begin with, but they were a pair for better or worse, the two of them against the world. Until her mother had snagged the most successful realtor in their small south Georgia suburb. She'd met him at church (*all that praying paid off*, Claudia had said, but her mother hadn't been amused by the joke). By the time Claudia was in high school, the realtor was her new stepfather, the three of them had moved into the nicest house in town, and all of the sudden they were living a life that was beautiful to her mother and fraudulent to Claudia. There were full-priced J.Crew sundresses in Claudia's closet and her mother was wearing freshwater pearls and doing things like making afternoon tea and signing Claudia up for horseback riding lessons. Claudia may have started college with bright red hair and a lip ring, but she also knew how to ride a damned horse.

She walks slowly to Paxton's door now, irrationally afraid that the coroner had been called away at the last minute and hadn't removed Paxton's body after all, afraid she might open the door to find him still inside. The thought of it is almost enough to send her back down to the lobby to mind her own business.

Almost.

She needn't have worried about the key this time. Apparently, in their haste to finish last night's investigation, the police had neglected to lock the front door at all. It pushes open with a simple twist of the knob. Careless. They'd remembered to turn off the lights at least, which makes it dark and shadowy despite the morning sunlight. She walks straight to the entry table. The smell of cigar smoke has all but dissipated, the ghost of a scent.

She doesn't see any letters.

She steals a cautious glance at the living room and is relieved to see that the body has, in fact, been removed. Still, she studiously avoids looking at the light fixture. Instead, she takes in the elegant décor. Gold-framed vintage movie posters above the sofa. Casablanca and Vertigo and The Graduate. An oversized emerald-green velvet sofa and a glass coffee table with slender golden legs. In the kitchen, a sleek round breakfast table with a pedestal base and two light brown leather chairs.

None of this fits with her perception of Paxton. He didn't strike her as the kind of person who cared much about *stuff*. She's a little surprised he could afford such high-end furnishings. Like most of her residents, he'd qualified to live here based on someone else's income—probably his parents—but somehow, Paxton always seemed like the kind of kid who had to work for the things he wanted. Clearly, Claudia had misread his situation.

A small stuffed rabbit is torn to bits in the living room floor, the soft white of its guts strewn about the hardwoods. No doubt the puppy's doing. Claudia wonders if Amberly will keep the puppy, or if he'll go back to the canine rescue where he came from. She can't remember the little dog's name, though she clearly remembers having a brief conversation with Paxton last month when he came down to her office to pay the pet fee. It was the last time she'd spoken to him. The shaggy little dog is part retriever and will probably grow to be far too large for a one-bedroom apartment. At the time, she'd thought that adopting the dog was an irresponsible move.

It nags at her that Paxton adopted a puppy so recently. Why would he have done that, if he was about to end things?

The rest of the apartment, aside from the sophisticated décor, is messier than she'd first realized. A pile of laundry on the fancy sofa. A bottle of multivitamins and opened cereal boxes along the counter beside the sink. This evidence of life—the mess, in particular, might as well be a neon sign flashing those obvious words: Paxton was here, and now he isn't.

It may be obvious, but she's having a hard time believing it, despite the fact that she saw his body with her own eyes. It still feels like he might walk in from class any second and find her here, among his things.

She opens drawers, picks up stacks of papers. Bills, homework. The letters aren't in his kitchen, and not in his living room either. Which means that, if she wants to be thorough, she needs to check his bedroom.

But she finds that she can't do it. She's gone far enough, and it feels too intimate somehow to trespass into the room where he slept. Claudia knows, rationally, that she won't find the letters in his bedroom anyway. The police took them, of course they did. She doesn't even know why it matters so much to her, like having this insight into the *why* of Paxton's death might help her understand Killian's. It won't, though. It won't change a thing.

Claudia backs up, retraces her steps into the kitchen area. Her hip bumps the breakfast table, and a stack of papers falls to the floor and scatters. She reaches down to collect the wayward pages. It's random scribbles mostly, but as she scoops them up, something smaller slips out from the bottom of the pile. For a moment, she thinks she may have found a goodbye letter after all, which is ridiculous because he wouldn't have hidden them, but then she recognizes the texture of the paper, the silver embossed script.

It's the same invitation she has at home, for her friend Ingrid's engagement party. Why would Paxton, a college senior, have been invited to a party for the president of the Wyatt McIntyre Birch Real Estate Group? She wishes Ingrid hadn't had to run off so quickly this morning; maybe then Claudia would already know the answer. She pulls her phone from her jacket pocket and sends a text to Ingrid.

> Hey, hope you got your dad home and settled, and that he's doing okay. I didn't get a chance to tell you this morning, but a resident at The Prestige died last night. His name was Paxton Gale. Weird question, but did you know him?

Claudia watches, expectantly, as three dots show up on her message screen. And then disappear. She waits another moment, then tucks her phone back in her jacket pocket. She turns the invitation over in her palm and sets it back down, then rifles through the papers again. There is nothing else here that has anything to do with WMB.

Reluctantly, she shows herself out of the apartment and locks the door.

***

Back at her desk, Claudia works on crafting an email to her residents. She stares at the blank email screen for half an hour before she starts to type:

Good morning.

I regret to inform you all that one of our residents passed away last night. Some of you may have seen emergency vehicles and uniformed officers on the property; however, rest assured that no foul play was involved in this terrible tragedy. Please join me in keeping the resident's family in your thoughts.

-Claudia Aldridge, Property Manager

When she's done, she feels mildly satisfied with what she's typed up. Succinct but heartfelt. She hopes. She presses send and prepares herself for a flood of responses.

A knock on her office door distracts her from her inbox. It's the mailman. "Morning. We've got some packages out here for you." Claudia follows him to the lobby, where he's left a stack of parcels on a nearby table.

She is gathering the boxes and envelopes to put away in the mailroom when one of them catches her eye. It's a medium-sized Amazon envelope; if she was guessing, she'd say there are books inside. But it's the recipient's name she can't stop staring at. Paxton Gale. Without thinking, she tears into the envelope. Two books fall out into her hand: *Dog Training 101* and *Enter Night: a Biography of Metallica*. Odd combination.

There's a Prime stamp on the envelope, meaning Paxton could have ordered this package as recently as Saturday. If Paxton planned to die, why did he place this order? If he planned to die, why buy a book about dog training?

She shakes her head, dismissing the questions. It's possible Paxton didn't order this himself at all. Maybe someone sent it to him, a gift he'll never receive.

It occurs to her that she needs to call Margo, her boss at the corporate office. There's a whole process for emergencies, a process that Claudia is only slightly familiar with because she's never had a real emergency before. The corporate office is in Huntsville, and Margo isn't scheduled to visit until October. She won't know what's happened unless Claudia tells her.

Margo will want a copy of the police report. The business card for Sergeant Grundy is still on Claudia's desk, so she picks up the phone and dials the number and extension listed there.

"Hi," she says when he answers. "Claudia Aldridge, from The Prestige at Ellen Point."

"Hi Miss Aldridge," he says. "We finished the investigation there last night. You get the key I left?"

"I did. Sergeant, was there any indication at all of *why* this happened?"

"Nope," he says. "Who knows, really? Not like it's uncommon. These college kids, they do it for all kinds of reasons. They think everything is the end of the world. Could have been a bad grade, or a fight with the girlfriend, or something else we don't even know about. It's a shame, but they're all so damned *sensitive*. What can you do?"

He's tapping the keys of his keyboard as they talk, on to some other case. She wants to tell him that there's more to "these kids" than he realizes. There was more to Killian, and probably more to Paxton too.

"Did Amberly say if they'd had a fight?"

"Who?"

She sighs. "Amberly? The girlfriend?"

"Oh. Nope. No fight this time, as far as we know."

"What about depression? Was he depressed?"

"As far as she knew he was fine. She was as surprised as anyone else."

"Oh." She can see that Sergeant Grundy isn't going to be any more forthcoming. So she asks about the police report, and the sergeant says he'll transfer her to the desk manager to request a copy.

"One more thing," Claudia says at the last second. "What about the letters Paxton left behind? Will they be passed along to his loved ones?" *What's in them?* Claudia desperately wants to know, though she's sure he won't tell her.

"Letters?"

"His suicide note. Or notes. The letters he left for his family. For his parents, I guess?"

"There weren't any letters, Miss Aldridge."

"There were. The other officer—Officer Stewart, I think—said so."

"Well, Officer Stewart was either mistaken or thinking of a different case," Grundy says. "The kid didn't leave anything behind."

"What?" Claudia sits up straighter.

"There were no notes."

"You're sure?"

"I'm the lead on this case. I think I would know."

The goodbye notes don't exist. She feels a chill creep up her spine. "But if he didn't leave any letters, how do you know it was a suicide at all?"

"Ma'am, we know a suicide when we see one. Didn't *you* see him too? Now, if you'll hold on a second, I'll pass you along to the front desk so you can get a copy of that report."

Before she can say anything else, there is a click on the line and Sergeant Grundy is gone, his gruff voice replaced by hold music.

Claudia stares out of the glass doors of the lobby, where a grocery delivery person stands outside fumbling with the callbox. Grocery delivery is new to the area and it seems like her residents enjoy the convenience, if the fact that Claudia has to help delivery people into the building twenty times a day is any indication.

She takes the cordless phone with her to the front door. "Come on in," she says to the delivery person, a college-aged guy with a frustrated look on his face.

"I've been calling the customer for ten minutes," he says. "No answer." His arms are weighed down with plastic grocery bags. "Can I leave these with you?"

Her least favorite part of the new grocery delivery app. "I guess." She sighs. "Who's it for?"

The delivery person looks down at his phone, scrolls. "Customer name is...Paxton Gale."

"That's impossible," she sputters.

"No, it says so right here. Delivery scheduled for Monday."

"When...when was it ordered?"

"Um, let me see. Looks like Saturday?"

Claudia is speechless. Why would Paxton have ordered *groceries* if he meant to die? She thinks of the email she just sent out to her residents, the one that confidently states *no foul play was involved.*

She watches the boy unload groceries right here in the lobby, but she's not really seeing him. What she sees, instead, is a golden puppy with big paws. An Amazon Prime package. A grocery order with no one to accept

43

it. She hears the sergeant's voice telling her that there were no letters left behind.

She feels the evidence building in her mind. She'd seen Paxton's body with her own eyes. And yet, suddenly she knows with complete, bone-deep certainty that no matter what the police say, Paxton Gale did not die by suicide. And if he didn't die by suicide, and if his death wasn't accidental and wasn't due to natural causes, that leaves only one conclusion.

Paxton was murdered.

CHAPTER 6

"So, like...can you say *how* he died?" Janie asks. Claudia is sitting at her desk, and Janie is perched in the chair across from her, an unopened Ipsy package on her lap. Claudia is annoyed at the interruption, and she obviously can't share her suspicions with Janie. If it *was* murder, Janie is the last person who should know.

Claudia hesitates. Even if she sticks with the story the police believe, it seems too personal to share.

Janie leans forward. "Let me guess. If I guess right, will you tell me?"

"Yes," Claudia says, sighing. Janie is relentless, and Claudia needs her to leave so she can concentrate.

"Alcohol poisoning."

Claudia shakes her head.

"Heart attack."

"No," Claudia says.

"Oh my God," Janie says. "He totally killed himself, didn't he?" Claudia flinches, and that must give it away, because Janie launches into a new guessing game. The game of *how*.

"Janie, I've got to get back to work. Just assume it was terrible."

"You seriously won't tell me?" She twirls a strand of hair around her finger.

"No," Claudia says. "I seriously won't. I'm not allowed to." It's a lie; she has no idea if she's allowed to or not. But the statement seems like an effective way to end the conversation. She should have thought of it sooner.

It's odd, how people are more curious than concerned about Paxton's demise. With the exception of Amberly Vance, it seems that no one else in the building really knew Paxton. They don't *feel* anything about the absence of one of their own. They're a rare breed, these kids. Are they truly so charmed that they think nothing bad will ever happen to them? Or are they so consumed with their own tiny tragedies that they don't have the time to devote to anyone else's?

Maybe, like children, they believe if they ignore the bad thing, it will go away.

Claudia has been thinking about the security camera feed for the building and how it implicated the electric-skateboard-riding sign thief just the weekend before. She only ever checks the footage when a situation requires it; it's tedious work and not nearly as interesting as one would assume. But this situation *does* require it. The camera feed could tell her more about Paxton, and what happened to him. When Janie leaves, Claudia opens the security camera app on her computer. The screen is suddenly filled with rows and rows of other tiny screens, each one recording some area of the building. She rewinds to Saturday night—the last time Paxton was seen alive. She's selecting the camera that records sixth floor activity when the phone rings.

"It's a great day at The Prestige at Ellen Point, this is Claudia," she says, with a smile on her face. She's programmed to smile when she answers the phone. It's fake, but people on the other end of the line can hear the smile in her voice and they don't know the difference. Plus, the Caller ID shows that the person on the other end of the line in this case is her boss, returning Claudia's call from earlier. Margo Spalding checks in every week or so, but Claudia rarely has anything to fill her in on. Today is different. She leaves out several important details when she describes the tragedy; she uses the word *suicide* without mentioning her recent certainty that Paxton didn't actually die that way, and she keeps her mouth shut about the fact that she saw Paxton's body. And that she entered his apartment this morning and went through his things. Margo is stunned by the news of a resident death and she's incredibly sympathetic, as Claudia knew she would be. When Claudia hangs up the phone, she sighs and closes out of the security camera app. She'll come back to it later. Liza, the new leasing consultant, is arriving for her shift.

"Hi!" Liza chirps. She's wearing a crop top that shows a line of skin across her midriff. Claudia shakes her head. It's a cute shirt—Liza is nothing if not fashionable—but company rules say that she can't wear it to work, and if she had read the employee handbook Claudia had given her and has since referenced at least five times, she would know that. Claudia will have to talk with her again about work appropriate attire.

"Hi Liza, sit down for a second please."

"Oh my God, am I fired already? I'm not fired, am I?"

"What? No." Claudia mentally files away the fact that Liza knows things aren't going great so far. But then she moves on, brings her up to speed on Paxton's death, and watches Liza's eyes well up with tears.

"I'm sorry," Claudia says. "Were you and Paxton friends? I didn't realize you knew him."

"I don't," Liza says, a tear rolling down her face and leaving a trail of mascara behind. "It's just so *sad*." Claudia passes her a tissue. "Yeah, it is. But we've got to keep going as best we can. Are you able to do that?" Then Claudia remembers that she herself had been crying into her latte just this morning. She shakes her head. "Of course you can't. This is...tough. Why don't you take the day off? If you need to talk to someone, I'm sure we can reach out to a counselor. We could all probably use it."

Liza sniffles, nods. "Thank you. For the day. I don't know about a counselor. I'll let you know."

"Okay. Well, go on home and I'll see you later this week."

"Thank you."

It's a relief to have her gone. With Graham off too, Claudia doesn't have to interact with anyone besides the residents. Today, she's grateful for that.

By the end of the day, though, save for the inquiries like Janie's and the police report in Claudia's inbox, it could be any other day. It's disconcerting. Every time Claudia sees her residents, they seem to flicker before her eyes. Most of them have no idea how fragile they are, how quickly they could fade away. Like Paxton.

She has a recurring thought, now, that she can't shake. If Paxton *was* murdered, his killer is still out there, possibly even living here in this building.

*****

Claudia walks through her front door at the end of the day, kicking off her heels the second she's inside. Wearing heels is a bitch. Beau is in the living room on the sofa, freshly showered and relaxed in shorts and a t-shirt. ESPN is on the TV, and he's reading something on his phone.

She gets home after Beau most afternoons, if he isn't traveling for work. Since Ingrid's father hired him on eight years ago, WMB has expanded into the neighboring states of South Carolina, Florida, and Alabama, and Beau's always got several regional projects going on. Travel has become more frequent. But not this week.

"Hey," she says.

He looks up, startled to see her there despite the noise she's been making. "Hi, babe. How was your day?"

"Strange." She tries to gather her thoughts to elaborate, to explain to him all the reasons she thinks Paxton was murdered, to express her complicated feelings on Paxton's death in general. But she's missed her brief window; he's turned his attention back to the iPhone screen. "Never mind."

"I'm listening," he insists. He drops his phone on the sofa cushion. "Promise. Tell me about it? What's the news on your resident?"

"There really isn't any news," she says. "Nothing much to tell." She's not in the mood to beg for attention, and suddenly she doesn't really care to share this with him anyway. Her affectionate, sympathetic husband from last night is someone different now, a tired man who wants to unwind with minimal drama after a long day.

Claudia goes to the bedroom and changes into sweats and a tank top, pulls her hair into a loose knot. When she gets back to the living room, Beau is on his phone again. She sighs and heads to the kitchen to pull something together for dinner.

The invitation on the fridge catches her eye. *Please join us for an engagement celebration honoring Ingrid Wyatt and Thomas McIntyre.*

Everyone and their mother has been invited to this party. Ingrid and her fiancé, Thomas, had only dated for a few months before the engagement, but Ingrid's father is Southern and old-fashioned and way too eager to marry off his only daughter. Willard Wyatt is the original founder of the WMB Real Estate Group, and when he wants a party, he gets a party. It's an unofficial celebration of Ingrid's promotion to President of WMB, too, which she'd had to fight for (*It was just business,* Ingrid said smoothly when it was all over, though Claudia knows it was more than that). Ingrid's father had been the charming face of the business for decades, and his business partners weren't sold on Ingrid as his successor. It had nothing to do with charm *or* experience. Ingrid has Southern charm oozing from her Southern pores, and she'd been working at WMB since she was a teenager. The geriatric men weren't sure they wanted a woman running their business. But it was what old man Wyatt wanted, and then when Thomas McIntyre (whose family put the "M" in WMB) and Ingrid became a couple, the McIntyre family backed her too.

What's incredible is that even though Ingrid stays mostly tight-lipped about the company drama and even her personal life, Claudia knew all about it anyway. Not because of Beau, since he doesn't get into office gossip, but because she'd read most of the details in the paper like everyone else. The people who live in Ellen Point are obsessed with the powerhouse real estate and development group, and regard the original WMB founding families as some kind of hybrid between local royalty and the Kardashians. You can't open a copy of the Ellen Point Press without catching mention of WMB. If it's not news of some new real estate rehab or development, it's lifestyle news or an opinion piece regarding the personal lives of the founders and their families.

Ingrid's engagement had been a huge surprise, though, and one Claudia wishes she'd learned about from the source. Ingrid had wanted nothing to do with Thomas McIntyre from the moment her father had tried to set them up. At least, that's what Claudia thought. Until she read a rumor in the paper that Ingrid had been spotted with a ring on *that* finger. *Enemies to lovers after all,* Ingrid admitted sheepishly when Claudia called her about it. *And you're sure about this?* Claudia asked. *This isn't* really *a business move, is it?* It was the kind of question Ingrid's high-and-mighty Foxglove Society sisters would never ask; they'd just gossip about it behind her back. Claudia was more upfront than that. *Of course not,* Ingrid insisted. *I know what I'm doing.* And even though

Ingrid kept things close to the vest, she usually *did* know what she was doing. So Claudia let it go.

Thomas McIntyre remains a question mark, though. Last month, Ingrid had invited a select group of work colleagues and their spouses out for dinner. Claudia was there in her capacity as Beau's spouse. It was shortly after the surprise engagement announcement, and it was the first time Claudia or any of the work people had met Thomas. He may have the company last name, but he'd never worked at WMB. The group of them, eight in total, sat at a white-clothed table in a candlelit restaurant in front of a picture window with views of the lush, green, tree-covered mountains.

Ingrid and Thomas weren't like Beau and Claudia had been, back when they were newly engaged and giddy with the novelty of it. But Thomas *was* charismatic. And handsome. He was tall and slim, light hair touched with gray, and dark, arresting eyes. A big smile and a hearty laugh. Despite all of the charm and good looks, though, rumors persisted that there was only one reason Ingrid wanted to marry Thomas. He was a McIntyre, and she needed the McIntyres in her corner.

"Claudia," Ingrid said from across the dinner table. Her gold necklace twinkled in the candlelight. "How's work going?" Even though she mostly knew already.

"Really well," Claudia said with a smile. What else *would* she say? That conversation had taken place weeks before a resident up and died in the building.

"Claudia manages The Prestige at Ellen Point," Ingrid said, to the other couples at the table.

"Oh, wow," one of the women responded. Her name was Emma, and she worked at WMB. "Beautiful property."

Claudia nodded and smiled. "You all know that better than anyone." WMB was the construction company responsible for building The

Prestige. Early on in construction, they'd sold the property to Southern Campus Collective, national luxury student housing brand and Claudia's employer. Claudia, tapped as the manager of the new facility, first met Ingrid during the construction phase, and was introduced to Beau at the building's grand opening ceremony six months later.

"I tell you what," Emma's husband said. "They didn't have apartments like that when I was in college."

Claudia remembered her own rundown flat from her college years. "The student housing market has changed a lot."

"Is it hard," Emma asked suddenly, "working around so many students?" At Claudia's blank expression, she elaborated. "They're just so *young*."

Claudia shrugged. "I enjoy it."

Ingrid's new fiancé raised an eyebrow. "Beau, don't you worry about Claudia being around those college boys all the time? I remember what I was like in college." He chuckled. Alone. It was his one misstep, serving up a bit of misogyny with dinner.

Beau glanced at Claudia and finally choked out a small laugh. "Not exactly."

Ingrid's hand stilled around the wine glass she'd been about to lift to her lips, and she glanced at Thomas with annoyance. It was a blink-and-you-miss-it moment, before the mask of bland happiness settled back on her face and Claudia realized that Ingrid had been wearing that mask all along. Even in private, when it was only Ingrid and Ruby and Claudia meeting for coffee.

"Darling," Ingrid said to Thomas, in a light tone that held a hint of warning.

"Why should he worry, exactly?" Claudia asked. "Are we women so without our own agency that we could be swept away by the first horny frat boy who spares us a glance?"

Beau elbowed her. Ingrid smirked and sipped her wine, but she didn't actually say anything. It stung that she hadn't come to Claudia's defense. The candle flickered in the middle of the table.

Thomas wrapped his arm possessively around Ingrid's shoulders. "Not sure I'd want Ing around that every day, is all."

Never mind that Ingrid commands dozens of *adult* men and does just fine.

Ingrid had apologized, after the dinner, for Thomas's behavior. He was nervous around her colleagues, that was all. *Are you sure about him?* Claudia had asked, and Ingrid had insisted that she was.

It nags at Claudia, now, this invitation in her hand for Ingrid and Thomas's engagement party and the fact that she saw an identical one in Paxton's apartment. She checks her phone. Ingrid had never texted back. As she pulls ingredients from the fridge, she thinks about possible explanations. Did Paxton have a connection to the Wyatts? Could he be a relative? Paxton told her once that he was from North Carolina, while the Wyatts have a long history in Ellen Point. Still, they could be family. Or Paxton could be a McIntyre relative. An intern at WMB? They take on new interns yearly. But Beau would have known if Paxton had been an intern. The home office isn't big enough not to at least know everyone's first name.

Claudia starts dinner, a balsamic chicken recipe she's made so many times she could do it in her sleep. She lets her mind wander. Cooking comes naturally to her. She's good at knowing, without searching Pinterest or looking in some family cookbook, which ingredients will work together. It was a talent that had served her well when she was behind the counter at Mocha Margaret's back in college.

She thinks of Killian, of their first wild kiss in the coffeeshop, of how he'd walked out in a daze and had returned only a few days later. He'd tried to be casual but had knocked over a chalkboard stand advertising winter drink specials, catching the attention of everyone in the place. Including Claudia. She remembers his pink cheeks and lovely smile and his sandy hair that was just a little too long, like he was due for a haircut but couldn't be bothered. On her fifteen-minute break, she'd beckoned him out behind the shop and dared him to touch her again, and he'd put the palm of his hand against her cheek and everything else disappeared. She'd pushed him against the yellow-painted brick wall and found his lips with hers, and he'd tangled his hands in her blue hair and murmured something about how fearless she was.

Oil pops from the skillet and splatters onto her arm, and she jumps, her skin burning. She turns on the water faucet and holds her arm beneath it.

She's not fearless anymore, and she should take this as a reminder to leave the past alone. There's nothing there for her but pain.

CHAPTER 7

Killian may be on Claudia's mind more than normal lately, but it's *Paxton* who shows up in her dreams that night, and she wakes up the next morning desperately curious. She suddenly needs to know as much about Paxton Gale as possible. As if knowing him now could make up for the fact that she didn't know him well enough when he was alive.

As if knowing him could lead her to his killer.

Once she's at work, she settles in at her desk and searches for Paxton's social media profiles. He doesn't have an Instagram account, but she finds him on Facebook. It's a surprise, since so many college kids avoid Facebook these days. The boy in the profile photo is hardly recognizable as Paxton, though. In the image, he's clean-shaven with a wry smile. He wears a gray Henley shirt and jeans, and he's leaned against a fireplace, the mantel of which is covered in holiday garland. He looks much younger, and Claudia wonders exactly how old this photo is. Someone has tagged a more recent photo on his timeline from a year ago, and in this one Paxton is straight-faced in a black and white caterer's uniform, in a group of four others dressed the same.

His page isn't private, so she's able to learn more than she should, even though he hasn't updated it in forever. She learns that he graduated from Wallace T. Brady High School, and since she has no idea who Wallace T. Brady *is*, she takes an internet detour to find out that Brady was a prominent mayor in Kelver Ridge, North Carolina about a hundred years ago, and that Kelver Ridge (which she's never heard of) is where Paxton is from. Interests: Hiking, riding four-wheelers, playing piano. Claudia never pictured him as outdoorsy or musical, but what does she know? The whole point of her little investigation is that she hardly knew Paxton at all.

News of his death has spread; friends and acquaintances have taken to his Facebook wall to leave condolences. Claudia has no idea why this is a thing. The messages range in content from simple (*Heard the news. Gonna miss you buddy.*) to thoughts so personal it seems absurdly inappropriate to share them publicly (*I'm so sorry I ghosted you back in high school. I think about you every day.*). She refreshes the page over and over, watching new posts trickle in.

Eventually, Claudia takes Paxton's spare key and returns to his apartment. It doesn't *look* like anyone has been in the apartment since she left yesterday, but something feels different and she has a hard time putting her finger on what has changed. She makes her way to the door to Paxton's bedroom and finally steps inside. There's something about seeing his bed like this, unmade, covers askew, that makes it too easy to imagine him lying across it in careless slumber.

There is a stack of books on his dresser, and she picks them up one by one. School books, business mostly. There's got to be a clue here somewhere, some hint of what really happened in this apartment less than 72 hours ago. There are no photos of Paxton or his family and friends, which is maybe strange and maybe not. So many pictures are digital these days.

She goes back to the breakfast table, pulls out the invitation for Ingrid's engagement party. It's a minor thing, but she can't stop thinking about why Paxton would have been invited to this event. She pulls out her phone and calls Ingrid. No answer. She stares at the heavy paper for another moment, then folds the invite in half and stuffs it into the pocket of her dress pants.

Back at her desk, she checks Paxton's Facebook page again and reads through the posts she's missed in the twenty minutes she was away.

> *Can't believe you're gone.*

> *So glad we talked recently.*

But then this one, from someone named Aaron Baxter:

> *How could you do it, man? I didn't take the easy way out, even after what you did.*

Claudia stares at the last post. What the hell? She doesn't know what Paxton could have done, but it's a chilling and insensitive public statement. From his picture, Aaron looks to be Paxton's age. His profile is private, so she can't see much, but the photo shows a bearded young man wearing a camouflage hat. She wonders what Paxton did to Aaron, and if it was worth killing for. But Aaron's post implies that he believes Paxton died by suicide. Unless he posted this intentionally, to cover his own tracks.

When she refreshes the page again ten minutes later, there is a response to Aaron's post. It's from Marilyn Gale, who upon further investigation, Claudia determines to be Paxton's mother. *Of course* she's monitoring the posts.

> *What happened to you was an accident. Don't make this worse than it already is.*

How long, Claudia wonders, until Marilyn has Paxton's page deactivated? Or will she do it at all? Killian's page disappeared shortly after his death, but Claudia had an acquaintance who died in a car crash a few years back and his Facebook page is still active now, people posting memories on his wall on a monthly basis, his profile picture and interests unchanged, frozen in time. It's creepy.

Curious to find out what happened between Paxton and Aaron, she types Paxton's name into Google. There's a new result, posted this morning by an North Carolina funeral home. Paxton's obituary. *Paxton Gale, 22, died suddenly,* it says, with details about an upcoming graveside service in Kelver Ridge and the family he left behind: His parents, a younger sister, and a grandmother.

The photo used in the obituary is the same one from his Facebook page. Claudia reads and rereads the short passage. She doesn't have a clue where Kelver Ridge, North Carolina is, but a quick search shows it's a three-hour drive from Ellen Point. It would certainly raise eyebrows if Paxton's property manager drove across state lines to offer condolences, Claudia knows that. Margo is pretty understanding, but even she would frown upon it.

Still, Claudia starts to consider going. She assumes a graveside service means a burial and not a cremation, but she doesn't really know. What she *does* know is that it would be unprofessional to attend. She'd have to call in sick, wouldn't be able to tell anyone where she was actually going. But if she stayed out of the way, if she didn't talk to anyone and didn't get too close, no one would even know she was there.

It's a bad idea. She won't go. She definitely won't.

But she enters the address into her phone just in case.

***

"Okay, what's the update?" Graham asks, later that morning when he's settled at his desk. Liza is supposed to be here too, but it's thirty minutes past her scheduled start time and there's been no sign of her.

Claudia hasn't seen Graham since the night Paxton died. Usually, even on his off days, he'll find an excuse to come by her office for a quick chat. He lives here in the building, after all. But he didn't stop in yesterday, and she knows why. She's a reminder of the tragedy they experienced together, just a few short nights ago.

"There's not much to tell, really," she says. She feels like a conspiracy theorist confessing her belief that Paxton was murdered, so she keeps it to herself. "Not much has happened since...you know." She looks at Graham in his navy dress slacks, at the slim fit of his white button-down shirt and how it wants to cling to his chest. The smart watch against the warm brown skin of his wrists and his dark hair pulled back in its ponytail. He looks composed. If he's distraught about Paxton's death, he's great at covering it.

"How are you?" she asks him.

"I'm okay. It's just...it's wild. It's...I don't know." He looks down. So, not as okay as he seems. He'd normally be jumping right into some lighthearted story or other; Graham always has things to say. But there's a solemn air about them both right now. "It's hard to believe."

"It doesn't seem real," Claudia says.

"Is everybody freaking out?"

"No. It's strange."

Suddenly, Claudia aches for one of those familiar innocuous touches that are entirely professional but still make her feel human. She keeps her hands to herself, but she can't help but think of the tender skin of Graham's wrist, where his watch sits, and what the flesh there would feel like right now beneath her fingers. She shakes her head, trying to rid herself of this unwelcome burst of yearning. It's wrapped up in sadness and is less about Graham than it is about comfort. She knows that. Claudia is married and Graham is...well, even in slacks and a tie and with this serious expression on his face, Graham is her twenty-three-year-old employee.

Losing Paxton has Claudia's defenses down, and her emotions are unpredictable.

"So he's dead, and no one around here cares?"

"No, it's like they don't really *get* it. They're only interested in the drama of it. It could be a TV show."

"That's messed up."

"Yeah."

Claudia enters rent and Graham follows up on new leads, and Claudia tries to focus on work. She usually enjoys Graham's company, but today she'd prefer to have the office to herself again. She remembers the security camera footage and the hours and hours of recordings that she's yet to get back to.

Claudia needs to talk to Amberly. Without knowing anything else, she knows that if Paxton really *was* murdered, his girlfriend is the most likely suspect. She's seen enough Law & Order to know that the people who are supposed to care about you are the ones most likely to end you. But Amberly's grief seemed real. And...there's the physical aspect of it; Amberly is petite, and Claudia can't imagine her setting up the scene the way the cops found it. Not on her own at least, unless she's much stronger than she looks.

Some time alone with the camera footage might give Claudia more insight. But there's no opportunity, not with Graham right here (and not even touching her). Her thoughts are interrupted by a buzzing sound that means someone is outside the lobby requesting entrance. From her office doorway, Claudia sees two young women dressed in designer athletic gear. Graham jumps up to greet them.

"Welcome to The Prestige at Ellen Point," Graham says, opening the door. "How can I help you?"

"Um, hi," Claudia hears one of them say. "We were supposed to have a lease tour with Liza today?" The girl looks around the lobby and then says in a conspiratorial whisper that's not really a whisper at all, "She told us what happened, like, how a guy *died* here."

Claudia feels her jaw clench.

"And she said she would show us around, and maybe even get us inside the apartment where it *happened*. That's still cool, right? Is she here?"

"Are you friends with Liza?" Graham asks. Claudia knows he's trying to gauge how bad the situation is, how many people Liza may have told.

"Well, no, not exactly, but she mentioned it to some of the girls in our sorority and *they* mentioned it to our roommates, and *they* told us and then Liza said anyone who wanted to look around should come see her."

Great, thinks Claudia. She'd hoped to keep this quiet, and her own employee was out in the world spreading the news.

At that moment Liza rushes in through the lobby, past the girls without sparing them a glance. "Oh my gosh oh my gosh," she says to Claudia, who is trembling with rage. "I'm so sorry, I totally overslept. It was a really rough night. I can stay later this afternoon to make up for it if you want."

"Sit down, Liza," Claudia says, willing herself not to yell. Tardiness is the least of her problems. She can hear Graham outside in the lobby, still trying to diffuse the situation with the two clients. "We need to talk."

CHAPTER 8

I t's a gorgeous day for a drive, even if it *is* a drive through the mountains to the middle of nowhere. She's surrounded on both sides, nestled between the dense tree-covered slopes as she winds along the highway. There's not a soul who knows what she's up to. She'd called in sick this morning, leaving the office in Graham's hands, with Liza there to help. Liza, who'd gotten a written warning and a stern lecture from a seething Claudia for sharing the news of a resident death to all her friends. Liza's on thin ice, but she still has her job. For now, at least.

Beau thinks Claudia's at work, like it's just a normal day. She'd considered confiding in Ingrid and Ruby but had decided against it when Ingrid had cancelled their Thursday coffee date via text without a single word in response to Claudia's earlier message. She doesn't know how she'd explain herself anyway, and Ingrid has understandably been so busy caring for her father she hasn't had much time to talk this week. Claudia had dropped a gift basket by the Wyatt home yesterday, but she hadn't seen Ingrid in person.

Kelver Ridge, located just outside of Asheville, is a smaller town than Ellen Point but just as mountainous. Claudia swings her car into the church parking lot. Her black dress is simple and conservative, a basic dress for blending in. The fact that the sun is glowing in the sky means she can wear her big Audrey Hepburn sunglasses to hide her face. Her hair is pulled back into a ponytail. She could be anybody who knew

Paxton from anywhere. Besides, she's never met Paxton's family. Most of Claudia's residents are the product of helicopter parents; she sees and hears from the parents almost as often as she hears from the residents themselves (and sometimes more). Paxton is an exception. She's never even spoken with his family.

She has a retroactive appreciation for his independence.

The only people she needs to make sure to avoid are Amberly and Mary Louise. Claudia gets out of her car and looks around. Quite a crowd has gathered in the cemetery beside the church, where a white tent has been erected with chairs lined up beneath. The closed casket rests on rails, ready to sink into the earth. Sunlight glints off of the waxy smooth wood. She thinks of Paxton's body, the way she saw it in his living room. He was there, and now he's here, inside this fancy box.

Every seat is taken, and a crowd hovers behind the chairs. Paxton must have had a lot of friends. Or else this is just the latest gossip-worthy event in this small town. Claudia finds her hiding place in one of several small clusters of trees, the leaves vivid green. It won't be long before the orange and yellow will creep in and then these leaves will fall. She's tucked away but not obviously so; she leans against a tree like it's as close as she can bear to get. She's concocted a bullshit story, if anyone should ask her how she knows the deceased. But she'd rather not talk to anyone at all.

She studies the people in the crowd—as best she can from this distance—and tries to gauge their relationship to Paxton. They're young people mostly, probably former classmates.

His killer could be right here among them.

Amberly and Mary Louise (Lou for short, Claudia remembers) are beneath the tent. Amberly wears a black sundress with dainty white flowers splashed across it. It's warm today, and most of the attendees are too young to own proper funeral attire. There are young men in ill-fitting suits that probably belong to their fathers or were hastily purchased for this occasion, and young women in light frocks like Amberly's or dresses that look like they've been worn here straight from a night out in Ellen Point—tight-fitting, shiny. A few men wear jeans and button-down shirts. To hell with the suits.

Claudia isn't close enough to hear the preacher's words, and she's glad. She can guess the Southern Baptist preacher's take on suicide. Claudia spent enough time in church as a kid to know there's—allegedly—no room in heaven for people who die that way.

Sometimes she pretends, though. Not only that there *is* a heaven, but that Killian is there, keeping tabs on her from above, even after everything that happened.

***

Claudia knows the funeral is over when the hum of the preacher's voice goes silent and people start to drift from their seats, leaving Paxton alone there in a wooden box. It's time for her to go too, but she's riveted. Only four people remain under the tent: Paxton's parents, a young woman (his sister, Claudia assumes), and the preacher. Marilyn Gale, Paxton's mother, won't take her hands off the casket. Paxton's father stands behind her, and Claudia watches him pull out a flask and take a long swig. Finally, Paxton's sister grasps her mother's hands and gently pulls them from the wooden surface, then steers her away.

Claudia gets in her car. There must be some kind of wake now. All of the other cars leaving the parking lot are headed in the same direction. On a whim, she turns right instead of left, following everyone else. She has no idea where the Gale family home is, if that's even the destination, but it's easy enough to slide into the slow caravan of cars.

They drive through a town with two gas stations (one open for business and one with obsolete gas pumps and plywood over the windows) and a series of small businesses, some in better shape than others, and then Claudia is bumping along down a dirt road riddled with rocks. Cars are parked in the dry grass around a large farmhouse that looks like it's one strong breeze away from falling apart. The copper of the roof has turned green from weather and time, the white paint is peeling off in short strips, and the bushes in front are leafless and skeletal. Acres of land slope down to one side, where cows dot the landscape like dark buttons on a faded green sweater. Claudia pulls her car into the grass and idles there, watching the visitors (some of them carrying covered food dishes) filter up the wide porch and through the front door.

She shouldn't get out of the car, and there's no way she can go inside the house. Sooner or later, Paxton's parents (or some other family members) will be making a trip to The Prestige to pack up his apartment, and while they may not recognize her now, they'll surely make the connection when they finally get down to Ellen Point. So she doesn't go in. Instead, she sits in the car with the window cracked until she no longer hears the sound of tires on the dusty, rocky drive. Then she swings open the car door and steps out into the sunshine. Her heels catch in the grass as she veers slowly away from the front door and around the side of the house.

The windows are bare, no blinds or curtains to provide privacy. Living out here with no other houses nearby must be privacy enough. Claudia bats a low-hanging tree limb out of her path as she sneaks around to the back of the house. She can't actually walk through the door of Paxton's childhood home, but she can't overcome this urge to be part of things. She's embarrassed by her behavior, spying on this family and their loved ones in their grief. She still doesn't know what she hopes to learn.

Claudia has to open the gate on a chain-link fence to get around to the back of the house, and she winces at the creak it makes as it opens and closes. Her heels sink into a half-dried mud puddle as she creeps closer to the house. She'll have to throw these shoes away when she gets home. It's easy to see into the kitchen now, the crowd of people hugging and eating and wiping away tears. Alcohol lines the butcher block kitchen counter, and the woman she's pegged as Paxton's mother is pouring herself a drink. With a pour like that, she'll be wasted by the time her company leaves. Good for her. Whatever it takes to get through. She's pretty, even with her dark hair limp around her shoulders. One glance up, and she'll see Claudia watching her. But no, she turns her back and rejoins the crowd.

Claudia creeps farther down, where she can see into the next window. The sister's, she guesses. The walls are painted eggplant, with abstract art on the walls and an unmade bed against one wall. She thinks of the girl she saw earlier. Younger than Paxton, according to the obituary, but she can't be younger by much.

The next bedroom must be Paxton's. There's a large black-and-white photo of the University of Alabama's football team from some vintage year, and a poster of a huge off-road vehicle spinning through the mud. This room hasn't been repurposed as an office or storage or anything else (when Claudia left home, her old bedroom became her mother's *craft room*), so Paxton must have come back to visit regularly on holiday or summer breaks, or even long weekends. Still, this room is so different from his apartment at The Prestige that it's as if the spaces belonged to two different people. Claudia would like to open the window, crawl inside, look around. The proprietary urge—the comfort she's acquired with Paxton's personal spaces—is so strong that she finds herself reaching out, testing the window. Locked. Claudia isn't prepared to crawl through someone's window anyway. She doesn't know what she was thinking. She shouldn't be here. Not in this town and certainly not behind Paxton's house. She's turning to go when, out of the corner of her eye, she sees the light change in the room. She stops.

It's Lou, Amberly's friend, opening and then gently closing the bedroom door behind her.

The last time Claudia saw Lou up close, in the lounge at The Prestige, the young woman's face had been streaked with tears. If there are tears this time, Claudia doesn't see them. Lou had seemed like a sweet, genuine young woman, but Claudia rethinks that assumption now that she sees Lou going through Paxton's belongings. She looks under the bed, pulls open desk drawers. She even lifts the pillows from his bed to look beneath them. Then she's on to the closet, pushing clothes aside. Claudia leans forward, and the window sill creaks. Lou jumps, and Claudia ducks down before she's spotted.

It's time to get out of here. Claudia hurries back to the gate and fights to get it open again. Finally, it swings open (loudly), and she's almost to the front of the house when a man rounds the corner in front of her. Claudia is in such a rush that she almost runs him over.

"Whoa," he says.

"Oh my goodness, I'm so sorry." She hovers there, trying not to seem suspicious. She can feel the sweat on the back of her neck.

He leans against the house's white siding and pulls a cigarette from his suit pocket. "Haven't smoked in years, but today calls for it, I think."

"It's...a tough day," she says. She's glad she wore the sunglasses so he can't see much of her face. She doesn't recognize him—why would she?—but she's still disappointed in herself for ending up in this situation, where this man can say he spoke with her. He is proof that Claudia was here. She starts to step around him but he speaks again.

"It *is* tough, isn't it? Losing someone so young." He holds out his hand. "I'm Derek. Paxton's high school football coach."

Claudia shakes his hand and takes in his reddish hair, light eyes, athletic build. "Hi," she says. "I'm a friend of the family. I'm..." she wracks her brain, her made-up story entirely forgotten. "Cece." Her old initials, *C.C.*, before she'd gotten married and taken her husband's last name like a good Southern wife.

"Nice to meet you, Cece. Wish it were under better circumstances."

"Same," she says. "Were you and Paxton close?"

He shakes his head. "Not as close as we should have been. I mean, you know how Paxton is—was." Claudia nods like this is true. "He was just a kid, getting into teenage trouble, until the accident with Aaron. I don't know, I guess I should have checked in on him. I wish I had. Hindsight and all."

"Accident?" she says. She thinks of the message Aaron Baxter left on Paxton's Facebook page.

"Yeah." He looks at her, more carefully now. "How well did you know Paxton?"

"How well do you ever really know anyone?" she stammers. "I'm sorry, I've got to get going. It's been...nice, talking to you." She holds up a hand to wave a half-hearted goodbye, and then walks as fast as she can back to the car.

She has more questions than answers. There had been some sort of accident involving Aaron, the young man who had left that odd Facebook message. Claudia hadn't seen him at the funeral. And what was Lou doing poking around in Paxton's childhood bedroom?

The three-hour drive home gives her more time to think. When her thoughts start going in circles, though, she lets them drift back in time, to Killian.

She'd scrawled her phone number in Sharpie on his to-go coffee cup one day, and she'd been sure he'd call. He was as drawn to her as she was to him. She knew it. He'd sought her out at the shop several times by then. The mix of passion and peace when they touched was intoxicating. But for a while, her phone didn't ring and maybe it didn't even matter. Killian wasn't her type; before him, the boys she dated were all spikes and ink: gelled spiky hair, thick leather bracelets with silver spikes, arms and legs covered in tattoos, barbed attitudes that matched her own. Killian was completely different, and yet she felt enamored with him in a way she couldn't imagine fighting. Fuck fighting it. She wanted to run right toward him, without a thought as to what came after. That was how she did things, back then.

But. Even if she couldn't see them, she would come to learn that Killian had sharp edges of his own.

***

Claudia presses her foot to the gas pedal. This isn't about Killian. She drums her fingers against her steering wheel. Paxton. Paxton was involved in some kind of accident. When? Was "accident" code for a suicide attempt? But his coach had implied that he'd been a carefree teen. Something had changed, and that something involved the guy who had posted on Paxton's Facebook wall. Aaron.

Claudia needs to know what happened.

Then there was Lou, in Paxton's bedroom. What was she looking for? Claudia had gotten the distinct impression that Lou was *Amberly's* friend. How well had she even known Paxton?

There's a note from Beau on the counter when Claudia gets home. *Out for a run.* So she changes into shorts and a t-shirt and pulls out her phone and her laptop. She doesn't know Lou's last name, but Amberly is easy enough to find online. An Instagram search brings up her account. The most recent post is a shot of Paxton and Amberly, the words RIP and a broken heart emoji in the caption. Paxton is almost smiling in the picture, a dull drunkish look on his face. Her timeline shows she added the picture two days ago. There's a smattering of sympathetic comments underneath. Further down, Claudia finds a photo of Amberly and Lou, with Lou tagged in the photo. Claudia clicks to her page, but finds that it's private. It *does* give her one thing though: Lou's last name. Chambers.

Next, she opens Google and searches for Paxton Gale and Aaron Baxter. Together. An article pops up that she didn't see before. It's from last summer, from the online version of the Kelver Ridge newspaper. *Two Wallace T. Brady Grads Injured in Rock Crawling Accident*, reads the headline. Rock crawling. She's heard of people doing this here in Ellen Point. From what she gathers, Paxton and Aaron, who it turns out was a prominent local high school football star who had gone on to play in college, were rock crawling in a utility terrain vehicle on an old mining trail when they lost control of the UTV. It was after dark (already dangerous), and alcohol was involved. Paxton sustained minor injuries, but Aaron's leg was shattered when he was pinned between the UTV and a boulder. An article a few months later shared the news that Aaron was doing rehab at a medical facility in Charlotte, but that he wouldn't return to the University of Alabama and that his football career was over. There is an old GoFundMe campaign set up to help with medical bills, with a photo on the page of Aaron Baxter giving a thumbs-up from a hospital bed.

That's where the trail of information on Aaron stops. He has no Instagram and his Facebook page is private. It seems clear from Aaron's message on Paxton's timeline that Aaron was understandably still affected—physically or mentally or both—by the crash. And that either Paxton was responsible for the accident, or that Aaron believed him to be.

What did it do to Paxton to know that he'd been involved in a crash that injured his friend so badly? His football coach said he'd changed. It couldn't be an easy thing to live with. But was the guilt so bad that it drove him to suicide, and if so, why over a year later?

Claudia reminds herself that Paxton *didn't* die by suicide. It's a false narrative. He was killed. Earlier this week, she'd wondered if Aaron could be a suspect. But she thinks back to the night she saw Paxton's body in his living room. Someone went to a lot of trouble to orchestrate it, to make it *look* like suicide. Would Aaron have taken the time to do that?

She closes her laptop. She's no detective. She clearly doesn't know her way around an investigation.

But there's a persistent voice in her head, telling her that there's more here. There's more to Paxton Gale.

Someone killed him, and no one knows it but Claudia.

CHAPTER 9

P axton's mother may have held it together for her son's funeral yesterday, but today there are gray-blue circles beneath her eyes, her hair is in a messy pile atop her head, and she wears a ratty white sweatshirt that's at least two sizes too big. She could almost be an undergrad, headed to class with a hangover, if not for the faint lines on her forehead and that haunted look on her face.

Claudia recognizes her the instant she materializes outside the lobby, though Mrs. Gale has no way of knowing that Claudia saw her just the day before, standing in the Gale family kitchen. Now that the funeral is over, Mrs. Gale has wasted no time getting to Ellen Point to clear out Paxton's apartment. Claudia had expected a phone call first, had dreaded the conversation. But Paxton's mother didn't call; she just showed up. Claudia hasn't had time to emotionally prepare herself for this face-to-face interaction, or to make one last visit to Paxton's apartment before everything gets packed up and cleared out.

"I'm Marilyn Gale," she says, when Claudia opens the door. Paxton's sister is standing behind her, wearing jeans and a tank top, and up-close Claudia can see that her hair is shot through with streaks of orange. "My son Paxton...well, he...and this is my daughter, TessAnne."

"I'm Claudia Aldridge. I'm so sorry for your loss." Which is probably the same inane platitude everyone offers them now.

Marilyn looks around the lobby like she's in a foreign country. "I'm in shock," she says. "That's what they tell me. I'm trying to figure this whole thing out."

Claudia nods. Marilyn Gale wanders the wide lobby, runs a hand against an armchair, stares into the fire burning in the fireplace. TessAnne follows her.

"The girl he was seeing said she lives here. Is that where they found him?"

"Pardon?" Claudia asks. Surely the police gave her all the details.

"In her apartment? Is that where he was?"

"No. He was in his own apartment."

"Excuse me?"

"He was in his apartment. Amberly wasn't there. At least, not until later."

Marilyn looks away from the controlled flames. "What do you mean?" She seems agitated. Claudia has obviously said the wrong thing, though she doesn't know what that is. "What do you mean, *his own apartment*?" she asks. "What the hell was he doing here?"

Claudia looks at her in confusion. "He lived here."

"No, he didn't," she says. "I'm his mother. I think I would know. Paxton lives in an apartment on the other side of town. He has three other roommates." She doesn't use the past tense when she says his name. "We're headed there next to get his things. He couldn't afford a place like this. *We* couldn't afford a place like this. He's not one of these entitled college kids, you know."

"I'm afraid I don't understand," Claudia says, as calmly as she can manage, though she feels that ache in her chest again. She looks from Marilyn to TessAnne Gale. "He's lived here for months. He moved in back in January."

"He doesn't," she insists. "He hasn't."

"Maybe you should have a seat," Claudia says. "Let's get you two something to drink. Coffee? Tea?" Paxton's mother is obviously confused. She's grieving, and Claudia doesn't want to push the argument. TessAnne doesn't refute her mother's story, though.

Marilyn sinks into a leather chair in front of the fireplace. The flames dance small and bluish. TessAnne sits on the arm of the chair, her hand on her mother's shoulder. "Tea would be nice," TessAnne says. Marilyn leans forward and her shoulders sink in; the chair seems to swallow her whole. Claudia takes two mugs from the lobby's coffee and tea station and pours steaming water from a carafe. Her hand hovers over the array of tea. "Green?" she asks. "Earl Gray?" Marilyn Gale seems more like an iced sweet tea kind of woman.

"Whatever," Marilyn says. Claudia opts for the Earl Gray. She sets the mugs and two sugar packets beside the women on a glass side table, and then she leaves them sipping tea while she slips into her office to retrieve Paxton's lease from her file cabinet. She opens it for good measure, just to make sure *she* isn't the one who is confused. But there's his name, Paxton Gale, and his signature at the bottom.

Claudia takes the file with her to the lobby and sits in the empty leather chair beside the Gale women, file on her lap. She slides her finger along the top of it. GALE – 607.

"Mrs. Gale," Claudia says, quietly. She opens the file so both she and TessAnne can see Paxton's name on the lease. Hopefully when she sees his name written there, everything will fall back into place. Her eyes follow the text to the bottom, where Paxton's signature is scrawled. She shakes her head in disbelief, and TessAnne looks confused as well.

"That's his signature," Marilyn says.

"Yes."

"I don't understand."

"Y'all really didn't know he lived here?" Claudia asks. Her Southern accent gets more pronounced when she's stressed. TessAnne shakes her head. Claudia can't imagine how this is possible, but then again, it's not *impossible*. Maybe Paxton and his family aren't close. He could have a wealthy aunt or uncle who has padded a trust fund for him. Stranger things have happened.

"That's...unusual." She doesn't know what else to say. "Would you two like to go up to the apartment?"

"I...I guess so," Marilyn says. Claudia leaves them to grab a key, and returns moments later to lead the way to the elevators.

"This isn't possible," Marilyn says. "How is this possible?"

"I don't know, Mom," TessAnne says.

"What were you doing here, Pax?" Marilyn whispers. TessAnne and Claudia share a look. Claudia can tell she's worried for her mother.

"I know there are no words," Claudia says, "But we're really going to miss him around here." It's not the *biggest* lie she's ever told. Paxton was perhaps the resident she knew the least, and yet, Claudia has found herself mourning him as if they were close. And he was a good resident. She never had to send him a noise violation, and he never left cigarette butts or beer bottles by the pool. Rent always came in on time. By all accounts, that made him one of the good ones.

Marilyn is taken aback by the architectural details and the chandeliers illuminating the building's carpeted hallways. Claudia twists the key in Paxton's door lock and stands back, allowing the other two women to go in first. On a normal day this could be a lease tour, and Claudia could be guiding prospective residents through the community, ushering them through the elegant model apartment. This is the morbid opposite. Marilyn hesitates in the doorway then finally steps inside. TessAnne and Claudia follow. The door closes softly behind them.

Marilyn stops at the foyer table, runs her hands over the books there, the car keys. Then she walks slowly down the hallway, looking at the art on the walls as though she's never seen it before.

In the open kitchen and living room, Marilyn picks up the same paperwork that Claudia's been through half a dozen times now. She studies the sofa, the sophisticated décor, the flat-screen TV attached to the wall.

"What the *fuck*?" she finally says.

CHAPTER 10

C laudia looks at Marilyn Gale with wide eyes.

"This apartment was provided furnished?" TessAnne asks. Claudia shakes her head. "No."

Marilyn spins around in the apartment slowly, taking it all in. Her eyes well up and Claudia looks away. She shouldn't be here right now—this moment is private—but she can't leave.

"Claudia," Marilyn whispers, like they're closer than they are, like they didn't meet moments ago. TessAnne grips her mother's hand. "This stuff isn't his. The paperwork is, I see his name on the papers. But all this expensive furniture, these electronics. They aren't *his*."

This whole experience is starting to feel like something out of a Twilight Zone episode. Claudia doesn't know what to say. "Maybe he bought it without telling you?" she suggests, in a feeble attempt to set this right.

"No," TessAnne says. "He did occasional gigs for a catering company. He didn't have this kind of money. So how the hell did he get all this *stuff*?"

Claudia looks around at the furnishings that have become familiar to her at this point. "I...I'm sorry, but I don't know." She wants desperately to give them a logical answer, but right now at least, she has none.

***

Claudia leaves Marilyn and TessAnne alone in the apartment to get their bearings, and to give herself a moment to think. Back in the lobby she pours herself a cup of coffee, stirring in a sugar packet, pouring a drizzle of cream. She sits at her desk and stares at the mug, at the cream swirling into the dark liquid.

Most students who live at The Prestige at Ellen Point don't have full-time jobs. That means the resident screening service usually requires a parent or other cosigner's income information. It's a standard practice among student communities to ensure rent gets paid. If Paxton didn't have a steady job—and Marilyn and Tess seemed sure he didn't—then *someone* had to provide income information for Paxton, or put down a hefty extra deposit to get around it. If Marilyn and her husband didn't provide that, then who did?

Paxton's file is on her desk. Claudia opens it, flips through the lease agreement and to the paperwork fastened behind it. There's an approval printout from the third-party website they use to screen residents. Paxton would have entered his application details directly into the site.

She'll need to contact Tenant Secure to get a copy of that information. But before she can compose an email request, TessAnne steps off the elevator. Claudia waves her into the office. TessAnne seems to be holding up better than Marilyn, though Claudia sees her hands trembling when she takes a seat in the chair across from the desk. "We don't recognize most of that stuff," TessAnne says. "We don't know where it came from. How weird is that? That's weird, right?"

"It *is* weird."

"Mom's still up there. Trying to figure out what to do with it all. Strange question, but was there a *dog* in there?"

Claudia blinks. To say Paxton hadn't communicated with his family must have been an understatement. "Yeah. Paxton got a puppy from the Humane Society um...last month? A little golden mix. I think it's with Amberly now, if you want to get in touch with her. If, you know, you want the dog. I don't know if y'all are dog people..." Claudia's getting flustered trying to wrap her mind around all of this. "You knew about Amberly, right?"

Thankfully, TessAnne nods, though her face hardens. "Yeah, we knew he was seeing someone. We met her for the first time at the service. I don't know how to reach her though."

"I can put you in touch with her. In case you want the dog."

"I'll talk to mom about it. We found an iPad in the apartment—don't ask me where he got that, either—and I bet Amberly's number is in it, but we haven't even taken the time to charge it. Mom says she can't bear to look at it. We probably won't take the dog though. Mom is allergic. Then again, I don't like the idea of that girl having it."

"You don't care for Amberly?" Claudia asks.

"I don't know her well enough to form an opinion. I just know they weren't together long, and she's not the kind of girl Paxton would usually go for."

"Oh?"

"I thought he was into girls who were more...genuine, I guess. I didn't get a good vibe from her." Claudia bristles. It's the exact kind of thing someone might have said about Claudia, once upon a time. Her own vibes haven't always been great.

"I get it," Claudia says, but she's not sure she does. Amberly seemed to really care for Paxton. "Were you and Paxton close?"

"I mean, I thought so. He's three years older than me, but we used to be tight, before he moved away to college."

"Are you in school too?"

"Yeah, I'm a freshman. Community college though. I'm not smart like Paxton. I couldn't get into Ellen Point in the first place, even if we could afford it. Not like Paxton with his scholarship." Claudia hadn't known that Paxton was on scholarship.

"There's nothing wrong with community college," Claudia says. "Had you and Paxton talked recently?"

"Two weeks ago. He never mentioned a dog. Or, you know, this place."

"Was he...*okay* though?" She can't help but ask, no matter her certainty that Paxton was murdered.

"He sounded the same as always. Claudia, can I be honest with you?" She nods.

"Not one bit of this makes sense. Mom is heartbroken. Dad is...well, too drunk to fully accept what's going on, as usual...and getting them through this is hard enough without saying what I really think. But I don't believe Paxton was suicidal. Sure, he'd had his dark moments, especially after last year, but I can't see this happening the way they say it did."

Claudia is quiet.

"I may be reaching," TessAnne continues, "but I don't think this was suicide. I think someone killed him."

It's on the tip of Claudia's tongue to agree. But despite her own certainty, she has no real evidence. Amazon packages, a grocery delivery, and a friend acting suspicious at a funeral don't add up to much. "You do?" she asks, instead, leaning forward. "But, who could have done that?"

"I don't know. But trust me when I say I'm going to find out."

Claudia reaches for a business card from her desk and passes it over. "Here. It's got my phone number and email. If I can help, let me know." She pauses. "I mean it."

***

"We're done here," Marilyn says a short while later, though Claudia hasn't seen TessAnne or Marilyn actually move anything out.

"Already?"

TessAnne nods. "We don't know where most of that stuff came from, and we don't care what happens to it. Trash, Goodwill, whatever. Can you have someone take care of it? Whatever it costs, just send us a bill. We hate to ask, but it's just too much for us to worry about right now."

Claudia wouldn't dream of actually sending them a bill. "Of course." Marilyn's eyes are red-rimmed. "Is there anything else I can do for you?"

"You can't bring my son back, can you?" Marilyn laughs, a hysterical sound. Claudia is speechless. "No, I know you can't. I'm sorry."

TessAnne puts her arm around Marilyn's shoulder. "Come on Mom. Let's go. Claudia, we appreciate your help."

"Of course," she says.

She watches the Gale women leave, certain she'll never see or hear from them again.

CHAPTER 11

G raham arrives at work to find Claudia still shaken from her meeting with the Gale women. She fills him in on the details and watches his jaw drop.

"Wait, they didn't know he *lived* here?"

Claudia shakes her head. "The entire thing was a complete shock to both of them."

"How is that even possible?"

"I'm trying to figure that out. I've sent a request to Tenant Secure for the income information he provided to try and find out how he qualified to live here in the first place if his parents didn't even know about it."

"Huh." Graham twists the watch on his wrist. "Did they clean out the apartment?"

"No, they didn't take much of anything." She's been back in there already. Paxton's family had left most everything behind: the clothes, the furniture, and all of the art on the walls. "I guess I'll call tomorrow to schedule a furniture pickup." The local Habitat for Humanity ReStore will come get it for free. "You don't want anything from up there, do you?"

Graham shudders. "Definitely not."

"I figured."

"Wow. I don't really know what to say about all of this."

"Yeah, me neither." After a few quiet moments, Claudia goes back to her rent roll and Graham starts returning phone calls. Liza is off today, and Claudia finds that she's relieved. She doesn't want to have to deal with any more drama. She should have fired Liza, she knows that, but she's invested so much time in Liza's training and she can't start all over again. Not right now. So when Liza had apologized profusely for advertising Paxton's death and swore to put more effort into her work, Claudia had reluctantly agreed to give her a warning instead of firing her on the spot.

Now, Claudia needs to get her own act together. She can't abandon her investigation of Paxton's death—she's onto something, she knows it—but she's got to stop adding Killian into the mix. Finding out the truth about Paxton won't bring Killian back, and losing Killian was painful enough the first time around.

Her heart can't take it again.

***

At the end of the work day, after Graham has gone home, Claudia locks up her office and takes the elevator to the eleventh floor of the building. There's a gorgeous model apartment up there. Decorated to the nines, fully done, and vacant. She looks around to make sure no one sees her slipping inside, not that it matters. She's gotten used to being furtive, but she has every right to be in *this* apartment.

It's chilly inside, the air turned down low to counteract the Georgia heat. She adjusts the thermostat, then fishes out the bottle of elderflower liqueur and the highball glass she keeps hidden in the back of one of the kitchen cabinets. A former resident had gifted her the bottle and a set of two glasses, and she's been sipping on the liqueur ever since. Sometimes she's not ready to go home when the day ends, doesn't want to drag her work stress home with her or face the loneliness that awaits her there even when her husband is in the same room. She doesn't remember when they stopped *really* talking.

Claudia starts a playlist on her phone, volume turned low, and settles into the uncomfortable sofa. The apartment is meant to look beautiful, not to actually be lived in. She kicks off her heels and looks out the floor-to-ceiling windows. The views from here are spectacular. In another hour or so, the sun will sink below the horizon, bleeding into the mountains as it goes and turning the sky red and orange. She sips the syrupy liqueur and leans back into the sofa cushions. Elderflower isn't really her thing, but she's not going to let this expensive bottle go to waste. She wonders how long she could stay here before Beau would even think to call her. He isn't the kind of person who worries. It's one of the things that used to fascinate her about him. Claudia was relaxed like that too once, before Killian, but now if someone is even ten minutes late, she's convinced a tragedy has occurred. Sometimes, when she starts to think of all the ways people can die, she forgets how to breathe and she has to remind herself to do it over and over for a few minutes until it becomes automatic again.

Claudia is finally coming down from this sad, hectic day. It's not smart, spending time up here on her own. She should call her friends, confide in someone. But she doesn't reach for her phone.

The sound of the apartment door unlocking makes her jump, and she hides the bottle of liqueur and the glass on the floor beside the sofa. The maintenance team has long since left for the day, and no one else outside of the staff has a key to the apartment.

Graham looks startled to see her there. He's still wearing his work clothes, the tie around his neck loosened to the point that it's absurd to still have it on at all.

"Hey," she says, trying not to sound irritated. She doesn't want to hide what she's doing, and she's not in the mood for company.

"What are you doing here? I thought you'd left for the day."

"Soon. What are *you* doing here?"

He looks sheepish. "My roommate's home. I kind of wanted some time alone."

I nod.

"I can go." He gestures to the door. "I'll go. Sorry for interrupting. I should be at the gym, anyway." When he's not at work or at school, Graham is an avid rock-climber who takes advantage of the giant climbing wall in the state-of-the-art Prestige gym when he can't get out to the actual cliffs.

Claudia watches his back, the tailored button-down shirt, the flex of his arms as he reaches for the door. She sighs. "Wait," she says. "You can stay, if you want."

He turns, smiling. "You sure?"

She nods.

"Are you going to share the booze?"

"What?"

"The fancy liqueur."

"How do you know about that?"

He closes and locks the door. "You've never noticed? I may have had a little bit on occasion. Didn't think you'd mind."

"Naughty."

"Makes two of us, I guess. For real, do you mind the company?"

"No," she lies. He removes the tie completely, finally, and drapes it over the back of the sofa. His hair is already free from its ponytail. She reaches for the glass and takes a long sip. Then she refills it and offers it to him.

"You okay with sharing?" he asks.

"Apparently I've already *been* sharing, I just didn't know it." She watches as he takes the glass, lips touching the exact spot where her lipstick marks the rim. He doesn't notice. It's intimate though, like a kiss but not. She thinks again of touching him, wonders how his skin would feel beneath the slow caress of her palm.

"Why do you think Paxton did it?" she asks, when he passes the glass back. It's a trick, a tactic to lead Graham to the same conclusion she's come to. That Paxton *didn't* do it at all.

"I don't know. I mean, why does anyone do something like that? Do you think he was depressed? I mean, he must have been, right?"

"I guess."

"He'd just rescued that puppy."

"Yeah."

"I knew someone," Claudia blurts. She doesn't know why she's sharing this. She sets the highball glass down too hard on the table and it almost tips over. No one knows about Killian. "We were close, in college. He...he died by suicide. That's the right way of putting it, isn't it?"

"Oh my god. What happened?"

"Pills. I didn't know. It didn't even occur to me that he needed help. Or, it did, looking back, but I ignored it because I was a terrible person back then. Maybe I still am." Graham opens his mouth to speak, but she keeps going. "Anyway, I found him. When he did it. It was..." she trails off, unable to think of a word that conveys what it had been like to find Killian that morning.

"Wow. Claudia, I'm sorry. That really sucks."

She can't hold back a rueful laugh in the face of this simple, basic truth.

It does suck.

***

"Late night?" Beau asks, when Claudia finally gets home from work. He's watching the news.

"Yeah," she says. "Why, were you worried?" She's been wrong about him before.

"Hungry, mostly." After a beat, he smiles. "Kidding. I'm glad you're home." The smile looks good on him. She forgets, sometimes, but she's as attracted to him as she was when they first met.

She shakes her head, but she smiles too. She doesn't mind being the one in charge of cooking; Beau does other things. They fell into their roles naturally, without ever really talking about it. She kicks off her shoes and heads to the kitchen, where she pulls vegetables from the fridge and heats the stovetop.

She wonders what had made her tell Graham, her coworker, about Killian. It had been such a relief to open up, to share things long hidden. A part of her wants to keep doing it: share things, talk to someone who is actually interested in her thoughts and ideas and feelings.

She doesn't know why she never told her husband about Killian. She thinks of telling him now. She could. If not about her past with Killian, then at least about Paxton, about how committed she's become to finding out the truth of his death. But Beau won't approve, if he hears her at all. If he loses interest in what she's saying before she's even revealed the depth of her convictions about Paxton, it will gut her.

Any of these excuses may be true, but it's also true that she doesn't want her husband to know how deeply invested she's become in learning Paxton's secrets.

Finding Paxton's killer is her own private pursuit.

CHAPTER 12

B eau is on the back porch sipping coffee when Claudia pads out of the bedroom the next morning. Her phone rings as she's pouring her cup.

"Morning sunshine!" Ruby says. "I know it's been a shit week," (and she doesn't know the half of it, since Claudia hasn't given either of her friends a full update on Paxton since Monday's coffee date), "but you'll still be at the Golden Hour Gathering tonight, right?"

"Of course, but is *Ingrid* actually going to be there? With everything that's going on with her father? Have you talked to her?"

"Only briefly, but she basically planned the whole thing. She'll be there."

"The rest of the Foxglove Society could handle it without her. With your help."

"I know, that's what I told her, but you know how Ingrid is."

"The entire world could be crumbling around her and she'd still show up."

The Foxglove Society takes pride in the work they put into their fundraisers, but they also have a contract with the best event planner in town—Ruby Duvall. Between Ingrid and Ruby, Claudia has been subjected to every detail of the planning for the Golden Hour Gathering for months now. Just like every year.

It's not enough for Ingrid Wyatt to be the president of WMB Real Estate. Overachiever that she is, she's also the president of the fancy local women's group. The Foxglove Society is a hoity-toity group of women all trying to one-up each other, if you ask Claudia. But fundraisers are their thing, and they do a damned good job.

Ingrid isn't in it for the good deeds, though, and they all know it. She's in the Foxglove Society because her father expects her to be, just like her mother was once upon a time, and her paternal grandmother before that. All "respectable" young ladies in Ellen Point are supposed to aspire to be members, but it takes more than aspiration to get you in. You also have to pass a rigorous interview process and put yourself up for a vote. A *vote*. Ingrid has been tireless in her efforts to get her two best friends to apply for membership, but Ruby's business keeps her too busy on the weekends, and Claudia doesn't think joining a club should require so much effort. Her small group of close friends is more than enough for her.

"Want to ride with Beau and me?" Claudia asks. Beau loves this event. Give the man all the charcuterie, the live music, the mountain sunsets. He's more excited about it than she is.

"No thanks. I'll be there early getting set up, and I'm bringing someone with me, so we'll just see you there."

"Ooh. Can't wait to meet him." Ruby forms casual attachments to the men she meets on dating apps, bringing them everywhere with her for a week or two before she just...lets them loose. She's upfront about her intentions, and so good-natured about it that she somehow rarely leaves angry exes in her wake.

Claudia is jealous of Ruby sometimes, of how untethered she is, but it was Claudia's own decision to be tied down. She wanted Beau and this stability.

"You'll like him, I think."

"I'll let you know. See you later."

Claudia ends the call and pushes open the door to the back porch. "Morning," she says to Beau.

"Morning." He's stretched out in an Adirondack chair, his empty coffee mug on the table in front of him.

"You remember the Golden Hour thing is tonight, right?"

"Of course. Is the food going to be as good as last year?" He smiles.

"Better, probably. Hey, how was Ingrid at work yesterday? Stressed about the event?"

"I don't know. I was tied up with meetings, but I think she left work at lunchtime."

"Probably to start setting up," Claudia says. "I've been trying to catch up with her and I'm starting to get a little worried."

"You know Willard fell, right?"

She nods.

"I think things have been worse than normal." Ingrid's father's health has been on the decline for over a year now. It's cancer, though her father doesn't want it broadcast all over town.

It seems like a lot of things are worse than normal, Claudia thinks, ruefully, as she sips her coffee and they settle into silence.

***

The Foxglove Society's annual Golden Hour Gathering is held on the property of a restored farmhouse in a mountainside meadow on the north side of Ellen Point. It's the perfect wedding venue for much of the year, save for when the bitter cold of winter rolls in and snow makes the drive impossible, or when the summer heat is so stifling no amount of decorative paper fans would make an outdoor wedding bearable. This evening, though, the light of the setting sun spills over rows of wooden tables set with flickering lanterns, wildflowers, and crisp linen runners. Small batch wines, craft ciders, and spiced pear cocktails and mocktails are served at a wooden outdoor bar, and appetizers of charcuterie cups and herb-buttered focaccia are delivered on trays by a catering team dressed like extras from Little House on the Prairie. A well-known local artist has set up an easel near the barn where he sketches the scene in delicate charcoal lines, a string quartet plays on the farmhouse steps, and woven blankets and low tables make small conversation areas for guests to lounge before dinner is served. Children in summer sundresses and linen pants rolled up at the bottom chase one another through the grass, their gleeful squeals competing with the music. The weather might still read summer, but the light has shifted, softer and richer. Women wear flowing dresses and men wear slacks with button-down shirts rolled up to the elbow. It's a last savoring of long days of summer, a celebration of nature, a fancy whimsical affair.

"Looks good this year," Beau says, admiring the set-up. "Want a drink?"

Claudia nods her head and Beau sets off toward the bar.

"Hey Claudia!" She spins around and finds Ruby, dressed in a long, bold floral print dress and sandals.

"You look fantastic," Claudia says, after a hug from her friend, and Ruby does a little twirl.

"Thank you, dear. And so do you." Claudia's dress is simple, sleeveless, dark and mid-length with a scoop neck.

"Thanks." Claudia looks around. "Where's the guy?"

Ruby shrugs. "He couldn't make it after all."

"You okay with that?"

"Yeah, just, you know, things didn't work out."

Beau returns, arms laden with drinks. He must have seen Claudia chatting with Ruby, because he magically has a stemless wine glass for her as well.

"Ah, wonderful," Ruby says, as Beau hands her the glass. "Thank you."

"My pleasure." Beau passes Claudia her glass. "I see Sawyer over there with his niece."

"Construction friend," Claudia explains to Ruby.

"Construction rival, more like," he says with a smile. "Owns a competing business over in Wildflower Glen. Anyway, I think I'll go say hey." He kisses Claudia on the cheek and heads off between the rows of tables.

"You picked a good one, you know," Ruby says, watching Beau.

"Hmm." She tilts her head as if to see her husband from Ruby's perspective. She hasn't told her friends about the distance between Beau and her. Ingrid was the one who introduced them, after all. Aside from that, there's a part of Claudia that can't bear to confess to her friends the depth of her loneliness. Maybe Ruby's right. Maybe Beau *is* a good one. Maybe Claudia is the problem. "Have you seen Ingrid yet?" she finally says, changing the subject altogether.

"No, I got caught up in the kitchen making sure the food was coming along." Dinner is all locally sourced, from the rosemary lamb to the butternut squash ravioli to the roasted vegetables. "She should be working on the lanterns."

They stroll through the meadow, stopping to chat with other guests as they make their way to a line of unlit paper lanterns that Ingrid is arranging in a sort of aesthetically-pleasing semi-circle. They don't actually release the lanterns into the sky, and the candles inside will be battery-powered, but when the sun goes down each guest is invited to symbolically "light" a lantern and make a wish for the season to come.

"Hello, gorgeous," Ruby says. "Beautiful event, as always."

"Thank you both for coming," Ingrid says. She's dressed impeccably in a waist-defining cream-colored sundress. But Claudia can see the exhaustion in her eyes.

"Hey, how are things with your dad?" Claudia says. "How can we help?"

"You're so sweet for asking," Ingrid says, quietly. "I appreciate the basket you dropped off, and so did he. I meant to call. He'll be okay, this time. It's just hard to focus on..." she gestures around at the festival, "all of this, right now."

"We could cover for you here," Ruby suggests. "As long as we don't get accidentally initiated into the Foxgloves."

"Thanks," Ingrid says. "But I really have to do this. It's...my job, as president. My dad's nurse is with him. I learned this morning that Kennamer Farms is going on the market soon, so this may be the last year we get this venue for the gathering."

"I didn't know the Kennamers were selling," Ruby says. She's coordinated dozens of weddings here.

"Yeah, last minute decision. New grandkid apparently, and they want to move closer."

"You're not interested in buying?" Claudia asks Ingrid. "It's a great property."

Ingrid shrugs. "I don't really know what we'd do with a farmhouse, so I think I'll sit this one out. We'll see what happens."

"Hey, I don't see your fiancé anywhere. Wasn't he supposed to be here?" Claudia asks.

"Oh, he is. He's around here somewhere. What about Beau?"

"Mingling. Or kicked back on a blanket by now, maybe."

"Ruby, weren't you going to bring someone?" Ingrid asks.

"I was," she says carefully. "But he *ghosted* me."

"What? For the Golden Hour Gathering? Are you kidding?" Claudia says, her eyes wide.

"Completely serious. It's like he fell off the face of the earth." Ruby's smile is just a bit less dazzling than normal.

"That's wild," Ingrid says.

Ruby shrugs. "It was good while it lasted."

"Claudia, how are you?" Ingrid asks, cautiously. "With work, and the boy who...who...."

"Died?" Claudia says flatly. "Not great."

"What happened, exactly?" Ingrid says, and Claudia remembers that Ingrid had left the coffee meet-up before she'd spilled all of the details to Ruby.

"Suicide," Claudia says. "That's what they say, at least."

Ingrid stares at her. "That's...horrible."

"Yeah, actually that reminds me," Claudia starts, but she's interrupted by Thomas McIntyre striding up to join them. She'd never gotten the chance to ask Ingrid about the invitation she found in Paxton's apartment, but she doesn't want to talk about Paxton in front of Thomas. Maybe it's because of the comment he made last month about Claudia's job, about how she might act when surrounded by younger men. She doesn't want him to know she's been rummaging around a resident's apartment, that she'd be anything less than professional.

"Ladies," he says, with a wide smile. "Doesn't Ingrid throw a great party?" He puts his arm around Ingrid's shoulders.

"I had Ruby's help," Ingrid says.

"You were the mastermind, though. You could put me out of a job," Ruby says.

"That's our Ingrid," Thomas says. "Excels at everything." He squeezes Ingrid's shoulder.

"You guys are adorable. It's sickening," Ruby says.

"Thank you, we'll take that," Thomas says.

The sun paints watercolors across the sky as it sinks, ambers and blushes and violets. This is it, the golden hour of another departing summer. Claudia looks around at her friends and even in this enchanting light, it feels like she can see through their smiles to the sadness lurking beneath. Ingrid's father is ill, and Ruby has a bruised ego despite her efforts to hide it. Claudia is investigating the death of a college student she hardly knew to ease her own guilt.

It's a perfect evening with a perfect sunset on a perfect mountainside, and yet Claudia is suddenly overcome with a sense of despair that no amount of celebrating can shake away.

CHAPTER 13

Amberly Vance, Paxton's girlfriend, shows up in the lobby of The Prestige two days later. It's the first time Claudia has seen her since the funeral. Lou is by her side, and they've brought along a stocky boy who introduces himself as Randall. Paxton's roommate. "At the other place, where he lived," he clarifies when Claudia looks at him strangely.

So it was somehow true that Paxton had two apartments. "Hi," Claudia says, shaking his hand when he holds it out. Then she focuses her attention on Amberly. "How are you doing?" she asks.

"Fine, I guess," Amberly says. She looks down, pushes her light hair behind one ear. Claudia has other residents who would plop down in a chair and talk her ear off. Janie would. Her job veers into counselor territory more often than she's really comfortable with. But it's clear Amberly doesn't want to talk. Claudia can't make her, but it's disappointing.

"I wondered if we could get the key to Paxton's apartment," Amberly says. "Mrs. Gale said it was okay."

"She did?" Marilyn hadn't mentioned anything about Amberly going into the apartment.

"Yeah, in case we wanted anything...of sentimental value." Lou and Randall nod.

Claudia feels uncomfortable giving a key to Amberly and company, but Marilyn *had* told Claudia to clear everything out. Is there harm in letting Amberly take what she wants? It's going to be tossed out or donated anyway.

Claudia retrieves the key and hands it over. Amberly, Lou, and Randall disappear into the elevator, and Claudia doesn't see them again until Amberly returns the key two hours later.

"Hey," Claudia says to her, when Amberly drops the key into her palm. "If you want to talk or if you need anything, I'm here. Okay?"

"Yeah, okay." Amberly doesn't say another word though, just spins around and leaves.

When Claudia goes up to the apartment an hour later, she finds that the entire place has been ransacked. She stares in shock. It wasn't tidy before, but it's a disaster area now. Books are scattered around the bedroom, dresser drawers are empty with their contents strewn about. Clothes from the closet spill out into the rooms, hangers idle. The bed has been completely stripped and the bedding is heaped on the floor. In the living room, knick-knacks that once sat on sleek shelves litter the hardwoods. Even the bathroom cabinets have been rummaged through, the cabinet doors left open.

Lou was searching again, and this time, she'd had help.

Claudia sits down on the living room floor and takes in the whole jumbled scene. She wonders if they found it this time, whatever it was they were looking for.

Back when Killian died, Claudia had searched and searched for a suicide note. She'd needed some kind of explanation for why he'd left her on purpose. Maybe that's what Paxton's friends were doing too. She might truly believe that, might *understand* that, if she hadn't already seen Lou going through Paxton's room at his parent's house in Kelver Ridge. Because Paxton wouldn't have left his goodbye letters there.

Paxton's friends have different motives than Claudia did.

She's angry suddenly, for Paxton and his family. She's angry at herself for trusting Paxton's own friends—his girlfriend, even—to respect his things. His mementos, his treasures. They'd trashed his home.

Claudia scrambles from the floor and leaves the apartment, locking the door behind her. Before she can think too hard about what she's doing, she takes the elevator up two floors, marches to Amberly's apartment, and bangs on the door. She doesn't expect an answer, not once Amberly sees her through the peephole, but Amberly surprises her. When the door opens, the dog scampers out and jumps at Claudia's legs. Claudia reaches down and runs her fingers through its soft fur.

"Get. Inside," Amberly mutters to the dog. Then she looks up at Claudia. "Sorry, Claudia. What can I do for you?"

"How could you?" Claudia asks. "Why would you do that to Paxton's apartment?"

"What do you mean?" she asks. Amberly looks puzzled. If Claudia hadn't seen the apartment herself, she might believe the act.

"Why bother lying? You knew I'd have to go back up there. You three are the only ones who had the key."

"Honestly, Claudia, I have no idea what you're talking about." Her eyes are wide and heavily made up, and her mouth is a thick, pink-lacquered line of fake sadness. Claudia recognizes it now, and she feels stupid for having felt sympathetic toward Amberly in the first place. For having felt a connection to her. "Did something happen in Paxton's apartment?"

Complete denial is an interesting, and infuriating, strategy. "You know what?" Claudia says. "Never mind." She leaves, fuming and confused about what to do next. She thinks of calling Amberly's mother, telling Mrs. Vance about her daughter ransacking her dead boyfriend's apartment. Amberly's mother is an overbearing financial manager in Atlanta who dotes on her daughter. Claudia can only imagine that a phone call to her would end up with Mrs. Vance chiding Claudia for upsetting Amberly, and not the other way around.

When Claudia gets back to her desk, she looks up Lou again on Instagram. Claudia rarely uses her own social media pages, but today she breaks that rule to send Lou a private message.

I know what you did to Paxton's apartment. We need to talk. If I don't hear back from you, I'll be calling his mother.

Ten minutes later, after Claudia has poured herself a cup of hot tea and started to calm down, it occurs to her that sending the message wasn't smart. Threatening a college student? Not great. Claudia wonders about Lou and Amberly's friendship.

Amberly's grief over Paxton's death now feels like a front. Could Amberly have been the one to kill him after all?

***

Claudia may still be wading through the mystery of Paxton's death, but it's time to clear out his apartment to get it ready for the next resident, whoever that may be. Claudia makes a list of what needs to happen. She'll call Habitat for Humanity and have them come and take away the furnishings. There is a local junk hauling company that will take the rest to the dump and shred the paperwork. The maintenance team will repair the light fixture in the living room.

Claudia can make the place look brand new again, but she can't imagine anyone else actually living there. Someone else will, though. It will all keep going.

She goes back up to Paxton's apartment to take it all in one last time before its official deconstruction. It's hard to find anything anymore.

The papers that used to sit on the breakfast table are scattered on the floor. Claudia makes her way to the bedroom, where the dresser drawers have been upended. A glossy corner of a photo peeks out from under the dresser and she leans down to pick it up. It's the first photograph she's seen in the apartment. It's of Paxton and three other guys, one of which she recognizes as Randall, the one who helped Amberly and Lou trash the apartment. She's never met the other two, but she thinks she recognizes them from the funeral. She can tell the photo was taken in a bar by the neon sign lit up behind them and the crowd dancing in the background. She doesn't know the place, but then again, she's long past her barhopping days. She tucks the photo in her pocket, takes one last look around Paxton's apartment, and closes the door.

"Graham," she says later, when she's back down to her office. She tries to sound casual. "Do you have any idea where this photo was taken?"

He comes over to her desk to take a closer look. His cologne is woodsy, with a note of citrus in there somewhere. She leans into him slightly without realizing she's doing it, and then straightens when Liza walks past. If Graham notices the closeness or sudden lack of it, he pretends not to. The fabric of his suit jacket rubs against her arm.

"Yeah, it's The Study Room. I used to see Paxton there every now and then."

"You go there?"

"I mean, sometimes. Occasionally. It's not really my kind of place, but some of my friends like it. Where'd you get that picture?"

"Found it in Paxton's apartment." She tells him how she'd let Amberly and her friends check out a key for the apartment, and how they'd left it trashed.

"Why would they do that?"

"Not sure. But I want to find out. Were these guys usually out with Paxton, when you saw him at the bar?"

He nods. "Yeah. I've never met them, though. Why, what are you thinking?"

"That I'd like to try to track them down. One of them was with Amberly and Lou yesterday. Maybe I can find out what's going on."

"I don't think you should do that."

"Why not?"

"I just don't think it's smart." He looks down. "I mean, after what you told me the other night, about your friend, I get why it's important to you. I'm not trying to tell you what to do. It's up to you. Paxton's death was horrific, but there's nothing you can do to bring him back. I see you trying to make it better, but you can't, you know?"

"Yeah, I know that," she says, too quickly. "You're right."

There's no reason to go to that bar. Graham *is* right, there's nothing she can do to fix this. But she keeps thinking about Paxton's friends, Randall and the other two.

It doesn't matter if it's pointless or not. She has to talk to them.

CHAPTER 14

I t's been a long time since Claudia has been out to a bar alone.

When Beau left town this morning to visit a commercial construction site in Greenville, South Carolina, Claudia knew she had to seize the opportunity. He's probably finishing up dinner with his colleagues from the Greenville office right now, after which he'll stay overnight at a hotel funded by WMB before driving home tomorrow.

Which means she's on her own tonight.

She checks her phone and sips her Maker's Mark. Wine was what she'd really wanted, but she remembers the college bar scene well enough to know that no one stands around sipping Chardonnay in places like this.

The Study Room isn't crowded yet, but she bets it will be. There aren't all that many bars to choose from in Ellen Point, and the students have to blow off steam somewhere. She sits on her stool and looks around. The music is already blaring, even though there are only two girls swaying back and forth on the makeshift dance floor. Red lights flash to the beat of the music.

The bartender has hair that hangs down to her waist and a halter top that shows off her belly ring. Every now and then Claudia catches her looking over. Probably thinking someone Claudia's age doesn't belong here. Claudia holds the photo of Paxton and his friends in one hand, and she studies the face of each person who makes it past the bouncer at the entrance. Would she recognize Randall and these other boys if she saw them again? It hasn't been that long since Paxton died. Maybe his friends aren't even *thinking* about partying again yet.

She bets they are, though. The shock of Paxton's death, the grief of it, will wear away and they'll go back to laughing and having fun and living their lives. One person short, but otherwise the same. Nearly whole. Not everyone is like her, carrying a ghost around with them everywhere they go.

Her mind drifts away from the bar, and she thinks of Killian again.

She gave him hell when he finally called her. He'd kept her waiting for weeks. But she still said yes when he asked her out on a date. They met at an outdoor artist's market on their college campus. There was something refined and radiant about Killian, even in jeans, a heather gray t-shirt, and Birkenstocks. He was a bright light, a shiny coin, a twinkling star. She wasn't the only one who noticed. Walking with him around the market, she could feel other students noticing him.

The booths at the market were filled with metal jewelry, homemade soaps, paintings, wood carvings. Claudia could hardly focus on any of it, with how ravenous she was for Killian, how starved for his touch.

Killian made small talk with the artisans in his Southern drawl that was even more pronounced than hers, flashing his disarming smile, and he'd purchased an odd, ugly sculpture of a cow made from magazine pages and Paper Mache.

Why'd you buy that? She'd asked him.

He'd shrugged. *I like cows.*

That is the most hideous thing I've ever seen.

The artist wasn't selling much and I wanted to make him feel better. This art is really...dark.

It's a cow.

You wouldn't make art this bad if you weren't in a bad place.

She'd laughed. He'd taken her hand then and his touch had been such sweet relief that she didn't spend a single second considering that maybe Killian hadn't been joking, that maybe he didn't love or even like cows or magazine art but he really had seen the art as an expression of someone's pain. That maybe there was a reason he was able to recognize it so easily.

***

By midnight at The Study Room, Claudia still hasn't seen Paxton's friends. She's acutely aware of how pathetic she must look, alternating between scrolling on her phone and reminiscing. She can't convince herself to stay any longer, so she tips the bartender, slings her purse over her shoulder, and leaves disappointed.

***

"Back again," the bartender says the next night, setting a napkin in front of her. "Makers?"

Claudia nods, impressed that she remembers. "Thank you."

Friday had been a bust, but maybe Saturday will be better. It has to be, since Beau is driving home tomorrow and she won't get another weekend to try this for a while. She was lucky to get a second chance as it was. Beau had been invited to join a golf game today with the head of the Greenville WMB office, so he'd decided to extend his trip. To Claudia, it had seemed like a sign.

The bartender sets the glass down in front of Claudia and smiles, dimples lighting up her face. "Here you go."

"Thank you," Claudia says again. "Hey." The bartender seems friendly enough, and Claudia is here early again. She pulls the photo from her jeans pocket and smooths it out on the bar. "Do you know these guys?"

The bartender studies the photo. "I don't know. Maybe." She leans closer. "Yeah, I think so. I mean, I don't know everyone who comes in here, but these guys are here *a lot*." She shrugs, shakes her head. "Kids, right? They think this is a cool place to be."

Claudia smiles. The bartender can't be much older than twenty-one herself. "Why do you want to know?" she asks.

"It's...complicated. I need to talk to them. Have you seen them tonight?"

"No, but they might show up later." She looks at Claudia. "Are they in trouble or something?"

It's too much—and too depressing—to explain to her. "No," Claudia says. "Nothing like that. Do you know their names? Any of them?"

"No, but you can ask them yourself." She winks at Claudia. "Must be your lucky night. They just walked in."

Claudia spins around. It's them all right. Three young men, one shorter and stocky, one taller and well-dressed, and one with very light blond hair. Now that they're here, she doesn't actually know how to approach them. Without thinking about it too much, she sends over a round of shots. Seems like a good way to make new friends. She has the bartender take them over, the small tray balanced on her shoulder. When the young men ask who sent them, the bartender tilts her head at Claudia. Claudia gives a little wave, then slides off her stool and walks over. She wills herself not to be self-conscious. Young men in a group can be intimidating. She knows that well enough from her job.

"Hey," she says to the three friends.

"Hey." It's Randall who answers her. The stocky one. He's wearing an Ellen Point University t-shirt. "I know you."

"Yeah," Claudia says. "Sort of." She feels a surge of anger at him for what he did to Paxton's apartment, but she tries to hold it back. That's not the way to get what she wants.

"She works at that apartment building. Where Pax stayed."

At once, their collective guard seems to go up. "Why are you here?" the stylish one asks.

"To talk to you guys. About Paxton."

"Why?"

"I'm trying to help."

He crosses his arms. "If you're a friend of *hers*, you can tell her to go fuck herself. Paxton would still be here if not for her."

"Who?" She asks. "Amberly?"

Randall looks uneasy, and the third boy, the one with the light wispy hair, stares at the table. He's barely looked at her at all. Randall finally shakes his head. "Nah, but like Devin said, we're not talking to you. Not to you, not to her, not to anybody."

"Well, that's a shame," she says, but she doesn't push. She *wants* to; this may be her only chance at getting this information. But if she keeps it up, they may never tell her anything at all. She can see their resistance. These guys know more than they're sharing, and she can be persuasive when she needs to be. She's determined to get to the truth about Paxton.

They *will* tell her. She'll make sure of it.

CHAPTER 15

"It's a great day at The Prestige at Ellen Point, this is Claudia. How can I help you?"

"Paxton *was* murdered. I'm certain of it."

Claudia's office door is wide open. She's not on speaker phone, but she still looks around to make sure no residents are in the lobby checking their mail, pouring coffee, watching the news. She glances at the Caller ID. "TessAnne, is that you?"

"Yeah. Someone definitely killed him."

Claudia is stunned. Despite having given TessAnne her business card, she'd been fairly certain she'd never hear from the Gale women again.

"What makes you so sure? Did you find something?"

"It's just not adding up," TessAnne says. "Isn't that what they say in movies? When the police were in his apartment, guess what they never found? What *we* never found when we came to collect his things?"

"What?"

"His phone. Isn't that strange? It wasn't in his car either when we brought it back here. You know how attached everyone is to their phone these days." A vision of Beau springs to Claudia's mind. "Why haven't we found it?"

"I don't know. You're right, that is strange. Did you try the Find my iPhone feature? That's a thing, right?"

"Not turned on. But here's the other thing: I finally charged his iPad, and Claudia, there are all these text messages."

"What kind of messages?" Claudia is riveted.

"Awful ones. Basically *telling* him to kill himself. Telling him how to do it, saying that the world would be a better place without him in it, saying he would be at peace. Who does that?" Claudia thinks she hears TessAnne sniffling.

"That's...wow. So you think he followed those instructions and did it himself after all?" Claudia can't decide if this proves or disproves her murder theory.

"Even if that's what happened, shouldn't the person who sent those text messages be held responsible? That's...murder by *suggestion*, or something."

"Did you call the number?"

"Of course. Disconnected. It's like something out of fucking CSI. Something else was going on here. Someone *wanted* my brother dead." A shiver creeps up Claudia's spine.

"Who do you think it was?"

"I don't know. One of his friends. Or someone else completely."

"TessAnne, why are you telling me this?" She appreciates every single scrap of information she can get about Paxton, but surely TessAnne has closer confidantes.

"Because you said you'd help, if you could. And you can. Don't you have security cameras in that fancy building?"

She'd gotten so wrapped up in other leads that she'd forgotten to go back and catch up on the security camera feed. She can't believe she hasn't studied every minute of the footage from that weekend already. "I do."

"Could you go through it? See if anyone else was with Paxton the night he died?"

"I can try," Claudia says, because she doesn't want to admit that she'd already started this project and then forgotten about it. "It takes a while. I'll need to spend some time on it."

"Okay. You'll do it though?"

"Of course." TessAnne may be sharing information with Claudia, but Claudia can't bring herself to share what she knows. About the letters-that-weren't, about the grocery delivery, about Amberly and her friends ransacking Paxton's apartment, about Claudia's own experience with suicide and her gut feeling that Paxton's death was something else entirely. She tells herself she doesn't want to upset Paxton's family, but the truth is that she needs to figure this out for herself first.

Claudia opens the security camera app. She'll know the truth soon enough.

***

She spends an hour scanning camera footage before her eyes start to cross.

The postmortem stalking of Paxton is getting to her. She needs a break, and she could use some better coffee. The gourmet stuff in the lobby turns lukewarm and stale after a few hours. Claudia still prefers a strong latte, even if she doesn't make them herself anymore. She grabs her purse and locks up the office, then slips her sunglasses over her face and drives the few blocks to The Gilded Mug.

She swings her car into the drive-through line but changes her mind and turns into a parking space instead when she sees Beau's truck. It's parked a few spaces down, the silver Chevy with the Ellen Point Alum sticker on the back window. School pride and all. It's not the first time they've bumped into each other here. The WMB building is nearby.

Claudia sees Beau standing in line, deep in conversation with Ingrid. It's not surprising to see them together. They often talk work business over coffee or lunch.

Claudia steps around the back of the line to get their attention and a college kid gives her a dirty look. She taps Beau on the back and he turns. "Claudia," he says, a smile on his face. He leans over to give her a kiss on the cheek, and then she spins to give Ingrid a hug.

"How's everything going today?"

Ingrid smiles. "Good. Beau says y'all had a good time at the Gathering." Claudia can't put her finger on what is different about Ingrid. Her blond hair is pulled back in a sleek low bun and her makeup is flawless except for the lightly smudged mascara, and still, something seems off in the same way it did at the Golden Hour Gathering.

Claudia wishes Ingrid would open up to her more about her father's condition. She's starting to worry that Willard is either not recovering from his fall as well as expected, or that his cancer has taken a turn.

"I have to hand it to the Foxglove Society," Claudia says. "To you, really. It was a great time."

"Sit down and join us."

"Okay. I can't stay long, though. I've got a lot going on at work. Just need my caffeine fix."

Ingrid nods. The three of them order and Ingrid insists on paying with her black company AmEx.

"So, what do you two have going on at work?" Claudia asks, once they're all seated at a small indoor table.

"A few things," Beau says. "We've been working on securing the property at the corner of Price and Forester for a large-scale renovation. The old office building there is a disaster. But the owner has concerns about our offer."

"I don't know why," Ingrid says. "It's a fair offer. How are things going for you, Claudia?"

"Not great," she says. "I've actually been hoping to talk to you." She looks at Ingrid. "The resident who died at The Prestige. Paxton Gale. Did you know him?"

Ingrid shakes her head. "No. Why do you ask?"

"He had an invitation to your engagement party."

Ingrid freezes, her coffee cup halfway to her mouth. "He did?"

Claudia nods.

"I don't know why that would be. I'll ask Ruby about the invite list. Maybe your resident knew Thomas somehow."

"You didn't tell me about the invitation," Beau says.

"I didn't? Must have slipped my mind." It hadn't; she'd just stopped talking to Beau about Paxton entirely.

"Let me know," Claudia says to Ingrid. "Some things aren't adding up, and I'm trying to get some answers for his family."

"You met his family?"

"Yes. They're devastated."

"Of course they are," Ingrid says. "And you're...you're sure it was suicide?"

"It's what the police said." She would confide in Ingrid, if Beau wasn't there.

Ingrid grips her coffee cup with both hands. "How awful."

"Yeah. Well, sorry for bringing down the mood. I should get back to work." Claudia kisses Beau lightly and stands. "It was nice seeing you both."

Claudia leaves, her mind still on Ingrid and that invitation. Ingrid didn't know Paxton had it. So how did he get it in the first place?

***

Back at work, she presses play on the camera footage. She's still on her own for a few more hours, and she's got nothing else on her to-do list that can't wait.

The best camera angle doesn't face Paxton's apartment directly; instead, it's focused on the sixth-floor elevator bank. But Paxton's apartment is close enough to the elevator that she has a decent view of the outside of his door. She'd left off on the Saturday evening before Paxton died. Going through the footage takes forever; even fast-forwarding only barely speeds up the movement. She should pitch camera upgrades to Margo at their next meeting.

Paxton finally shows up on camera around 5:00pm. Claudia switches from fast-forward to slow-motion, even though it looks like he's only taking the puppy out for a walk. The little dog keeps twisting around to try and fit the leash in its mouth, trying to walk himself, and Claudia smiles. Still, seeing Paxton on camera is unnerving. He is clearly alive here and doing alive-person things: pressing the elevator button, playing with the dog while waiting there, pulling his cell from his pocket and making a call. Nothing here suggests that by this same time the next day, Paxton will be gone.

His phone. On Saturday evening Paxton had his phone. But according to TessAnne, no one ever found it in his apartment.

She watches him get on the elevator, and then she switches cameras to follow his progress through the lobby and presumably out to the designated doggy play area, though the camera doesn't go far enough to verify. She keeps her eyes on the screen until he returns. At a little after 7:00pm he does the same thing, takes the dog out, brings the dog back in. It's nearing 8:00pm on the camera screens when she sees something surprising—Amberly stepping off the elevator on the sixth floor and knocking on Paxton's door. Funny, she doesn't remember Amberly ever mentioning that she'd been with Paxton on Saturday night, though maybe she gave those details to the police. Paxton opens the door and the puppy bounds out to see her, jumping on her legs and wagging his little tail. The three of them—Paxton, Amberly, and puppy—disappear into the apartment.

Claudia watches the comings and goings of other sixth-floor residents for what amounts to almost another hour. By the looks of it, Janie was hosting a party at her apartment down the hall. People spill off the elevators toting cartons of beer and hard seltzer. Finally, Paxton's apartment door opens again and Amberly stomps out. Her body language suggests she's arguing with Paxton, though Claudia can just barely see Paxton's face inside the doorway. Amberly gestures with her arms, then points at him. If only the cameras captured sound. Claudia wishes she could at least zoom in to see Amberly's face better, to try to read her lips. As it is, all she can tell is that Amberly appears to be shouting. After about ten minutes, Paxton slams the door and Amberly leaves, muttering something as she waits for the elevator.

Claudia *knows* Amberly didn't disclose an argument to the police. A wild scenario plays out in her mind: Amberly and Paxton fighting, Amberly becoming enraged, Amberly...somehow staging a hanging?

There's no point in continuing that line of thought, because argument or no, Paxton is alive when Amberly leaves. At 9:17pm, he makes another trip outside to walk the dog.

She can't stop thinking about what happens next. Is it possible that her instincts are wrong and Paxton died by suicide after all? Did he go back inside his apartment after arguing with Amberly and just...do it? If that's the case...she finds herself willing time to rewind like the security cameras do, so she can go back to the night when all of this played out, so she can knock on Paxton's door and say something, *anything*, to distract him from the argument or whatever it was that caused him to do it. She's read that despair can sometimes be ridden out like a terrible wave. Claudia doesn't know if she believes that. But she'd have liked to be there, just in case.

The truth is, though, that if she *could* jump back in time somehow to make a change, she'd go back a lot farther. It wouldn't be Paxton she would save, if she had to choose. It would be Killian. It would always be him.

On the screen, Janie's party spills out into the hallway. It must be noisy, but the security guard is nowhere to be found.

When Claudia was in college the good parties were always at rental houses with big yards and plenty of space for debauchery. She remembers the first time she'd invited Killian to one of those big, messy events she used to love so much. It was only a few days after they'd visited the student market together. She had a group of friends who lived for big strange themed parties, the out-of-control kind where anything could happen. She remembers standing outside on a back porch shivering in the olive green military jacket she wore over her flapper dress, the flames in the firepit making everything glow in a wild, dancing sort of way. Dave Matthews blared from the speakers, incongruent with the Roaring Twenties party theme. The house was big and old, and someone had probably called it charming once upon a time, before it aged into a rundown college rental with bright red camping chairs on the front porch where rocking chairs should have been and Solo cups perpetually scattered across the lawn.

Claudia remembers people dancing in the living room between the ratty sofas, the beer pong tournaments in the dining room. She remembers a drunk boy standing too close to her, talking her ear off in that pretentious college-boy way. Remembers the moment she'd turned her head and spotted Killian in the kitchen, looking out at her, and how she'd pushed past the other boy and rushed inside. She couldn't hide her excitement at seeing him there. She'd come to know a little bit about him by then, enough to know that this wasn't his scene.

Hey, she said to Killian.

Hey.

You came.

Yeah. You didn't tell me I was supposed to wear a costume.

She looks down at her gold dress, barely visible beneath her jacket. *I'm sorry. I didn't think you would actually turn up.* She had to hold herself back from jumping into his arms right then and there.

I texted.

You did? She pushed her hands into the pockets of her jacket, but her phone wasn't there. *My phone is missing, apparently.* She grinned at him with a shrug.

I should maybe go, he said. *I just wanted to say hi.* His unbuttoned shirt was rolled to his forearms, a navy t-shirt underneath. He was a ray of sunshine in the dirty kitchen. But there were dark circles under his eyes and a frown on his face. She could practically see the glow of him starting to diminish.

She felt a surge of panic. She wanted him smiling too. *Hi. Let's get you a beer.*

I don't really drink.

She pulled two beers from the fridge anyway. *Here.*

Thanks. Killian took the beer and nodded toward the porch. *Is that guy your boyfriend?* He ran a hand through his hair.

She laughed. *Definitely not. I don't do relationships.* She thought she sounded edgy, independent.

No?

No.

She opened a cabinet and pulled out two shot glasses and a handle of Mr. Boston's. Craft beer and cheap liquor. She poured, then held up her shot glass for a toast. *To not doing relationships*, she said, even though Killian was almost certainly the relationship type. She stared at his shot glass until he picked it up and clinked glasses with hers. He swallowed his shot pretty smoothly for a guy who didn't drink, and she told him so.

I should have said I don't like *to drink. It makes me...too much myself.*

You look the perfect amount of yourself *to me.* She led him down a hallway to an empty bedroom.

She closed the single window in the room, muffling the shouts from the yard. Killian watched her from the doorway. *Come in*, she said. She gestured toward the bed, but he sat on the floor and she settled beside him.

Killian took a drink of his beer. *It's different*, he said. *Seeing you like this.* He wasn't exactly the same boy she'd met at the artist's market, all charm and smiles. He was quiet that night, different. She still ached for his touch.

Like what?

He gestured toward her dress, then to her hair, which was styled in finger waves with an embellished hairpiece. It occurred to her that up until now, he'd only seen her in leggings and oversized t-shirts, with her Converse tennis shoes or her unlaced black boots.

At least you're still wearing your jacket, or I might not recognize you.

Ha. Her blue hair made her pretty easy to spot.

He looked around the room. *It's really...green in here.* There was a lava lamp on the dresser and the blobs inside swirled up and down, melding together and breaking apart and then coming together all over again.

Right?

*So...*he said.

So...tell me something. About you.

Um, okay. Well, I'm from Dallas, and—

Not like that.

Like what, then? What do you want to know?

A secret. Something no one else knows.

Are we close enough for that?

We could be. Come on. I'll tell you if you tell me.

His eyes were glued to the lava lamp. *Okay. Well. This is hard to explain, but I died once.*

What?

Well, not really. But sort of. It was a long time ago, but it sort of stuck with me. I was a kid and I was crossing the street with my mom and this car came speeding around the corner and drove right through the window of a CVS. It missed me by inches, but the thing was, it felt *like it hit me. Like part of me was crushed beneath the back tire. I could feel all the broken pieces of myself but I wasn't under that car at all. I was standing there with my mother's arms around me and she was in tears because of how close the car came to hitting us, and she kept saying how lucky we were. How lucky I was. And I didn't tell her. That I was lucky...but also not?*

The car didn't actually hit you.

No. It was...a feeling. Even when I think back on it, it's hard to remember that I wasn't actually hurt.

That's...unusual.

The thing is, ever since, I feel like I die all the time. I don't know why or how, but something split inside me that day and now the things that could happen sort of do happen. I see it all play out. I feel it. Every disaster. The pain of it, you know, but the relief of it too. I feel it all.

That must be scary, she finally said. She stared at him and tried to determine what it meant.

Anyway. See what happens when I drink? He shook his head. *Let's talk about something else. What's your secret?*

She'd bartered to know him better, but she didn't really have anything worth sharing. *I got a new tattoo recently.* She shrugged out of her jacket and slid the strap of her dress down over one shoulder to display the small dagger there.

I like it. He leaned so close that she could feel his breath on her skin, right above the fresh ink. *You've got goosebumps.*

Killian, she said. *Please.* She couldn't take him being that close and not having his hands on her. It was a wonder she'd held out this long.

He lifted his head to her, pushed a wayward strand of hair behind her ear and tilted her chin up with one fingertip. Even that was enough. His face glowed green in the strange light. They were so close already, but she leaned in slightly and Killian wrapped her up in his arms. The kiss started out soft, but then came the desperation she already knew so well, his hands clutching at her like he was sinking and she was a lifeboat. Her hands in his hair, and that desire to touch him and touch him and keep on touching him. The frantic need to hold on.

The rattle of the doorknob interrupted them but it was still hard to pull away.

Hey assholes! A voice shouted from the other side of the door. *Whoever you are, get the hell out of my room!*

A grin broke across her face, and then she threw her head back and laughed. Killian looked uncomfortable at first, but soon he was laughing with her. The throaty, half-drunken melody of their shared mirth was the best sound she'd ever heard. The only things she cared about in that moment were Killian and herself and the charged air around them.

And then only him.

***

Claudia jumps at the ping of the elevator opening. It's a resident, checking his mail. She's fallen too far into her memories. It's hard, sometimes, to reconcile the girl she used to be with the woman she is now. She's become an entirely different person, but then again, that was the point.

A quick check of the time tells her that Graham will be in for his shift soon, so she closes out of the playback program and clicks back to where the cameras are recording in real time. Her screen fills with small squares, each capturing time in a different area of the property. Voyeuristic as she's become, she scans each camera before ending the program. It's midday and there's not much going on. Kara Leonard is jogging on the treadmill in the expansive fitness center, and someone whose face she can't see is watching TV in the resident lounge.

The last person Claudia expects to see is her husband, especially after running into him at the coffee shop, but a Chevy identical to his is pulling into the visitor section of the parking garage. Sure enough, Beau gets out and walks toward the elevator. Before he can press the button to call the leasing office—to reach her—the elevator opens and a blond-haired girl steps out. Amberly Vance.

Claudia expects them to sidestep each other and go about their respective business, but for some reason they start talking instead. Beau smiles big, like Amberly has just said something hilarious. Claudia can't imagine what these two would be chatting about. Beau's face lights up when he smiles like that. It's been a while since she's been the one to make it happen, and she wishes it was directed at her and not at a resident. Especially not *this* resident.

She closes the camera program and heads for the elevators. One carries her down and the doors slide open, revealing Amberly and Beau in what appears to be mid-flirt. Surely not, and yet here they are: Amberly laughing, Beau laughing, it's a whole goddamned laugh riot and Amberly's hand, fingers coated with shimmery silver nail polish, rests lightly on Beau's arm. She doesn't look much like a girl who recently lost her boyfriend.

"Hey," Claudia says.

"What do you wa—" Amberly starts to say, at the same time Beau says "Hey, babe." There's a strange flicker of something like guilt that crosses his face before the easy smile returns, smaller now, and that's how Claudia knows that she wasn't imagining things. Her husband was indeed casually flirting with a college student.

Beau's endearment throws Amberly off-guard. "Amberly," Claudia says. "I see you've met my husband."

Amberly covers her shock with a smile quickly enough. "I didn't realize you were married to Claudia," she says to Beau. "I'd better get to class. It was nice meeting you."

"Yeah, you too."

"What are you doing here?" Claudia asks Beau, once Amberly has walked away.

He holds up Claudia's wallet. "You left this at the table at the coffee shop."

She hadn't even realized it was missing. "Thank you."

"Of course. I'd better get back to work."

"What were you and Amberly talking about?"

"Who, that girl? Nothing really, just making small talk."

"You know who that is, right?" At his clueless expression, Claudia tells him that Amberly had been the one to discover Paxton's body.

"Poor girl," he says. "What a thing to go through."

"Yeah." Exactly what Claudia first thought about Amberly. Except now she knows better. Claudia thinks of telling Beau about what Amberly and her friends did to Paxton's apartment, and how she's starting to think Amberly is the last person in the world who deserves sympathy. But she finds that she still can't. These secrets are kind of *hers*, now. Hers and Paxton's. And Paxton wouldn't want her to tell.

So she keeps her mouth shut.

CHAPTER 16

O n Friday evening, Claudia lies to her husband. He's at home this
weekend, but it doesn't matter. She can't resist the urge to return
to The Study Room to keep pushing for the answers she needs from
Paxton's friends. She concocts a story about going out for drinks with
Ruby. Too risky to use Ingrid as an alibi. She can't exactly *tell* her friends
about the lengths she's going to in order to solve Paxton's murder—she
knows how it would sound—and if Claudia mentions Ingrid then it
could come up in conversation between Ingrid and Beau at work.

In the end, it doesn't matter anyway: If Beau doubts her story, he
covers it well. Probably too excited to have a night alone to bother with
questions.

She takes her spot at the bar, looking around. Working with college
students on a daily basis usually makes her feel young, but in this bar
with this particular clientele, she feels ancient.

"You again," the bartender says, with a wink and a grin. "Your usual?"

Claudia nods. She's a character in some seedy detective novel. Hanging out in a bar alone. Having a *usual*. Trying to solve a case. "Are you
the only bartender that works here?"

"No, just the only good one."

"What's your name?" Claudia asks.

"Zoe."

"Hey Zoe. I'm Claudia."

Zoe sets down the Makers Mark and leans forward. "So, Claudia, did you get what you wanted from those boys last weekend?"

"Not yet."

"They don't really seem like your type."

"They're definitely not." Claudia doesn't mention that she's married. Her wedding rings are tucked in her purse. Nothing screams *old and boring* like a wedding band.

Zoe's eyes are green and sparkling, and tonight she's wearing a cropped tank top. Her belly ring glints in the red light. She must know how pretty she is. Kudos to her for using it to her advantage. She pulls out two shot glasses, fills them with tequila. "Well, whatever those boys mean to you, they aren't here now." She slides one of the glasses to Claudia, keeps the other for herself. "So, in the meantime...cheers?"

"Cheers."

They toss back their shots, and then Zoe gets called away to the other end of the bar by two rowdy young men. Claudia watches the way the bartender moves, the way she talks. The attitude, the mischievous twinkle in her eye, the sly smile, that unnamable *something* she has that Claudia herself used to have. Right now, Claudia would do almost anything to be that version of herself again. The version of herself from before she met Beau and before she got her first grown-up job and even before she met Killian and he up and died on her.

Claudia sips her Maker's Mark.

Too late for all that now, of course.

***

She's got a nice buzz going by the time Paxton's friends roll in. She's more relaxed because of it and it makes her better in her approach; at least, she thinks it does. It occurs to her that if she keeps drinking there's a chance she won't remember the full scope of what they tell her, even if they decide they *can* trust her.

"Good luck!" Zoe shouts over the noise of the crowd, when she sees Claudia standing.

Claudia tries to channel a younger version of herself, that confident girl who never questioned she would get exactly what she wanted.

"Hey," she says to the young men. Same table as last week. Predictable. They look at her without speaking. *They* may be buzzed already too, because Randall actually smiles.

"Look who's back."

She zeroes in on him. "Happy to see me?"

"Depends on why you're here. Why do you care so much about him anyway?"

"Why wouldn't I?"

"You have a thing with him too or something?"

"What? No. Why would you say that? Did Paxton have a *thing* with someone besides Amberly?"

Randall shrugs. "Maybe. I don't know."

Something clicks. "There was another woman. You were talking about her the other night. Who is she?"

"The older chick," one of them says, then blushes. "Older than us, anyway."

"And they were...romantic?"

"If that's what you want to call it."

"Who is she?" she asks again.

The well-dressed friend nudges Randall and gives him a warning look.

"We don't know her name, actually," Well-Dressed Friend says. "We might remember something else important though...if you hang out a while. Come on, dance with us." His grin is a challenge.

"Why would you want that?" she asks, warily.

"Why wouldn't we? Come on," he says. "You scared?"

They expect her to turn them down, but they don't know that dancing actually sounds perfect to her right now. It's exactly what a younger Claudia would do. The pulsing red lights have turned friendly and welcoming.

"Fine," she says. "Let's do it."

There's a hip-hop song playing and she can feel the beat of it beneath her skin. The young man—whose name she knew, last time she was here—puts his hands lightly on her hips as they dance. Another of Paxton's friends join them. She laughs. It's funny, really. The red light flashes on her face and she blinks and of course these men aren't Paxton, but they're *like* him. The hands on her waist keep her from falling over. All four of them are dancing now. This is it. She's earning their trust and she'll get to the truth. For Paxton.

A scene flashes through her mind but it has nothing to do with Paxton Gale at all. It's Killian, lying on a bed, barefoot. She blinks it away.

She's dancing, jumping up and down now to a different song, moving and moving and she doesn't have to be still ever again if she doesn't want to. She doesn't have to think about a thing. "Hey," Randall says. He's dancing closest to her now. He leans in so she can hear him. "The woman's name. The one who was messing around with Paxton. It's Ruby."

Ruby. "Wait. *What?*" She turns to him, but it's too loud for questions and now he's singing along to the music and she's spinning or the room is, and suddenly a cool hand grabs hers. The hand—it doesn't belong to one of these men, she can tell that much—pulls her out of the circle.

She's indignant. Who would drag her away at such an important time? But it's Zoe, the bartender, and she's been so nice to her. Zoe pulls her down a hallway. There's some kind of closet at the end, but they don't go in there. It's quieter here. Claudia leans against the wall.

"Claudia, right?" she says. "It's probably not my place to say so, but I think you've had enough to drink."

"I have?" Claudia asks. "I can't tell. I don't really do the bar thing anymore."

"I figured." She hands Claudia a plastic cup, and Claudia drinks from it eagerly. She wants this feeling to last and last. She's disappointed to realize the cup is filled with water, but she drains it anyway. It turns out she's thirsty.

"Oh god," Claudia says. "I'm drunk. What an idiot."

Zoe laughs. "It happens all the time. Is there someone I can call to come get you? I could get you an Uber."

"Why are you helping me?"

Zoe shrugs. "Just don't want you to do anything you'll regret."

"Claudia? What are you doing here?" She turns her head to see that someone else has invaded their hallway. It's Graham, in those relaxed khakis and a dark t-shirt, looking like he actually belongs in a place like this after all and not in a business suit behind a desk.

"It's Graham," she says to Zoe. "Graham from work." Like the bartender knows, or cares.

"You a friend of hers?" Zoe asks. Are Claudia and Graham friends? They must be, or Graham must have said they were, because Zoe asks if he can get her home.

"No," Claudia says, because Graham is her employee and this is all extremely inappropriate. But they ignore her.

"I've got to get back to work," Zoe says. "Take care of yourself, okay?"

"Yeah, I'll try."

"I'll see you next time."

"Okay." Claudia says. *Of course* she'll be back. She can't remember the last time she's had this much fun. Soon Zoe is gone and Graham has taken her place in Claudia's field of vision and she's not unhappy to see him there.

"How much have you had to drink?" he asks. Claudia can't tell if he's amused or disgusted. There are muscles beneath his shirt that she's never really noticed before (rock-climbing muscles?) and she flattens her palm against his chest.

"A little."

He looks down at her hands. "Let's get you out of here." Graham takes her by the wrist and leads her down the hallway. He stops and says something to a small group of people who must be his friends, and then he guides her through the crowded fray. She stumbles along behind him. She has no idea if Paxton's crew is still here; if they are, they've moved on to other, more age-appropriate women.

"What are you doing?" he asks, when they're outside in the humid night air. It feels like it could storm soon. He leads her away from the bar and stops beneath the awning of a store that's closed for the night. "You're not actually here alone, are you?"

"Is that so strange?" she asks. "I used to do things like this all the time." A million years ago, she'd be closing down the bars, alone or with friends, on a night like this.

She closes her eyes—she's *tired*, suddenly—but then Graham's voice is in her ear. "Claudia. Look at me." When she does, she finds him staring at her, his copper coin eyes gone dark.

"Oh," Claudia says, in an almost-whisper. It seems obvious—why hadn't she noticed before? "You *want* me."

"No, I…"

"You do." The top Claudia is wearing, loose at the neckline, slips off one shoulder and she watches his eyes follow the movement. "You want to touch me," she breathes. God knows she's thought enough about touching him.

"Claudia..."

She takes his hand and puts it there on her shoulder, palm on her skin, his fingertips grazing the dagger tattoo. Her sigh sounds as loud, to her, as the music inside the bar. She can feel the heat of his skin.

"I can't," he says quietly, but his fingers scorch along her shoulder, to her neck. "You know I can't."

"You're afraid."

He leans forward, close enough that she can feel his breath along her skin, following the same path as his fingers. "You think I'm afraid? You think that's what this is?" he murmurs into her ear, his sleek dark hair brushing against her cheek. There's beer and lime on his breath. She can *almost* feel his lips there, against her neck. He's going to kiss her; she knows he will, and for some reason she's surprised, despite the fact that she's basically dared him to do it. It's amazing how fast she's forgotten about Zoe the bartender and Paxton's friends and everyone else. Even Killian. The blankness of her mind in this moment is welcome and wonderful. This wildness, this emptiness, this anticipation, this is what she's been missing. *Yes*, comes a voice hidden somewhere inside.

Graham steps away from her suddenly and takes the heat of his body with him. "I want to," he says, his breath ragged. "I want to, Claudia, but it's not right."

His words sink in, and the spell is broken. The lightheaded delirium fades away, and with it that all-consuming desire to be touched and kissed and *wanted*. The thrill of it. But Claudia understands immediately what Graham didn't say. That she's married, that Beau is at home, trusting that Claudia is out with Ruby and not kissing her fucking colleague.

She's not her younger self. She's not selfish like she was before Killian; she *cares* about the people she might hurt. She can't work through her angst with a meaningless fling, the way she would have years ago. She's horrified that a part of her wanted to try.

"I know," she says to Graham, blinking furiously and wishing her hungry skin didn't ache from the absence of his hand on her body. "I know. Shit. I'm sorry." She should have left Graham out of this, whatever *this* is that she's going through.

"I can take you home," he says. The desire is still there, in his eyes, and she looks away. "I've only had a few beers. I can grab a coffee. Let me drive you home."

But she can't let him do that. If she knows Beau, he's asleep and dead to the world, but she can't risk it. Beau isn't the jealous type, but Graham wasn't part of her alibi.

Instead, she orders an Uber and allows Graham to wait with her until the driver arrives. She tries to ignore the dark mountains beyond the small downtown area and the way they seem to loom over her. She's coming down quickly from her high, but she still has to fight the mortifying urge to ask him to touch her again. What would Ingrid and Ruby think? She knows something about Ruby now, but she can't remember what. Embarrassment is setting in, and she knows that no matter what she'd told Zoe, she obviously won't be returning to The Study Room. Ever. Bad enough that she'll have to face Graham on Monday and pretend that she can still command some sort of authority.

"I have to ask," Graham says, after a long beat of awkward silence. His hands are stuffed in his pockets. "Is all of this about Paxton?"

She raises her eyebrows.

"I'm not talking about you and me, and what happened just now—"

"*Almost* happened," she corrects.

"Almost happened. Right. But you were here, at this bar, where he used to hang out. I saw his friends in there."

She's quiet.

"Why are you still so wrapped up in this? In him?"

"Because," she says. It's a relief to have something else to talk about, and the words come tumbling out. "Because I know he didn't kill himself. It sounds...impossible. But he didn't. Someone killed him."

CHAPTER 17

B eau is asleep when Claudia gets home. She brushes her teeth and
rinses her face, and the cold water helps her sober up. She lies in
bed, wide awake, watching the steady rise and fall of Beau's chest as he
breathes. What kind of reckless person would do the things she's done,
and the things she's *almost* done? She thought she was better than this
now. Claudia falls asleep finally, guilt settling around her like a blanket.

She jolts awake in the middle of the night, every part of her body
buzzing and for a moment she's certain she's traveled back in time and is
the passionate, obstinate girl she used to be. That if she turns her head,
she'll see strands of her own blue hair on the pillow. But no, she's a grown
woman, and that's her husband snoring softly beside her. This is what is
real.

Having someone else's hands on her has stirred that primitive knowledge of how intimacy can drown out other things, like pain and confusion and sadness. It's not the person she yearns for, it's the *drowning*. She
could straddle her husband right now, wake him with her mouth and her
body and maybe achieve the same thing.

Maybe.

But she doesn't try. Everything is tangled up. And at the core of it
all, here in the quiet of the night, what she wants most is just another
moment with Killian, the boy who left her for good and in doing so,

taught her that passion—her kind of passion—is dangerous. Deadly, even.

She lets the memories come. It's 2:00am; who's to know? Who else but her *could* know about how she'd brought Killian to her old, rundown apartment and how he'd looked standing there, his Birks sinking into the rust-colored shag carpet. How drunk with relief she'd felt when she finally had him in her bed. How he looked so clean-cut, so kind, and he *was* those things, and also how he'd ravaged her as if he was as starved for her as she was for him.

Should I stop? He'd murmured, and she'd put a finger to his lips. *I'll die if you do. I need every bit of you.*

Killian spent a lot of time at her apartment after that. She'd wake up in her bed with their bodies tangled together like clothes fresh from the dryer, morning light pushing through the cheap blinds of her bedroom window.

It was more than lust. They went to parties together, and museums, and concerts. There was the pure sweetness of his hand in hers. He sent flowers, and he bought her extravagant gifts, like an onyx-encrusted dagger pendant on a white gold chain. *To match your tattoo.* Claudia may have insisted she didn't do relationships, but she and Killian were as close as two people could be.

They were fucking happy.

They were.

But. The nightmares came, occasional at first and then for several days in a row. Claudia would wake in the middle of the night to Killian thrashing around the bed. He had vivid dreams, wild and scary. The terrible things that didn't come for him in the day found him in his sleep. Sometimes he tried to keep the dreams at bay by not sleeping at all; he'd lie beside her while she slept, but he'd read a book by lamplight or stare at the ceiling in the darkness. Some nights he'd shake her awake. *Let's do something*, he'd suggest, as if there was a world of things they could get up and do at 3:00am. He kept a pair of running shoes by her front door, in case he wanted to go for a middle-of-the-night run down the seedy street where she lived.

When they weren't together he'd call her sometimes in the middle of the night, wide awake and desperate to talk. About anything, he said. He wanted to hear her voice. And so she'd make herself a cup of coffee and they'd talk on the phone until the sun came up.

They were consumed by one another, and the good times were so good that she ignored the other times when he was withdrawn, when he seemed to be lost in another world entirely. When they had plans and he didn't show. The times when she called him and days passed before he called her back. Killian's disappearing act. She pretended like it didn't hurt. She'd probably been just as thoughtless herself, before she met him.

He spent so many nights in her bed, but he never invited her to his place. *Roommate,* he said when she pressed. Finally she surprised him there, at his apartment. She wanted to see where he lived. His roommate let her in, and he was so welcoming that she wasn't sure why Killian used him as an excuse to keep her away. Killian was typing on his laptop at his computer desk when she knocked on his bedroom door. He jumped, but he smiled when he saw her. *If I'd known you were coming I would have tidied up*, he said, and he stood up and started doing exactly that. He carried a stack of schoolbooks, a magazine, a picture frame, and a few wayward papers over to a dresser drawer and dumped them all in. There was a line of shopping bags in one corner. She peeked into them and saw t-shirts and socks, notebooks and pens, two pairs of running shoes and new Birkenstocks, hardback novels. All unopened, still in boxes, or with tags and price stickers. *I...like to buy things*, Killian said with a sheepish shrug.

I see that. Killian's family was wealthy, but it wasn't something they talked about.

His bed was neatly made with a plaid print comforter. He pulled her down on it and she fell into him, into a soft kiss on his soft bed. It was comfortable there, in his room, and she wondered why he'd tried to keep her away.

What she'd give, now, to go back to the wondering of it all. To do more when it mattered. Before Killian, she'd never hesitated to speak up if something or someone bothered her or hurt her or pissed her off. But she wanted so badly to hold onto what they had that she held her tongue, and it all crumbled anyway.

She made such a mess of things then.

She thought she'd learned her lesson.

***

Claudia crawls out of bed on Saturday morning with a pounding headache and a churning stomach that could be the alcohol or the sour feeling of regret, or some mix of the two. The feeling grows when she has to ask Beau to drive her downtown to pick up her car. She and Ruby had a little too much fun last night, she lies. She cringes when she thinks of how the night had truly played out, but then a blurry memory surfaces: Paxton's friend, whispering a name in her ear. *Ruby.* A woman named Ruby was involved with Paxton. Surely not her Ruby? It has to be a coincidence. Ruby isn't the *most* common name in the world, but it isn't exactly rare either.

When she's alone in her car, Claudia calls her friend. No answer. She tries a text instead.

Call me when you can.

Ruby responds a few moments later.

Busy day! Let's catch up on Monday!

Claudia spends the rest of the weekend with Beau trying her best to pretend everything is the same as always, but she can't quite look him in the eyes. She should tell him about the moment with Graham, the one that felt so intimate. She knows she should, but every time she opens her mouth to confess, the words get stuck in her throat.

CHAPTER 18

TessAnne Gale calls Claudia at work on Monday.

"Have you had a chance to look through the security camera footage yet?" she asks.

"Some of it," Claudia says. "Did you know that Paxton and Amberly argued the night he died?" She tells TessAnne what she's seen so far. "It may not mean anything," Claudia cautions. "It doesn't mean she killed him."

"It doesn't mean she didn't. Why wouldn't she have mentioned that she argued with him? To the police, or to us? She was here for Paxton's funeral. She was in our house."

"Maybe she feels guilty. Because they fought. Maybe she thinks it's all her fault." Claudia can't believe she's defending Amberly Vance, but she knows firsthand what it's like to feel responsible for someone's death.

"Or maybe she feels guilty because she's guilty."

"Or that. But TessAnne, think of the logistics." Claudia hesitates, because who would want to hear these details? "It would take more than just Amberly to get Paxton into the position he was in when he was found. I don't see how she could have orchestrated it on her own."

"So you're saying she had help."

"I'm saying don't jump to conclusions. Look, I'll keep going through the feed and let you know what else I find."

"Thank you." TessAnne wouldn't be so quick to thank her if she knew about Claudia's botched attempt to get information from Paxton's friends. She seems to interpret Claudia's willingness to help as friendship, because she doesn't hang up the phone. Instead, she starts talking about Paxton. Not that Claudia minds. It makes her feel like she's helping just by listening.

It also feeds her obsession.

"Here's the thing. He was confused about what he wanted to do with his life. There's the family insurance business, and he was planning to take it over. That's why he was getting his business degree in the first place. But my dad has basically run the business into the ground. I swear, half the time he's got the "Closed" sign in the window because he's either over at the bar across the street or sleeping off a hangover. Then Paxton and his friend, Aaron, got into this stupid accident and Aaron was badly hurt. People in town thought Paxton was responsible, that he was a drunk too, like our dad. You can understand why he wouldn't want to move back here. Mama told him he didn't have to, that we would support him no matter what. But he didn't know what he wanted to do, and he thought he should know."

"I don't think anyone knows at that age." Claudia had gone through a handful of jobs after college, before she'd moved home in defeat and let her stepfather use his connections to get her into property management.

"That's what Mama said. No one knows. But he was a little lost, I guess. And he felt bad because of the whole deal with Aaron. But he got a catering job and things started looking up. There was a minute when he thought he'd lost his scholarship and was going to have to come back to Kelver Ridge no matter that he didn't want to, but he got things turned around. After that, it seemed like things were good. Really good. He told me was going to stick with the business degree even if he didn't take over the insurance business, maybe even stay in Ellen Point for a while and go for his MBA. He had plans, Claudia."

"Catering job?" Claudia thinks of the photo she'd seen on Facebook of Paxton in a black and white server uniform. Ruby owns an event planning company. Is it possible that Paxton worked for her? If that was the case, then it wasn't completely inconceivable that her Ruby was *the* Ruby.

"Yeah, he did events and stuff."

Claudia can't discuss Ruby with Paxton's sister, so she changes course. "You mentioned an accident. What happened there?" Even though she already knows.

"It was a rock crawling accident, of all things," she says. "It's like, when you ride across the rockiest parts of the mountain, on purpose. Kids do it all the time around here. Anyway, it was last summer. He was out riding with Aaron. They used to be best friends. It was dumb to be out there that late at night. Anyway, their UTV flipped, and Aaron was hurt pretty bad. It wasn't Paxton's fault, but he felt like it was. Didn't help that Aaron blamed Paxton, and told anyone who was listening that Pax was responsible."

"How terrible."

"Yeah. Aaron's okay now, mostly, but he moved out west to work at his uncle's ranch once he could move around well enough. His immediate family is still here, though, and still holding a grudge."

Aaron is hundreds of miles away. Did he hate Paxton enough to come all this way back to kill him? And if so, why now? Claudia had originally been suspicious of Aaron, but these details don't exactly add up to murder.

"Was Paxton hurt in the accident?"

"Bumps and bruises. Nothing serious. But he lost a bit of himself after that, couldn't wait until summer was over so he could get back to college and away from this godforsaken town. I don't blame him."

"I'm sorry."

"You know the police won't even consider reopening his case? They didn't question anyone else in the building, besides Amberly and that friend of hers."

The night they found Paxton dead, Claudia hadn't thought it strange that the police didn't question anyone else. It looked like suicide. They'd said suicide.

"I keep asking them to take another look, to consider that things are not as simple as they seem. The detective told me that no one wants to believe someone they love could die that way. So nonchalant, like Pax is just one more statistic."

"That's how they are," Claudia says. Though she guesses that if the police thought too much about how unique and irreplaceable each victim is, how tragic and horrible every crime, how devastating every death, they probably couldn't do their jobs. They'd never be able to drag themselves in for another day of heartbreak.

***

The next day, Claudia is surprised by an Instagram response from Amberly's friend, Lou. *I got your message, but I don't think I can help.* Claudia fires off a succinct response. *I think you can. Meet me at The Gilded Mug today at 5:30.* Fake confidence. She has no idea if Lou will actually show. Still, it feels promising. Hopefully she'll do better with her than she's done so far with Paxton's other friends. Although. Paxton's friends had given her one lead. *Ruby.* There must be a dozen women named Ruby in town, right? But how many had a catering staff on payroll? Claudia allows herself to consider the possibility that her friend, Ruby Duvall, had a relationship with a college student seven years her junior. Would it be such a surprise? Hasn't Ruby said, more than once, that age is nothing but a number? But if Ruby was seeing Paxton, why would she have kept it from Claudia and Ingrid in the first place? Claudia's kept her share of secrets, even from her best friends, but Ruby isn't like her.

If Ruby was involved with Paxton, does that make her a murder suspect? And where does that leave Amberly?

The clack of Graham's shoes on the tile floor as he steps off the elevator pulls her out of her thoughts.

"Hey," he says. He doesn't look at her as he walks to his desk.

She could pretend that nothing is different between them, and after a while the awkwardness might pass. Graham is the best assistant manager she's had.

He's also the only one she's ever considered kissing.

"Hey." Things are quiet between them for a moment. "Can we talk?" She's winging it, hoping the right words will come. "This weekend. What happened. *Almost* happened. It was inappropriate. On my part. I should not have put you in that position. If you feel like you need to report it...to HR, that would be understandable. I don't want you to be uncomfortable here." Jesus Christ, don't let him report her.

He looks up. "No. I mean, I'm not. I don't want either of us to be uncomfortable. But you didn't take advantage of me or anything, if that's what you're thinking. I knew you'd had too much to drink. I know you...you know...have a husband. If anything, *I* almost took advantage of you."

"No, I don't think that's—"

"Claudia, I'd never report it. We were both drinking, things nearly got out of hand but they didn't. I'm sorry."

"Me too." She sighs.

"Okay, we're both sorry. Did you...uh, did you tell Beau?"

"No." She feels a fresh wave of guilt. But nothing had actually happened. Graham hadn't kissed her (would she have stopped him, if he had?) and touching her shoulder wasn't exactly illicit, despite the effect it had on her. It wasn't worth shaking up her marriage over. "I didn't think it was necessary."

Graham looks relieved. "Okay."

"Okay." She tries not to think about things like sexual harassment claims or blackmail or the fact that Graham basically holds her job—maybe even her marriage—in his hands from here on out. Their company has rules forbidding supervisors from fraternizing with employees. Not that they were fraternizing. It was just a moment. One heated, reckless moment.

Which is probably enough to get her fired. Possibly divorced? She's always trusted Graham in the past, just never with anything this serious.

He takes a seat across from her. "So, I know it's not my place, but I'm going to say it one last time. I think you should leave the Paxton thing alone. For good."

Her shoulders tense. "There are questions that need answers. His family needs me."

"I know you think that, but the thing is, they might never get answers. *You* might never get answers. Not about Paxton, and not about your college friend either. That's what happens when people die, especially like that. They leave questions that can't be answered."

Claudia looks at him, trying her best to remain professional and unfazed by the intense gaze he's leveling at her. "This has nothing to do with Killian," she says. "And Paxton didn't die by suicide at all." There's a wild bit of pleasure at letting the words out. Then she wishes she could take them back.

"Yeah, you said that the other night. I thought it was the alcohol talking."

"No. I mean yes, but no."

"You know that's not what happened. Don't you think the police would know? You *saw* his body, Claudia."

"TessAnne said someone wanted him dead."

"TessAnne, Paxton's grief-stricken sister?"

"I know what you're thinking," she says. It was a mistake to tell him.

"I worry about you, is all."

She bites her lip. She knows exactly how to say the words people want to hear. "You know what? You're right. I should stop. I will."

He doesn't look all that convinced. "I *will*," she says.

"Okay. I won't mention it again."

"Thank you." And then she changes the subject. She doesn't tell him about her conversation with TessAnne earlier, and she doesn't mention her scheduled coffee date with Lou. Because it doesn't matter what Graham or anyone thinks. She can't change course at this point, not until everything is resolved.

Not until she has justice for Paxton.

***

The Gilded Mug isn't crowded this afternoon, and Claudia is glad. When grad students are here studying with their lattes and laptops, they have ways of letting you know that your voice is a disturbance. Those side-eyed, pissed off glances; the pointed action of smashing earbuds into their ears.

Claudia is well aware that she has no authority to question Lou, but there has to be something here, something that forces these strange puzzle pieces into a complete picture. She arrives early, gets a latte for herself, and takes a seat on the patio.

Lou looks nervous when she appears. She's surprisingly punctual.

"Hi," Lou says.

Claudia nods toward the coffee counter. "Hi. Grab a drink if you want."

"I'm okay." Lou pulls out one of the iron chairs and takes a seat. She's perched on the edge of it like she might bolt, like she thinks she's in trouble. Claudia relishes this tiny bit of misplaced authority.

"What's going on, Lou?" she asks.

"I don't know what you mean."

"Things aren't adding up. Something's not right."

"*Nothing's* right about what happened. How could it ever be right?"

"I know. I shouldn't have said it like that. But I saw the state you left Paxton's apartment in, and I know Amberly and Paxton were arguing the night he died."

"Why is any of this your business? Why do you even care?"

"Because Pax was my resident," Claudia says, realizing belatedly that she's used his nickname out loud. "His family is hurting. They need answers. I know you were snooping around his childhood bedroom the day of his funeral. I don't know if that's enough to reopen his case, but I bet his mother and sister would want to try...if they knew."

"How do *you* know?"

"I just do." If she thinks Amberly told, or that someone else at the funeral saw her, then all the better.

"You've talked to Paxton's family?"

Claudia nods.

Lou looks down. She looks scared, but her words are defiant. "Well, I can't help. And if they want to try to reopen Paxton's case that's up to them. I have to go."

"Lou," Claudia says. "*Tell me* what's going on."

"No." The chair legs scrape the ground as she stands.

"What were you looking for?" Claudia calls after her, but she's already gone and Claudia has to fight the instinct to chase her down.

Her younger self would have done it. As she sips her latte, Claudia can't help but think of what she'd have done a decade ago in a situation like this. She wouldn't have taken no for an answer.

But that was then.

CHAPTER 19

T he next afternoon, while Graham is on a call and Liza is away on a lease tour, there's a buzz at the lobby door.

She's not expecting to see Lou again so soon, especially not after the pointless coffee shop meeting. But here she is, standing in front of Claudia, wringing her hands together, her freckled cheeks even paler than normal.

"Hi," Claudia says.

Lou walks past her and starts pacing back and forth across the lobby, weaving in between the leather armchairs and side tables. Her hair is in a braid down her back. She's quiet for a long time. "So, here's the thing," she says, finally. "I shouldn't be telling you anything. I swore to Amberly that I wouldn't tell." She looks around, like she expects Amberly to step off the elevator any second. "She's in class," Lou says. But saying it doesn't seem to make her any less anxious. She looks down at her shortish fingernails. A silver bracelet jangles on her thin wrist.

"You guys are friends, right?" Claudia asks.

"As much as anybody *can* be friends with Amberly." Lou spins the silver bracelet anxiously. She doesn't seem to realize she's doing it. "I don't want to be on her bad side. But, this whole thing is wrong, and I don't know what to do." Lou looks at Claudia finally, and Claudia wonders if she's been crying.

"Are you *scared* of her?" It sounds ridiculous, but Lou looks terrified and Claudia doesn't know why she would be.

She doesn't answer, so Claudia tries a different question. "What were you looking for? In his bedroom? In his apartment?"

"His iPad. Amberly forgot he had one, so she insisted we go back and look." The answer comes out so easily this time that it makes Claudia think Lou has been aching to talk to someone. "We didn't find it though."

Because Marilyn and TessAnne have it.

"Why did you want it?"

"So we could erase the texts that Amberly sent."

"What texts?" Oh. *Oh.* Claudia thinks of the messages TessAnne had told her about, the ones from the disconnected number. The ones that told Paxton to kill himself, and suggested ways he could do it. The ones that urged him on. "*She* sent those?"

"You know about them?"

"His sister told me. She has the iPad. Why, though? Amberly and Paxton were together." Lou's bracelet glints in the afternoon light. The spinning motion is oddly hypnotic. "You don't know Amberly. She was like, attached to Paxton. From the minute she saw him, she thought he was hers. She thought she meant something to him. But then she found these pictures on his phone, of Paxton and some other woman. He had them stored on a photo app, so they were kind of hidden, but Amberly is suspicious like that. He left his phone sitting out one day while he showered, and she went through it. It was clear from the photos that Paxton and the woman were...involved. And the pictures weren't uploaded all that long before he met Amberly. Anyway, Amberly couldn't deal. She confronted Paxton. She wanted to know all about the woman, but he wouldn't talk about it at all, and he refused to delete the pictures. They had this huge fight. After that, Amberly kept trying to find ways to prove

146

that she was in control, and to prove to herself that Paxton loved her more than he loved the mystery woman, whoever she was."

Claudia can't help but wonder if that mystery woman was Ruby.

"Why would Amberly want Paxton to kill himself? That seems pretty extreme."

"At first the texts were just out of anger or whatever. But then it turned into this twisted experiment, to see what she could make him do. I don't think she really expected him to do it, but it made her feel powerful to think he might. She basically killed him just to see if she, like, *could*. I mean, she didn't kill him with her hands. But he's dead anyway."

Claudia sways. So Paxton really had killed himself, because some girl told him to? It's hard to believe. "What happened that night?"

"They argued all the time, once Amberly found the pictures. Paxton said the woman was part of his past but Amberly wouldn't let it go. Anyway, they fought that night, there at his apartment, and then she left. And she started sending those text messages. It wasn't the first time. He usually ignored them. But this time...he just did it. Once Amberly had cooled down the next day, she went to his place to apologize, and there he was. She called me, frantic, and I came over. She'd already swiped his phone while we were waiting on the police, but she remembered about the iPad later, and she thought they were linked. I don't know. She was freaking out, thinking she'd get into trouble if someone saw the texts. We looked around his apartment and his bedroom at his parents' house after the funeral, but the iPad had vanished. Paxton had deleted her from his phone after their last fight anyway, but she deleted all of the messages too and cancelled her own phone plan to be on the safe side."

"Surely it can still be linked to her."

"Well yeah, I guess, if anyone was actually looking."

"*I'm* looking."

"I meant like, the police. Someone who matters."

147

Claudia shrugs off Lou's dismissive words. "You're saying Amberly killed Paxton."

"Yeah, sort of. I mean, I guess it depends on how you look at it. But it feels like murder to me."

"And you think...what, that she would do something like that to you? Is that why you're so afraid?"

"How would I know? I've never been friends with a murderer before. Amberly has this way of finding the things you're worried about and using them against you. Plus, now that Paxton is dead, now that he actually *did* it, she's on a power trip." She looks at Claudia. "That's why *I'm* worried. But I mean, you should be worried too."

"Why's that?"

"Because Amberly was already mad at you. She knows you've been asking questions. And then she met your husband in the parking garage the other day."

"So?"

"So, when Amberly is attracted to someone, it's not just attraction. She becomes completely infatuated. It's what happened with Paxton. And ever since she met your husband, he's like, her newest obsession. The fact that you think he's yours is just a bonus."

Claudia shakes her head, so surprised she actually laughs. "My husband isn't *mine*. He's a human being. I don't own him. And I'm not afraid of Amberly. I'm pretty sure my husband isn't interested."

Lou's arms are crossed over her body. "She's got his phone number already. There's more to her than you think. And if you're not afraid, you should be. Didn't I just tell you she killed Paxton?"

"You did. And Paxton's family needs to know. They want that phone. If you give it to me, I can make sure they get it." The truth is that *Claudia* needs to see it. She needs to see the messages, and the photos, and the proof of Paxton's relationship before she confronts Ruby. She thinks of

TessAnne with the iPad and wonders if the photos would be there too. Claudia could call her, tell her what to do, where to look. It would be the right thing to do.

And she will. Right after she figures things out for herself.

Lou shakes her head. "I can't get you that. Amberly has it."

"You don't know where she keeps it?"

"No, I do. But if I take it, she'll know it was me."

"I can help you, if you bring me the phone. You know Amberly can't get away with this. If you keep helping her hide what she did, you'll go down with her eventually."

"I can't do this." Lou stands up. "I shouldn't have said anything to you."

"You did the right thing. Think about it. Bring me that phone, Lou.

***

It turns out that the phone isn't the only piece of evidence out there. At 11:30 the next morning—the last day of August—an email from Tenant Secure Resident Screening Services shows up in Claudia's inbox.

Thank you for your applicant inquiry. Per your request, we are able to provide you with the following information about the applicant at your community:

NAME: Paxton Jonah Gale
SS#: xxx-xx-1028
PREVIOUS ADDRESS: 400 Lumar Street Unit 408 Ellen Point, GA
EMPLOYER: Champagne Toast Event Planning

SUPERVISOR: Ruby Duvall
INCOME: Not required*
*(Applicant paid additional deposit to waive credit check)

Claudia actually gasps. It was true that Paxton had worked for Ruby. Claudia has it now, real honest-to-goodness proof tying them to one another. Ruby was Paxton's boss, and, according to Paxton's friends, they'd had a relationship. A fling? Something more? Claudia glances over at Graham in his adjacent office. No, it isn't far-fetched. But if Ruby had purposefully kept this secret from Ingrid and Claudia, then she could be keeping other things from them too. But why? If Paxton died by suicide, and Amberly had pushed him to do it, how did Ruby fit into this story?

"I'm going to lunch," Claudia says. "Want anything?"

Graham looks up from his computer and shakes his head. "I'm good, thanks."

She collects her purse and takes the elevator to her car. Ruby runs Champagne Toast Event Planning out of her house, so Claudia heads in that direction. Ruby may be able to avoid Claudia's calls and texts, but she can't blow her off in person. It hits Claudia, suddenly, that both her friends have been avoiding her lately. She hasn't thought much of it with everything else going on, but now she wonders. Is it possible that Ingrid knows Ruby's secret already and, for some reason, they don't want Claudia to know? Or has she alienated her friends in a way she doesn't even know about?

She tries to shake off the thought. Instead, she turns her thoughts back to Ruby, to her deliciously carefree attitude. Ruby doesn't hold back from spilling the details of her love life (the good, the bad, and the ugly) to Ingrid and Claudia during their monthly coffee dates and happy hour meetups. If she was serious about someone, Claudia would surely have known. It's not hard to imagine Paxton falling for Ruby. But Ruby is passionate about her work, so passionate that it *is* hard to imagine her dating an employee, if that's what she was doing.

First time for everything, though.

Ruby lives in a charming little cottage, and her full-service event planning business makes up the downstairs level. The second floor is her apartment, and she has a large shed out back where event supplies are stored. Ruby allegedly keeps a detailed record of her inventory, but Claudia has been in that space before and she knows for a fact that there is no order whatsoever to the items stashed in there. Chairs and popcorn machines are stacked on tables, with tablecloths and napkins strewn over the top of it all. Whatever her system, it seems to work for her. Ruby is single-handedly responsible for most of the events in Ellen Point these days. Fancy wedding? Five-year-old's birthday party? Sorority social? Check, check, check.

Claudia pulls into the driveway. The periwinkle siding of the house is cheerful, and the sign in the yard twinkles in the sunlight: a golden champagne glass (the company logo) and the business name written in fanciful script.

Except for the graffiti on the side of the house, which definitely wasn't there last time Claudia visited. One word is slashed across the siding in messy bold red letters.

MURDERER.

Claudia stares. It's too big of a coincidence for this to be about anyone or anything besides Paxton. Someone else has been following the same leads she has. If the person behind the graffiti didn't know about Amberly's text messages yet, and if it's true that Ruby and Paxton had a relationship, then this other player might have pinned the whole thing on Ruby. And if that person wanted revenge, Ruby could be in danger. Is it possible that Lou had it wrong and Ruby played a role in Paxton's death after all?

Even if Ruby *is* a murderer, she's still one of the few friends Claudia has. Claudia does a quick scan of the inside of her car, looking for something that could be used as a weapon, if the graffiti artist has Ruby inside somewhere. She ends up with nothing but car keys, tucked between her knuckles like she's walking through a parking lot alone after dark.

She walks up the plant-lined path to the front door and rings the doorbell. She waits. For a long moment no one comes to the door, even though Ruby's Prius is in the driveway. Claudia is about to walk around to check the back door when Ruby finally answers. She smiles. "Hi, Claudia." She casts a look outside in both directions before opening the door wide enough to allow Claudia to enter. "You scared the shit out of me." She takes care to close and lock the door again behind them. "Guess you saw the new artwork. Apparently I'm a murderer?" She lets out a short laugh. "I'm headed to Sherwin Williams later. It seems I have some painting to do."

"Ruby," Claudia says. "Why is that there?"

"I don't know. I've been working on a big project, and I went out today to finalize some details and when I got back...the graffiti was just...there. Obviously it's some kind of prank, but I'm not going to lie. It's been a stressful week, and this has me rattled. I've never been called a murderer before."

"You really don't know why someone would do this?"

"Um, *murderer*? I killed a spider last week, but I don't think his family is out for revenge."

"So you have absolutely no idea at all?"

"What? No." Then she looks closely at Claudia. "Why are you asking like that? Do *you* know something?"

"It's about Paxton."

"Who?"

"It's okay. I know about the two of you."

"The two of who? Claudia, I am deeply confused."

"Paxton. Paxton Gale."

"I. Don't. Know. Who. That. Is."

"Come on. Paxton Gale, the resident who died at The Prestige. I know he worked for you."

"He *what*?"

Claudia stares at her friend, trying to determine if Ruby is as perplexed as she appears, or if she is a better liar than Claudia realized.

"He was part of your catering staff."

"He...really? Damn, what a small world." When Claudia raises her eyebrows, Ruby says "I don't do the hiring of the catering staff. That's David. You know, my catering manager?"

"You didn't know Paxton worked for you? But then, what about the relationship?"

"What relationship? What are you talking about?"

"Paxton's friends told me that the two of you had a...thing. He said your name. And Paxton had an invitation to Ingrid's wedding, and you sent those out."

"I'm not seeing this guy. Wasn't. I can't imagine why someone would say that. Are you telling me this boy's friends thought he and I were sleeping together or something?"

"That's what I'm telling you."

"And he died. And..." she trails off. "And let me guess. *They think I fucking killed him.*"

"Or..." Claudia stammered. "More like led to his downfall, in some nonspecific way."

"Well, guess we know who tagged my house. And...is this something you believed too?"

Claudia looks down, embarrassed. "I'm sorry. I've been trying to get in touch with you for days. I've gotten involved in trying to find Paxton's murderer, and I guess my imagination got away from me. And I saw that invitation, and his employment details, and then his friends said he was with a woman named Ruby. It didn't seem farfetched."

"Claudia, I didn't know that guy. And I thought he died by suicide, anyway."

"That's what everyone thought, at first..." Claudia trails off. "But if you didn't know him and everything is fine and there's nothing strange going on, then why have you been avoiding my calls and texts?"

Ruby's cheeks turn pink and she smiles. "I didn't say *nothing* was going on. I was working on something for Champagne Toast. I didn't want to say anything until I was sure."

"What is it?"

"I put in an offer on Kennamer Farms, the Kennamers accepted, and we closed on it today. Champagne Toast Catering is going to have its own event space!"

"Ruby, that's amazing!" Claudia's excitement for her friend briefly overrides her desire to untangle the Paxton puzzle. "You should have told us, though." Claudia had known business was booming, but she hadn't realized Ruby was even interested in the Kennamer property.

"I didn't want to get too invested—emotionally—I mean, in case it didn't work out."

"I'm so happy for you." Claudia gives Ruby a hug. "Let's put something together to celebrate. I'll call Ingrid. And sorry. You know, for this weird mix-up. Do you need help, painting the house?"

Ruby shrugs. "Thanks, but I think it's a weekend project. Hopefully it doesn't scare off my clients in the meantime."

Claudia's confusion is back. She needs to think, to work through everything she knows about Paxton, and Amberly, and his friends, and how Ruby's name was drawn into this mess in the first place.

CHAPTER 20

C laudia has been so wrapped up in the mysteries surrounding Paxton Gale that she hasn't spent any time considering the ridiculous possibility of her husband falling for Amberly Vance. Lou had warned Claudia, but Claudia had promptly discarded that warning and the discomfort that came with it. The whole idea would be funny, actually, if not for the fact that one person who was involved with Amberly has died already. Beau's not the type to stray.

She reconsiders that stance, though, when she pulls up to The Gilded Mug after her visit with Ruby and sees Beau standing in line. He's chatting with a woman Claudia first assumes to be Ingrid. She's heading inside to say hello, door handle in her grip, when she takes in a few details at once: The jeans the woman is wearing (too casual to be Ingrid's workwear) and the blond-to-the-point-of-platinum hair, where Ingrid's is honey-hued. Ingrid is taller. The woman turns her head and her face is in profile and Claudia realizes that no, it is certainly not Ingrid.

It's Amberly Vance. In line at The Gilded Mug next to Claudia's husband in the middle of a work day. She's smiling, he's smiling, and all at once the idea of them together isn't so funny.

Claudia is too stunned to enter. Instead, she turns on her heel and goes back to her car. She has flashes of herself, drunk to the point of stupidity, in a bar with kids a decade younger than her. Graham's warm breath on her skin. How exciting it had felt to be wanted. What an ego boost it must be for Beau, to be fawned over by a pretty college girl.

She needs to tell him what Amberly is capable of, before she ends up with a dead husband on her hands. Would he actually fall for Amberly and her supposed tricks? How many "tricks" could a twenty-one-year-old young woman actually have, anyway?

"How was your day?" Claudia asks him, later that night while she's making dinner.

"Fine," he says, as usual.

"Anything interesting?" If running into Amberly was a coincidence, this is the perfect opportunity for him to tell her all about it—Amberly *is* one of Claudia's residents, after all. He'll tell her about running into that girl again, and she'll tell him how Amberly is sort of a killer. Depending on how you look at it. Then Claudia will tell him how she's gotten tangled up in finding answers about what happened to Paxton. She'll even come clean about how she and Graham almost kissed.

"Same as always," he says, instead. He's looking at his phone, and now Claudia wonders if he is really reading articles, or if they're text messages. "How was yours?"

She smiles and hides the disbelief she feels. "Same as always."

They start a movie after dinner, but Claudia's not really watching. This day has kept her so busy that she's been able to avoid it, but now she can't help but think back to this night so many years ago. This night, the last night of August...the last time she saw Killian alive.

Claudia's college friends, the ones who inexplicably loved theme parties, hosted a Victorians & Vampires kegger for their back-to-school party. Killian had worn a costume that had taken her breath away, a long black cape and a top hat, with liner around his eyes and a timepiece hanging from his brocade vest.

*You look...*she'd stammered. *What* are *you?*

156

A Victorian watchmaker. Or Victorian architect. Or Victorian magician. Whatever you want, really. What are you? The vampire version of Tinkerbell?

Claudia had worn a short black dress with a strange swirling pattern and tall lace up pleather boots with a pair of huge sparkly black wings attached to her back and fake fangs in her mouth.

Something like that. What do you think?

You look great.

We *look great.*

Claudia drove Killian's car to the party. Killian was a slow and careful driver, too careful. *One wrong twist of the steering wheel and anything could happen,* he'd said once. It was a powerful idea. Killian drove a Land Rover that was shiny and new and only hypothetically made for outdoor adventures. But Claudia loved driving it, loved the idea that she *could* do exactly as he'd suggested, if she wanted, twist the wheel and take the car right off the highway and into god-knows-where. Killian knew all of that, and he still preferred Claudia to take control.

He was quiet on the ride over. His phone rang and he declined it, and then it rang again. Again, declined.

Who are you avoiding? She asked.

What? No one. He looked up at her with a brilliant smile. And yet, he wasn't quite himself. She noticed and she didn't ask.

They danced together at the party. Claudia's friends passed around Jello shots. Killian made a face at them (the shots and the friends), but he took the first shot with her. The lights were low in the living room, music burst forth from the speakers, and they danced and danced.

You are incredible, Killian said into her ear, his breath hot there. *Irresistible.*

She kissed him, long and slow, pulled him so close to her that they were one dark blur and she couldn't discern where her black skirt ended and his black cape began. His arms were around her back and her body was buzzing in every place their skin connected. When she pulled away from him, her red lipstick was across his lips and she didn't wipe it away this time. He looked like the vampire then, lips wet with fresh blood.

Killian had stopped drinking after the first shot, so he'd been the one to drive them home. Claudia was happy and a bit stumbly as she followed him to the car, his black cape swishing behind him. Time got tangled and twisted for her when alcohol was involved, and the ride to her apartment felt like it happened at warp-speed, even with Killian's careful driving. One minute she was beside him in the car and the next they were in her bedroom and he was unzipping her boots and peeling the fairy wings from her back. She pulled him onto the bed with her.

You sure?

I'm always sure about you, she said.

Claudia, he whispered, pulling away the rest of her costume as she fumbled with his. He pulled her to his chest. Finally, her naked skin against his. His body connecting with hers. *I love you,* he murmured.

He pressed his lips to her cheek and it must have been the alcohol wiping out the filter between her thoughts and her words. *I love you too,* she said, into his ear. *I do.*

She fell asleep curled against him, his lean arms pulling her to his chest. But in the middle of the night she felt him stir, leave her bed, pull her covers up around her.

You aren't staying? She whispered.

Not tonight, he said. *You rest.* She drifted in and out of sleep as he pulled on his clothes in the darkness. *Don't forget what I told you.*

And then he was gone, and she tumbled back into sleep with a smile on her face.

She woke up in the morning, hungover and thinking of Killian and remembering the words they'd said. She texted him to ask if he wanted to get breakfast.

But he didn't respond.

CHAPTER 21

Work is hell the next day. Graham calls in sick, even though Claudia would bet a hundred dollars that he's fine. It's out of character for him to make excuses not to come to work, but despite their promise to forget just how close they'd come to crossing a line, it's been uncomfortable lately. Claudia wishes she'd never gone out that night at all and embarrassed herself. But it's done, and there's no going back, and now she's stuck with only Liza here in the office, and Liza is screwing things up left and right. Today alone, she's quoted the wrong prices twice and forgotten to show the resident lounge on a lease tour. Ever since Liza used Paxton's death as a way to advertise, Claudia can hardly stand to be in the same room with her. She should have fired Liza, she knows that. It was wrong to let her stay. *One more strike*, she promises herself. *One more strike and I'll do it.*

The afternoon has turned busy, crammed full of lease tours and re-ports due. In the middle of it all, the Habitat for Humanity folks arrive to remove the furniture from Paxton's apartment. It's still unreal, showing prospective residents around the building, knowing someone died here. But despite Liza's careless attempts at gossip, the word hasn't spread as far as it could have in a town like this, and even the residents don't ask about it anymore.

It's raining outside and getting dark earlier and earlier every afternoon. It won't be long before it's pitch black outside by the time she leaves work.

The first of September is a bad day for her, worse than August 31st even. August reminds her of how naïve she was all those years ago on that last night with Killian, when she didn't know what was to come. But September comes with knowing.

September 1st is the day Claudia went to Killian's apartment and found him there, in his bed. How long she'd stood there like an idiot, admiring him, assuming he was sleeping, thinking of how she'd said the word *love* and he'd said it back. He still wore remnants of his Victorian costume, the shiny slacks and a white undershirt.

And then she noticed the pill bottles in a neat line along his nightstand and the world fell apart, piece by fucking piece. Things happened after that, but it was all a grief-stained blur: her blue hair falling into Killian's face as she listened for breath that wasn't there, her pleading to him to wake up, a call to 911, her sudden manic certainty that there had to be some explanation if only she could find it, a frantic search around his room for a note that didn't exist. At some point Killian's roommate arrived home from spending the night away and Claudia didn't know the roommate well but she still gripped him in a desperate hug as he stared, wide-eyed, at the scene in that room. Police arrived. Things happened, and none of it changed the fact that Killian, beautiful Killian, had abruptly left the world. Left her. On purpose.

The loss of Killian is etched into her skin as permanently as her dagger tattoo. Sometimes the memory of him is so painful she can't believe she can feel it all and still be walking around like she isn't shredded inside. It's amazing what the human body can endure. And what it can't.

Claudia takes her time closing up the leasing office at the end of the day. She tries to think about Paxton. But she's useless there too; she couldn't do anything to help him when it actually mattered. She'd been so sure that there was another woman in the picture. Paxton's friends had given her bad information, and she'd latched onto it like the eager little amateur detective she's been pretending to be. She still doesn't know what Paxton was up to that was so lucrative he'd had an apartment on the side. She still has no proof that he was murdered. As of now, the only thing she knows is that Amberly was behind the text messages, but she doesn't actually have any evidence of that either. Meanwhile, her husband is having coffee dates with Amberly, and she can't even get up the nerve to confront him about it.

Maybe Graham is right after all and there are no answers in a situation like this. Maybe it's just a shitty thing and that's that.

She's turning out the lights and getting ready to drive home in the rain when she sees movement out of the corner of her eye. She looks up. Someone is outside the lobby door. Someone wearing a rain jacket.

For a split second she sees Paxton, not dead after all but standing out there rain-soaked. She imagines letting him in, and him explaining that the whole thing was one big, strange mix-up. But then she blinks, and it's Randall, Paxton's friend, the one who inexplicably showed up here with Amberly and Lou the day they ransacked Paxton's apartment. The boy she danced with in the bar. He doesn't look like Paxton at all. She feels her cheeks burning as she walks slowly to the door and pushes it open.

"Hi," she says. "Can I help you?"

"Hey Claudia." He runs a hand through his rain-damp hair. "Can I come in?"

She steps aside, even though she really doesn't want to. She's ready to get home. It's dim in the lobby, only the decorative sconces glowing and the controlled fire flickering in the fireplace. She thinks of apologizing to Randall for the night in the bar a few weeks back, but instead it's her frustration that comes out.

"You and your friends lied to me," she says. "You told me there was another woman in Paxton's life."

"What?" he says. "I didn't lie. There *was* another woman."

"Not Ruby Duvall."

"Yes. Ruby Duvall. That's her name."

"You're wrong," Claudia says. "She's my friend, and I asked her. She doesn't even know who Paxton is."

"Look, I don't know her. But Paxton said her name was Ruby."

"Well he lied, and now you and your friends have spray painted her home. And her business. You're lucky she hasn't filed a police report yet."

Randall shifts his feet and looks down. "Okay, maybe we didn't do the mature thing. We thought she had something to do with Paxton's death. But then Lou told me what Amberly did. And she told me that you really are trying to help Paxton's family." Claudia nods. Let him believe that's her only goal. "I've always liked Marilyn," he says. "TessAnne too. The other guys feel the same way. We want to help. We didn't know, when we first met you. We thought you had something to do with the other woman, *Ruby,* the one who hurt Paxton. Emotionally I mean, or whatever. She's the one who set him up in this apartment in the first place, so it's not, you know, super off-base for us to think that. He would have done anything for her. Honestly, anything. They were hot and heavy and he was on top of the world...and then they weren't and he wasn't. He jumped into this thing with Amberly, to try to get his mind off the breakup, I guess. But Amberly...she's *scary.* I didn't know, the day I helped her and Lou. I didn't know what Amberly had done. They asked me to help with moving some things, and then we got up there and Amberly started tearing the place apart and ordering Lou to do the same thing. I didn't know she was looking for the iPad. Lou only told me after." Randall shakes his head. "Women. Fuck."

"You and Lou are close?"

"We weren't. I only know her through Amberly. But she's not like Amberly. She's different. Better, I think." He shrugs. "I mean, *I hope*."

He still hasn't said why he's here.

"Just, you know, get to the truth, okay? Make sure Marilyn and TessAnne know. I don't know if what Amberly did was illegal, but it doesn't seem right for her to mess with people's heads like that and get away with it." He digs around in his pocket and produces an iPhone. "This might help. Lou said you needed it."

"Paxton's phone?" she asks in disbelief.

Randall nods. "Yeah. Amberly's going to shit when she realizes it's missing. Lou really went out on a limb to get it. Password is his birthday. Here, I'll open the photo app and you can see for yourself." He moves his finger around the iPhone screen and an app opens, and then an album, and then he puts the phone in her hand. "And there you are. Good luck, Claudia."

She hears Randall walking away, footsteps squelching in the rain, but she can't pull her eyes away from the first photo in the album. It's a man and a woman, both in swimsuits, embracing on an unfamiliar beach. Sun-kissed skin, windswept hair, bodies pressed against one another. There's no doubt that the two people in the photo are intimate. An outstretched arm—Paxton's—captures the selfie.

It's Paxton there, in the photo, but the woman beside him is *not* Ruby Duvall.

***

Claudia is still scrolling through Paxton's photos when her own phone rings.

It's Beau, calling with a story about a rain-related crisis at a job site that he has to leave the office to take care of. *Don't expect me home until late,* he says.

If she hadn't seen him at The Gilded Mug with Amberly yesterday, she may not have been primed to spot the lie. But Beau is a terrible liar. His voice takes on a different tone that's easily distinguishable from its normal tenor. Claudia understands, too well, how easily people lie, how easy it is to omit details. She's done it herself.

Claudia hangs up the phone and grabs her raincoat, then leaves work early and speeds over to the lot next door to WMB Real Estate Group. It's what any suspicious wife would do, probably. She's afraid that she's missed him already, but no, there is his truck. Ingrid's SUV is there too and Claudia could take this opportunity to go in and see her, if not for the pressing matter at hand.

She's never tailed anyone before. Claudia is only just learning how to be covert. But it shouldn't matter. Beau would never expect her to doubt him. Back when they were newlyweds, they'd touted the fact that they trusted each other so implicitly. Never mind that she hadn't been completely honest with Beau about the most painful part of her life. She'd never mentioned Killian. At all. The memory of Killian is with Claudia every single day, and Beau has no idea he ever existed.

Now Beau is lying to her about spending time with Amberly Vance. Because she knows, deep down, that he's going to see Amberly and not to a job site. It's chilling to think that Amberly was involved in Paxton's death, and now she's spending time with Claudia's husband. It makes her feel better about following him to tell herself she's more than a jealous wife. She's protecting her husband from a potentially dangerous woman.

She watches Beau leave work, then waits what she assumes is an appropriate amount of time before following. She tries her damnedest to leave three car lengths between them so he won't notice her, won't see the black shine of her car hanging back but keeping close. The rain slows, making it easier to keep him in her sights.

When did she become this person?

This sneaky, suspicious woman.

An almost-cheater.

A woman obsessed with the death of a college student she barely knew.

A person with oh so many secrets.

It always seems easy to tail someone in the movies. She watches Beau's truck turn left from Price Avenue onto Lumar Street. She feels momentarily triumphant when she realizes that she doesn't know of any new construction in this area. She follows him two miles before he turns into the parking lot of a Mexican restaurant. Beau's truck is one of only five in the lot, so Claudia has to keep driving past until he's gone inside. She makes a three-point turnaround that becomes five, and then finally she swings her car into the parking lot of the gas station next door. From here, she can see right into the restaurant without being obvious. Bright chalk paint spells out food words—Nachos! Tacos! Enchiladas!—on the big windows. Past the words, Claudia sees a line of booths. It's getting dark outside, and the darker it gets, the easier it is to see inside the restaurant.

Beau sits alone in a booth tucked in the front corner and stares out the window, obviously waiting for someone. It occurs to her that some part of her *wants* to catch Beau cheating. She thinks back to the night outside The Study Room, leaning into a dimly-lit storefront with Graham's lips so close to her skin. It would make her feel better to know she isn't the only one capable of straying.

She stops analyzing her feelings when a white Mercedes sedan pulls into the parking lot and parks right next to Beau's Chevy. Claudia doesn't know if Amberly would recognize her car, but she's glad she parked at the gas station anyway. There she is, Amberly Vance, a big brown leather purse slung over one shoulder and a cell phone to her ear. She wears jeans and a light sweater with a deep v-neck, her hair long and wavy down her back. As she approaches the door of the restaurant, she ends her call and tucks the phone away in her bag.

Claudia watches as she approaches Beau and slides into the booth across from him. No handshake or hug. Claudia doesn't know what to make of that.

A waitress approaches with chips and water, and then disappears. Beau and Amberly fall into what looks like an easy conversation. He's smiling at her. She keeps leaning forward, hair spilling over her shoulders.

Is Beau on an actual date with a college student? Is he really doing this, on purpose, with intention? Claudia stares, transfixed. She gets out of the car, not sure what she plans to do.

She imagines Beau and Amberly leaving here and heading...where, to a hotel room? Is that how it would go? They can't go back to Amberly's apartment. Surely Beau would worry Claudia would see them on security camera footage, and that's assuming they didn't run into Graham or one of the other residents who have seen Beau at community events and would recognize him.

Her husband is cheating on her. Wanting to cheat, at the very least. The reality of it sinks in. And unlike Claudia's intimate moment with Graham, Beau had planned this. He'd lied to her to meet another woman. It's hard to accept, even with the evidence of it before her eyes.

"Excuse me," a voice says. She spins around and realizes she's preventing a man leaving the gas station from reaching his driver's side door.

"Sorry," she mutters. She steps back to her own car. She could wait, see if Beau and Amberly leave together, where they go next. Or she could go in there, confront Beau. She doesn't know what she'd even say. She doesn't know what she *wants* to say.

Behind her steering wheel with her hair damp from the light drizzle, she feels like she's supposed to cry. But she can't summon the tears.

She doesn't go home, not for a while. Instead, she drives. She heads toward her neighborhood, but when she gets there she speeds right past and ends up on backroads and in surprise mountain subdivisions she hadn't even known existed. She passes elegant little Southern castles with acres of forest separating one from the next. She twists and turns down roads she's never explored, past antique malls and roadside diners. She knows she'll turn around, but she entertains the idea of not. This could be it, the night she disappears. The night she runs away and never comes back.

A small, logical voice in her head whispers that maybe things are more innocent than she'd first assumed. Maybe Beau will get home before she does, and he'll wonder where she is.

She keeps checking her phone, but it never rings.

***

It's not readily apparent now, but Claudia and Beau have always been a surprising match.

It all started with Ingrid. Claudia had been working for Southern Campus Collective as an assistant property manager in Atlanta when she got the offer to come to Ellen Point to run a new community for Ellen Point University students. She didn't know much about the college town other than it was exclusive and mountainous, but she had no reason to stay in Atlanta. Nothing—and no one—worth staying for.

Claudia's boss, Margo, introduced her to Ingrid when she took them both to lunch in downtown Ellen Point to finalize the details of the property transfer. Ingrid and Claudia were both youngish, single, and career-focused. Margo left after lunch to go back to Huntsville, but Ingrid and Claudia stayed at the restaurant for another hour, finishing a bottle of wine and talking. Claudia was her best self after a glass of wine, but it was clear that Ingrid didn't let loose very often. Before they knew it, evening had rolled in and they were giggling together like schoolgirls. *Thanks for this,* Ingrid said. *I haven't laughed like this in a long time.*

Months later, at the Prestige open house, Ingrid introduced Claudia to Beau Aldridge, the WMB Construction Manager. With Claudia in her cocktail dress and Beau in his gray suit, you couldn't see right away how different they were. They started talking at the champagne bar. Beau was smart, and laid back, and he had a great smile. They discussed their work but also the books they'd read recently. After a few glasses of champagne, he asked for her number. It was the first time since Killian that Claudia remembered feeling...not smitten, exactly, but curious about someone in a romantic sense. She wasn't celibate; there had been other men and even women and lips and hands and skin to quench her thirst for human connection. But they were one-night stands, all of them. She couldn't risk her passion destroying anyone else.

Over the years since Killian, though, she'd worked to conquer the part of herself that was careless and wild. As she did, those one-night stands became less frequent. She'd reigned in that desire for touch until it couldn't consume her. Meanwhile, she'd found her footing professionally with apartment management, and she'd become moderately successful.

Beau was interesting, and handsome, and just plain *nice*. Usually, the combination was an automatic red flag, because she'd allowed herself all of that once and look how it turned out. Flirting with Beau felt okay though, mild and pleasant without that sharp edge of need she used to be so familiar with, and she could suddenly see how her life could be different with someone like him. If she wanted it to be.

He called her the day after the open house and asked her out for coffee, and she said yes.

She'd done such a thorough job of hiding what a disaster she used to be that Beau had no way of knowing that he and Claudia weren't the same. She'd long since washed out her vivid hair dye and invested in half-a-closet's-worth of business attire for work. She watched Beau and she listened to him, and she intentionally used all of that information to become the kind of person she thought he'd like. Pretty soon they were staying in together and cooking dinner and watching Netflix and doing all of the other sweet and mundane things that couples do.

After a year of dating, Beau proposed. Claudia said yes, and why not? He got down on one knee when he asked, and she believed she could commit to this life they'd made. She was ready for it, and an opportunity like Beau Aldridge might not come along again. They got married in the Virgin Islands with only their families present. Claudia and her mother had reconciled after college, and even though her mother wasn't pleased that she hadn't gotten the Southern wedding she'd always dreamed of planning, she and Ronald made the trip. Her mother loved Beau. Of course she did. Everyone did.

Things were as good as they could get, then, and Claudia was happy. She would have sworn she was.

No one who attended the wedding knew about Claudia's relationship with Killian and it didn't matter. Claudia was bright white in a beautiful gown. She was brand new.

But when she looked down that aisle, she still thought of running, like they do in movies. Disappearing so no one could find her again—not Beau or her mother or anyone.

All these years later, and still she thinks about it.

***

The next night, Claudia meets her friends for drinks at a trendy restaurant in a downtown hotel.

Claudia and Ruby arrive at the same time, and Ingrid waves to them from a booth farther back in the restaurant where she's already getting friendly with her vodka tonic.

"I'm so glad you suggested this, Claudia," Ingrid says. "I really needed this drink." A server comes by and Ruby touches him lightly on the cuff of his sleeve. "Sweetie, can we get two more of those please?" She points to Ingrid's drink.

"Sure thing," the waiter says with a smile.

"Ingrid," says Ruby. "I don't know if you've heard the news yet, but I'm about to be the new owner of an event space! Oh, and I'm also an alleged murderer."

Ingrid raises her eyebrows in surprise. "I don't know where to start with that."

"I'm buying Kennamer Farms. I didn't even know it was on the market until the Golden Hour Gathering, and I knew it would be huge for my business to have an event space. So I pulled together every penny I had, and I made an offer."

"Ruby!" Ingrid says. "Congratulations! Why didn't you tell us? I would have been happy to invest!"

Ruby looks sheepish. "I know. That's part of the reason I didn't say anything. I really wanted to do this on my own. But I knew it was impulsive, and I didn't want anyone to talk me out of it. And then, you know, I wasn't sure it would actually work out, and I didn't want to jinx myself by saying how much I wanted it."

"I can't believe you went out and bought a farm," Claudia says.

"I know. But it's going to be so great. For weddings, and parties, and photo sessions, and everything really. I'm so excited. Or I *was*, until I got home from the closing and saw that someone had spray-painted the word MURDERER on my house." Ruby fills Ingrid in on the situation. "Turns out, according to Claudia, some college boys thought I was sleeping with their friend—that poor guy who died at Claudia's building—and that I killed him."

"Isn't that strange, Ingrid?" Claudia asks. "Isn't that the most bizarre mix-up?"

Ingrid looks at Claudia, eyebrows raised. "It is. So strange."

"You lied to me," Claudia says to Ingrid. "About the invitation. About knowing him. You could have told me. I wish you had. It would have saved me a hell of a lot of trouble."

"Wait, what?" Ruby asks.

"It's...complicated. And I didn't know you'd be so interested in him," Ingrid says.

"Well, I am."

"What's going on?" Ruby says.

Ingrid clears her throat. "Ruby, I'm sorry. For the mix-up. Um. It was me. I was the one with the...connection to Paxton."

Ruby's mouth drops open.

"The photos I saw suggest a pretty strong *connection*."

"You've got to be kidding," Ruby says. "Ingrid, my god. But he's...I'm so sorry that he's...you know, deceased now." She reaches out to touch Ingrid's hand. "You've been going through all of this without saying a word. Why?"

"It doesn't matter," Ingrid says. She drains her vodka tonic. "Not when he's not even here anymore."

Paxton wants me to know, Claudia almost says, before stopping herself. How selfish of her. Ingrid is the one who had the relationship with Paxton. By comparison, Claudia didn't know him at all. "Ingrid. You didn't kill him, did you?" She has to at least ask.

"What? Of course not. I...I loved him."

"You weren't that polite when you accused *me* of murder," Ruby mutters.

"But...what about Thomas?"

"My relationship with Thomas is...not what it seems."

"Listen," Claudia presses. "If you really don't want to talk about it, I understand. It's not my business and it never was, and I've gotten too involved and the not knowing...well, it's almost all I think about. But if you say it's not *for* us to know, then...then it's not."

Ingrid looks at them for a long moment.

And then she tells them one hell of a story.

PART TWO

(ONE YEAR AGO)

CHAPTER 22

Ingrid Wyatt is done with this wedding. After months and months of fanfare (how many bridal showers can one person have before everyone agrees that it's just poor taste?) Elodie Rose Reynolds is married. Hallelujah. Ingrid has been here every step of the way. She's not close friends with Elodie Rose like she is with Claudia and Ruby, but since Ingrid is the Foxglove Society president and Elodie Rose is secretary, Ingrid felt obligated to be a part of it all. She'd even hosted the first shower at the Wyatt mansion. And then she'd proceeded to attend, gift in hand, the six subsequent showers—one of which Elosie Rose'd had the nerve to host *for herself.* Has anyone ever been so pleased to be lawfully wed?

The jazz band out of Atlanta plays on one side of the hotel ballroom. After the four-course meal, the dining tables have been cleared to make way for the dance floor. But Ingrid won't be dancing. She doesn't need to make a complete fool of herself simply because it's a wedding.

She grabs a glass of champagne from a tray that glides past balanced on the arm of a server in the usual black-and-white attire. Thank God for the bubbly, at least.

She's here alone, and that's how she'd wanted it. There are men she could have asked to accompany her to the wedding. But it's a badge of honor not to need a date to get through life. Usually. Tonight feels different for some reason. Maybe it's because Elodie Rose was the last unmarried woman in the Foxglove Society besides Ingrid. Now Ingrid is the only one without a husband. She doesn't even want one, for crying out loud. She's married to her work, and she's damned proud of it. Wyatt McIntyre Birch Real Estate Group is thriving, and that's in large part due to her.

But there was this moment, earlier, during the first dance between Elodie Rose and her new husband where Elodie Rose was gazing up at him and he was looking down at her and pushing an intentionally loose strand of hair behind her ear and this stupid slow song was playing that Ingrid had never heard before. For a second, Ingrid wanted that moment for herself.

She takes her champagne and slips out a side door, near the lot where her car is parked. She walks over, enters the code on the door and slides into her Lexus. There's one emergency cigarette inside and she desperately needs it. She lights it and tucks the lighter back into her glove compartment. Then she walks back to the hotel, puffing her nicotine lifeline and hoping no one else sees her. The smoking is a rebel habit she's picked up recently, but she tries not to let herself get carried away. She leans against the gray stucco of the hotel and watches the sun sink behind the lush mountainside. In between pulls, she drains her champagne.

The only things her Foxglove Society sisters care about are marriage and babies. No matter how successful Ingrid is, no matter how high she climbs at Wyatt McIntyre Birch, the only thing these women will ever notice about her is that she's single. As if that's something she should care about. Thank god these aren't her only friends. Claudia would have something cynical (but accurate) to say about this spectacle if she was here, even though Ruby is the event planner behind it all. Everything was done exactly to Elodie Rose's specifications. *The bride wants what the bride wants*, Ruby is fond of saying. But now that the ceremony is over and the reception is well underway, Ruby's work is done for the evening and she's gone home. Ingrid wishes she was still here. Ruby doesn't stop long enough to socialize during her events, but it had still been comforting to have a friend—a *real* friend—nearby.

Ingrid would like to escape too, leave this reception and go relax in her hotel room. Even though the wedding is here in Ellen Point, she'd booked a room at the hotel hosting the reception. She needs a night away, and her father's caretaker had assured her that he would be okay without her there for one night.

A member of the catering staff walks past and no, she doesn't imagine it. He rolls his eyes at her. "Those things will kill you, you know," he says drily. He pauses at the door and she studies him. He's young, sexy in a careless sort of way. Too sexy for his own good. His dark hair sticks up in a way that's styled but also somehow natural. He has dark eyes with strong brows and sharp cheekbones, and his black and white catering uniform flatters his lean body in all kinds of nice ways. She'd seen him serving champagne inside. The reception is nowhere near over, not yet, but his black bowtie is already loosened around his neck.

"I've heard. Thanks for your concern."

He shrugs. "Can't smoke there, anyway." He points to the sign behind her that she hadn't noticed, the red one that says NO SMOKING in big letters. "You're right underneath a sprinkler and if it senses that smoke, your friend's wedding is going to be evacuated. Or flooded, one or the other. But I get it. The usual rules probably don't apply to people like you."

Her amusement at the mental image of Elodie Rose and her wedding guests running out, dresses soaked and hair-sprayed coifs collapsed, is muted by his biting comment. Still, she smiles.

When Ingrid was a little girl being shown off by her father, wearing some frilly dress she'd hated, her father would always lean down to remind her to fix her face. *Smile, Darling*, he'd say after her ballet recitals, when proud parents were snapping photos. It wasn't just him. *Your presentation was great,* a (male) college professor said to her once. *But I think you'd connect with your audience more if you tried to smile.* A lifetime of men telling her to smile when she's sad, when she's angry, when she's nervous. So now she can hardly do anything *but* smile. Her jaws ache at the end of the day from smiling so much. And the smile is genuine—it's a habit too ingrained, at this point, to break—but the smile doesn't mean what they think it means. Her smile has no relation, anymore, to her own happiness. She's even more likely to smile when she's *unhappy.* That's what these men have taught her.

"You're right," she says, just to piss off the server. "They usually don't. And maybe I shouldn't be smoking here, but sprinkler heads aren't directly triggered by smoke. It takes heat, a lot of it. So, unless I set these bushes on fire, we're probably going to be just fine, you and me, and all of those people in there too."

"Well." He smirks. "Thanks for setting me straight." He walks through the side door to the ballroom. Men. Always trying to *teach* women things. Once he's left, though, she finds that she's acutely aware of his absence. People don't talk to her the way this guy did. Oh sure, they'll explain things to her that she already understands, but they don't usually do it with such a shitty attitude. It had been *delicious* to tell him he was wrong, to drop her polite Southern persona for one moment and just be. And despite her irritation, she's intrigued, and her smile turns into a laugh even though he's no longer there to see it. It hardly has anything to do with him anyway.

When she goes back inside, the Foxglove Society ladies are on the dance floor, dancing to some R&B cover the jazz band is playing. They move in a circle with Elodie Rose in the middle, all of them looking drunk as skunks at this point. June Pressman is the only other member of the Foxglove Society sitting it out, probably because she'll want to point out later what idiots they all looked like. The self-appointed Foxglove

Society gossip, she'll also be the one to let them know who was flirting with another member's husband and who breached etiquette to wear a white dress to the wedding. At least Ingrid knows she didn't do either of those things. Her silvery gray dress is appropriate for this late summer wedding; not flashy like June's (for someone who is on top of everyone else's transgressions, the woman has very little self-awareness), nor matronly like Elodie Rose's sister-in-law (who is only twenty-eight but whose dress makes her look sixty). Ingrid looks good in this dress, and she knows it, and the furtive glances from other husbands in the room confirms it. As if she'd dressed for any of these boring, suited, overgrown frat boys. And the women all want to know why she doesn't want a husband of her own.

She takes a fresh glass of champagne and mingles, making small talk with these same men about work and the stock market and college football season. They think they know more than she does, but she can't call out *these* men, because even if she's the vice president of a regional empire, she's also a Southern lady with a role to play. So she smiles through the *Well, actually*s and marvels, as usual, at the unbelievable—*unearned*—confidence of men.

Ingrid excuses herself to go to the restroom, though what she really wants is an escape.

In her haste to get out of the ballroom, she runs, quite literally, into a member of the catering staff. She watches, mortified, as the champagne flutes balanced on his tray clatter to the floor and spill across the ugly hotel carpet.

"Oh," she says, stunned. She reaches for the empty glasses and helps corral them back onto the tray before looking up. It's the same sarcastic manboy from outside. "You."

"Um, yeah. And you too." She'd gotten the impression he'd left their earlier conversation mildly amused, but he's obviously annoyed now. He reaches for the two glasses in her hand.

"Let me help." She's almost yelling over the noise of the band. In the celebration, no one notices them huddled by the ballroom doorway.

"I think you've helped enough." He lifts pieces of a broken champagne flute from the carpet. "Anything I break comes out of my paycheck, you know."

"I'll take care of it," she says, quickly.

The handsome server gets to his feet, with four intact flutes and one broken one balanced on his tray. He pushes on the double doors and she follows him. "As if my boss would ever allow a guest to pay."

"Oh." She makes a mental note to follow up with Ruby on it later. Ruby doesn't work directly with the catering staff anymore, but she'll be able to put Ingrid in touch with the catering manager so Ingrid can make sure the glass is paid for. Ruby buys in bulk; it can't cost much. Ingrid wonders if the glass will really come out of the server's paycheck or if it's a story he's telling her to make her feel worse.

"It's fine, don't worry about it," he says and walks away. She opens her mouth to say something, but he's already gone.

Suddenly she knows she's done with this wedding. Elodie Rose, surrounded by her other girlfriends, won't notice she's gone. Ingrid strolls down the hallway to where the hotel opens up into a big, elegant lobby with traditional details and an upscale restaurant. She makes her way to the bar, enjoying the way her heels clack against the waxy hardwood floors after the hush of the carpeted hallway.

She orders a vodka tonic with lime, smiles at the bartender like she isn't a little bit pissed off at the entire world. She wishes she'd made up an excuse to get out of attending Elodie Rose's over-the-top wedding.

(As if she could have done that.) Then she wouldn't have to be here in the first place.

She'd left her phone in the hotel room (purse too, everything but her tiny silver clutch), so she has nothing to keep her occupied now. The Southern-style restaurant (appropriately named OKRA) is crowded with couples, a few business people, and college students around big tables. Three months ago, OKRA was featured in Garden & Gun magazine, and now even Ellen Point residents who aren't staying at the hotel come here for dinner, and Ellen Point University students come in groups and post pictures of their food on Instagram. Ingrid takes it all in. When the bartender asks her if she wants another drink, she nods.

"You haven't found anything here to break yet?" There he is, the server, bow-tie gone, shirt untucked and unbuttoned with a white undershirt beneath. Ingrid looks at him. That hard, angular face, like he's seen some shit though he probably hasn't. Old enough to have lost the cute boyishness she can tell was there once, but young enough to make her wish *she* was several years younger. Not that she would have had the confidence to go after someone like him, back then. When she was in high school, she'd had a crush on a boy who still pops up in her dreams from time to time. He was a bad boy cliché, leather jacket and motorcycle, and she'd wanted him so badly. He'd liked her too. But she was afraid of what her father would think, and so she'd never even agreed to a date. She regrets that now.

This server reminds her of him.

"Hmm...not yet." She's had more to drink than she would normally allow. If she'd stayed at the wedding, she would have stopped at her two-champagne limit. Nothing harder. But the wedding must be winding down or Server Boy wouldn't be here beside her, and she's not going back anyway. She still shouldn't be drinking like this; somebody—June Pressman, most likely—could see her and then it would get out that

Ingrid Wyatt is a lush and then no one would take her seriously. Aren't they always looking for a reason not to?

The server is staring at her. "What are you looking at?" she asks. This guy really seems to dislike her. But suddenly she wonders if he's fantasizing instead, if he's thinking of working her slim-fitting silver dress up around her hips, pulling her hair free from the loose chignon and watching it fall around her shoulders. Probably not. But she hopes he is.

She doesn't know what's gotten into her tonight.

He shrugs. "Are you off work?" Ingrid asks. When he nods, she orders him a drink. Same thing she's having. "Seems like you need it."

"Thanks," he says. He stands up, grabbing his drink from the bar. "Hey, sorry for being a dick earlier. It's...been a long day. You didn't deserve all that."

"Hmm. Make it up to me by sticking around for a while, if you want." She doesn't know why she says it, why this young man and his attitude are almost as intoxicating as the alcohol.

He raises one thick eyebrow in surprise. "Why?"

"I don't know...just seems like maybe you should."

"Don't you have a husband around here somewhere?"

She raises her eyebrows.

"Okay, no husband." He sits back down. She catches him glancing at her legs where her skirt has ridden up. Maybe he *is* fantasizing about her, after all.

"You a student?" she asks.

"Junior."

She does some quick math. He must be more than a decade younger than her. "Jesus, you *are* old enough to drink, right?" The bartender hadn't ID'd him because Ingrid had been the one to order.

"*Of course*," he says emphatically, and she doesn't know yet that while he *is* twenty-one, he'd only recently hit that milestone. "What's up with that wedding?" he asks. "Friends of yours, or family?"

"Friends. Sort of."

"Nice wedding."

"Is it?"

"I mean, yeah, if you like that sort of thing. I've worked five others this year pretty much exactly like it."

Ingrid laughs. "The bride wants what the bride wants. Are you telling me that Elodie Rose is *not* as special as she thinks she is?"

"I hate to break it to you, but no, Elodie Rose is not special."

He's grinning at her suddenly and he has this look on his face like it hasn't occurred to him yet that she's untouchable. Tonight, maybe she isn't. She's never propositioned a man before, but what the hell? She'll never see him again. The air around her is gold and shimmery and she's warm, almost happy.

"So here's the thing," she says. "I have a room upstairs."

"Oh yeah?"

"Yeah."

"I bet it's a nice room."

"It's *very* nice."

"So is this goodnight? Are you heading up to your room now, all alone?"

"That's not quite what I had in mind."

The server leans close to her, runs his fingertips up her leg, on the exposed skin between her knee and the hem of her dress. It's a bold move. "Then what *do* you have in mind?" He's trying to play it cool but she can tell he's nervous; if he's misread the situation, she could slap him. Or worse.

"I think," Ingrid says, sounding braver than she feels. "We order an-other round of drinks, take those drinks upstairs to my room, and see what happens after that. Are you...interested?" She thinks of her younger self, the girl who never got the boy she wanted.

Fuck all of that.

He looks into her eyes. "Yeah. Hell yeah, I'm interested."

She orders another round and tosses down some cash. He takes the drinks and follows her to the elevator. He's eager to touch her, she can tell, but his hands are occupied with the drinks. She leans against the cool elevator wall, watching him. She takes one of the drinks from his hands, sips, her crimson lips against the glass leaving an imprint behind. He could say something now— *You're so beautiful. So sexy*—but he doesn't, and she's glad. It would all be trite. She wonders if he's expecting some-thing from her, some kind of disclaimer. *I never do this.* But she doesn't say it either. She's not that girl, and she doesn't care all that much what he thinks of her.

She wonders if he feels used.

Ingrid has stayed at this hotel before, after late night downtown char-ity events or networking dinners, nights when she wasn't quite ready to go back to her father's house. She's always been alone, though. She has a condo of her own, a few miles from campus, but she'd rented it out last year when Willard first got sick so she could move back into the mansion where she grew up, to help take care of him when he'll allow it. He's got nurses and a cook, but he likes having family around, even if he doesn't say it outright.

The walls of the hotel room are painted light blue, the headboard fancy, a plush rug atop the hardwood floors. Ingrid tosses her clutch on the floor in the entryway and tips back her drink. For the first time, she feels uncertain. She licks her lips while he stares.

She wants him to be the one to do it, to make the first move, and he somehow seems to know this. He sets his glass on the entry table and dives for her, his lips against her mouth, and her empty glass falls from her hand. Everything seems to speed up. He lifts her, sets her on the table. She pushes off his button-down shirt. He's exactly what she'd hoped for and also different. Better. She didn't realize how *hungry* she was, how long it's been since she's touched someone this way, with abandon. Has she ever? She gets his undershirt off, bites into his shoulder, runs her hands along the contours of his stomach.

The bed is plush and luxurious and comfortable, but they don't make it there, not the first time at least. Instead, they tumble onto the rug. With one errant hand Ingrid produces a condom from her purse. She may not do things like this often, but she's nothing if not prepared for the unexpected.

Car horns beep on the street outside.

Her dress is around her hips, and his clothes are in a heap beside them.

She wraps her legs around him. She's been starving for this kind of intimacy and now that she has it, she's insatiable. They make it to the bed eventually.

"Damn," he says, later, a lazy grin on his face. The pleasure has relaxed them both. Ingrid slides from between the sheets and bends to get her purse from the floor. She feels his eyes on her. It hadn't occurred to her to be embarrassed, to hide her body like some schoolgirl. She brings back a cigarette, lighter, and her phone and slips beneath the covers, her legs sliding against his. He trails a hand up her leg.

"Isn't this a non-smoking hotel?"

"Jesus," she says. "You have a real problem with cigarettes, huh?"

"Not exactly." He kisses her, sucking smoke from her mouth. "It's just surprising. You don't seem like a smoker." He bites her lip.

"Yeah?" she says. "What *do* I seem like, to you?"

"Fucking incredible," he murmurs.

"You don't know me very well," she says. "You're not completely terrible yourself." She passes him the cigarette. He takes a drag, even though he clearly isn't into it. She checks her phone. No missed calls, thank goodness. Whenever she's away from home, she worries about her father.

The server trails kisses down her stomach and before she knows it, they're entwined again.

It's after midnight when he kisses her goodbye. "This was...really something," she says. She thinks of thanking him—is that the thing to do?—but she doesn't. She could have asked him to stay the rest of the night, but she doesn't do that either. She enjoyed the experience, but she still wants the room to herself now.

"Yeah," he says, that smirk on his face again. "Something." The door clicks closed behind him, and she goes to bed wrapped in a hotel bathrobe with an easy smile on her face.

CHAPTER 23

N
o matter how much she'd hated it, Ingrid would rather attend Elodie Rose's wedding every day for the rest of her life than give a speech in public. Actually, if the repeat weddings ended like the original, that might not be so bad.

Public speaking, on the other hand, will never stop making her uncomfortable. It doesn't matter how often she does it. Today she's on the Ellen Point University campus, preparing to speak to a Real Estate Business class. The course professor had been her mentor when she was in college herself, so she goes back once a year to give another boring speech to his class. It's good for recruiting new talent to WMB. Even before her father got sick, it was one of the things he didn't like to think about anymore. He would rub elbows with the other old white men, play golf and take lunch meetings, and leave the speeches to his shiny, pretty daughter.

Today is her thirty-third birthday, and damn is it dreary out. She's having dinner with her friends tonight to celebrate. Not the smug, fake Foxglove ladies but her real friends. Ingrid's birthday, and here she is, smoking outside before the class starts, and sulking, and feeling strangely nostalgic for her own college years, which weren't even that great. She watches kids dragging themselves to class—half of them hungover, probably—and she wants to tell them to stop looking so glum. Honestly, don't they know this is as good as it's going to get? She hadn't even had the good sense to have fun while she was in school. Her friends went to bars and she was home studying, trying to make her father proud. She'd finished her undergrad early and jumped right into her MBA program.

It was all to impress Willard Wyatt and earn her place beside her older brother Harley, helping to run the Wyatt McIntyre Birch real estate empire. She should be happy that things had turned out even better than she'd planned, that Harley is out of the picture and she's the one in charge. She's the person her father always expected her to be—the person he wanted *Harley* to be—and it should mean something. But Willard, who spent so much time teaching her to be like him, isn't as impressed with her hard work as she thought he would be. He used to be the most ambitious man Ingrid knew. Now that he's ill, he barely leaves the house. He hasn't turned the company over to her yet, but it won't be long before he makes the decision himself or his health makes the decision for him.

Willard's business partners, Theodore Birch and Carter McIntyre, have been hands-off since they came on board decades ago, more silent investors than anything. But occasionally they drag themselves off the golf course to offer their special brand of unprompted feedback, like last week, when it came out that they didn't like a company decision Ingrid had made. WMB had been in the process of acquiring a beautiful piece of rugged land, where Ingrid and her team had planned a live-work-play development. But at last month's Foxglove Society meeting, Mindy Richmond had sheepishly informed Ingrid that the Ellen Point Friends of the Stream (of which Mindy was also a member) had a petition circulating to stop WMB from purchasing the land. In addition to the peaceful little stream (that would have been great for the development's planned nature trail amenity), the land was home to a rare variety of wild mushroom and several other native plant species. Rather than have the reputation of WMB muddied by moving forward with a plan that was unpopular, Ingrid had scheduled a meeting with representatives from

Friends of the Stream and had ultimately agreed to find a different piece of property for the project. She'd also committed to making sure the project was green-certified, once they found a new location for it. Being environmentally friendly *was* important, and the whole thing hadn't been worth the bad press anyway. Afterward, the president of Friends of the Stream wrote an Op-Ed in the Ellen Point Press thanking WMB for the decision. Now Ingrid is on the Friends of the Stream email list, too, and her inbox is inundated with weekly e-newsletters about plants she was glad to save but whose growth habits and Latin names she doesn't necessarily need to know.

Making the deal was the right thing to do.

Except apparently Mr. Birch and Mr. McIntyre thought she should have ignored Friends of the Stream and moved forward with the development anyway. They worried she was being "pushed around" by environmental interest groups. They hadn't even had the good grace to tell her about their disapproval to her face, no; instead, they'd had their monthly breakfast with her father and told *him* all about it, and then he'd sat her down to discuss their concerns.

She knew what she was doing though, and she wasn't going to change her position because three old men didn't appreciate the environment. Or good PR.

It doesn't matter. The company will still be hers, even if Birch and McIntyre disagree with her decision. They certainly don't know enough about the business to run it themselves, they're too attached to sell, Willard is all but completely retired, and there's no one else they can trust to run WMB. She should be happy about that. She's put everything aside: friendship, dating, hobbies, all to be the face of Wyatt McIntyre Birch. Someday, it will all be worth it.

Ingrid is standing outside of Alvey Hall when a vaguely familiar college student stops on his way into the building. He's wearing a beat-up leather jacket over a hooded sweatshirt. Despite the hood, his dark hair is wet with rain.

It takes her a second to place him, out of context, and without the black and white catering uniform. It's been a while.

"Those things really will kill you," he says, frowning.

"Hello to you too."

He'd programmed his number into her phone that night in the hotel room when she wasn't looking. She'd laughed when she found it later. *Guy From the Wedding.* But she hadn't called him. Their encounter had been meant for one night only, one night born of alcohol and frustration. She has no regrets, but she also didn't think she'd ever see him again.

And yet, here he is.

"It's actually a smoke-free campus."

"You are just too much, you know that?"

"What are you doing here?" he asks.

"Business."

He shrugs. "Well, good to see you and all. Take care."

She goes back to her cigarette, leaning against the red brick of Alvey Hall. Well surprise, surprise. She hadn't *planned* to ever see him again, but she's not unhappy about it.

It turns out he's in the class she's speaking to. Ingrid spots him when she takes the podium, registers his surprise when she's introduced. Good. She talks about connecting with clients, about networking, but her mind keeps wandering back to this guy, his body against hers, that night they'd spent together in her hotel room. She discusses numbers, management, commercial interests, the market, bullshit, bullshit.

The ugly florescent lights shine down on the classroom full of students and on her too, and her mind starts to spin scenarios that would never actually happen. She imagines stopping her lecture, walking right up to this Guy From the Wedding, kissing him on the mouth with everyone watching.

She really doesn't know what's gotten into her lately.

Class ends and she smiles and everyone claps, and she has no idea if she's been even the least bit interesting. Most of the students pack up their laptops, but he doesn't. He just sits, staring at her.

Ingrid pretends she doesn't notice, loads her sleek briefcase and looks around the room. Her eyes meet his and she smiles. She walks toward him. He's seated, so he ends up eye-level with her waist. "Hey," she says. He stands.

"Hey." He slings his bookbag over one shoulder. "Good talk, or whatever."

"Wow, thanks." With her heels on, she's taller than him.

"Hey, what are you doing now?" she says, on impulse. "Let's go get a drink." She doesn't know where the suggestion comes from. He looks at her like she's playing a joke on him.

"I'm serious."

"No, you're not, *Ingrid Wyatt*. You're you, and I'm me, and if you wanted to have anything more to do with me, you would have called. You didn't. It's been *three months*. Not to mention that you're apparently this super important person. And isn't it a little early in the day for a drink?"

"Okay. Point taken." She walks away, hoping he'll be watching. In a few steps she'll be gone from this auditorium and she can wallow in the sting of rejection alone in her car. He was interested once; it's not like she could have known that he wouldn't be interested again. She wonders if she's less appealing to him now that he knows she's successful. It's disgusting, but it happens all the time.

"Hey," he calls out. "I'm sorry, I didn't mean all that. I just...you really want to get a drink. With me."

She stops. "Why, you change your mind?"

"Maybe."

"Well, figure it out."

She's got other things to do, and she's getting impatient watching the indecision play out on his face. But finally he shrugs and says, "let's get a drink then."

"You have an umbrella?" he asks Ingrid as they leave Alvey Hall.

"No, but my car is right here." She points to a small private lot next to the school building.

Parking on the Ellen Point campus is a nightmare. There are only a few lots around, and you need to buy a special pass and sacrifice your firstborn to park in any of them without getting towed away. But as it happens, Ingrid *does* have a special pass, and her Lexus hybrid SUV is parked a few steps away.

"Incredible," he says. "The rules really don't apply to you, huh?"

Ingrid pulls a key from her briefcase and taps a button, and the car unlocks. "Throw your bag in the backseat." He does as she says, and then he settles himself in the passenger seat next to her. She starts the car and the music blasting through the speakers makes him jump. He looks at her funny and she shrugs. "Sorry." She adjusts the volume.

"Metallica?"

"I'm...a fan."

"Cool. So you realize you just let a stranger in the car with you, right?"

"Are you a stranger?" *I know you intimately,* she almost says, but doesn't. It's not like that means anything anyway.

"I mean, yeah, I pretty much am."

"Okay." Her fingers tap the steering wheel. "So was that a mistake, then? Are you going to do something...bad?" But she's teasing; she's not afraid of him.

"I could."

"Please. You're a real estate major."

"I'm a business major. And so was Ted Bundy."

"Not true. Did you even watch the documentary?" The rain taps against the windshield, the wiper blades silently whisk the water away, and then it all plays out again.

"Do you want to know my name?" he asks. "Or anything about me at all?"

"Sure." She doesn't know yet if she cares. "What's your name?"

"It's Paxton."

"Hi Paxton, I'm Ingrid." She's maneuvering the car onto a winding road and hardly glances at him.

"Yeah, I know that now. So is this, like, a thing you do?"

"What?"

"You know, pick up random guys?"

She looks at him. His luck is about to run out if he doesn't shut up soon. "Why yes, I do, actually. All the time. If you think you're special in some way, you're wrong."

"Liar."

"Hmm." She *is* lying, though. She never does this kind of thing. It's funny, actually, how unlike her it is. She'd sheepishly told Ruby and Claudia about the one-night stand, the week after it happened. Ruby is one of the most sex-positive people Ingrid knows, and Claudia had her fair share of casual sexual encounters before she met Beau. They were happy she'd had a good time, like she knew they would be. And yet, Ingrid found herself hesitant to share too many details. For some reason, she held back the age difference and even though she'd originally intended to tell Ruby about the broken glass, she didn't mention that either, or the fact that her lover was a member of Ruby's catering staff. Part of it was embarrassment; what if the age difference *was* too taboo, even for her friends? But another part wanted to keep it for herself, the magic, the surprise of it all.

This particular manboy has caught her on two occasions where she's had too many feelings, and too many thoughts about the things she's missed out on, like that boy from high school and his confident smile. His name was Ace. And Paxton, well, he's just a convenient substitute.

Ingrid doesn't respond to him. She swings the Lexus into a parking space in front of Hotel 283. "You coming, or what?"

There's a surprised look on his face. Honestly, after their first encounter, he didn't anticipate a hotel?

She feigns innocence. "They have great drinks at the bar. Lunch too, if you're hungry. I'm not here for a room, if that's what you're thinking."

She is absolutely here for a room.

He scrambles out of the car. The sidewalk is slick with rain but she's a pro at walking in heels. This hotel is bright and modern, big strange-shaped chairs and a simple bamboo block of a registration desk. But true to her word, she walks right past it, down a few steps, and into a trendy little bar.

"What do you drink?" she asks, sliding onto a bar stool. The place is practically empty at this time of day. It's only the two of them and two women at a corner table. The bartender places napkins in front of them.

This place is different than the hotel where Elodie Rose got married. That hotel was regal, overdone, huge chandeliers dripping crystals, real gold fixtures and bannisters. Hotel 283 is sleek, simple, modern. The office of WMB more resembles the former, but Ingrid prefers this.

"Whatever you're having is fine."

Ingrid looks him over, sizes him up. Things are different in the daylight. He looks right back at her. She orders the same as last time, vodka tonic with lime. Grey Goose, she specifies. The bartender asks for their IDs; he's a younger guy himself. He checks their licenses, smiles a flirty smile at Ingrid, and raises an eyebrow at Paxton.

"Happy birthday," the bartender says to her.

196

"It's your birthday?" Paxton asks.

"It is."

"It's your birthday, and you're giving a speech to a college class and hanging out with...me? Don't you have anything better to do?"

"Obviously not. So...Paxton." His name feels good in her mouth, sharp.

"Ingrid."

The bartender delivers their drinks. Ingrid sips hers, letting it coat her tongue before swallowing.

He follows suit, or tries to. "Okay. Want to tell me why I'm here? Not that I'm complaining."

She rolls another sip of vodka around her mouth. "Actually, I'm looking for an intern."

"What? Really?"

"No." She looks him up and down again. "You really think it would be you, if that's what I was looking for?"

He deserves a joke at his expense after all of his barbs, but she still feels guilty once she sees the hurt on his face. He's not Ace, that tough pretty boy from her high school years. Perhaps Paxton is more sensitive than she gave him credit for. He drains his drink in one long swallow. "You know what? I don't need this. I don't know what the game is here, but I don't think I want to be a part of it."

"Don't you?" she asks. She pulls him in by the hood of his sweatshirt. "Paxton," she whispers, her lips against his ear. "It's my *birthday*."

The whisper, the close proximity of their bodies, the way she murmurs against his skin—it's effective. "Jesus," he mutters.

This time they can't wait; their hands are all over each other by the time the elevator doors slide shut. She's procured a room, just like that, and the key is in her purse. She didn't realize how much she'd wanted this again, the intimacy of being with someone but also the intensity of being with *him*.

The minute they're inside the hotel room, he's got her pressed up against the door, one hand on her thigh and his mouth scorching against her own. He sinks to his knees, kissing his way down her body as she quickly takes in the room. Sleek gray walls, a bamboo headboard and pillows shaped like squares. His hands find the clasp of her suit pants and he slides them down her legs, and her attention is quickly redirected back to Paxton: his hands, and his mouth, and his lean arms holding her body against him, and his black hair, slick from the rain. She winds her fingers through it. This is it. This is what she's been missing.

Afterwards, she checks her phone and sees she's missed a text message. It's from her colleague, Beau, sent a half-hour ago. *Meeting starts in 5. Did your speech run long?*

"Shit," she says. She's gotten caught up here, with Paxton. "I have to go. She tosses her phone on the nightstand before swinging herself off the bed.

"Don't. What's the rush?"

"I missed a meeting."

"I'm sure they'll wait for the VP of the company."

"You don't understand how it works." Punctuality is important to Ingrid, and it's not a good time for missteps.

He climbs from the bed, grabs his boxers and jeans. "Guess I'm pretty clueless, right? I should probably get out of here so you can get back to your important shit."

"Hey." She thinks of kissing him again, but she doesn't. "It's not like that."

"Happy birthday, Ingrid Wyatt." He dresses and leaves while she's still pulling her hair back into a bun. The door clicks closed behind him.

***

"Explain to me again why we need to 'network," Claudia grumbles. "Especially here."

"To further our business interests, of course," Ruby says brightly and with only a hint of sarcasm. She takes a bite of a greasy potato skin. This quarter's Women's Networking Luncheon is at a bar and grill where a soccer game is airing on five different TVs. Men in jerseys alternate between shouting at the TV and appraising the women in their workwear. It really is a terrible choice of location.

"I don't think I *have* business interests," Claudia says. She pushes her hair behind one ear. Claudia is disenchanted with her job lately. Ingrid understands; Claudia's residents are so damned needy that she's practically on call 24/7.

"Look at it this way," Ingrid says. "One day you might want to change jobs, or you might need a professional favor. And then you'll be happy that I forced you to be social." Ingrid is faking positivity. She doesn't enjoy the networking events either. They've gotten less and less interesting over the years. For all the schmoozing and speeches and board meetings Ingrid is part of, she's an introvert at heart.

She used to attend these things on her own, which was its own special brand of hell. But she did it, lest anyone forget that she was, in fact, a professional. Then she met Claudia. Ingrid had never had a real friend before. Sure, she'd been practically born into the Foxglove Society circle, and she might call those women "friends," but she can't be herself with them. She performs for them, as the version of Ingrid Wyatt her father wants her to be: a lovely and sensible—yet demure—lady who happens to have a business mind. Hidden away, when she's in Foxglove company, is Ingrid's naked ambition, her apathy toward romance and especially marriage, her hard and fast loyalty to her father even though it sometimes seems he doesn't deserve it. The Foxglove ladies see the shiny veneer of her. The day she met Claudia, that veneer fractured and fell apart. All it took was a bottle of wine and a kindred spirit. Ingrid had recognized something in Claudia, a certain ability to read the room and become exactly what the occasion called for. When Margo, Claudia's boss from Southern Campus Collective, was seated at the table Claudia was reserved and professional. But once Margo was gone and it was only Ingrid and Claudia and the bottle of Pinot Grigio, it turned out that Claudia was wry and witty and sharply cynical. Something about watching Claudia's true self break through was freeing, and Ingrid found *herself* sharing things she'd normally hide away. Her father wasn't sick back then, but she still felt the weight of his expectations. Ingrid even shared her dream, which had remained unspoken up to that point, of being the one in charge of Wyatt McIntyre Birch. Harley had been gone for a few years by then, but Willard hadn't yet recognized that he was gone for good, and that Ingrid was the best choice for the WMB legacy.

Men hardly ever know what they need, Claudia said. *Or they think they know, but they're usually wrong.* Her voice was laced with bitterness, and Ingrid wondered about the man who had hurt her. There was always some man, somewhere, who had left or lied or done some other kind of betraying. Claudia seemed self-sufficient to Ingrid then, too jaded to ever fall in love. But six months later, Ingrid introduced Claudia to a work colleague, and she watched Claudia slip on a new persona adapted specifically for Beau. And Ingrid didn't say a word because the whole thing seemed to make Claudia happy and so love, or some semblance of it, must have been what she wanted after all.

"Or. We might make a new friend here," Ruby says, gesturing around the restaurant at the same ladies they always saw at these events.

"Yeah, right. You were an exception, and you know it."

Ingrid started dragging Claudia along to the networking meetings shortly after they met, and they waded through the sea of female realtors and floral designers and professors together. Then, one day Ruby rushed through the door, not quite late but barely on time. Her long light brown hair was caught up in her purse strap and Ingrid and Claudia watched her try to discreetly untangle it while she chatted with Mindy Richmond. Claudia and Ingrid were charmed by her, and when Ruby got trapped in a conversation with Dana Redding, dominant personality and the number two realtor in Ellen Point (which she was fond of telling people, for some reason), Ingrid and Claudia jumped in and pulled Ruby into a conversation of their own. The rest was friendship history.

Ruby's business was brand new then, and Ingrid and Claudia and probably ninety percent of the women at the networking lunches underestimated Ruby and her intelligence and what a hard worker she was. It was part of Ruby's magic to make it all look effortless. She never took herself too seriously, but she knew what she wanted, and now everyone in town wants Ruby's name behind their special event. The former local event planning go-to had quietly gone out of business last year, driven to closure by the popularity of Champagne Toast Event Planning.

"So anyways," Ruby says. "I had a date last night."

"Oh yeah?" Claudia says.

"He's a tattoo artist at that shop downtown."

"And?"

There's a twinkle in Ruby's eye. "It was a good date. His name is Tanner."

"Of course it is," Ingrid says. "Are you seeing him again?"

"I think so. We'll see how it goes."

"Hey ladies." A large man in a red soccer jersey leans over their table. "Y'all here for some kind of business meeting?"

"Something like that," Ingrid says.

"Sounds serious," the man says with a grin. "Too serious." Claudia rolls her eyes. "Why don't you let me buy y'all a round of drinks and y'all can try to relax a little?"

"We're good," Ingrid says. "We're actually in the middle of a conversation, so if you'll..." *leave*, she thinks but doesn't say. Instead, she waves her hand in a gesture that has the same effect.

"You sure are pretty," the jersied man says, focusing in on her. "You married?"

"I'm seeing someone," Ingrid says, flatly. She doesn't know why she says it; she doesn't usually lie to ward off unwanted advances. For some reason she sees a flash of Paxton's face in her mind, even though they're strictly friends with benefits, minus the friends part. They're strictly benefits.

"Lucky man," he says, and wanders back to his friends at the bar.

"Anyways," Ingrid says to her friends, as if they hadn't just been interrupted. She hasn't told them about her one-night stand becoming a one-night-plus one-day stand. It's not like she has anything to be ashamed of. To the contrary, she's proud of herself. She saw what she wanted and she went for it. In her business life that's just another day; in her personal life it's quite the departure.

"That was a lie, right?" Ruby says. "There's no one you need to tell us about?"

Ingrid shakes her head. She loves her friends, but she finds she still wants to keep this secret for herself.

CHAPTER 24

Paxton's number is there, programmed into Ingrid's phone. She hadn't thought she'd ever use it, but she hasn't been able to stop thinking of him since her birthday. She only holds out a few days before making the call. It's a Thursday night, eleven thirty, late for her but not for the younger people of the world.

"Hello?" he basically shouts. It's loud in the background. She's caught him in the middle of something.

"Paxton."

"Yeah, who's this?"

She ends the call. She pictures him in a bar somewhere, music thumping and girls his own age leaning toward him, arms around his shoulders, dancing against him. She shouldn't have called.

Seconds later, her phone lights up with an incoming call. *Guy from the Wedding*. She answers without saying anything.

"Ingrid," he says. "Ingrid, I know it's you, I'm sorry. I'm always fucking things up. It *is* you, right?"

"Why'd you put your number in my phone if you didn't want me to call?"

"I did want you to."

"Where are you?" she asks.

"Downtown. A bar."

"Are you with someone?"

"My roommates."

"What bar?"

"The Study Room. Where are you?"

If this is going to happen again, he's going to admit that he wants it, too. "Do you want to see me, Paxton?"

He doesn't even try to play it cool. "More than anything. Come meet me."

"I'm not hanging out at a bar with you." Though they've been at bars together twice now, Ingrid has a sense this is a different kind of bar with a different kind of clientele.

"Then let's go somewhere else. Wherever you want."

She takes a deep breath. "Look for me. I'll be there to get you in fifteen minutes." She hangs up without saying goodbye.

Exactly fifteen minutes later, she pulls up to the curb, where he's standing outside the college bar. She's pleased that he doesn't make her wait.

She rolls down the passenger side window. "Get in."

His eyes are on her. She's dressed differently now than the times before, not dolled up for a wedding or professional for work. Tonight she's in comfortable jeans and a soft t-shirt. 90s rock music plays at a low volume through her speakers.

"Hey," he says.

"Hey yourself."

"So. Where to?"

"You'll see." She takes the same winding road that led them to Hotel 283, but she drives past it and further up into the mountains. She could keep going here and, if they wanted to park and hike a ways, take them right up to Ellen Point, the mountaintop the city is named for. From there, you can see the entire town and far beyond.

"It would be funny if you were the dangerous one," Paxton muses. "If you brought me all the way out here to the middle of nowhere and killed me or something."

"You worried?"

"Not really."

"Killing you isn't in my plans, if it makes you feel better."

"It does. Much." He's quiet for a moment. "You know, I tried to tell my roommates about you."

She turns her head to him. "You did?"

"They said I was full of shit." He must see the alarm on her face. "I know, it probably wasn't very gentlemanly of me, but we were all drinking at the apartment the other night, and it was right after you and I...well, it just felt surreal and I...I needed to say it. But they didn't believe me anyway."

"Did you tell them my name?"

"No, we didn't even get that far."

Ingrid thinks of how gossip spreads in Ellen Point, especially when it involves her family. "Do me a favor," she says. "If you talk about me again, don't use my name. The newspaper would find a way to run a story like this, and I don't need that kind of publicity right now."

"You embarrassed?"

She shrugs. "I wouldn't say that. But reputation means a lot in my family. Look, talk if you want. Just don't use my name."

"You mean like, make up a fake name?" He laughs.

"I don't know, maybe," she says. "Call me...Ruby." She doesn't know why she chooses her friend's name, except that Ingrid herself has never had much of a love life and this adventure, or affair, or whatever it is, seems much more like something Ruby would do.

"Can we pick a different fake name? That's my boss's name. Or my boss's boss's name. Still...weird."

"I actually forgot you work for her."

"You know Ruby?"

"She's one of my best friends."

"Oh yeah? Weird. She seems cool. Career-focused and all."

Ingrid laughs. If he thinks that about Ruby...

"She is. She's still a lot more fun than me, though."

Paxton rests his hand on her denim-covered leg. "I think you're pretty fun," he says with a grin.

"You, this...is an anomaly."

"If you say so."

"Tell me more about your roommates," she says.

"Terrance, Devin, and Randall. They're idiots."

"And your apartment?"

"A dump. About what you'd expect. Well, maybe not you. I looked you up online, you know."

"Oh yeah?" There's a lot about her, out there.

"Yeah. Only daughter of Willard Wyatt, the founder of Wyatt McIntyre Birch Real Estate Group. Sounds to me like you're calling the shots at this point, though. I saw the article about you in Georgia Trend magazine, and that picture of you in the dress and blazer and the pearls..." he trails off.

"And?"

"And it was sexy as hell," he says.

Ingrid feels her entire body heating up. She's never heard herself described that way before. She turns off the main road and her Lexus bumps along a dirt path. They end up parked in the middle of a forest. Her family owns twenty acres of this undeveloped land (she's having studies done on whether it could be a site for her live-work-play development after the original location fell through), but she doesn't tell him that. Let him believe they're trespassing, pushing boundaries, crossing lines. When Ingrid and her brother were young, her father would bring Harley out here to hunt deer. She'd been jealous then, of the way they'd dress up in their dark camouflage and paint their faces the color of the trees and dirt, how they'd spend early mornings together, quiet but also bonding somehow. She was jealous of the unapologetic power of their bows and arrows as they aimed to kill.

She turns off the car but leaves the radio on. "Come on," she says. He gets out of the car and looks around, but then he sees that she's lifting the hatch of her SUV and climbing into the back. The second row seats are pushed down already. Paxton climbs in beside her. She pulls him to her by the lapels of his leather jacket and kisses him. He tastes faintly of alcohol. His hands reach for her hips, pull her close.

"You're gorgeous," he whispers into her neck.

"So are you."

The back door of the SUV is open to the night air. She tugs his clothes off slowly, one item at a time: the jacket, the crimson henley with the dark buttons at the top, the white t-shirt underneath that. There's no rush tonight. He pulls at her jeans, at her shirt. She's brought a blanket and she drapes the fabric around them. It's colder out here than she'd expected.

It's magic, almost. Paxton isn't anyone's idea of Prince Charming; then again, that's not what she's looking for. Being around him makes her feel *excited* by the well of possibility that is his life—his path isn't set, he doesn't have to be anything or do anything he doesn't want to do. Later, she'll marvel at how easily she makes this assumption, since she knows practically nothing about him in this moment. When she's wrapped all around him and he's breathing her name, she starts to think she wants to know more after all.

"Tell me about yourself," she says, when they're lying side-by-side on top of the blanket. Sweat beads on his forehead now, even in the chilly night air.

"Isn't that the kind of thing you ask someone *before* you sleep with them?"

"I wasn't sure I wanted to know."

"What changed your mind?"

"I don't know," she says. "Forget I asked."

"No. What do you want to know?"

"How old *are* you, anyway?"

"Twenty-one."

"Jesus," she said. "You're so young."

"Isn't that what you were looking for?"

"I wasn't *looking* for anything."

"No?"

"No."

They're quiet for a moment. "You're in school. How's that going?" she asks finally.

"It's fine I guess. What's left of it." Ingrid assumes he means because it's almost Christmas break, but he starts telling her about how he screwed up and lost his scholarship and how he'll be leaving Ellen Point soon. It turns out he's a smart guy with a full ride. Or he *had* a full ride. But when he came back to school in the fall, he drank too much, partied too hard, missed too many classes. She wants to know what happened to prompt all of that destructive behavior, but she doesn't ask. Some girl probably broke his heart. He learned the hard way that a GPA can fall fast; he got the letter last week about the loss of his scholarship. His room is all packed up except the furniture, and he's got an ad out for a sublease to take his place in the apartment. Paxton is going home to

Kelver Ridge, North Carolina this weekend and he isn't coming back after the holidays.

"Not like you care," he says. "Not like you should. It's just what happened."

"What about your job? Doesn't Ruby pay well?"

"Yeah, but I'm just one member of a whole catering staff. And jobs are sporadic. I make enough for gas and groceries, but not for a whole semester of school."

"And your family? They can't help?"

Paxton laughs. "The only one of them who knows is my sister, TessAnne. If my mom knew, she'd probably try to sell a kidney on the black market to get me the money. She's that proud of me. Don't ask me why."

"Surely there are student loans you could get?"

He shrugs. "Yeah, maybe. But I've missed the deadline to apply for this semester. Maybe I can work something out for next fall."

"So...you screwed up."

"I mean, yeah. Definitely."

"And you're leaving. This weekend. And you're not coming back."

"No. At least, not for a while."

It's interesting how disappointed she feels. "Then I guess we'd better make the most of tonight." She climbs on top of him and leans her head back. Through the sunroof, she can see the stars beyond the canopy of trees.

"Nice knowing you Paxton," she says later, when she pulls up in front of his apartment. It's as he described—one of those older cookie-cutter buildings. WMB would never build anything like this. She reaches for him and kisses him, soft and slow.

"Goodbye Ingrid."

***

She sits in her office the following Monday, reading emails but barely processing them. She skims the Friends of the Stream newsletter, subject line: *Getting to Know the Swamp Chestnut Oak.* It's a momentary distraction. Finally, she gives in and grabs her phone from the desk drawer and pulls up Paxton's number on the screen. She sips her lukewarm coffee and decides that she definitely will not call him.

She's going to call him.

If she *doesn't* call him, he'll be gone and there won't be a thing she can do about it.

She puts the phone aside.

The offices of Wyatt McIntyre Birch are located in a spacious old house, white brick and columns and oozing Southern charm. Her private office is upstairs. It used to be two separate bedrooms, decades ago when this was an actual family home for some long-ago family. Willard Wyatt's office of equal size is across the landing and next to it, a third office. Smaller, and empty. The small one was supposed to have been hers, and this one was supposed to have belonged to Harley. It took years before her father gave in and let her move her things into it. In between the three rooms, there is an open landing where Ingrid's assistant has a desk. The managers' offices, associates' cubicles, and the receptionist's desk are all downstairs.

Ingrid taps her heel against the hardwood floors as she gets back to the emails. Her fingernails make a clicking noise against the keyboard as she sends curt, professional responses. But her mind is on Paxton. He's probably sleeping right now. She thinks of his lean, athletic body, sprawled across a mattress.

She doesn't know anything about him, not really. She's turning to mush over some college student. It's pathetic.

She leans her head back against her desk chair. Her office is new-Southern, masculine with a touch of rustic. Her brown leather desk chair matches the supple leather sofa in the sitting area. An oriental rug covers an expanse of the refinished hardwoods. Nothing frilly about this room. She doesn't do frilly.

"Ms. Wyatt?" Her personal assistant's voice buzzes in through the phone on the desk.

"Yes?"

"Your nine-thirty appointment is here."

"Thank you," she says. "Send him in."

Before her client makes it to her office, she reaches for her cell phone again. Quickly, before she changes her mind, she sends Paxton a text:

Meet me for lunch

She includes the time and the name of an Italian restaurant downtown. It's not a question; there's no opportunity for him to say no.

Not that he would.

***

She's sitting in a booth near the back when he arrives. She might have decided on a whim to help Paxton, but she still isn't sure she wants to be seen with him in public.

"Hi," she says, when he shrugs out of his leather jacket and takes a seat across from her. The restaurant is filled with old memorabilia, a mix of vintage US and vintage Italy. Empty wine bottles line a ledge along the wall.

"Hey."

"Hungry?" she asks. "I ordered a pizza."

He nods.

"Here's the thing, Paxton. I've decided I'd like for you to stick around." She can't believe she's doing this, any more than she can believe that she seduced him at Elodie Rose's wedding. She's recently become a completely different version of herself.

Paxton laughs. "Yeah, I'd like that too. But I can't. I thought I made that clear. I can't afford rent, much less another semester at Ellen Point."

Ingrid taps her finger along the table, and he watches her hands.

"About that."

"About that," he repeats.

"I'm going to make you an offer."

"An offer I can't refuse?" He laughs, but there's no lightness to it.

"I'd like to pay for you to stay in school."

"Right," he says. "Good joke. If you're trying to make me feel worse, it's working."

"I'm serious."

"No, you're not. College is expensive, Ingrid."

"I can afford it."

"I'm sure you *can*, but I can't accept that kind of gift. And what's the catch, anyway?"

"There's no catch, Paxton. I just don't want to see you throw away your future, and I've got to admit, I've been enjoying having you around."

"You don't have to bribe me to hang out with you."

"I'm not. But you can't 'hang out' with me if you're leaving town and going back home to...*where* did you say you're from?"

"Kelver Ridge."

"Yes, wherever that is."

"It's north of here, past—"

"I don't care. Do you want to stay in Ellen Point, or don't you?"

He twirls his straw around in his glass of water. "I don't know, Ingrid. So, you'd be like my sugar mama or something?"

"No. More like a..." she searches her mind for the right word "*bene-factor*. You don't have to spend time with me, Paxton. If you want to, great. If not, that's okay too. There aren't strings attached. If the idea of this whole thing bothers you, maybe you pick up extra catering shifts on occasion. It's up to you. But at least you get to be here, finish your degree, do something better than whatever you were planning back home."

"I'm supposed to take over my dad's insurance business."

She raises her eyebrows. "And is that important to you?"

"No," he says. "You have no idea how *not* important it is to me." He tells her then about how his alcoholic father is ruining the family business, and how his mother is too busy carrying on an affair with the high school football coach to care. "And there was this accident I was involved in over the summer...and there's this *way* everyone in Kelver Ridge looks at me now. Let's just say it's the last place I want to be. If it weren't for my sister, I'd never go back. Not even to visit. And now you're sitting here saying I don't have to. But how do I know I can trust you? What happens when you get tired of me and change your mind? Then I'm screwed. Again."

"I won't take the money away," she says. "We can write up a contract, if you want. I'll make sure you're covered through the rest of this year and all of next. What you do after that is up to you."

"You can't be serious. This can't be real."

"It's real if you want it to be. Think about it. If you decide you don't want to take me up on my offer, then leave tomorrow like you planned."

"I'll still have to go home for Christmas. My family is expecting me."

She smiles. "Of course. But this way, you can come back."

The waitress appears and sets a pizza on the table in front of them.

"Jesus," Paxton says. "This is exactly the kind of pizza you'd order." He shakes his head. She looks at the strategically-placed circles of mozzarella, tomato slices, thin ribbons of basil.

"What's that supposed to mean?"

"That it's the prettiest damned pizza I've ever seen."

"Wait until you taste it."

***

The deal. I'm in.

Ingrid is on the sofa in the family room of the Wyatt mansion, reading the Friends of the Stream newsletter on her phone, when she gets Paxton's text. Her father is in his room asleep already.

She breathes a sigh of relief. She'd thought Paxton would say yes. Who would turn down that kind of offer? But she'd started to get anxious when she hadn't heard from him eight hours after their lunch. She wonders what to do next, what to say. She's never done anything like this before.

Ingrid wonders what Paxton will tell his roommates, the ones who expect him to leave. Maybe he'll make something up; maybe he'll be embarrassed that he's relying on someone else to pay his way.

She doesn't really care. She feels giddy. Whatever comes next, she's gotten what she wanted.

CHAPTER 25

It's the aimless, winding week between Christmas and New Year's, when longing and nostalgia and hope and despair get all mixed together like a potent cocktail. Ingrid only knows one way to keep those feelings at bay. She turns into the parking lot of Paxton's run-down four-bedroom apartment. She could tell he was nervous about inviting her to his place, but it makes sense this time. The EPU basketball team is involved in some kind of holiday tournament, and every hotel within a fifty-mile radius is booked. She'd never risk bringing Paxton to her father's house, and it's gotten too cold outside now to go back up the mountain. Her car isn't roomy enough for them to be comfortable without the back hatch open and she's not about to contort herself for car sex like some fumbling teenager. She's considered all the options. Paxton's roommates aren't back from Christmas break yet, but Paxton had rushed back after the holiday. To Ellen Point, to school, to *her*.

Ingrid understands the kind of life the average college student lives. Sort of. She'd lived at home during college, so it's not like she has *first-hand* knowledge. But, she knows not everyone can be living it up at The Prestige.

"Don't judge," Paxton says, laughing uneasily, when he opens the door for her. And she tries not to. She really does. She suspects he only suggested his place because he expected her to say no.

The door creaks open as she steps into the living room. One of the fan bulbs is out and the glow is muted, unpleasant. He looks up at it like it's the first time he's noticed. The floor is covered with beige apartment-grade carpet, flattened from years of wear. The sofa looks like someone's hand-me-down, and the coffee table has one leg missing. It's propped up with a cinder block and some magazines. "There was a party, and one of my roommates broke it," Paxton says.

Ingrid strolls through the galley kitchen with the laminate countertops. Even here in Ellen Point, these kinds of apartments used to be the best you could hope for if you were a college student. The fancier things were reserved for the homeowners or the weekend tourists. Until Ingrid collaborated with Southern Campus Collective on the building of The Prestige, that is.

"Where's your room?" she asks, finally, and he takes her hand and leads her down the hallway and into his bedroom. The furniture consists of a twin bed, a dresser, and a computer desk with a laptop perched on top. There's no overhead light; a chrome floor lamp shines its feeble light on the room.

She hesitates, and Paxton looks at her, clearly expecting her to walk out. Her eyes settle on the keyboard pushed against the wall.

"You play?" she asks, nodding to it.

"More or less. My mom made me take piano lessons as a kid. Some of it stuck."

"Play me something," she says, and he slides the keyboard close to the bed so he can play while seated there.

"I'm not very good."

It's a lie, though. He plays *The Unforgiven* by Metallica.

"You like this song, right?"

She nods, wondering if he learned it for her.

He trails off before the song is finished, and she stands up and pulls her sweater dress over her head. Everything suddenly feels strange and raw and real.

He touches her. Hands on her shoulders, lips on her neck. They tumble onto the tiny bed.

***

"I could really go for a cigarette," Ingrid says, mostly to tease him. She's propped herself up on his only pillow, and Paxton has one hand under his head. He watches her.

"Have a cigarette, if you want one."

"I'm not going to smoke in your bedroom. I'm not a monster."

"I can think of other things you can do with your mouth..."

She hits him with the pillow and he laughs. She looks around his room. "It doesn't make sense for you to live here, you know," she says, casually. She was trying to save this conversation for later, but the words slip right out.

"I'm sorry?" That embarrassed look returns to his face.

"I'd like for you to think about moving. Just consider it. I can't come here when your roommates are back in town. And you can't come to my place, and it's not practical to keep renting rooms all over town."

"I'm sure it gets expensive."

"It's not that. Eventually I'm going to run into someone I know. And they might suspect something." She imagines bumping into a client, or one of the Foxglove Society ladies, in a hotel setting. She shudders at the thought.

"Something like what?"

"Something like what's actually happening."

"Well, I'm sorry my place isn't good enough for you," he says. There's an edge to his voice. "I can't pick up and move."

"Sure you can. I'll take care of everything."

"No, I mean, I won't. I can't bail on my roommates. I already almost did that to them, when I thought I was leaving town. I literally just told them I'm staying right before I left for Christmas break."

"Okay." She's quiet for a moment, thinking. "So, keep your place here. This is where you live, as far as everyone knows. But we'll find you another place too, one that's more...welcoming, for guests."

"You mean for you."

"Yes."

"What if I say no?"

Ingrid shrugs like it doesn't matter. "Then you say no. It's just an idea. You don't have to do anything you don't want to do." She leans over, nibbles his ear. "But it would be so much easier for us to see each other if you had your own place, alone. Think of all the things I could do with my mouth, then."

He groans. "So you just want to, what? Control my life now?"

"Nothing you don't want."

"I want it. You know I do. Whatever you think is best."

***

Ingrid sends Paxton to The Prestige. It's the nicest apartment building in town, after all. She plans to call Claudia to let her know she's sending someone (a family friend, she'll say), but she loses her nerve. She's going to tell her friends about this relationship...just not yet. It's one thing to have a few nights with a younger lover; it's another thing altogether to pay his way. It's a narrative that will take exactly the right framing. In the meantime, Paxton is armed with a credit card Ingrid has put in his name that will cover whatever fees are necessary to hold an apartment. *Claudia will take care of you*, she tells him. *Just don't mention me.* The whole idea is dangerous. Claudia has cameras all over that building, even if she only checks them when there's an incident. Moving Paxton there means they could be caught anytime. It's risky, Ingrid knows, and yet she feels a certain thrill about the whole thing.

Paxton tells Ingrid all about his appointment with the "business bro" who offered him coffee and was dressed in a suit even though he was probably Paxton's age. About the apartment that's a far cry from the flat he shares with his roommates and how they would shit a brick if they saw him. He'll have to tell them something eventually, about this arrangement. They'll start to wonder where he is all the time.

The guy had shown him a one-bedroom apartment on the sixth floor. It turned out to be the only apartment available for immediate move-in. *Strange time of year for the college community*, the guy had explained. *Most apartments come open during the summer.* W

"They wouldn't even have this one if the guy that lived here hadn't transferred to a different school," Paxton explains. "Lucky for me. It's a really nice building."

"Only the best for you."

"Only the best for *you*."

"Either way." Ingrid remains proud of The Prestige. She'd always liked the big rooftop pool, hot tub bubbling in the corner. She pictures the steam rising up into the still gray air on the day they'd handed the building over to Claudia and Southern Campus Collective. From there you could see the town below and the mountains above. From there, the world felt like a fairytale.

Ingrid wants Paxton to live there, and when he is telling her about it she realizes that yes, he wants that too.

"So anyway, I put down the money, like you told me to." And maybe it never mattered what he thought about the building; he was always going to do exactly what she told him to do. What Ingrid wants, Ingrid gets.

"Fantastic."

He explains the process to her, but she already knows. He receives an email link to an online application that they complete together. *How's your credit?* Ingrid asks, and when he shrugs she suggests he choose the option to pay an additional deposit to avoid a credit check altogether. She could provide her own information—her credit is impeccable, of course—but then she'd be Paxton's cosigner, which means she'd be involved. On paper.

In the end, he goes through with the whole process and before they know it he has a new apartment. She wonders, idly, what else she could make him do.

CHAPTER 26

"Hi Dad," Ingrid says, loudly. Sometimes it takes her father a minute to register her presence.

"Ears work fine, Ingrid."

And sometimes it takes no time at all. The lights in the family room are dimmed and her father is settled into his favorite recliner, the TV playing an old black and white movie.

"How are you?" She takes a seat on the sofa. She's still wearing heels and a skirt. She knows he likes seeing her like this, in her professional work attire. It reaffirms his confidence in her as the new leader of the company.

Willard Wyatt doesn't make it to the office most days, though every now and again there is a good day when he makes his nurse help him into his business suit and Ingrid drives him over. He walks with a cane when he's at work, wouldn't dare have her push him in the wheelchair, despite the fact that it's much safer with how tired his body is right now. He doesn't want anyone to see his weakness, so most of the time he stays home and lets Ingrid handle things.

If someone has to handle things, he'd rather it be Harley. But Willard's health is on a decline, and Harley is nowhere to be found.

Harley's the oldest child and Willard's favorite. He was always the one with her father's full faith and confidence, the one Willard chose to drive the boat out on the lake during the summertime. Even when Ingrid was older, Willard never let her take the wheel. *Sit back and enjoy the ride, princess*, he would say. She was never denied a place at WMB—it's a family business, after all—but Harley was meant to be the one in charge. It used to sting (still does, if she's honest) to know she wasn't Willard's first choice. She should have been. She's better at numbers, and planning, and leadership, than Harley ever was. She'd never crack under pressure the way he did. The day after Harley graduated with his MBA, he loaded up his car and drove off into the sunset. Going to find their mother, the letter said, but that was nothing more than a bad excuse. Their mother was dead to all of them the minute she left them behind.

Harley was the second-generation charmer, the one who had smiles for everyone, smiles that meant something different than Ingrid's. They were both Wyatts, but as with so many old Southern families, the boy meant more.

The boy wasn't around anymore, though, so Willard Wyatt had no choice but to let the girl step up to the plate.

Ingrid's father used to be the strongest man she knew, but the cancer has taken a toll. He seems small in his recliner now. "Your mother used to love this movie," he says, pointing at the TV with the remote. Ingrid glances over. It's Casablanca. He doesn't see her roll her eyes. He never used to talk like this. When her mother left, the three of them—her father, Harley, and Ingrid—made a collective agreement (though they didn't actually say it out loud) that they'd forget she ever existed. But since Willard got sick, he talks about her more and more. Like he can only remember the good parts now. Like he's forgotten that she left them all, not for anyone or anything in particular, just for herself. She told Willard that this life was suffocating her, and she took off. And that was that.

The past is the past. Ingrid checks the email on her phone and sees a new Friends of the Stream newsletter. *Know Your Mushrooms: The Amanita Cormeuma*. The newsletters are strangely soothing; last week before bed she actually went back into her email and read about the Swamp Chestnut Oaks that grow along the stream bank. She'd fallen into a peaceful sleep with the phone in her hand.

"The deal for the Barringer land went through today," Ingrid says.

Her father smiles. "Good job." She's embarrassed by how much she relishes his praise.

"Your nurse told me Carter McIntyre was here to visit."

Willard's smile disappears. "Didn't ask for visitors today, but that old fool came by anyway." Even friends and business partners don't have the right to see Ingrid's father, not unless he's planned for company so he can be well-dressed and seated at a desk or a table and not tucked into his recliner.

"And how is Carter?" she asks, even though she doesn't care, as long as he has no further complaints about how she runs WMB. Carter and his family are pompous and elite, even by Ellen Point standards. Even by Wyatt standards.

"Limping. Hurt his knee last week, and now he's walking like a damned invalid." He's smug when he says it. "He's not over your agreement with the Friends of the Water—"

"Friends of the Stream, Dad."

"Whatever they are. He made a comment I didn't like, said his son just moved back from Portland, and that he could be an asset at WMB, help you fend off those pushy environmentalists."

Ingrid bristles. She'd been playmates with Thomas, Carter's son, when they were children; or rather, Harley had, and Ingrid had followed along waiting for the boys to give her the time of day. They'd all attended the same private high school, but Thomas had moved west for college and no one around here has seen him in years. He's been gone from Ellen Point even longer than Harley. "Does he even have any experience in real estate?"

"Guess so. Sounds like he was building some kind of workshare space before he moved back."

"Huh." *Workshare?* This guy from *Portland* was supposed to help her fight off the Friends of the Stream? Who didn't need fighting off anyway, but not the point. Thomas McIntyre was probably a card-carrying member of his local chapter of Friends of the Stream himself, or whatever the Portland equivalent was. "Now's not the best time to bring somebody new on board."

"I told you I didn't like the comment, princess. I don't want a McIntyre there either. I see what he's trying to do. We didn't make any plans, so don't go getting upset."

"I'm not upset," she says, with a sigh of relief. "I'm open to whatever you think is best, of course." As long as what Willard thinks is best is keeping the McIntyres (and the Birches, for that matter) out of her business.

"He did say he'd like for you and Thomas to get together. The boy doesn't know anyone around here anymore."

"That's great, but I'm not really interested." He didn't *say* the word date, but the implication is there. She tries not to think of her twenty-one-year-old lover. With or without Paxton, she's not interested in dating. It just gets in the way of everything else.

"So to shut him up, I gave him your cell phone number, told him he could pass it along to his boy."

"Dad!"

"Think of it as networking. Or hell, think of it as a date for all I care. You're not getting any younger, princess."

Ingrid shakes her head and opens her mouth to argue with him before he cuts her off.

"The McIntyre boy should be calling once he gets settled in."

"If you say so." She'll deal with Thomas when he calls. *If* he calls. Maybe he's as interested in Ingrid as she is in him. She leaves Willard watching TV and heads upstairs. Willard should have sold this house years ago. It's entirely too much for one person. But no matter how cavalier he tries to be about it, Ingrid knows he holds onto a belief that one day the people who are missing—Harley and her mother—will come waltzing back in and they'll all be one big family again. And he wants this house here when it happens.

Ingrid sleeps in her childhood bedroom. It's very pink. It's what she loved as a preteen, but she can't stand being in it now that she's a woman in her thirties. She changes into jeans and a t-shirt and looks at her watch. Edna, the housekeeper and cook, will have dinner waiting downstairs. Ingrid will eat dinner with her father, and then they'll watch one of the old movies he likes until his early bedtime. She's there to keep Willard company more than anything else.

Once her father has gone to bed, she'll call Paxton and see what he's up to. Whatever it is, he'll drop it for her. She knows he will.

She counts the hours before she can feel his warm, eager hands on her and forget everything else.

***

"Hello?" Ingrid is walking into the gym with Ruby for their evening spin class. One thing she gained when Ruby came into her life was an exercise partner. The gym isn't Claudia's thing. *Absolutely not,* Claudia says, any time Ingrid invites her. *You two go have your fun, if that's what you want to call it.*

Ingrid had been reaching to turn off her phone when it rang in her hand.

"Hi, is this Ingrid?"

"Yes, who's this?" She can hear the impatience in her own voice. She waves for Ruby to go on in without her.

"It's Thomas McIntyre. I'm Carter McIntyre's son. He...uh, well, this is awkward, but he gave me your number. From your father?"

"Oh, hi Thomas." Damnit. It's been a few weeks since Willard mentioned Thomas, and she'd forgotten all about him.

"Hi there. So, before you say anything, I know it's lame to be set up by your parents. But, I'm just hoping to make some friends and network a little. I haven't lived in this area since I was a kid, and I'm trying to get the lay of the land. You probably don't really remember me, but we used to hang out when we were kids, so I'm not a complete stranger." He laughs.

"I remember," she says. The class is about to start.

"At the risk of sounding like...well, like a complete loser, I'm hoping I can convince you to have dinner with me, tell me what I need to know about succeeding in this town? From what I hear, you're killing it at WMB."

Ingrid feels some of the tension leave her shoulders. Networking she can handle. Plus, Willard had really wanted her to connect with Thomas. It will make him happy if she does it. How bad can one dinner be, anyway?

"To be clear," she says. "I'm not interested in anything *other* than networking."

Thomas laughs again. "Networking only, promise."

"I'm free on Thursday," she says. "How do you feel about sushi?"

***

Ingrid walks into the sushi bar. She's come straight from work, still in her work clothes. Pants, blazer. Just to reinforce the idea that nothing romantic will come of this.

"Ingrid," Thomas calls, the minute she walks in the door. He's wearing slacks and a button-down shirt and sitting alone at a table for two.

So this is Thomas McIntyre, whom she hasn't seen in person since they were high schoolers, but who has clearly taken the time to look her up if he recognizes her so easily. She can't decide if she's flattered or annoyed. She tries to give him the benefit of the doubt. It's not unusual to be prepared. If he was a new client, she would have done the same thing.

"Thomas?" she asks as she approaches him. She holds out a hand for him to shake, and he clasps it in both of his.

"So great to see you again," he says with a smile. He's handsome. His light brown hair is short and stylish and his mouth is full of perfectly straight, gleaming teeth.

Ingrid pulls her hand back from his overly familiar grip. He pulls a chair out for her and makes a show of sliding her in like she's a child.

"Thanks so much for meeting me."

"My father tells me you moved back here from Portland," she says. "Quite a transition."

He chuckles. "Tell me about it. It's nice, though. I'd forgotten about Southern hospitality. Everyone around here is so *nice*." He says it like it's amusing.

"They are."

The waitress approaches with two glasses of water and asks if they'd like anything to drink.

"Bottle of Chardonnay, please," Thomas says smoothly. "Two glasses."

Ingrid despises when men attempt to order for her. "Actually, no glass for me," she says to the server. "Just water is perfect." She turns to Thomas with a smile. "I'm not drinking tonight, and even if I was, Chardonnay isn't my preference." She's skilled in sounding sweet when she needs to, but she doesn't like this man's audacity.

Thomas shrugs. "Suit yourself." He winks at the waitress. "Let's make it a single glass of Chardonnay for me, then."

"I hear you're in real estate development yourself," Ingrid says when the waitress departs.

"I am, or was. We were doing a workshare project. You know the kind, I'm sure. A space with fully-equipped private offices and cubicles for entrepreneurs and freelancers to rent as needed. My role had more to do with marketing than building, though. We actually sold the concept a few months ago, before construction had even begun."

"So what's next for you?"

"I'm working on an idea for something new."

"Fascinating. What?"

"It's still in the early stages, so I'm not quite ready to discuss it."

She smiles. "Well, it must be keeping you busy." He's either lying about having a business idea, or he's pegged her as too stupid to understand.

His wine appears, and he takes a sip. "And you work for your father."

"I run the business that my father started, yes."

Thomas nods. "Sounds...tedious."

"Does it?" Ingrid has been craving sushi, but this man has made such a first impression that she suddenly can't stand to spend another moment in his company. She makes a show of checking her phone. "Oh goodness. Speaking of, I've got a work emergency I'm going to have to go deal with. Anxious client. I'm sorry, Thomas, but I've got to run."

He looks disappointed. "But you just got here."

"I know. Maybe we can try again sometime." Lie. If he was anyone besides the son of Carter McIntyre, she'd tell him the truth: that there's no way she'd do this again.

He stands with her. "Well, thanks for meeting me." For a moment, he looks like he's going to try to hug her, but she reaches out a hand and pats him on the arm before he has the opportunity.

"Of course. Welcome back to Ellen Point."

The minute she's in the car she calls Paxton.

"Hey," he says.

"Hey you. How do you feel about going furniture shopping for your new place? It's not too late to head towards Atlanta. I know of a great storeroom."

"Just tell me when to be ready." His voice, his eagerness to be with her, is a breath of fresh air.

"Let me go home and change. I'll see you in a half-hour."

"You got it."

CHAPTER 27

"What are you doing for Spring Break?" Ingrid asks. Paxton has been in the new apartment for a few months now, and she's lying beside him in his new queen-sized bed. Maybe it should bother her that she's funding it all, but it doesn't. Being in control suits her perfectly.

She's got to be more careful, though. Last week, she let Paxton take her out to some of his favorite downtown bars. It was a Tuesday, so the whole scene should have been dead. They danced and drank and Ingrid had the kind of fun she imagined most people had during their college years but that she'd foolishly missed. They were at The Study Room when Paxton's three roommates approached them. At first Ingrid thought Paxton had set the whole thing up as a way to introduce her to the other people in his life, but then she caught his alarmed expression. He wasn't afraid of his friends knowing about them; he was afraid that *she* would be afraid. That the reality of it all would change her mind. *Hey man, where've you been lately?* One of them asked. *Hey,* Paxton stammered, doing those handshake-to-hug things that men do with their friends. *This is...*he trailed off, glancing at her. *Ruby*, he finally blurted out. She raised an eyebrow at him, but smiled and shook his friends' hands.

Lucky for Ingrid, Paxton's roommates had been drinking already and they didn't care who she was, not really. Instead, they all did shots together at the bar and she and Paxton danced close—so close—and it felt, for a moment, like they were a normal couple. *I thought you weren't going to use your boss's name*, she told Paxton later, back at the new apartment.

I panicked, he admitted, with a shrug and a grin.

"No plans," Paxton says now. Spring Break at EPU comes so early—it's the second week in March this year—that it can hardly be called a "spring" break. But that doesn't stop most of the kids from loading up their cars for a long drive down to Panama City or Daytona and freezing their asses off on the beach.

"Want to go somewhere?"

Paxton leans over her and she pulls him close, kisses him. She runs her hands down his chest. He's been working out in The Prestige gym. "Anywhere with you," he says, which is the perfect answer.

She thinks of all the places they could go. She's not a Florida kind of girl. She thinks of destinations more tropical, farther away, places where they could touch and kiss in public like they had downtown that night, without her worrying about running into a client or someone from the Foxglove Society. The idea of having a reputation to uphold at her age is laughable, but here she is.

The truth is, she doesn't want to have to explain herself. Not to the Foxglove women, not to her father, not even to her friends. *Why him?* They might ask, and there is the obvious: He's young, and fun, and sexy. And that might have been enough for one night. But there's more than that. Paxton doesn't expect anything from her, unlike the other men in her life. She gives him more because she wants to, but Paxton only wants *her*. It's endearing. There's something to be said for the way he teases laughter out of her now, how it feels like she doesn't have to fake it.

And yet.

Running WMB is the goal she's been chasing her entire life, and if she has to keep her reputation shiny and clean to get there, then that's what she has to do. She can't be like her mother or her brother, folding under pressure and disappearing when things get hard.

So what if she needs her own tiny rebellions to keep moving forward with everything else?

It doesn't matter. What matters is the delicious touch of Paxton, the feel of his skin against hers, the sensations she thought she'd missed out on entirely. Her younger self would have given anything for this.

And *this* Ingrid, the grown-up, appreciates that she can leave when she's ready. She doesn't have to stay for the bad habits he surely has. She doesn't have to know him *like that*.

"Do you have a passport?"

He looks at her. "Ingrid, do you think I've been out of the country before?"

"Okay, I guess that's a no." She thinks for a minute. Spring Break is next week. It's too late to have one expedited. She thinks of where they could go without one.

"What about Hawaii?" she suggests. "No passport required."

He laughs.

"What?" "You really think you can stay away from work that long?"

"For you, maybe I could." She has years of vacation time she's never used. It wouldn't be irresponsible to take a little break.

"Then let's go to Hawaii." He kisses her neck, licks the skin there.

"I'm serious. Let's go. I'll have my assistant work out the details."

"She knows about us? And you're okay with that?"

"She doesn't know about us."

"And she won't question you if you want her to book a trip for yourself and a mysterious second party?"

Ingrid shrugs. "I'll just have her do the legwork. I pay her well enough not to ask personal questions. But I don't really want to talk about my assistant." She kisses him. "Let's not talk at all right now."

"You're the boss."

***

From her desk at work, Ingrid texts Paxton photos of an upscale resort.

Does this work?

A little shabby, but it will do

Funny boy. Pack your bags.

They stay at the beachfront resort, and she somehow forgets for one week about WMB and all of her responsibilities. She *does* check in on her father every day. He thinks she's on a work trip, which goes to show how far removed he's become from the day-to-day business at WMB. She hates herself a little for not admitting to him that she's gone on vacation. She texts pictures to Claudia and Ruby, the only people who know where she really is. They think she's on a self-care solo trip, taking some much-needed time for herself.

There are a lot of lies involved, but Ingrid has never felt so free. She and Paxton drink frosty drinks that never seem to run out, and they chase each other up and down the beach. The nights are chilly, but they keep each other warm.

She wants to press pause on this moment, so she can keep it, golden, and nothing ever has to change.

CHAPTER 28

When Ingrid pulls into the driveway of the Wyatt mansion, there is an unfamiliar car parked outside. It's a Subaru hatchback, crimson red, and it's blocking her way to the garage. She'd talked to Willard on the phone as she was leaving the airport in Atlanta, but her first thought is that something has happened to him in the few hours since. Maybe he's taken a fall and Edna or the regular nurse has called someone in to help. She swings to the side of the Subaru, tires sliding into the well-manicured grass. It's probably nothing. He's probably entertaining a friend, or acquaintance, someone she'll have to smile pretty for. Still, he hadn't mentioned that he was expecting company. Ingrid cuts the engine and grabs her purse. The rest of her things can wait.

She's still coming down from her vacation. When she'd caught her reflection in her rearview mirror, she'd looked happy, refreshed. Even now, the sun is shining and springtime is on the horizon and she has a great job and a man she likes spending time with and maybe things don't have to be so serious all the time.

As long as nothing bad has happened to her father while she's been away.

The front door is unlocked. She can hear voices from the family room. Willard and another man. Ingrid breathes a sigh of relief. She follows the sounds, and then stops in her tracks in the family room entryway. Willard is in his recliner, like always, but looking suddenly healthier and more animated than she's seen him in months. And near him, on the sofa is a man in khakis and a polo shirt, supple leather loafers on his feet. He's got blond hair—like hers, but sandier—and he's making himself awfully at home, leaning back with one arm splayed out on the sofa, an ankle crossed over his knee. The sense of lightness she'd felt only moments ago abandons her. She feels her face growing hot with anger, and she has to remind herself that a tantrum won't help. She's better than that.

The men are so caught up in conversation that they don't notice she's there until she pointedly clears her throat.

"Ingrid, my girl," her father says, a wide smile on his face. "Look who's here."

"Ingrid!" The long-lost Harley Wyatt jumps from the sofa and crosses the room in three short strides to envelope her in a hug. She instinctively starts to step back before forcing herself not to. She returns his hug, but she can't manufacture a drop of enthusiasm.

It's been eleven years since Harley up and left town the day after he graduated with his MBA. Ingrid has occasionally wondered if Willard had ever hired a private investigator to find Harley or their mother, or both. Her father is about as comfortable with a lack of control as Ingrid is. But if he ever knew their whereabouts, he'd never told her. She'd never asked.

Harley steps back and looks at her, his hands on her shoulders. "My god, you're a grown up. Dad says you've been away on business. Things must be going well for the company."

"*So* well," she says, dazed. She's suddenly aware that in her tank top, blue jeans, and flat strappy sandals, she doesn't look like she's just coming back from a business trip. Her skin is sun-kissed, shoulders pinkish from so much sun. The whole thing hadn't been carefree like she'd thought; it had been careless. To dress like this, coming home. To go on a spontaneous trip with her lover, to abandon her responsibilities so someone else could swoop in and grab them from her. This is exactly what she gets.

"Harley, what are you doing here?" she asks. It's a little like seeing a ghost. A ghost she's been in competition with for years.

They used to be close, sort of. Harley's only two years older than Ingrid, after all. She remembers them wading in the creek down the hill from their backyard, Harley picking up worms with his fingers and flinging them at her. Her, catching them with her bare hands to prove she wasn't scared. Her mother used to get so mad about the mud caked on Ingrid's frilly dresses.

"It felt like time to come home," Harley says, which sounds like complete and utter bullshit. Somehow he found out that Willard is sick. Harley has come home to claim what he thinks is rightfully his.

It isn't his anymore, though.

"Harley tells me he's been living it up in Charlotte," Willard says. "He's been just a few hours away for years now."

"Fascinating," she says. "And yet he hasn't been in touch?" It's too much to sit next to her brother on the sofa; instead, she takes a seat in one of two armchairs across from him. Her father's recliner wasn't originally meant for this room. They'd had to rearrange furniture to fit in it. *I don't care what you have to move,* he'd grumbled. *I don't think it's too much to ask to be comfortable in my own damned living room, Ingrid.*

"Oh, I'm sure we'll get to that," Willard says, waving a hand like it suddenly doesn't even matter that Harley's been gone for nearly a decade. "And what do you know, Ingrid? He's been working in real estate after all."

"Well, for about five years now," Harley says. "Thought it was time I finally put those degrees to use." He smiles his megawatt smile. "Listen, Ingrid, I told Dad, but I'll tell you too: Leaving when I did was immature.

I was intimidated by the responsibility of running things at WMB, and I ran away instead of stepping up."

"Fears are natural, son," Willard says.

Ingrid is going to be sick if this keeps up. *Fears are natural?* Willard had been devastated when Harley left, and now he's acting like it's no big deal? She thinks of how *she'd* stepped up when Harley disappeared, how she'd spent her entire summer at WMB learning every bit of the ropes, how she'd continued working there every second she wasn't in school. Taking on all of that responsibility that Harley was so afraid of.

"Hmm," Ingrid says.

"I know me being back here is a lot to take in," Harley says. He looks at his watch. "Actually, I should get going."

"You're not leaving already, are you?" her father asks, too quickly.

"Just for now. I got a hotel room in town."

"This is your home too, you know. You could stay here."

"I appreciate that. We'll take it one day at a time, see how things go." He leans over and gives Willard a hug, and then he hugs Ingrid again. "It's so good to see you both."

The front door clicks shut behind him.

"Well well," her father says. "What do you think of that?"

"It's certainly...unexpected."

"I always knew he'd be back one day."

"You know, I've had a long day of traveling. I think I'd better unpack and get showered."

"Sure thing, princess."

Harley's back, and that can only mean one thing. He wants the family business for himself.

Then again, maybe not. Maybe Harley genuinely feels guilty for leaving his family. Maybe he realized it was time to swallow his pride and reunite with them. Except the Harley she knew wasn't like that. The

Harley she knew was casually ambitious, entitled. The Harley she knew had what could only be described as a full-blown meltdown eleven years ago and disappeared off the face of the earth, so how is she supposed to know who she's dealing with now?

In any event, they're only a few months away from the official announcement that Ingrid will be the new president of WMB Real Estate Group. There's a luncheon planned at the Wyatt office. Caterers are booked. Her father knows how hard she's worked for this. Surely he wouldn't change direction now, give the company to someone who knows nothing at all anymore about how it works, just because that someone happened to be the prized Southern son.

Would he?

***

"And *then* he says, 'We'll take it one day at a time.' Like he might be here indefinitely." Ingrid doesn't know why she's doing this, recounting to Paxton the return of Harley Wyatt like he cares. Except if he doesn't, he does a great job of pretending. They're strewn across each other on his velvet sofa the next evening, binge-watching a TV series but not really paying attention. Paxton's arm is tight around her waist.

"What do you think he wants?"

"I know what he wants. His company back."

"That can't be it. He's been gone forever. Plus, there's no way your dad would consider that, right?"

"That's what I want to think, but you don't know how persuasive Harley used to be. You didn't see how happy my father looked to have him back. He'd give just about anything to make sure Harley sticks around."

"Well, what can you do about it? There must be something you can do."

There must be, but she doesn't know what yet. She'd been so anxious after seeing Harley last night that to settle herself, she'd read an entire Friends of the Stream newsletter before bed, and now she knows way too much about the Amanita Cormeuma mushroom that grows along the stream bank. She's actually looking forward to the next newsletter. Maybe she'll join the Friends of the Stream after all.

Ingrid doesn't know when Paxton became someone she could confide in. There was a time when she'd never think of discussing work with him, or the complexities of her family. Things are different now.

Paxton rubs her shoulders with his thumbs. "Why don't you try to relax for now? That company is yours. I know you're not going to let anybody take it from you."

She sighs. He's right. She's *not* going to let anyone stand in her way. She'll do whatever it takes.

***

Her father is chipper at breakfast the next morning, and Ingrid knows it's because of her brother's reappearance. Is he whistling?

"Nice seeing Harley again," she says, testing things out. "You two must have talked for a while. Any idea how long he'll be in town?" She'd had a lot of catching up to do at work the day before, and Willard had been asleep by the time she'd gotten home. So instead of getting more intel on Harley and his plans, she'd changed out of her work clothes and gone to visit Paxton.

Her father takes a bite of his oatmeal and nods. "Don't know. He's welcome here as long as he wants to be here, though. He's turned into quite a man, hasn't he? Quite a man."

"He certainly has. But didn't he say he's working in Charlotte now? Surely he has a job to get back to."

"Well, if he's working in real estate, he can do that here can't he?" Ingrid sets her spoon down and dabs at her mouth with a napkin. She's suddenly lost her appetite. She knew it would come to this.

"Sure he can, if that's what he wants. Did he say that's what he wants?"

"Well, no." Willard chuckles. "But he wouldn't have come back if it wasn't, would he? Always pictured the two of you running WMB side by side. Looks like I might live to see it after all."

"But Dad, *he left us.* After all this time, you'd just let him back into the business? Back into our family?"

"Princess, you know family is all about forgiveness. It doesn't matter so much now, that he left. I'm sure he had his reasons. What matters is that he's come back."

"Is that what you'd say if Mama came back too?"

Her father's face clouds over, and she regrets opening her mouth. "Don't bring your mother into this. Can't we just be thankful for the things we've got? That Harley came back? That he's here with us now?"

"I don't know if we can trust him."

"Stop worrying so much, Ingrid. I know what I'm doing. You should loosen up. You know, that Thomas McIntyre was really taken with you when he met you a few months back. You should give that poor boy a chance. I raised you to be ambitious and to work hard, but I fear that the company has become your whole life. It's not healthy, princess. Take it from someone who knows. A woman your age should have a husband who wants to take care of her, and a family she's proud of. Those things are important too."

"I don't need anyone to take care of me," she says, working hard to keep her tone even. "I take care of myself. Now, if you'll excuse me, I need to get to work."

"Good, good. Harley said he'll be by later for lunch. I'm going to talk to him about visiting the WMB office soon, try and refresh his memory on things there. He might even be interested in checking out the Florida or South Carolina offices eventually." The satellite offices she'd set up.

"Of course. Great idea. Bye, Dad." She kisses his cheek even though she'd just as soon strangle him. He's really thinking of bringing Harley back into the fold, probably making them co-presidents unless he takes away her position entirely and puts Harley right there at the head of the company.

She has to keep it from happening.

***

Ingrid isn't planning to answer the phone when she sees Thomas McIntyre's number on her caller ID, but then she thinks of her father and how much he'd wanted her to give Thomas a chance, and how much she needs to be on her father's good side right now. She reluctantly answers, and sure enough, Thomas wants to get together again. If not for Harley's reappearance, she would have said no. Firmly. As it is, she makes plans to meet Thomas for drinks on Friday after work.

"Let's do something tomorrow," Paxton says that Thursday night. They're in his kitchen, eating dry breakfast cereal out of the box even though it's 10 o'clock at night. "Want to go to a movie? We could do that little drive-in everyone's always talking about. It's out of the way, right? I bet no one there would recognize your car."

"I can't."

"Why, what's on your schedule?"

"I've got drinks with someone after work."

"Ah. Like a work thing?"

"No, he's not a colleague. Just this guy my father wants me networking with."

"Ingrid. Do you have a *date*?"

"It's not a date."

"No? It's got a real 'date' sound to it."

"It's just drinks."

"Yeah, okay." His smile has disappeared.

"Paxton," she says. She runs her bare foot up his calf. "It's no big deal. You know how important it is for me to keep my father happy right now."

"Are you like, *seeing* this person?"

"No." She sits up. She doesn't like the implication that she owes Paxton something, but she also doesn't like the hurt look on his face. "Paxton, what you and I have...it's good. I don't want to lose it." She doesn't *want* to be with anyone else, least of all Thomas McIntyre, but it's the principle of the thing. Paxton doesn't own her.

He shakes his head. "Yeah, okay. You should probably get going now, though, shouldn't you? It's getting late."

"Yeah, I guess so." She could reassure him, but she doesn't. What she does is her own business. It is.

CHAPTER 29

"Family expectations are a lot to live up to, aren't they?" Thomas says. This time they're at a local bar and grill. They're having a decent time, and Ingrid thinks she may have misjudged Thomas initially. She tries to shrug away thoughts of Paxton.

"Tell me about it."

"You wouldn't believe the things my father puts me through," Thomas says, and his face clouds a little. "For example, I have a trust fund I was supposed to be able to access when I turned thirty-five, but it turns out there is a clause in it that says I have to be *married* to get it. I mean, can you get any more archaic?"

Ingrid raises an eyebrow. "And I thought my father was bad."

Thomas holds up his pint glass and clinks it against hers. "Cheers," he says. "To the old-fashioned families we love, no matter the hell they put us through."

"Cheers to that."

"Anyway, I don't suppose you want to get married, do you?"

She laughs so hard she almost chokes on her craft beer.

***

Later that night, Ingrid sees the email in her inbox. Paxton has never emailed her before.

To: Ingrid Wyatt
From: Paxton Gale
Sent: 3/19
Subject: (no subject)

Ingrid—
You're on a date or whatever it is with someone else tonight, and here I am waiting again. I won't pretend to like the idea of you with someone else, but I know better than to try to stop you.

Thing is, I'm always waiting for you. You're off in some big meeting or home with your dad or doing something with that society you're in. You have so many things in your life that have nothing to do with me. I like that you have your own stuff. Your own kickass career. I just never considered that if you weren't with me, you might be out with another man.

It stings, is all.

You've done so much for me, between school and this apartment and the vacation and jesus, everything. You make me feel like I'm important or something. Like I'm even worth all this money and trouble.

The shit you've got me believing, Ingrid.

A week ago we were on a trip together and I swear I thought it all

---

> *meant something. Now here I am waiting for you to turn up at my*
> *door again.*
>
> *Have a good night.*
> *-Pax*

It's something, reading Paxton's raw thoughts.

> **Got your email**

she texts.

> **Want to get together, talk?**

She had a not-entirely-terrible time with Thomas, but she still feels pulled to Paxton. She wants *him*. And she hadn't meant to hurt him.

But he's holding a grudge. Or maybe he's feeling vulnerable now after sharing his feelings. It takes five minutes for the thought bubbles on her text message screen to turn into words and when they do, they aren't what she'd hoped.

> *It's not a good time. We'll talk later okay?*

***

"I heard you and Thomas McIntyre saw each other last night," Ingrid's father says at dinner the following evening.

"Word travels fast."

"Carter called."

"Hmm." She eats her salmon without comment.

"Listen, Ingrid. I didn't want to tell you this, but I don't have a choice. Carter is questioning your leadership of the company, and he wants to put Thomas up for consideration as the new president of WMB."

"*What?*" She'd been preparing herself for a battle with Harley for control of the company, but *Thomas?*

"I know, I know. I told him no one but a Wyatt would take over as the face of my company, but if he can get Birch on board, I'll be outnumbered, and I'll at least have to entertain a discussion."

Ingrid feels like yelling, but stops herself. Willard seems legitimately uncomfortable having to share this news. She notices he looks tired today, and wonders if he has it in him to fight this battle on her behalf. If it's even on her behalf at all. It didn't escape her notice that he'd mentioned a "Wyatt" taking over, and not her specifically.

"That's the dumbest thing I've ever heard. Thomas McIntyre doesn't know the first thing about what goes on at WMB."

"I know that, princess."

"Well, we have to stop it. Does Thomas even want WMB? He certainly didn't mention it last night."

"I don't know. I don't know how serious Carter is. It's possible he hasn't even discussed it with Thomas yet. It might be in your interest to woo the boy a bit, find out what he does and doesn't want. You could talk him out of the idea."

"Maybe."

"I don't want him running my company and I'm not going to let it happen," Willard says. "But he's not a bad kid, Ingrid. And he's been through a lot."

Never mind that the "kid" is in his mid-thirties. Her daddy thinks of a man like Thomas as a child, all the while reminding Ingrid that she isn't getting any younger. The double standard makes her want to scream.

"I never said he was bad. What do you mean, anyway? What's he been through?"

"He didn't tell you? Guess it's a sensitive subject. His business partner out in Portland died suddenly. Car accident. They were good friends, from what I hear."

"How awful," she says. "Thomas didn't mention it."

"From what Carter told me, Thomas was pretty torn up about it. Couldn't bear to stay out west after that and run the venture on his own. He sold the project to get as far away as possible."

She feels a beat of sympathy for Thomas. "Well, that's terrible. But you know what's not going to make him feel better?"

"What's that, princess?"

"Trying to take our company out from under us. The *nerve*. I'm going to put a stop to this."

"That's my girl."

***

"So wait a minute," Ruby says, sipping her Matcha latte. It's a gorgeous spring morning and Ruby, Claudia, and Ingrid are at an outdoor table at The Gilded Mug. "Your *brother* is back in town after all this time?"

"Honestly, I'd almost forgotten you had a brother," Claudia says.

"Yes, well, I wish *I* could forget. Of course, my father would never let me."

"So what does he want?"

"The company. I'm sure of it."

"Did he tell you that?" Ruby asks.

"No, but he doesn't have to. Why else would he be back? And if he doesn't want it, Thomas McIntyre has put his hat in the ring. Imbeciles."

"The pompous hot guy you went out with?" Claudia asks.

"I thought he was...well, maybe not so bad, after we went out again the other night. I thought he liked spending time with me, but turns out it was all some kind of ploy."

"Or *maybe*," Ruby says, "this is all a big misunderstanding. Or, or! You're in an enemies-to-lovers rom com and you just don't know it."

Ingrid rolls her eyes.

"Or," Claudia says. "Have you considered that you're just surrounded by assholes?"

"Well yes," Ingrid says. "It's occurred to me."

"What are you going to do?" Ruby asks.

"She's going to fight it, obviously."

"But surely your dad wouldn't let anyone else take over?"

"*Let*?" Claudia says. "No one else has a clue what all Ingrid does there. They'd have no idea where to start. If anyone else takes the reins, it will be the end of WMB. Honestly Ingrid, I don't know how you haven't exploded with rage already. This whole thing is absurd."

"It's not easy," Ingrid admits. "But I'll handle the situation. It's...what I do."

***

Ingrid is at the office later that day when her father stops in with Harley. Willard is walking with his cane and he doesn't even look embarrassed by it. Of course he wouldn't, not when he's got his vibrant and virile son beside him.

She walks down the massive steps to the main level, her expensive heels clacking against the marble. There is a small handful of people who have been working at WMB since before Harley left, when he was in grad school and interning here. Those people hug Harley and slap him on the back. The ones who've come on board in the years since shake his hand and shoot uneasy glances at Ingrid as she approaches. Every one of them wonders the same thing she does: Whether Harley is back to attempt to claim his title, the title Ingrid is so close to having for herself. They wonder what it means for them, for their jobs, for the future of the company. It's all written there, in their eyes.

She won't give them the petty family drama they think they're going to witness. Not here, in public. This place, this building, this is where her reputation matters most. Instead, she leans over to give Willard a light hug (so as not to cause him to lose his balance) and then she embraces Harley as well, even though it pains her to do it.

"Welcome back," she says with a smile. If she could kill Harley and get away with it, she would.

"This place hasn't changed a bit," he says, with his charismatic grin. It's changed *quite* a bit, actually; Ingrid has made plenty of upgrades, both decorative and functional. Obviously nothing grand enough to warrant notice.

"Why don't I give you a tour?" she suggests. "I'm sure everyone would like to meet you." Everyone who isn't already gathered in the entryway, that is. "Dad, would you like to have a seat?"

Willard scowls at her and shakes his head. "I'm fine and dandy dear. You lead the way."

Ingrid takes Harley lightly by the arm and guides him through the lower level, past the lobby, through accounting and HR, introducing him to anyone he may not know yet and reintroducing him to those she's sure he's forgotten. Everyone is charmed by Harley, like always. Willard walks slowly along beside them. She'd love to put her arm around her father to hold him steady and make sure he stays upright. He'd hate that though, especially here.

Once they've finished the downstairs tour, Ingrid leads them to the elevator behind the stairs. No way she's going to let her father attempt those wide marble stairs. His pride—and other things—would certainly suffer if he were to topple down. The upstairs level consists of the open sitting area with a few cozy chairs and her assistant's desk, with three offices off the sitting area.

"Now *this* looks different," Harley says when they step inside Ingrid's office.

Willard chuckles. "Could have been yours, you know." Ingrid's cheeks feel hot. She knows Willard is thrilled with Harley's return, but she can't believe he would say something so blunt, not with her standing right here.

"Looks nice," Harley says. Ingrid smiles stiffly and leads them to the other offices—her father's office, which he hardly visits anymore. And the other one, the office that *would* have been Ingrid's, the smallest of the three, now stuffed to the brim with file cabinets and banker's boxes.

"Well, what do you think, son?" She knows what her father is looking for: an admission of regret for leaving all of this behind. Ingrid can't help but feel that if Harley has any remorse at all—and it's not clear that he does—then it should be for leaving his family and not the family business.

Harley puts his hand on Willard's shoulder. "Looks great, Dad. You've got a lot to be proud of."

"You still have a place here. If you want. Ingrid would probably like the help." She knows what Willard is thinking, that he could put Harley in charge of things instead of her and that would quiet the Birch and McIntyre families. Everyone would feel better about a man at the helm. She's surprised her father hasn't come out and said it yet.

She'd like to kill them both at this point. Instead she smiles and says, "There's always a place for family."

***

"Thomas McIntyre, are you out of your mind?"

"Ah, Ingrid. You must have heard."

She'd almost decided she wasn't going to dignify the McIntyres' ridiculous takeover attempt with a response. Honestly, who do they think they are? But after seeing her father proudly showing off WMB to Harley, and Harley to WMB, she knew she had to do something. With the threat of takeovers coming from both of these ill-equipped and stunningly overconfident men, she has to get a handle on the situation—and fast.

How nice to be a man who wants something. Forget about all the years Ingrid has spent learning the ropes at Wyatt McIntyre Birch. She knows what everyone does there, from the receptionist answering calls to the HR manager processing payroll. She's sacrificed everything for this business, *her* business. These men are grossly underqualified to run her company, but that doesn't stop them from thinking that yes, maybe all of this could be theirs.

"Listen, it's not what you think," Thomas stammers through the phone. "Well, not really. Let's meet for lunch and I'll explain."

"I'm sorry? You think I'm going to have a nice lunch with the snake who's trying to steal my company right out from under me?"

"It's Wyatt *McIntyre* Birch. It's at least a little bit my company too."

"No, it's a little bit your father's company. You've never set foot inside this business." She tries to keep her voice down; she's at her desk, after all, and she doesn't want anyone else to overhear. The last thing she needs is for everyone to start thinking there's a tug-of-war at the top. Even if it's true.

"I think this is all a misunderstanding. Meet me for lunch, seriously. At least give me a chance to explain."

"I will give you a half-hour of my time, and not a minute more. I have a business to run. No matter how much you might want to get your hands on it, it's mine today, and today I have work to do."

"Understood."

***

Ingrid sits across from Thomas at a sandwich shop on Price, not far from the office. She has to fight the urge to leap across the table and wring this smug bastard's neck. Even if he looks more sheepish than smug at the moment.

"Did you want to order something?" He asks her.

"No, I do not want to *order something*. I haven't had much of an appetite since I learned that you're trying to take over my company. It's not enough to have Harley back—"

"Oh, right. My father told me about that. How's Harley doing?"

"You can call him and ask him yourself," she snaps. "Thomas, why am I here?"

"Look," he says. He rubs his forehead with two fingers. "I don't *want* WMB. For some reason, my father wants me to have it. Like he thinks it will make me feel better or something, about my project—my life, really—falling apart back in Portland. He's the one who started this whole thing. Man, you really pissed him off with your Friends of the Stream agreement, huh?" Thomas chuckles.

"So you're going to tell your father you don't want to be part of the company?"

"I didn't say that."

"*No?*" She wishes she'd ordered a drink so she could throw it in his face.

"Okay, here's the thing: I'm broke."

Ingrid laughs. "Right."

"It's true."

"Please. You just sold your project."

"I didn't. I lied. It didn't sell. The whole thing fell down around me after my business partner...well, he died."

"I heard."

"Well, you didn't hear everything. He'd taken out a huge loan I didn't know a thing about, and everything got tied up in an insurance investigation after his death. I haven't gotten back a single cent of the money I invested in our project. I can't even sell the land until the investigation is finished, and even when it's sold the money will go toward the loan. It's a nightmare. Not only did I lose a friend, but I lost what we'd been working towards for years."

Ingrid stares at him. "That's...terrible. I'm sorry you had to go through that. But what, exactly, do you expect me to do about it?"

"Look, I don't want to admit to my parents how bad things are for me right now financially. They'd be more than disappointed. They'd be...well, angry. They gave me part of the investment money to begin with. They told me to use it to make something of myself. I can't tell them it's gone. And as you know, I can't have my trust until I'm married. But...I bet my father would bend those rules a little if I were, say, engaged. All I want is that trust, so I can start over. Here, or somewhere else. It doesn't really matter."

"Engaged."

"Yes."

"Well, good luck finding yourself a fiancée."

"I'm looking at my fiancée."

"I'm sorry?"

"Too far-fetched?"

"Look Thomas, I don't want a relationship with you, and I certainly don't want to get married. I can't possibly have given you the impression otherwise."

"No," he says. "That's not quite what I mean. I don't particularly want a relationship myself. But I want my money."

"So..."

"How do you feel about pretending to be engaged? Just for a little while. Until I talk my dad into giving me the trust. If we're engaged, he'll certainly understand why I won't be moving forward with the takeover attempt. I'll explain to him that we're in love, and that we've been spending time together, in secret, ever since I came back."

"We're not in love."

"Yes, I know that. But it will be the exact thing he wants to hear."

"That's...an incredibly stupid plan."

"Oh, come on. They do it in rom-coms all the time."

"You watch rom-coms?"

"Not the point. This could benefit you too."

"And how is that?"

"Well, aside from the fact that my father won't expect me to challenge your leadership anymore, there's the Harley factor, right?"

"You don't know anything about Harley anymore."

"I know that he's mysteriously returned after a decade or so away. Why do you think that is? Has he come out and said he wants back in at the company?"

"No."

"But you know he does."

She's silent.

"Well, what's better than one Wyatt son?" When she doesn't answer, he continues. "One very experienced Wyatt daughter with a McIntyre by her side. Plus, if your dad wants you married off as badly as my father wants me wed, then you'll make him so happy with engagement news that he won't do anything to upset you. It's a good idea, Ingrid. It gives us both exactly what we want."

"It's the dumbest thing I've ever heard of."

"Okay, then I'll let my dad know that I might be interested in putting my hat in the ring for the WMB President title after all. I think I can make a good case for myself. I'm willing to give it a shot...if I have to. I've got nothing—and I mean nothing—to lose. I don't think the old men would actually go so far as to hoist you out and make me president, but I bet the suggestion of it would cause a whole lot of uncertainty and turmoil for your employees, especially if Harley makes a play for the job too."

"You are unbelievable."

"No, I'm practical. And desperate."

"So either I pretend to be engaged to you...or...you're going to try to take over my company?"

"It sounds bad when you say it like that."

"That's because it *is* bad, asshole. Don't threaten me. If you think you're so good at a job you've never even *attempted* that you could take it out from under me, then go ahead and try." She stands up, grabs her jacket, and stalks out, leaving Thomas McIntyre sitting at the table alone.

CHAPTER 30

I ngrid stands at the elevator bank in the visitor parking garage at The Prestige. It's the first time she's seen Paxton since the night she went out for drinks with Thomas. She can't believe she gave someone like Thomas her time in the first place. Paxton has been curt in his text messages to her all week, but Ingrid knew he would relent. He can't go long without her.

The elevator door opens and there he is, in his t-shirt and jeans. "Hey you," she says. He's such a refreshing sight, his dark hair a bit disheveled, looking at her warily before a grin spreads across his face.

"Hey."

There are no cameras in the elevators, so when she steps in and the door closes, she lets Paxton pull her into a tight embrace and press his lips to hers. It's only been a week, but she's missed this so much.

The elevator slows and then stops on the lobby level and Ingrid reluctantly pulls away from Paxton just before the doors slide open.

Her eyes widen when she sees Claudia standing on the other side of the elevator.

"Ingrid," Claudia says, looking confused. "What a nice surprise. What are you doing here? Hi, Paxton."

Paxton nods hello while Ingrid works frantically to come up with a response. This scenario shouldn't be possible. Ingrid only comes to the building when she knows The Prestige leasing office is closed, to avoid an encounter like this one. She hears the slight change in Paxton's breathing. He's wondering what she'll do, if she'll come clean. She could. She could just say it. *Paxton and I are seeing each other. I'm here for him.*

But...would Claudia think of Ingrid as desperate, or worse, as a person taking advantage of power dynamics, of preying on this younger man?

Ingrid has never had a secret like this before, or friends to keep it from. She's scared half to death of how it could all play out.

"Surprise!" Ingrid says brightly. "I was in the area, and I thought it was a nice evening to grab a drink downtown, and I hoped you might join me. You've been working so hard lately. What do you think?"

Claudia's brow furrows. She hates surprises, and Ingrid knows this. Paxton sighs. "Um, yeah," Claudia says. "You caught me just in time. Late night here. I was headed out. I just need to call Beau and let him know."

"Sorry to interrupt," Paxton says, "but if you all aren't going up, can I...?" he trails off, gesturing upwards and looking to where Claudia's hand is on the elevator door, holding it open.

"Oh, sure," Claudia says, stepping back. Ingrid steps off the elevator, with a quick glance back at Paxton. She hopes it communicates how sorry she is. "Have a nice evening," Claudia says to Paxton before the elevator whisks him away.

> I'll come back

Ingrid texts Paxton, but when she tries to reach him later that night, he doesn't respond.

***

257

The next week Willard Wyatt makes dinner reservations for the family, which now includes Harley. Ingrid wants to protest, but it's the first time in a year that her father has been excited about leaving the house.

"Looking lovely tonight, princess," he says, as they gather their things. He's in a particularly cheerful mood once again, and Ingrid is annoyed by it.

"Thanks, Dad." She *had* put on a nice dress for the occasion.

There's a moment of struggle getting him into her SUV. He needs her help but doesn't want to say so, and so she helps him while they both pretend she isn't doing a thing. Finally he's situated in the passenger seat, and she climbs behind the wheel. No Metallica when Willard is in the car; Ingrid has already got her jazz pre-set playing softly. They pick up Harley from the modest inn where he's staying, and then there is an awkward drive to the restaurant (with Willard and Harley talking and Ingrid mostly silent), which happens to be in the same hotel where Elodie Rose Reynolds got married back in the fall. It's easier to get her father out of the car with Harley's help.

"This restaurant was featured in Garden & Gun," Willard boasts to Harley, though he's certainly never cared about Garden & Gun magazine before. In fact, he only knows this tidbit because Ingrid shared it with him.

"Wow," Harley says. "I'm excited to try it."

"We have a reservation," Ingrid tells the hostess. "Wyatt." The hostess leads them to a table in the middle of the restaurant, and to her shock, she sees Thomas McIntyre already sitting there.

"Thomas," she says. "What are you doing here?" She hasn't spoken to Thomas in the week since he suggested a fake engagement and then tried to threaten her. She'd even gone so far as to block his number. She would like nothing more than to never, ever speak to him again.

But there's a grin on her father's face. "Well, I know you two have been spending time together, so I asked Thomas to join us." She thinks of Willard's urging to get closer to Thomas, to see what he's up to. Maybe this is all part of that, but still...inviting him out to dinner?

Her face must be giving her away, because Harley is watching and he's got a wary look of his own. So she rearranges her features and produces a smile. "What a *nice* surprise."

Willard pats Thomas on the back, and Harley shakes his hand. "Good to see you again, man," Harley says, though he still doesn't look at ease about the situation. Ingrid begrudgingly has to wonder if something about the sibling bond sticks, even after years apart. Because it seems like Harley can feel her energy.

"The long-lost Harley Wyatt," Thomas says. "What have you been up to?"

Harley proceeds to tell Thomas the same story he'd given Ingrid and Willard. Willard listens in and interjects with funny comments, and Ingrid remembers how charming her father used to be. Harley had gotten it directly from him.

Ingrid lets her mind, and her eyes, wander away from the table. To their left is the bar where she'd had drinks after Elodie Rose's wedding, where she'd met Paxton and where he'd touched her for the first time. She flushes, thinking about his hands on her body. Suddenly she yearns for him so intensely that it's all she can do to sit here at the table.

The server brings them a round of drinks, craft beer for Harley and Thomas, white wine for her, and sweet tea for Willard (who can't drink alcohol with his medication). They toast to Harley coming home. "And to Ingrid, the future president of Wyatt McIntyre Birch," Harley throws in, and Ingrid is so stunned that she almost spills her wine. Even Willard looks surprised. So he's been expecting Harley to make a play for the position too, then. She feels an unexpected surge of pure hatred for her father. All of the ways she's constantly proving herself, and yet she's still nothing more than a placeholder.

They order from the nouveau Southern menu, shrimp and grits and deconstructed this and fried that. The waiter brings their appetizer platter of pimento cheese and fried okra with water crackers and the conversation stops, mercifully, while everyone nibbles their food.

When they've finished their appetizer and then their entrées, Willard Wyatt asks for the check ("On me, on me,") he insists when they all reach for it.

"Thank you all for letting me join you this evening," Thomas says, folding his napkin and placing it on the table. "Though I have to admit, I do have an ulterior motive."

Here we go, Ingrid thinks, clenching her fists. This is the part where Thomas McIntyre pitches himself to Willard in his bid to take over WMB. Will Harley admit to wanting it too? She thinks of getting up and leaving, walking away from all of this *shit*.

"Ingrid, we've spent a lot of time together lately," Thomas says. *No we haven't*, she thinks. "And I can't deny my feelings. You're smart, you're beautiful, you're talented." She braces herself for the *but. But I can run WMB better than you. But I have the confidence of 2/3 of the founders of WMB. Blah blah blah.*

It doesn't come. "I know it's sudden, but I can't imagine waiting another day to tell you how I feel." Thomas stands up, looks around the crowded restaurant with a smirk on his face, digs into his pocket to produce a ring box, and drops dramatically to one knee in front of her. "Ingrid Wyatt, I'm a desperate man. I'm so in love with you that I can hardly stand it. Will you be my wife?"

She stares at him.

And stares.

And stares.

Many of the other diners have noticed the spectacle and now watch her with expectant, excited looks on their faces. Thomas has played her. He's bet on her not making a scene, not throwing her drink in his face and storming out. Not in this crowd. Not in front of her father. She thinks about doing it anyway. Different scenarios play out in her mind in rapid succession as she stares at the hideous ring Thomas holds out before her.

He expects her to reluctantly agree. He thinks he's won. She can't let it play out this way. So she does the one thing she's sure he's not expecting.

"Oh, Thomas!" She gushes. She puts her hands to her chest like she's overcome with joy. "What a *perfect* surprise!" She grabs him by the arms and hauls him up with her when she stands. "*Of course* the answer is yes. I can't wait to be your wife." And then she kisses him, there in front of God and Willard Wyatt and everyone else just trying to enjoy their trendy dinner. She is repulsed by his lips on hers, and she has to hold back a gag. Thomas is so taken aback by her response that he drops the ring box and it clatters on the table.

"Thank you...for making me the happiest man alive," Thomas stammers, when they separate.

"I'm the happy one, darling." She's going to kill him.

"Well, I think a round of celebratory champagne is in order!" Willard is smiling a knowing smile that tells Ingrid that he was in on the proposal, and supported it (without knowing the whole story). Harley, however, obviously was not. He watches the scene play out with a suspicious look on his face.

She'd underestimated Thomas, how conniving he could be, how manipulative. He's bested her this time by putting her in a situation in which he knew she couldn't refuse him. But she won't let him get his way. Thomas McIntyre has picked the wrong person to mess with.

***

Harley joins Ingrid and Willard for breakfast at the Wyatt mansion the next morning. Willard has requested that Edna cook up a feast. *None of that damned oatmeal this time. Fix up some waffles, some grits, something with some flavor. We're celebrating.* No matter that the steel-cut oats with fruit and honey were part of the customized diet the nutritionist had recommended for him. No matter that Ingrid's stomach is still churning from the night before. In the middle of the table is a pile of waffles, a dish of butter, a plate stacked with bacon. Ingrid pours herself a glass of juice.

"So, Harley, I was thinking about a golf outing," Willard says.

Ingrid looks up. "You think that's a good idea?" Swinging a club could tip the poor man over. Even Harley looks skeptical.

"Of course I do, princess. I know what's best for me." He looks back to Harley. "Anyway, thought I'd invite Thomas and Carter to join us. We've got a lot of things to discuss now, don't we?" He chuckles.

"I'm sorry, are you going to plan my wedding during a round of golf, without even inviting me to join?" Ingrid can't hold back her words, and she can't keep the annoyance out of her voice. The idea that the men will handle everything is more than she can tolerate, even for a fake engagement. Not to mention that her own golf game is flawless.

Willard looks properly chastised for once. "Oh, now princess, I'm sorry, of course you're involved. You're the bride-to-be!"

Harley stands abruptly. "Ingrid, can I speak to you for a moment? In private?"

Ingrid looks up at him, confused. But she follows him into the kitchen. Edna's there already, hands covered in flour, preparing rolls for dinner. She takes one look at the two of them, rinses her hands, and wipes them on her apron.

"I believe I'll just step out for a moment," she says. Edna and Ingrid aren't close, but they share a certain suspicion in regards to Harley's motives.

"Man, this kitchen," says Harley, looking around. "Brings me right back." He taps Ingrid lightly on the arm. "Hey, congratulations on your engagement. But, is this really what you want? Because, I don't know, something seems off."

She shrugs. "Look, you can drop the concerned brother act. I know you want WMB, I just don't know why you won't come out and say it. You know I'll fight for it if I have to. The company may not have been promised to me since birth, but I've worked hard enough to have earned it ten times over. I know more about it than anybody else at this point, including our father. There are literally no lengths to which I won't go to make sure it's mine." She can't help but hold up her gaudy engagement ring as proof.

To his credit, Harley has the good grace to look ashamed. "Okay, this is what I was afraid of. You don't have to go to any lengths, Ingrid."

"What?"

He shakes his head. "I don't want the stupid company. I *never* wanted it. I didn't mean to mess things up for you."

"I don't understand."

"Look, I don't even work in real estate. I said that because I knew it's what Dad wanted to hear. I work at a coffee shop in Charlotte. I'm a barista, for crying out loud." He gestures to his outfit, the khakis and short-sleeved blue-striped golf shirt. "You think I really dress like this? This is all for him."

Ingrid is dumbfounded. "You...you're a barista?" She's incredulous.

"Yeah, and you know what the crazy part is? I love it. Not everyone is like you and Dad. Not everyone is driven by ambition. Not everyone wants work to be their entire lives."

Harley says *ambition* like it's a dirty word.

"Then why are you here?"

He looks down. "I missed my family, okay? I wanted to see you guys." He looks back up, forcing himself to meet her eyes. "And, well...I need money."

"Are you kidding me?"

"I wish I was."

"So, let me get this straight. Ambition is bad, but money is good?"

"Look, normally I get by just fine. But there are...extenuating circumstances."

"You should be ashamed of yourself, Harley Wyatt. Dad's out there slowly dying and you pop back into our lives and make him think you actually give a damn when really it's all because you need money. The money that everyone under this roof has worked for, except you."

It had been so, so stupid to let Thomas McIntyre put this ring on her finger. She should have said no, should have made a scene. He'd played not just on her instinct to protect her reputation, but on her unease that Harley was lurking, waiting for a chance to step back into the role she'd worked for. She's angry at herself, and with Thomas and with Harley. And yet, she's relieved that Harley doesn't want control of WMB. Money is easy, compared to that. But she needn't have gone to such extremes to ensure Willard's loyalty, to make sure the company remained hers.

Now that her father is expecting a wedding, she'll have to come up with a good reason why she and Thomas will be ending their engagement immediately.

"There's this woman," Harley says.

"There always is, with you."

"She's an artist. A sculptor. We're in love, and she's pregnant."

"Wow. Congratulations." If he expects the idea of being an aunt to make her feel all warm and fuzzy, he'll be disappointed. The way Harley got around in high school and college, Ingrid is a little surprised there aren't dozens of little Harley Wyatts running around the Southeast.

"Yeah, thanks. The thing is, she doesn't think we can afford a baby. She wants to move to Colorado, to live with her parents in Denver. And her parents don't want me there, if I can't support my family. I mean, maybe I *should* have been more ambitious. So I need to be able to step up, financially, show her that I can provide for this kid. I don't know if I still have an inheritance, after skipping out on everyone, but if I do, I'd like to have it. Early. Or a loan, even, something I could pay back over time. I don't deserve it, but it's not for me. It's for the baby."

"And then what? You get the money and you disappear until you're broke again?"

"It's not like that. It doesn't have to be like that. I did miss Dad. And you. And I regret not being here. But there was so much expectation, and I guess I'm more like Mom than I thought, because I couldn't handle it. Every time I thought about coming back, I thought of how disappointed Dad would be. You know that look he gets." She does, in fact, know that look, but their father hadn't been disappointed at all to see Harley. He'd been overjoyed. "I swear, every time I planned to come back I saw that look in my mind, and I just couldn't do it."

"He's your father."

"And I'm a big ole coward, okay? Do I have regrets? Of course."

"You could have just called, if you needed money. I would have gotten it to you, without you coming back here and getting Dad's hopes up that you were back for good."

Harley winces. "I didn't know he was sick. I didn't know you were in charge of everything now."

"That's the point, Harley! You. Should. Have. Known. Family doesn't abandon one another." Except Harley had. And so had Ingrid's mother. "Dad doesn't have a whole lot of time left, and I'm not going to let you run out on him...again."

"I won't do that. Despite what you think about my actions, I do love the man. He's my father. I'm not staying in Ellen Point—living up to the Wyatt legacy isn't in my DNA. But I'll keep in touch, come back for regular visits, even bring Mia down with me—assuming she'll still have me. Dad will be happy to know he's going to be a grandfather, right?"

"He'll be thrilled, of course. What are you going to tell him? About not staying?"

"You think I should come clean, tell him the truth?"

She pauses, working through things in her head. Is she prepared to help Harley, now that she knows he doesn't want to take WMB from her?

"About being a barista? No. Let him believe you have a real estate job you enjoy, and that you have to get back to it. Tell him about Mia if you want. Tell me how much money you need, and I'll do my best to get it for you. Don't mention it to him at all. If you do, he'll think you only came back for that. As long as you keep in touch and you're good to him, then I won't tell him either."

"He won't notice, though, if you pull money out?"

"I have my own accounts, Harley. I don't need to dip into Dad's funds or even into your 'inheritance' to help you out." She's been investing since she got her first paycheck. She shakes her head.

"Damn. You really are the one in charge here. Thank you so much." He hugs her, but it's still so new to have him back that she can only return it stiffly. He looks at her. "Did you really get engaged just to secure your spot at WMB?"

She shrugs. "It was...an impulsive decision."

"Call it off, okay? I never trusted that guy, even when we were kids."

"We'll see what happens." There's no way she'll actually marry sleazy, conniving Thomas, but she can't forget the look on Willard's face, the bliss etched there in the age lines. He was so happy. He'd feigned annoyance that she hadn't told him how close she and Thomas had gotten, but he was already going on and on about the big engagement party they'd throw to celebrate.

Ingrid thinks of Paxton, of how devastated he would be if he knew what she's agreed to, even if it's all a big lie.

He'll never need to know.

She did all of this. She created this madness. With Paxton. With Thomas.

Now, to get it all back under control.

CHAPTER 31

I ngrid calls the Foxglove Society meeting to order. She doesn't have time for this today, but she made a commitment to the Foxglove Society ages ago and she can't push it to the side now. As soon as it's over, though, she's going to meet Thomas.

She's returning the ugly ring and telling him she won't go along with his stupid plan. *Let* him try to take her company. He's the one who will come out looking worse for it. Everyone knows Ingrid lives and breathes WMB, and Theodore Birch and Carter McIntyre can't *actually* overrule her father even if they want to, since it was Willard's business in the first place and he still holds the majority share. She could kick herself for letting these takeover attempts (one of which existed only in her imagination) get to her. She's never doubted her own abilities before.

The ring is going back. And in the spirit of honesty—and in the spirit of no longer pretending to be someone else to please the men in her life—Ingrid is going to tell her father the truth. That Thomas manipulated her into a fake engagement and that she's simply not having it. If Willard is upset, so be it. Soon enough he'll learn from Harley that he's going to be a grandfather, and he'll be too excited about that to care about Ingrid calling off an engagement that only just began.

Fundraisers are on the Foxglove Society agenda today. The Golden Hour Gathering is coming up at the end of the summer and after that, they've got a masquerade ball in the winter to raise money for the local women's shelter. Another silly excuse to play dress-up, to be fancy, and to feel good about it because it's all for a good cause. Not that Ingrid has any room to judge. God knows she enjoys the finer things in life. But lately, in the same way that Paxton has started to see the world through her eyes, she's started to see the world through his. And through his eyes, this kind of thing feels...idiotic. What if, instead of buying fancy dresses and masquerade masks and decorations and entertainment, all of that money went to the women's shelter in the first place?

Maybe she's not cut out to be the Foxglove Society president anymore.

Ingrid rushes through the event schedule and eagerly draws the meeting to a close. This month's meeting is being held at Elodie Rose's new house, which is nearly bare and which Elodie Rose keeps reiterating is "a work in progress" until her decorator gets back from vacation. When the whole thing is over, Ingrid grabs her purse and starts to make her getaway.

She is promptly blocked by June Pressman and her big magenta smile.

"Ingrid, what a treat to see you here. Seems like we never see you anymore, outside of the meetings," she says.

"I've been working a lot." Ingrid looks at the door. The last thing she wants is to get caught up chatting with June.

"And that's not the only thing taking up your time, I hear..." she says, with eyebrows raised and a grin on her face.

"I'm not sure what you mean." Ingrid's pulse picks up.

"Well, Dana Redding told Elodie Rose that she was antiquing a few weeks ago and she saw you outside a restaurant, *canoodling* with a man. A *much younger* man."

Ingrid freezes. She remembers the night well. She'd thought they were safe in Wildflower Glen, the next town over. They'd had a few glasses of wine with dinner and outside the restaurant Paxton pulled her under an awning in the spring heat that felt more like summer and kissed her and she'd wrapped her arms around him and kissed him back. She was feeling so giddy from the wine that she'd nearly wrapped her legs around him too. She'd only just managed to refrain. Thank god. Paxton drove them back, and when they were passing the mountain road that led to the acres of land owned by the Wyatt family, Ingrid had insisted he pull in. They'd made love there, in the grass while the sun set.

She mentally chastises herself now, for having been so goddamned stupid.

"Hmm, I'm afraid I don't know what you're referring to," Ingrid says smoothly. "Dana must be mistaken."

"That's what I told her. She didn't seem confused. Said you two were practically tearing each other's clothes off right there in public. She claimed to have a picture of it on her phone but it was too blurry to tell if it was you. Dana wanted to pass the story along to her sister at the paper, but I told her to wait a minute. I told her you aren't the type to go gallivanting around, being indiscreet. And with who? Some young stranger? 'Ingrid is our Foxglove president, for heaven's sake,' is what I said. 'She'd never be so tawdry. She cares too much about her reputation." Still, June is staring at Ingrid like she does, in fact, believe Ingrid was out "gallivanting." June looks like she's positively starving for details. And something about the way she describes what Ingrid and Paxton were doing makes it sound dirty, and wrong. Ingrid is hit with an unexpected wave of shame. She thinks of all of the times she's seen middle-aged (or older) men with much younger women, and how she always assumes those relationships are driven by money, not love. And that's exactly how it is with Paxton and her. She's bought him, paid for him. It's an excruciating thought, and it hits her right in the chest. Paxton couldn't possibly care for her the way she's grown to care for him.

It's that shame, and panic, that propel her forward. "Actually," she says. "I'm surprised you haven't heard. I've been seeing Thomas McIntyre, Carter's son. Surely you know he's back in town?"

"Oh?" Her eyebrows lift. "Eugenia McIntyre *did* mention that he was home, but I didn't know you two were...enjoying each other's company." It's a heady feeling, having a piece of information June doesn't, and Ingrid would appreciate it more if she wasn't lying through her teeth.

"We are." Ingrid rummages through her purse frantically. "There's no other man but Thomas, and he's not all that young anymore—but don't you tell him I said that." She fakes a giggle and pulls out the ring, slips it on her finger. "In fact, Thomas and I aren't just dating. We'd planned to wait a bit longer before sharing the news, but I'd rather you ladies hear it first. We're engaged."

June grabs Ingrid's hand and gasps, and then goes to town cooing over the jewelry. Ingrid hates this fucking ring. Before she knows it, all 23 members of the Foxglove Society are crowded around her like excited buzzards and it's all she can do to hold her hand steady and smile.

***

Ingrid knocks at the door of Paxton's fancy apartment. Seems like he never stays at his other place anymore. She wonders how often he sees his friends. She's made it so he enjoys the same quality of things she does, and in return, he's always available for her.

He opens the door with a small smile. "It's been a little while," he says, stepping back so she can enter.

"God, I've missed you," she says. "I would have come back here, the night Claudia caught us, but I didn't hear from you..." she trails off.

"And then with the Harley situation...it's been busy. But good news: You were right. He doesn't want WMB, and he's not staying."

"That's great. I knew it would work out." She follows him to the sofa and sits, and he leans in to kiss her like he just can't wait. The stubble on his face scrapes against her skin and she could cry.

She pulls away. "Paxton. There's something I need to tell you." There's a crack in her voice and he notices.

"What is it?" He asks. "Is it your dad?"

She shakes her head. "I did something. It's not a big deal, not really. It's all pretend, but it was a mistake anyway. I haven't found my way out of it yet, but I will."

"Tell me."

Ingrid swallows and holds up her left hand, where there now rests one ill-fitting and ostentatious engagement ring.

If we're doing this, you have to wear the ring, Thomas had told her when they met after the Foxglove Society meeting. When she should have backed out but didn't, all because she couldn't stand up to June Pressman and her father and everyone who expects her to be perfect in the exact way she's taught them to expect it of her. What a coward she is. *I want everyone to know you're mine.*

I'm literally pretending *to be yours*, she'd corrected, waving cigar smoke out of her face.

Cigars are for celebrations, he'd said. *And this is quite a moment to celebrate.* They have a deal now. This engagement is for show, until Thomas gets his trust and Ingrid gets her promotion. At least, that's what Thomas thinks.

We have to pretend the right way. Would Ingrid Wyatt ever marry someone who couldn't provide her with a proper ring?

Paxton's eyes are glued to the jewelry. His face grows pale, then red. She could have just taken the ring off and not told Paxton about it at all. She could have withheld the information. It's not like she's really getting married. And yet, it had felt wrong to keep it from him once she'd committed to the charade.

"Ingrid." He's almost growling. "What the hell is that?"

Composure, she thinks. She's the one in charge. "I'm fake engaged. It's only for a few months."

His jaw is clenched. He stands, backing away from her.

"It's not what you think," she says. "It's not real. It's...I made a deal, with Thomas McIntyre. I...someone in my women's group saw you and me together and I panicked...and I needed to secure my spot at the company, and he has this trust fund he can't get unless he's married. It's all temporary." She's babbling like an idiot. The plan sounds as stupid now as it did when Thomas first suggested it.

"So what? You're just going to *marry* him? What about you and me?"

"It's not going to get that far." She swallows. "We aren't really going to get married. And you...you have nothing to worry about anyway. My deal with you is in writing. I wouldn't go back on it. You'll still have your apartment, your tuition, your stipend. I made you a promise."

"That's not what I mean and you know it. I'm not talking about the money. Not everyone cares about money the way you do, Ingrid. I'm talking about us."

Lo and behold, there's at least one man in the world for whom money isn't everything. She gets up, follows him, puts her hand to his cheek. "Nothing changes between us either," she says.

It's her left hand she's put to Paxton's face, and he flinches against the feel of the metal on his skin.

"There's an engagement ring on your finger, and I didn't put it there."

"I told you, it's all pretend."

"Is that a real ring, Ingrid?"

"Yes."

"And did you tell your father about it?"

"Yes, but—"

"Then you're engaged. That's not pretend. And that means I can't do this with you. You know about my mother, and how I feel about cheating. I can't."

He runs a hand through his dark hair. Anguish is written on his face, and she feels guilty for finding him sexy this way.

He paces the room. "It could have been me, you know. If marriage is what you wanted." And then he stops, stares at her. "Oh wait, it couldn't have been me, though, right? I'm not good enough to please *your father*."

Ingrid shakes her head, even though he's right. "Paxton, you've got your whole life ahead of you. I couldn't drag you into this."

"But you already did drag me in. I thought I was part of your life. I thought...Jesus, what a stupid kid, right? I thought I meant something to you." She hears what he's saying, but she also hears what he doesn't say. He doesn't say he loves her. He's twenty-one years old, what on earth does she expect?

"You do."

"Just not enough. I'll never mean more to you than that stupid company."

"It's the company that's allowed me to do this for you," she says. It's too much all of a sudden, and she can't hold back her frustration. "You'd think you'd be more appreciative."

He stares at her, shocked. She immediately wishes she could take back her words. "You've never made me feel like a charity case before."

"I'm sorry. I didn't mean that."

"I think you did. And I think you should go. Or, am I even allowed to kick you out, since you pay for this place? Am I not being *appreciative* enough?"

"It's your place, Paxton. I'll go."

She doesn't know how this got so out of hand. She'd hoped that things didn't have to change between her and Paxton, but she knew, deep down, that he'd have a problem with her engagement. Even if it's fraudulent. She'd told him anyway.

"It doesn't matter what the contract says." Paxton is behind her as she heads for the door. "If you want me out, say so. I'll get by without your pity money."

The door clicks shut behind her, and she's alone in the hallway of The Prestige at Ellen Point. She's always thought of this place as so luxurious, but now the lights feel too dim, the black and white photographs impersonal. Claudia has always joked that this whole place is staged to make people feel important. It's the exact ambience Ingrid prefers, and yet she finds herself wishing they were back in Paxton's old place, crushed together on his twin bed. She finds herself longing for something that isn't put together *just so* for her pleasure. She thinks of going back, knocking on Paxton's door, of suggesting they run away, the way Harley did. Hop in the car and ride off into the sunset. They could get by for a while. She imagines sleeping in hotels across the country, a cottage on the beach.

Harley did it. Her mother did it. Why can't she?

Even if Ingrid *could* bring herself to leave it all behind, she suspects that Paxton wouldn't actually agree to go. The horrified expression on his face when he'd realized she was engaged told her more than she wanted to know. He won't touch her while she has a ring on her finger, while she's committed—even *pretend* committed—to someone else.

She knew this thing with Paxton couldn't last. He's too young, too real, for this life. It could never be anything more than a fling.

She knew it all along.

***

The email shows up in her inbox a week later.

To: Ingrid Wyatt
From: Paxton Gale
Date: 5/1
Subject: (no subject)

Ingrid—I know I told you to go. But every single thing in this apartment makes me think of you. I should go back to my old place, if my friends would even still have me there.

I'm wallowing, I get that. It's immature of me I guess, emailing you and all. But since no one else knows the truth of us, I don't exactly have anyone else to talk to. Maybe I should try talking to my friends.

I don't know the details, but I keep thinking that if I was just a different person, maybe you wouldn't have said yes to an engagement to a man who isn't me. If I was from a well-to-do family, if I dressed in nice slacks and button-down shirts and wore leather loafers and had a bitching fucking golf game, would my age have mattered as much? Could it have been me putting that ring on your finger? Funny thing is, I have all of the right clothes now, purchased on your dime. You set me up for success, like you said you would. You wanted me because I was different, but you turned me into someone else. Someone more like you. I could pass as well-off now, but it wouldn't be enough. Fancy clothes and slicked-back hair wouldn't be enough to fool your father, and you'll never be happy without his blessing.

It's enough to make me hate my own family sometimes. If not for them, if not for being brought up in Kelver Ridge, if not for my father who screws up everything he touches and my mother who's always looking for something better, if I'd been born someone else altogether...

But it was me, wasn't it, rough background and shitty attitude (your words, not mine) and all, who attracted you in the first place? You could have anyone.

But it was me.

And now it's not.

There's this pool party coming up, here at the building. It sounds silly, but maybe I'll go. I can't just sit here, thinking. It's become such a habit to wait for you and now you're not here and you're not coming, and I'm still waiting.

I just don't know what for.
-PG

To: Paxton Gale
From: Ingrid Wyatt
Date: 5/1
Subject: RE: (no subject)

It doesn't have to be like that, if you'd let me explain. You don't have to wait for me. I could be there tonight.
-IW

To: Ingrid Wyatt
From: Paxton Gale
Date: 5/1
Subject: RE: RE: (no subject)

I want that, Ingrid, But I can't. Not now.

To: Paxton Gale
From: Ingrid Wyatt
Date: 5/1
Subject: RE: RE: RE (no subject)

If you change your mind, let me know. Have fun at the party.

To: Ingrid Wyatt
From: Paxton Gale
Date: 5/4
Subject: RE: RE: RE: RE: (no subject)

Ingrid—You were honest with me even though it hurt, and I owe you the same.

I fucking messed up. I met someone. At the party. She's different from you in every way that counts. I thought I needed that. She laughed too loud and flirted too much and I couldn't help thinking that you would never try so hard. You'd never have to. But the more I drank, the more I thought she was trying exactly hard enough. I brought her back here and for a minute I felt like I won.

And then I woke up and there was a girl next to me who wasn't you, and all I wanted was to take it all back.

I wish I could.
-PG

To: Paxton Gale
From: Ingrid Wyatt
Date: 5/5
Subject: RE: RE: RE: RE: RE: (no subject)

Paxton—
There are a lot of things you don't understand. I would tell you, if you'd let me. We don't owe each other exclusivity. You can date whoever you want. But, for the love of god...
Don't tell me about it.
-IW

CHAPTER 32

It's the day of Ingrid's promotion luncheon, the day she's waited for now for months, years. No one is standing in her way. Not anymore.

True to his word this time, Thomas had told his father he wasn't interested in working at WMB in any capacity, and that he wouldn't fight his fiancée for the spot at the top anyway.

Harley has been driving down from Charlotte on weekends to spend more time with Willard, and he'd stood by quietly during the planning of the luncheon. Ingrid can't help but wonder if Willard is disappointed that Harley hasn't expressed interest in returning to WMB, if Willard would have changed course entirely if he'd thought Harley could be at the top. Maybe she'll always wonder.

There's a big conference room on the main level of WMB, and that's where the luncheon is being held. The caterers are in the office kitchen pulling the meal together, the décor is simple but perfect, and Willard is here to symbolically hand off the torch.

Ingrid is ready. She's *so* ready. This is where she shines. She stands at a table at the head of the room, her father seated on one side of her and Harley on the other. Who would have thought? The WMB employees are starting to trickle in. Excitement is in the air. Ingrid looks around the room. She wants to take it all in, remember this moment. Best of all, her friends are here too. They're not WMB employees, but they wanted to support her. Claudia has just walked in, waving excitedly to Ingrid, and Ruby is in the back with the catering manager.

Everything is going according to plan, until Ingrid's eyes land on Paxton Gale, leaning against the back wall near the door. He's wearing a navy-blue suit she picked out for him months ago. *Everyone needs at least one nice suit*, she'd insisted. She just didn't know he'd wear it *here*.

Ingrid leans down to her father. "I'll be right back," she says. Then she makes her way to Paxton.

"What are you doing here?" she all but hisses at him, taking his arm with one of her fake business smiles and leading him out, past the chandeliered lobby and out a door at the back of the building. There's a small courtyard here. It's a beautiful early summer day.

"You look great," Paxton says to her, with a small smile. She's over-the-top professional today. Heels. Blazer. Hair pulled back. All part of delivering the message that yes, she's obviously the right person for this job. "I could have worked this event, you know. Wouldn't that have been wild? I turned it down."

"Paxton, why are you here?"

"To support you, obviously. I know how much this means to you."

"You shouldn't be here."

"Why not? You invited me. I got an invitation." He pulls it out of his jacket pocket. Ingrid stares.

"That is...an interesting mistake."

"You're still engaged, right? Is your fiancé here?"

She flinches, but she doesn't answer. Paxton's email—the one about the other woman—had hurt her. She'd actually cried, like a lovesick idiot. She was disappointed with herself for caring so much and disappointed with him too for giving up on her so easily and jealous of a nameless, faceless young woman who could be with Paxton without having to hide.

And yet, a small part of her is buzzing, alight with joy at seeing him for the first time in over a month. Her business brain knows he doesn't belong here, but her body hasn't gotten the message.

"Look, Ingrid, I was wrong. You told me you were engaged, and I panicked. I reacted badly. But I trust you, and I trust your plan. I've thought about it a lot, and I don't want things between us to end."

"Now isn't the time to talk about this." She stiffens, pushes down that part of her that wants to wrap her arms around him. Her business brain is in charge today. It has to be.

"Maybe not, but I had to come. I should have told you ages ago, but I love you. You know I do."

She doesn't know if it's the truth or desperation, but either way, it hits her harder than she lets on. He *loves* her. Maybe. "Let's talk about this later," she says quietly.

He looks frantic. "Why not now? Don't you want me here? Don't you want me in your life?"

Something hardens inside her, then. She's spent a lot of nights missing him. But this scene—this, him, here, now—is inappropriate. He may be much younger than her, but he's never acted this childish before. She doesn't have time for this today, and she can't allow this kind of behavior. Not now, not ever. This is the kind of drama that could topple everything she's worked for. She looks around quickly, making sure they're still alone. "Paxton," she says. She can tell he knows he's crossed a line. "You were right. This was never supposed to be a long-term thing. It's over now. It has to be."

Paxton's face goes pale. "No, it doesn't. You know that. Look at me, Ingrid." He reaches for her. "You *know* me. You know what we have. Don't do this."

She looks down at his hand, gripping her arm. This is all wrong. He must know it too, because he lets go, holds up his hands in surrender.

The door opens behind them and Thomas, of all people, steps out. "Hey," he says. "Your father is looking for you. He'd like to get started." Thomas takes in the situation, looks at Paxton with suspicion. "Everything okay?" Thomas is wearing an impeccable suit but (it doesn't escape Ingrid's notice) it's not as well-tailored as Paxton's. The yellow paisley print of Thomas's tie is flat-out offensive.

"Everything's fine, Thomas. I'll be right in." He waits there, clearly expecting her to make an introduction, but she doesn't.

"That's him, isn't it?" Paxton asks, the moment Thomas has disappeared back inside. "Your fiancé?"

"Paxton, you need to leave, and you need to do it now."

"But, Ingrid—"

"Enough. *Listen to me.* If you're expecting me to play along in—what is this, anyway?—some attempt at a big romantic gesture? It's not happening. I've never threatened you before, but I am telling you now: If you ever pull this kind of stunt again, showing up at my office and even *thinking* about causing a scene, everything you have, everything you enjoy...will be gone. Contract or no. Go back to your new girl, the one who tries *exactly hard enough.*"

It's so hard to leave him there, but that's what she does, turns on her heel and abandons him in the courtyard of WMB, tears in his eyes.

She's three minutes into her speech from the head table in the conference room, smiling despite her emotional turmoil and her hatred of public speaking, when she catches a glimpse of him through the window. He's leaving, just as she'd asked.

And here she is, with everything she's ever wanted.

***

"You okay, Dad?" Ingrid asks. Harley has just left after a weekend in Ellen Point. Finally, he'd had the long overdue conversation with their father. He'd told Willard about his pregnant girlfriend and his intention to stay in Charlotte. Willard's delight in hearing the news of a grandchild had helped soften the blow that Harley had no interest in coming back to WMB, that he was "fully committed to his real estate job" in Charlotte. Ingrid had processed the bank transfer as Harley was climbing into his Subaru for the drive home.

"I'm fine, princess," Willard says. "Don't you worry about me." He's in his recliner with a glass of iced tea in his hand.

"You're not upset that Harley doesn't want to move back?"

"I knew he wasn't going to. But it's been good having him around again, nevertheless. Here's hoping he does what he says, keeps on coming back for visits and brings that girlfriend and baby down too."

"But I thought you wanted him to come back to Ellen Point for good. Wasn't that what you said?"

"Well sure, Ingrid, I hoped he'd come back. Thought for a minute he'd gotten tired of that insipid coffee shop or that he and Mia had broken up. Or even that they were getting married and wanted to move closer to family." Willard shrugs. "He was meant for more. But a baby is nice enough, even if they're doing it all out of order. Harley's a grown man, and he's got to make these decisions for himself."

Ingrid starts to reply, and then stops. "Wait. The coffee shop?"

"I'm not an idiot, princess. I know Harley doesn't work in real estate. He needed money, I guess? He must, if he has a baby on the way. And I suppose you took care of things, as you do."

"How did you know? About his job? About his girlfriend?"

"Surely it won't surprise you to know I've had folks keeping me updated on Harley for years. Helps me sleep at night to know where he is, and that he's okay. Never had to worry about that with you."

"So you've always known what he's up to? Where he was?"

"I've always known."

"Why didn't you just go get him and bring him home?"

"Wasn't up to me to do that. Harley had to come back on his own time."

"Dad! Why didn't you tell me?"

"You didn't need to know. You've been thriving outside of Harley's shadow all these years. You two may be siblings, but you're better off with a little space between you."

She tries to hold her tongue, but she can't. "If that's the case, then why did you make it so clear that you'd prefer his leadership at WMB to mine, even after all this time?" The hurt and anger must show on her face.

To Willard's credit, he looks guilty. "The loyalty to the firstborn son is hard to shake. Thinking of you two working together at WMB got me excited, but I know there's no one better suited than you to run the business. It's been *your* business for years now. I've never given you your due for that."

"Thank you." She's quiet for a minute. "That means a lot to me. But...I have to ask. If you've known where Harley was all these years, that means you know where Mom is too, doesn't it?"

"If I did, would you want to know?"

She thinks about it. She'd long ago accepted that her mother was not meant to be part of her life, not if she got in the car and left them behind.

"No, not right now. It's enough that you do."

"That's what I thought, princess. That's what I thought."

***

To: Ingrid Wyatt
From: Paxton Gale
Date: 6/20
Subject: (no subject)

Ingrid—I don't blame you for blocking my number, but I'm desperate to hear your voice. I screwed up at your lunch, and it's changed things. You could have stopped the money too. It's what I deserve.

You don't know much about this because it's usually the last thing I want to talk about, but the summer before I met you I was in this accident. I was rock crawling with my friend (not that he's my friend anymore) and the UTV flipped. It was stupid, but we used to do it all the time. Kelver Ridge has mountains like Ellen Point, and my friend's family had these old mining roads on their land that led to some rugged terrain on the mountainside. It was a thrill driving over those rocks. I bet you'd like it. Maybe you've even done something like it before. Anyway, my friend got hurt, and it messed up his football scholarship. I try not to think about it, but when it comes to all the ways I've messed up, that accident is pretty high on the list. My friend was really popular in our town and I...wasn't. Everyone knew about my family. The accident wasn't really my fault, but it's easy enough to believe it was when everybody in Kelver Ridge blames me.

It has nothing to do with what happened between you and me, but in a way it does. Both are about the way I feel now. Like I'm nothing, and if you put me next to something, people will always be able to tell the difference. You may have dressed me up like your own private Ken doll (it's not an insult, I wanted you to) and put me up in this swanky apartment, but you still know the difference.

I know how I sound and I'm sorry. I hate it too. Pathetic, right? It's okay. I'm okay. Or maybe I'm not, but I will be.

Thinking of you.
  -PG

CHAPTER 33

The McIntyre family home is out in the country, a few miles outside of Ellen Point proper. Where the Wyatt mansion is nestled in one of the oldest—and best—neighborhoods at the base of the mountains, this estate stands alone, at the end of a private drive and secluded in a way that makes Ingrid uneasy.

It's an imposing white house, stucco with a Mediterranean vibe, out of place in this part of the south. The structural details are more fitting for Miami, or the actual Mediterranean.

Carter and Eugenia McIntyre have invited Thomas and Ingrid over for evening cocktails. Thomas is there already, and he opens the front door as she steps out of her car. "Darling, welcome!" he says, loud enough for his parents to hear. This his voice turns quiet and low as Ingrid approaches the doorway. "Don't fuck this up," he reminds her, the smile still broad across his face.

She doesn't reply. He attempts to pull her in for a hug but she side-steps him and makes her way into the large formal living room where Carter and Eugenia sit. It's Ingrid's turn to play the role of happy fiancée now, but inside she's seething. The scene with Paxton at the promotion luncheon is still fresh in her mind. None of it would have happened if Thomas hadn't ruined everything by dragging her into this sham engagement.

"Ingrid!" Carter exclaims, standing. He wears a jubilant smile. "Congratulations on the promotion." As if it wasn't Carter who'd questioned her leadership at WMB after the Friends of the Stream agreement. As if he hadn't offered up his son as some potential savior of Wyatt McIntyre Birch.

It doesn't matter. She's the president of WMB, and no one is taking her position away. She could have called off the engagement now; what could Thomas do? And she will. Once she shows Thomas how much she appreciates everything he's done for her.

All of the McIntyre family's animosity towards Ingrid has apparently evaporated, now that she's going to be part of the family. She allows a hug from Carter, and then one from Eugenia. "We are so happy for the two of you," Eugenia says. She's wearing a light pink sweater set and slacks, a thick pearl necklace around her neck. "Imagine, the two of you used to play together as children!" She clasps her hands in delight, and it's all Ingrid can do to keep from rolling her eyes. Eugenia wouldn't know any of what they'd gotten up to as children, since she was usually indoors with a martini in her hand. Ingrid's own mother had despised Eugenia, and had said so on many occasions. The two of them had been in the Foxglove Society together, decades ago, before Ingrid's mother said *screw it all* and took off.

Carter pours drinks for Thomas and Ingrid, whiskey on the rocks for Thomas and white wine for Ingrid.

Thomas will ask about his trust tonight. He's told her as much. He thinks they're co-conspirators now. He'll do it with her there, so Carter can see them together, the happy couple, and he'll believe that Thomas is about to be a happily married man. Thomas expects her to back him up. It's the point of the ruse, after all.

The small talk is absurd and mostly revolves around wedding plans. "We thought we'd get married next spring," Ingrid says smoothly, as though she and Thomas have discussed this in detail—which, of course, they haven't.

"Actually," Thomas says, "that reminds me of something I've been wanting to discuss with you all. It's...a bit delicate, but it's about my trust. I know it's technically not to be accessed until I'm married, but now that we're engaged, it would be so helpful to have those funds in advance. For the life we'll want to build together. So much of my own money is tied up in my next project, and I want to spoil my bride properly."

"Hmm," Ingrid says. She has to bite back her distaste at the open discussion of money. Her father taught her that it was tacky to talk money socially, that these kinds of talks were done in private or in a boardroom. The only person she's had any kind of real financial discussions with, outside of her business, is Paxton—when she'd offered to pay his tuition, and that had been well outside her comfort zone.

"Don't we all?" Carter says with a chuckle. "I guess you're right, son. We always wanted to make sure you were settled first." He looks to Ingrid. "I was a wild bachelor back in my day, before I met Eugenia. The things I got up to..." Carter lets out another laugh then turns his attention back to Thomas. "I wouldn't have been able to handle that kind of wealth. But, you're not like me, and perhaps it hasn't been fair to withhold the trust all this time. You're a grown man, after all."

"Actually..." Ingrid puts her hand on Thomas's arm. It's a precise dance she has to do now. "While we *have* discussed accessing the trust early, Thomas and I have recently come up with an alternative proposition that we'd like to suggest." She pauses.

"Always the businesswoman, our Ingrid," Carter says. "Okay then, let's hear it, you two."

"We'd like you to consider repurposing the trust entirely. Right, darling?" She looks into Thomas's eyes with a bright but timid smile on her face. Then she turns back to Mr. and Mrs. McIntyre. "The truth is, we don't *need* anything extra right now. I've got my own accounts, and Thomas is so modest, but he's done quite well with the sale of his project out west. Once we're married, we hope to have children right away. A whole houseful, even!" The lies pour from her mouth. "What would be wonderful is for you to turn any trust you intended for Thomas into one...for our future children. What better way to recognize Thomas as the responsible, capable adult that he's become?"

His parents' faces light up. She knew mentioning grandchildren would do the trick. "Well, that's a marvelous plan," Carter says. "Thomas, you're in agreement on this?"

Thomas's expression is calm but she sees the flush of red at his collar. Ingrid has no doubt that the McIntyres have plenty of funds to provide Thomas with his trust *and* start one for their hypothetical children. They have more money than they know what to do with. But. If Thomas contradicts her now and says he needs the funds after all, he'll have to explain why: That he didn't sell off the project out west and has no money of his own. She waits to see what he'll do.

"Um. Of course," Thomas finally stammers.

"Then that's exactly what we'll do. Cheers to family!"

"Wonderful," Thomas manages a smile through clenched teeth. "Perfect. Cheers."

"Cheers!" Ingrid murmurs, holding up her wine glass. Finally, Thomas McIntyre is getting what he deserves. A part of her feels giddy, triumphant. But it's not enough to shake away the loathing that has settled in her stomach.

Not for Thomas, but for herself.

***

You're smarter than I gave you credit for, Thomas told Ingrid, after that night. He'd said it with a wry smile and a gleam in his eye.

And you, not so much, she'd replied. *You shouldn't have brought me into this.*

I'll still get what I want.

I don't think you will.

And even though she'd been victorious in keeping the McIntyres from giving Thomas his trust, something about the look on his face made her uneasy.

Take your ring back, she'd told him, pressing the hideous thing into his palm.

We agreed not to call things off until after the engagement party.

You actually still want to go through with that?

Of course I do. Why not? It's not like either of us has anyone else. We're the same, you and I. We aren't stupid enough to fall in love. Who would love people like us, anyway? The invitations for the party have already gone out. We had a deal that the engagement lasts until after the party. We'll do the Golden Hour Gathering and the engagement party like we planned, then we'll go our separate ways. Your father wants a party, Ingrid.

What about what she wants?

***

To: Ingrid Wyatt
From: Paxton Gale
Date: 8/5
Subject: (no subject)

Hey Ingrid—It's been a while. It's embarrassing how deep of a funk I fell into. I'm finally starting to crawl out of it.

It finally occurred to me that things don't have to be this way. It's too late to change things with us, probably. I don't expect you to respond to my emails, after everything, but it still seems right to tell you how I feel. Even if you're not listening, even if I'm blocked and these messages are sitting in your junk folder.

Anyway. Maybe I can fix other things. Maybe that's supposed to be the takeaway. I don't have to be nothing, maybe. I might never be good enough for someone like you, but damn, that's a pretty high bar. Fall semester is about to start and you gave me these tools to succeed, or whatever, even if you were unintentionally preparing me for a life without you in it. Maybe it was intentional, even. I don't pretend to know, honestly.

I'm hanging out with my old roommates again. They asked about you (about Ruby actually, haha). I tried not to say too much, other than things ended. I know you wouldn't want me talking. They all treat me like I'm heartbroken or something. Anyway. I've picked up more catering jobs and on a whim, I filled out an adoption form for a dog. I know. But they had this dog rescue event downtown and there was this friendly little retriever mix. I haven't told anyone else, in case it falls through. It takes forever to get approved. I don't know how you feel about dogs. We never talked about it. My sister would try to talk me out of it, if I told her. She'd say to focus on school. I never had a pet growing up. My mom is allergic.

And...I know you don't want to hear about it, but I've been hanging out with that girl from the party. She's not you, no one is, but the existence of her in my life keeps me distracted. Keeps me from making another sad gesture of my undying devotion to you. Haha.

What it all comes down to, I guess, is that I'm trying to pull myself together as best I can. But I'm missing you still.
-PG

Are you sure you want to delete all messages from Paxton Gale?
Messages from Paxton Gale deleted.

***

We aren't stupid enough to fall in love. Who would love people like us, anyway? Thomas's words stick with her, churning in her stomach.

She *is* stupid enough.

Even after everything, even after the deleted emails and the knowledge that Paxton has been with someone else, she can't stop thinking of him. She hadn't counted on it being so hard to let go of him. She even misses seeing his email confessions in her inbox.

She let herself get caught up in this devious game with Thomas, with one-upping him into submission, but none of it actually matters. She'd known it when the jubilant feeling she'd gotten from convincing Thomas's parents to withhold his trust disappeared in moments. The winning of it means less than she'd thought. She's done nothing good by lowering herself to Thomas McIntyre's level, or by blaming him for every single thing that's gone wrong. If she'd had the courage to turn down his proposal in that restaurant, she could have stopped this whole thing before it ever started.

Ingrid finds herself yearning for Paxton. Elodie Rose and her husband will celebrate their one-year anniversary this month, which means it's been almost a year since Ingrid and Paxton first met. When she lies in bed at night, she reads all of the archived Friends of the Stream newsletters on her phone to keep herself from calling him. Endangered pitcher plants. Something about regional bees. The newsletters hardly soothe her anymore.

Paxton had been wrong to come to the WMB building the day of her promotion luncheon. He has growing to do. Ingrid thinks of how she'd felt when June Pressman confronted her about being with a younger man. She'd felt dirty, and powerful but not in a good way. Don't men do this all the time? The emails from Paxton were a glimpse into his soul, all the messy and genuine parts. She'd wanted so badly to reply, to spill the contents of her heart too, but she couldn't bring herself to put it in writing. When she'd deleted his emails, it was with a renewed resolve to move on. To let him move on, too.

It hasn't stuck, though. She can be without him. But maybe she doesn't want to.

It's impulsive, but before she can stop to think it through, she's getting in her car to go see Paxton.

***

Ingrid knocks on his door and holds her breath. She should have called first, but she hadn't known for sure that she was going to go all the way through with it until this very moment. Someone down the hall is having a party, and she can just hear the hum of the music, the voices, the laughter. Paxton may not even be home. Or home but not alone. He may even be at the party. A dog barks inside of his apartment. The pet adoption must have worked out. A beat passes when she thinks Paxton truly isn't there. She has a key to his apartment, but she'd never use it now, not after everything.

Finally, the lock turns and there he is. He's got a rattled look on his face that turns to pure astonishment when he sees her there.

"Ingrid."

"Am I interrupting something?"

"What? No, I...I thought you were someone else."

"Your new girlfriend," Ingrid says, softly. It shouldn't surprise her that he would date someone more age-appropriate. What will she do, though, if he has well and truly moved on?

"You read the emails," he says. "I didn't think you would. It's been so long..."

"I read them."

"I'm glad. I think. Maybe embarrassed. I deleted them all. I didn't want to see what a fool I'd made of myself. I maybe...overshared. But there's no girlfriend. It's over with her. That was...a mistake."

"Oh."

They stand there, staring at each other. Ingrid is suddenly self-conscious, and she wonders how Paxton sees her. Her hair is loose around her shoulders, her clothes casual. And she's aware of *him*. His dark hair, those expressive eyes. Her heart is pounding.

A dog pounces on her legs, scratching at her knees and practically begging for attention.

"Who is this?" Ingrid asks. She sinks down to the dog's level and rubs behind his ears, allows him to give her wet kisses on her cheeks.

"This is Charlie. He's new here, obviously."

"He's a sweetheart." She can't hide her delight. She never had dogs growing up (her parents wouldn't allow it) but she always wanted one. "Can I come in?"

"Of course." Paxton swings the door open wide. "It's kind of a mess. I wasn't expecting you."

"I should have called."

"You never have to call. I'm so sorry, Ingrid. About showing up at your promotion luncheon. You were right. That was your moment and I was...over the top." Charlie runs circles around them in the living room.

"Yeah, you were. But I'm sorry too."

Paxton looks like he wants to take her in his arms, but he doesn't. She admires the restraint. "I know I surprised you, with the stupid fake engagement. I was terrified of losing my company, and my fear clouded my judgment. And then I got caught up in the game of it. But I'm going to come clean to everyone. I can't do this anymore."

"What about the engagement party? Isn't it coming up?"

"Next month. How did you know?"

"You probably need to touch base with Ruby about the guest list you provided. I assume whatever mistake got me on the invite list for the luncheon also got me this little gem." To her horror, Paxton holds up an engagement party invite. "Looks like it will be a nice party. But I assume you don't actually want me there?"

Ingrid flushes. "Ruby said she'd put together a list from my email contacts. I was supposed to edit it, but I've been so busy and I really didn't think the engagement sham would get this far and...well, I didn't realize you were on the list. I wasn't thinking."

"That's a first."

"That must have hurt, to receive."

"It doesn't matter."

"It does. You matter."

"I don't know what to say to that."

"The party isn't going to happen. I'm going to call it off."

"What about your dad?"

"He'll be disappointed, but he'll be okay. I'll tell him everything tomorrow. Thomas McIntyre is a bad person, and playing his game is turning me into one too. And frankly, being away from you is tearing me apart."

Paxton stares at her, a stunned expression on his face.

"You've made some stupid decisions. So have I..." she trails off. "Let me ask you a question. Assuming you still have any feelings for me at all—"

"I do," he interrupts.

"Would you still have feelings for me if I *wasn't* paying for your school? Were you in this with me because you thought you *had* to be? Would you still care for me if...if I had nothing to offer you?"

"Ingrid. I fell for you before I knew any of that stuff, before paying for school was ever on the table. I appreciate it, I do. But you have so much more to offer than money. I'm in love with you because you're *you*."

"You are?"

"Of course I am." Her cheeks are flushed; she feels warm all over.

"I'm...I'm in love with you too. Am I too late?"

"No. Never too late."

She's in his arms in an instant. It's exactly where she wants to be.

***

"So...what happens next?" Paxton asks later, after they've made love in his bed. Charlie is happily destroying a toy in the living room. Being here like this, with Paxton, feels like coming home.

His phone chimes with the sound of an incoming text.

"Anything you want," Ingrid says. His phone chimes again. "Do you need to get that?"

He flings an arm over the side of the bed to grab his phone from the floor. He groans. When Ingrid raises her eyebrows, he mumbles, "you don't want to know." He looks at her. "You said you didn't."

She thinks of the last email she'd sent to him. "Just tell me."

"It's...the girl I was seeing. It was...a huge mistake. I thought it would be easy, you know, something to take my mind off...well, you. Obviously, I realized my heart wasn't in it and I broke things off. But you wouldn't believe the things she's been texting me. I think she wants to kill me. Seriously. Or wants me to do the job for her, more like."

He shows Ingrid his phone screen. "Jesus," she says. "Should we be worried? Is she dangerous?"

Paxton shakes his head. "No. She's just trying to get my attention. I made her feel used. I shouldn't have. She thought we were serious and I told her it wasn't like that for me, and...she's not handling it well."

"Hmm," Ingrid says. She tries to sound neutral, no matter how much she hates the idea of someone else being with him in her absence. It's not for her to get involved in this, but the girl sounds like a real piece of work. Then again, Ingrid is full-on fake-engaged to a manipulative prick, so she doesn't have much room to talk. Still, the texts from Paxton's ex are unsettling.

Paxton drops the phone on his nightstand and rolls to face her. "I'd rather talk about *this* relationship, though."

Ingrid kisses him. "I'm tired of hiding. I don't care what June Pressman or the other Foxglove women think."

"Who?"

"It doesn't matter. Screw them all. I got the company, and I think I deserve some happiness to go along with it. Let them talk all they want."

"So...you want us to be what, like a real couple?"

"If that's what *you* want, too." Ingrid knows it's what she wants. She wants to tell Claudia and Ruby all about Paxton, all about the sham engagement and being in love with a younger man. She wants everything that being with Paxton entails. "What will your family think? Will they be freaked out?"

"I don't know," Paxton shrugs. "My dad will be proud of me, probably. My mom and sister...maybe not so much. They're protective. But they'll warm up. What about your father?"

"You know," Ingrid says. "I don't recall Harley ever asking for Dad's approval of any woman he's ever dated. I love my father, but I'm done letting his opinion dictate my choices. Maybe he won't even have a problem with the idea of us, who knows?"

"And...if I want to take you out to dinner, here in town?"

"We can do that."

"And if I want to kiss you on the sidewalk outside the restaurant?"

"You can kiss me anywhere you want."

"I think I will."

Ingrid doesn't want to leave him, but she has breakfast with her father the next morning and a Foxglove Society meeting after that. It's hard to peel herself away. There's a lengthy goodbye kiss at Paxton's front door before she leaves him with a promise to see him again the next night.

She's been motivated and ambitious and focused all her life. Now she's going to try adding *happy* to that list.

She'll look back on this moment later, on her love-saturated, post-orgasmic blissful ignorance. Paxton's eyes on her, dark and lovely as she steps in the elevator and he waves goodbye. How he calls out he loves her and it feels like something warm and magical has settled around her.

She'd never guess that it's the last time she'll ever see him.

PART THREE

(NOW)

CHAPTER 34

Claudia and Ruby sit across from Ingrid in the booth at OKRA, stunned by the story they've heard. Ingrid's cheeks are streaked with tears.

"Oh, sweetie," Ruby finally says, moving closer to Ingrid and putting her arms around her. "Why didn't you tell us you were going through this?"

"I don't know," Ingrid says. "Damnit, I don't know." For a moment, Claudia expects Ingrid to pull herself together, the way she always has in times of stress or pain. But she collapses into Ruby's shoulder instead. A couple at a nearby booth turn around to look. "I was finally ready, and then he was just...gone."

Claudia squirms in her seat. She should join Ruby in comforting Ingrid, she knows that. But there's an ache in her chest, and suddenly it's hard for her to breathe. Claudia hasn't had a full-on panic attack in years, not even on the night she saw Paxton's body, but she recognizes the signs of one now. She tries to remember how to ground herself in the present. She grips the table. Rough wood. She focuses on the air around her, warmed from the kitchen and the crowd. She sees Ingrid and Ruby, her two best friends. Her only friends. But she doesn't really *see* them. What she sees is *her own* broken love story. One night a long time ago, a boy told her he loved her and he left her bedroom and the next time she saw him he was dead. She remembers the feeling Ingrid described, of being soaked in love and drenched in possibility, only to have it all ripped away. Final, abrupt, like there must have been some mistake and surely the error could be repaired if only you could figure out how.

But there's no repairing it. The damage is done.

"You loved him," Claudia finally says. She takes a sip of her vodka tonic, cool and dry, and tries to keep from choking. "You loved Paxton." Even when they'd sat down at the table tonight, Claudia hadn't expected love. She hadn't realized how emotionally ill-prepared she was to hear about Ingrid's pain.

"I loved him. And I didn't even know that he'd died. Who would have known to tell me?"

"Who *did* tell you?" Claudia asks.

Ingrid looks up at her. Even with her face tear-streaked, she somehow manages to look poised. "You did."

"*What?*"

"I was supposed to tell my father everything, that Sunday. Then the Foxglove meeting, and then Paxton and I were supposed to meet. But my father..." she trails off.

"Your father's fall," Ruby says, her eyes wide. "It happened that day."

Ingrid nods. "That morning. We were at the hospital all day and I was trying to reach Harley and get him down here and I meant to take the time to text Paxton and I...didn't. I was exhausted by the time I got home and rushing to meet you two at the coffee shop the next morning. I tried to call him then, but he didn't answer. I was so busy with my father that I didn't think much of it...and then I got *your* text message later that day." Ingrid looks up at Claudia. "You told me his name. It was a Monday, and Paxton was gone. Just like that. Elodie Rose's husband is a police officer and so I called in for the report. And I read it, and it was horrible, and I wasn't there. I went back to the apartment that night. I hoped somehow it would all be a terrible mix-up and he'd be there, shaking his head about

304

the whole thing." Claudia remembers the odd sense she'd gotten that someone else had been in Paxton's apartment in those first few days after his death. Of course Ingrid would have a key. "But Pax wasn't there and neither was Charlie and everything was trampled over by police and it was horribly real."

Claudia finally reaches out to take Ingrid's hand. "I'm so sorry you found out like that. I'm so sorry this whole thing happened."

"It's okay. I mean it's not, actually. It's not okay at all. But it's what I get, for making a secret of him. Don't judge me, Claudia, not everyone has what you have. I fell for someone...unconventional. But it was real."

"We'd never judge you, honey," Ruby says, but Ingrid is watching Claudia for confirmation.

"Of course we wouldn't," Claudia says. "Never. I can't imagine what you're going through." She doesn't correct Ingrid's assumptions about her relationship with Beau. Now isn't the time.

"Losing him *hurts* so much. I've never felt grief like this before. My stomach churns, I cry all the time. Even when my mother left us, I still knew she was out there somewhere in the world. But Paxton...and no one knew about us, so I have to keep acting like everything is fine. But it's not fine. Nothing is fine and it won't be fine again. Not ever."

"Oh, sweetie," Ruby says.

"It was the girl," Ingrid sniffs, "That girl he'd been seeing wanted him dead. I've read the police report, and I know what the police believe happened. But Paxton didn't die by suicide. We were *happy*. He didn't do it himself, I know it."

"I believe you," Claudia says. "I don't think it was suicide either."

"It was Amberly. He told me she wanted him dead. She killed him, and I'm going to make sure she pays for it. I just don't know how yet."

"She didn't kill him," Claudia says, softly. "Not with her own two hands, at least." Claudia starts to explain the contents of the text messages that Amberly sent to Paxton, but Ingrid cuts her off.

"I know. I saw the messages with my own eyes. But trust me, Paxton wouldn't have hurt himself, and no one could have convinced him to. She had to have been back to his apartment that night, after I was. She killed him then."

"According to her friend, Amberly didn't go back to the apartment," Claudia says. "Plus, I saw Paxton. Um, when the police found him. I'm not sure Amberly could have set it all up without help."

"You saw him," Ingrid breathes. A fresh stream of tears spills from her eyes.

"Yes."

"Tell me," she says. "No, don't."

Claudia takes a deep breath. "I won't."

"Maybe the girl had help," Ingrid says.

"Maybe." Claudia thinks. "I'm not sure."

"Well, if she didn't kill him and he didn't die by suicide, then *how did this boy die*?" Ruby asks.

"I don't know," Claudia says.

"Okay." Ruby pulls a fresh tissue from her purse and passes it to Ingrid. "Let's go over everything you two know about that night. Ingrid, can you do that? Or is it too much?"

"I can do it," Ingrid says.

"Tell me how *you* found out about Paxton's death," Ruby says to Claudia. So Claudia walks them through that night, how she'd rushed over to The Prestige. She remembers the way her hands had trembled. How she'd sneaked into Paxton's apartment when no one was looking.

"Did you notice anything unusual?" Ruby asks.

Other than the body hanging from the ceiling? Claudia thinks but doesn't say, out of respect for Ingrid. She walks herself through the same grounding techniques she'd used to calm herself a few moments ago. She closes her eyes. What did she see? What did she hear? "He was in the living room. I...I wasn't supposed to be in there. The dog was outside in the hallway with Amberly and Lou. I searched the foyer table. I was looking for a goodbye note. There wasn't one. There was a smell...cigar smoke. The cops were talking in the hallway, but I couldn't make out the words."

"Wait," says Ingrid. "Cigar smoke?"

"Yeah."

"Claudia." Ingrid grips the tissue in her hands. "Paxton didn't smoke. Not cigars, not cigarettes. Not anything."

"Maybe he was feeling celebratory? You two had just reconciled."

"No. He has—had—strong feelings about smoking. He wouldn't celebrate with a cigar. He wouldn't. But...I know who would. It's just...surely it's not possible. Even *he's* not that terrible."

"Who?"

"Thomas."

"Wait. Wait wait wait." Ruby reaches for her vodka tonic and takes a long drink. "You think your fake fiancé is a *murderer*?"

"It's a stretch, but who else?" Ingrid says. "It's not like Paxton had a whole lot of enemies."

"If Thomas was there, it would be on the security camera footage," Claudia says. "I didn't know there was more to see..." She has a sudden urge to go back to The Prestige right now, to scour that footage until she's seen every second of the night Paxton died. "I'll find out. And then we'll know for sure."

"And if it's true...what do we do about it?" Ruby asks. "The engagement party is just a few days away. Are you going to call it off? Go to the police?"

"Why didn't you call it off already?" Claudia asks, suddenly. "You told Paxton you were going to come clean, call off the fake engagement with Thomas. But you didn't. Why?"

"I meant to. Then my father fell on his way to breakfast that Sunday, and the ambulance came. Then he was in the hospital and it didn't seem like the right time and I promised myself I would tell everyone as soon as he was home from the hospital. But by the time he was discharged, Paxton was..." she takes a deep breath. "Dead. Paxton was dead, and then none of it seemed to matter anymore. Why *not* go through with the stupid fake engagement? But if it's true...if Thomas killed Paxton, then Paxton's dead because of *me*." A look of horror settles on Ingrid's face. "This could be all my fault. I made Thomas angry when I blocked him from getting his trust."

"You think he killed Paxton to punish you?" Ruby asks.

"Women are punished all the time for the things they want," Claudia says. "For wanting things at all."

"Fuck. That," Ingrid says slowly. "It's not right." She dries her eyes and suddenly there's an anger there, a look in her eyes that's fierce and hard. "Get me that footage, Claudia. If it's possible, if it's really true, that Thomas took Paxton away from me...he's going to get every single thing he deserves."

There's no doubt she means it.

***

Claudia calls TessAnne Gale the next morning and leaves her a vague message that she has new information about Paxton's death and that she'll be back in touch when she knows more. After that, she boots up her computer and settles in to watch the rest of the security camera footage from the night Paxton died. She skips ahead to the argument between Paxton and Amberly. This was where she'd stopped before. But now she moves forward. She sees Ingrid arrive. It's a jolt to Claudia's system, seeing her friend with Paxton Gale, involved in what Claudia now understands was an intimate conversation. They step inside together, and time passes. When Ingrid eventually leaves, Paxton kisses her in the doorway. Claudia feels her stomach twist at the sight, knowing how it will end, how much pain is yet to come.

And then…nothing. Claudia watches. And watches. And watches.

The office phone rings, and she drags her attention away to the caller ID. Her breath catches. "It's a great day at The Prestige at Ellen Point," she manages to choke out.

"Hello, this is Alice with the Ellen Point Police Department. I'm calling for verification that Jacob Morris is a resident at your complex."

Community, Claudia thinks. Not *complex*. The word *complex* implies issues, troubles, complications. Still, given that she's on the phone with the police *again*, it's a bad time to make the correction. "He is," she says, cautiously.

"Apartment 532?"

"Yes."

"Okay, that's all I need to know."

"Wait," Claudia says. "That's not all *I* need to know. Can I ask what's going on?"

"We're sending an officer over to do a welfare check," she says. "Some friends are worried he might hurt himself, and he's not answering his phone."

"No. Oh no." It's happening again.

"I'm sure everything is fine, Ma'am," she says. "It's likely just a precaution."

"Right. A precaution." Just a precaution. Jacob is another law student who lives in the building. He's probably fine, like the woman on the line said. He is not dead. *He's not dead.* Claudia repeats it over and over in her head. "Thank you. I'll wait for the officers."

But she doesn't wait for them. She goes straight to Jacob's door and knocks. If he answers, she'll be able to let the police know that he's okay and they won't need to even come inside the building and stir things up again with the other residents.

The chihuahua in the apartment next door, the one who is well-behaved as long as you don't make too much noise, starts raising hell. But Jacob doesn't answer. Claudia thinks of what she knows about him. More than she knew about Paxton, but what she knows only makes her more concerned.

She takes the elevator down to the parking garage to check for his car. It's noon, and Jacob has an internship at a law firm on the other side of town; it's very possible he's at work right now.

Except his Tahoe is parked in its regular spot in the garage. She swallows. It's real. It's happening again. She takes the extra step of checking out the key to his apartment from the box in the back. Nothing is stopping her from taking the key and going into his apartment to check on him, with or without the cops. But she's seen too many dead bodies in her life already. If Jacob is lying dead in that apartment right now, she doesn't want to be the one to find him there. She imagines Jacob, hanging like Paxton or lying in his bed like Killian. Or on the floor, bile pooling in the corner of his mouth.

Jacob may be twenty-four years old and a law student, but he's also a recovering alcoholic. Claudia remembers the night he drank too much and kicked the elevator doors off track, back before he started outpatient rehab. He's been sober for a few months now, but she can't help but wonder if alcohol is involved in whatever is happening now.

Instead of unlocking the door to find out what's going on, she sits at her desk and waits. She stares at her emails; they blur into gray and white on the screen. She wishes Graham or even Liza were here to share this worry. But Graham doesn't come in for another hour, and Liza's shift starts even later.

The officers take forever to get there, and when they arrive she finds that she recognizes one of them as Sergeant Grundy.

"Hi there," he says, and remarks on it being his second time at the property in as many months. "Hope this one turns out different," he says casually.

"Yeah, me too," Claudia says, and escorts the two officers to the fifth floor. She can't look at them.

The elevator chimes and they all head straight for 532. Grundy knocks, the dog next door goes crazy, and no one answers the door to Jacob's apartment. The cops ask about his car like she knew they would, and she tells them it's in the garage. She hands over the key to the apartment, but still the officers spend fifteen more minutes knocking loudly on the door and calling for Jacob before they finally decide to make a move. Claudia stands there, wringing her hands and pacing up and down the hallway.

She feels cold, even though the temperature is set to a comfortable 72 degrees in the hallways. Chill bumps rise along her arms. Her chest aches. It's happening again. Jacob is dead in there, she knows it.

Like Paxton.

Like Killian.

By this time, other fifth floor residents—the ones home at this time of day, at least—are starting to open their doors to see what all the shouting is about. Claudia tries for a reassuring smile but something about cops yelling into an apartment doesn't inspire reassurance.

She looks at her watch. It's 1:05pm. Graham should be in the office by now. She checks her phone to see a text from him. *Just clocked in. Where are you?*

She responds, trying to communicate the situation in as few words as possible. To her credit, she doesn't *say* that Jacob is dead. Two minutes later an elevator stops on five and Graham hurries out.

"What's happening?" he asks, and she's opening her mouth to tell him when she hears it: the sound of one of the officers finally turning the key in the lock. The officer pushes the door open and they all wait as he steps inside. He returns a moment later with Jacob, who looks dazed but *alive* and muttering something incoherent. The officers ask to go back inside to talk and he obliges, stumbling aside to allow them passage. Sergeant Grundy nods to Claudia; her job here is done.

Claudia looks at Graham. They can get back to work now. Everything is okay, except she's shaking. She can't make it stop. She can't breathe. She crosses her arms over her chest as if to hold herself together somehow. She tries to call up her grounding techniques but it's too much. It's all too much.

"Claudia," Graham says. He puts his arms around her and she lets him pull her close because it's either that or sink to the floor. "Hey, are you okay?"

She can't speak, but she wants to. She wants to tell him that she's frantically, hysterically happy that this time, *this time*, no one is dead. The ecstasy of it could overtake her. A laugh bubbles out.

"I'm fine," she says finally. She steps back. She can feel the ghost of his touch on her skin. "Go on down. I'll be right there."

"You sure?"

Claudia nods, and he takes her word for it. Once Graham is gone, she rides the elevator up instead of down and soon she's in the model apartment. She pulls out the elderflower liqueur and drinks straight from the bottle.

She's not okay. She should call someone, Beau or Ruby or Ingrid, instead of hiding up here all alone again. She takes the bottle with her into the master bedroom, where she kicks off her heels and removes her suit jacket, then curls herself onto the bed with the rock-hard mattress and ten thousand pillows. She pulls one of the pillows close to her chest. The sun is gleaming through the windows. She's never been in this bed before. She closes her eyes tight and wills herself to be still, to just be.

To just breathe.

***

The sound of the apartment door opening jolts Claudia awake. The soft orange-gray of twilight spills in through the windows; her phone confirms that she's missed the rest of the work day. She scrambles from the bed. How mortifying, to be found in here—barefoot, suit jacket draped over a chair with an empty bottle of booze on the table—by a maintenance tech. Graham knows how she hides up here. Maybe it's him, checking on her.

She hears voices from the living room as she struggles into her heels. If it is Graham, he's not alone. She thinks of hiding in the closet. Graham could be on an after-hours lease tour. It's not unheard of. They've stayed late for clients before. She hears laughter. If it's a tour, they'll make it to see the bedroom eventually. She has to get out of here. Claudia pulls on her suit jacket and gathers her things, removes her heels again, then tiptoes down the hallway to the living room.

She stops in her tracks when she sees Graham and Liza on the sofa. This is *not* a lease tour. Liza is leaning into Graham like the two of them are more than work colleagues and it suddenly occurs to her that maybe they *are*. Graham has a hand on Liza's knee and then before Claudia even has time to process this information, they are kissing and Claudia stands there watching in stunned fascination.

In the moment, in her half-awake and alcohol-addled stupor, she hates that it's Liza there on that sofa. She wants it to be *her* instead and it almost feels like it could be. *She* wants to feel Graham's cold, expensive tie beneath her hand as she pulls him to her own mouth. To kiss him with the fervor she feels right now. It's wrong, but tonight she just might do it anyway.

Graham would kiss her neck, the way he's kissing Liza's, and Claudia would frantically unbutton the pearly white buttons of his shirt. He'd put his hands on her again.

Her own shirt would end up on the floor, dress pants at her feet. Graham's shirt would hang from one shoulder and he'd be naked below the waist. He *is* that way, now. Claudia would bite his lip and pull him as close to her as he could possibly be.

Their rhythm would be made of confusion and elation and despair and the light from the balcony would twist and twinkle around them. Claudia would make noises, or Graham would. Both. He would say her name, arms wrapped so tightly around her that she would hardly be able to breathe but this time it would be okay.

Claudia squeezes her eyes shut, and when she opens them the fantasy has evaporated like gray mist and it's Graham and Liza, it's only ever been them, devouring each other like eager animals there on the sofa. She tiptoes to the door—they won't see her now—except as she eases the door closed behind her, Graham looks up and their eyes meet. He looks guilty but she doesn't know why. He's not hers.

He never was.

***

In her car on the way home that night, Claudia thinks of Beau and Amberly, of how she saw them sitting together in that Mexican restaurant, of what she can only assume they did together afterward. Maybe Claudia should have gotten to Graham before Liza, should have let that one desperate caress turn into something more. Maybe her marriage is nothing but wreckage anyway.

Jacob, the law student whose crisis sent her spiraling today, is going to be okay. There was a series of texts on her phone from Graham from earlier in the afternoon, explaining. An ambulance came, and took him to get inpatient treatment for alcohol. He'd relapsed after all, but he's getting help. He's *alive*.

Claudia pulls into her neighborhood, the rows of cute houses in neat lines, small yards, identical mailboxes. The red or pink or blue-haired girl she used to be would shit a brick if she could see this place. Things turn out differently than you expect. *Claudia* turned out differently. When she took Intro to Philosophy in college, she'd studied some philosopher—don't ask her who—who said you can't trust anyone, because people are always changing. You can't even trust yourself, because you're changing too. The you of yesterday isn't who you are today or even who you'll *want* to be, and she is proof of that. The things you swore you'd never want can become appealing in the right circumstances. And vice versa.

Sometimes, she wonders: if Killian hadn't died, would they still be a part of each other's lives? She wonders if his secrets would have ever come to light, or if he would have eventually carried them right back home with

315

him to Dallas. If she'd still be creating disasters wherever she went, or if some other consequence would have led her to see how much damage one human can do.

Maybe Claudia would have ended up here in this exact same spot, all the same.

CHAPTER 35

I t's the morning of Ingrid's engagement party, and Claudia is trying her damnedest to get through the remainder of the camera footage from the night Paxton died. Yesterday's crisis (and her unexpected reaction to it) had derailed her plan, but Ingrid's counting on her. Claudia's already planning on leaving work early for the event, so she doesn't have much time. And yet, resident issues keep demanding her attention. It's lunchtime before she can sit down at her computer to get started.

Let's do this, Claudia says to herself. She's got her flash drive ready. She skips ahead to the part where Ingrid arrives, then fast forwards until Ingrid kisses Paxton goodbye. Claudia thinks of how possessive she'd started to feel of Paxton over the course of these weeks, and how silly she'd been.

She watches.

Claudia slows the footage and leans forward when she sees yet another person step off the elevator and approach Paxton's doorway. The third person to arrive at Paxton's apartment that night. It could be Thomas. Or not. The person is wearing a hood that prevents her from seeing a face clearly, but the build and bulk suggests male. Claudia watches as Paxton opens the door and there is a pause, and then the man steps swiftly forward and he and Paxton are both out of view.

The door closes.

Claudia gasps. This is what she's been waiting for, something to solidify her conviction that Paxton was murdered.

The elevator chiming and the sound of heels clacking against the lobby floor pull her attention away from the screen. She looks up, expecting a resident, but instead it's Margo Spalding. *Her boss.* Claudia slams her laptop closed and stands.

"Hi Claudia," Margo says smoothly. Surprise visits aren't uncommon; it's one way supervisors can check up on the staff and the properties. But Claudia certainly isn't prepared for this today.

"Margo," she stammers. "What a nice surprise." She reaches out to shake Margo's hand. Margo is all business with her ice-gray glossy hair, skirt suit, and heels. She's older than Claudia by fifteen years or so. Margo and Claudia have a good working relationship, but Margo is the kind of no-nonsense professional who wouldn't approve of...well, anything Claudia's been up to around here lately. Claudia tries not to look shell-shocked by Margo's presence, here in front of her while she desperately needs proof of a murder at The Prestige.

"I know you're leaving early today, but if you're not too busy I thought we could go over your numbers, take a tour of the community, see how things are going around here. Everything looks lovely." Margo says it like the thought to drop in had just occurred to her, but the drive from Huntsville to Ellen Point takes a few hours. Plenty of time for a heads up, but Margo had decided not to give her one.

Claudia works on channeling Ingrid. Her friend is skilled at staying calm and collected, and hiding her emotions when she needs to. "I'm so glad you did," she says, with what she hopes passes for a smile. "Please, have a seat." She guides Margo to the sofa in front of the fireplace. "Can I offer you some coffee or tea? Sparkling water?"

Margo nods. "Coffee sounds wonderful."

"Still with cream and Stevia?"

"Yes, that's right." Margo looks pleased that Claudia has remembered this detail.

Claudia leaves Margo on the sofa while she pours coffee. Margo is shorter than Claudia, and Claudia can just barely see her head over the back of the sofa.

There's a tap at the lobby door, and Claudia looks up to see TessAnne Gale standing there. What terrible timing. Claudia walks to the door and pushes it open slightly, hoping to stop TessAnne there. But no, TessAnne pulls at the door and comes right on in.

"I got your message from yesterday about Amberly Vance and I just got in the car and drove. Do you know who did it? Who killed Paxton? What should we do? Go back to the police?" Her words come out in a frantic jumble. Claudia's eyes widen and she tries to cut her off. From the corner of her eye, she can see Margo's head turn to take in the conversation.

"TessAnne," Claudia says, struggling to remain calm. She touches TessAnne's arm. "Why don't we talk about this later? Now's not the best time."

"What?" she says. "You're the one who went into his apartment and went through his stuff and confronted Amberly and did all of the things, and now isn't a great time?"

Shit.

Margo has now spun all the way around on the sofa and is watching intently. Finally TessAnne notices her sitting there. "Oh, you're with someone," she says. "I'm sorry. I'll come back later."

She turns to go. The minute she's outside of the lobby doors, the elevator chimes and Claudia hears footsteps rounding the corner. "Hey Graham," she says, grateful it isn't someone else with some other disaster. She can at least count on him to be professional. "Guess who's—"

"Wait," he says. "Before you say anything, I have to get this out. It's about last night. I know you saw Liza and me together and it was only sex and—" Claudia widens her eyes and gestures frantically with her head, doing everything she can to alert him to Margo's presence, but he's not catching on. "Honestly, Claudia, I was only with Liza because I knew it couldn't be you. But I've always wanted it to be. I don't know what's between us, but it's *something*. I know you felt it too, the night we almost kissed." Claudia drops the coffee carafe and the metal clangs against the lobby tile, spilling coffee everywhere. Margo jumps up from the sofa and Graham freezes.

"Claudia." Margo's voice is stern and Claudia knows she's in trouble. Deep trouble. Her head is spinning and in the midst of all of this chaos, she knows with pure clarity that the most important thing right now is to make sure Ingrid knows what happened to Paxton.

"I..." she stammers. "I'm sorry, I have to go."

She grabs her purse, the work laptop, and the flash drive from her office in record time, while Margo and Graham stand watching, speechless. Claudia runs from the lobby and into the stairwell, nearly twisting her ankle in her goddamned heels.

She gets in her car and drives. She doesn't know where to go, but she's got to finish watching that camera footage, and she sure as hell can't do it at work. The parking lot at The Gilded Mug is mostly empty this time of day, and Claudia pulls in on a whim. Inside, the shop is alive with indie music and two laughing baristas. She hurriedly orders a coffee and takes a table, puts her phone on silent, then opens up the laptop and gets back to her task.

She starts the camera footage right where she left off, when the unknown man steps into Paxton's apartment. He's in there for over an hour. Late night turns to early morning hours, and Claudia almost can't watch because she is certain, now, that on the other side of that door,

Paxton is being killed. And it's far too late to do anything about it. She feels a tear slide down her cheek. It's too much to bear. Finally, onscreen, the door opens and the man steps out, alone. His hood is down this time, and she can see his face clearly. She stares at the screen.

Ingrid was right.

Thomas McIntyre turns back to the door, and she can see him studying the door frame and then the door mat. He leans down and lifts the corner of the mat, pulls out a spare key. She notices that he's wearing gloves. It causes him to fumble with the key for a moment before he uses it to lock the door, then he slides it back under the mat.

He glances down the hallway. It's amazing that he doesn't encounter anyone. After all, Janie's hosting a party right down the hall. Claudia keeps expecting Thomas to look up, but somehow he doesn't notice the camera. Instead, he hurries to the elevator and then he's gone.

Paxton hadn't walked him to the door. Paxton had been clearly alive when Thomas got there, and yet he hadn't walked Thomas out. And Thomas had purposefully looked for a key to lock the door behind him. He'd wanted people to believe the door was locked from the inside.

Claudia doesn't know exactly *why* Thomas wanted to kill Paxton, but it seems apparent that he did. She has to get the proof to Ingrid. She rummages through her purse for the flash drive and downloads the footage, then closes the security camera program. *Stay focused,* she reminds herself, when the reality of how deeply she's screwed up at work threatens to overtake her. She'll deal with that later.

Claudia gets in her car and dials Ingrid's office phone number, but she's not in. Of course she's not. She tries her cell but it goes to voicemail. There are four text messages on Claudia's phone.

Well? From Ingrid. *Did you watch the cameras yesterday?*

Was it him?

Claudia, I'm running out of time here, I've got to get ready soon.

And from Ruby: *Did you get the proof??? Was it him???*

Claudia's phone rings in her hand and she sees Margo's number flash up on the screen. She declines it. Surely Margo is calling to fire her. There can't be any other outcome. All of the years she's put in at The Prestige have come down to this. Claudia wonders what will happen to Graham. She shouldn't have left him there all alone with Margo. She should have stayed there to explain. Explain what, though? There's no good explanation.

Claudia drives toward Ingrid's office, racing down the streets at a good twenty miles over the speed limit while she tries to text Ingrid and still keep her eyes on the road. Her phone rings again, and this time it's Beau. Her first thought is that he's found out about her work debacle already.

"Yes?" she says. She wonders if he can hear the panic in her voice. She feels like a thread with too many frayed edges. She is coming apart.

"Claudia, where are you?"

"What?"

"Did you leave work early, like you'd planned? Ingrid's engagement party, remember? It starts in an hour." She looks at the clock. 5:00. Finishing the security camera footage had taken longer than she'd thought.

"Shit," she says. "I got behind, things happened at the office..." she trails off, unsure how to explain.

"I don't care what happened at the office." Beau's annoyance is evident, and she thinks of calling him on it, of airing her grievances with him now. Everything else is out in the open, why not this? She could tell him how she knows he's been seeing Amberly, that she'd almost crossed a line with Graham, that this marriage was in shambles even before other people were involved. "It's important that we're on time to this party, Claudia."

"Don't you think I know that? Ingrid is my best friend."

"And she's my *boss*."

"I know that, and I—"

"*I don't care*," Beau says. "Get home, get ready, and let's get to this party."

Claudia ends the call. "Fuck," she mutters. She makes a u-turn in the middle of the street and heads toward home, ignoring the car horns blaring behind her. She'll find Ingrid and Ruby at the party.

***

Claudia slips into the navy dress she's had steamed and ready for this occasion for weeks, since before she knew that her best friend was fake-engaged to a killer. Thank goodness Claudia had prepared, since Beau is already downstairs waiting for her. She looks at her reflection in the mirror. She has the answers now, about what happened to Paxton. He was murdered by Thomas McIntyre. Claudia should be able to move on, now that she knows.

But she'll never have what she really needs. In the end the only thing Paxton and Killian had in common is that their lives were both cut abruptly short. And the people who loved them were left searching for answers that were either entirely inadequate...or that never existed at all.

***

Beau is unusually surly on the way to the Wyatt mansion. "If traffic is light, we can still make it on time," he says in a quiet voice.

Claudia smooths her dress. She thinks of telling him what she knows about Thomas, about how this entire party is nothing but theater. It's only important to Ingrid in the context of setting Thomas McIntyre up to take one big fall.

But she doesn't tell him that. "We'll make it on time," she says, instead.

"No thanks to you."

Beau isn't usually so confrontational, and his words ignite something inside of her. She's going to explode if she keeps holding everything in, so she turns her head to look at him and just blurts it out. "I know about you and Amberly Vance."

"*What?*" He looks away from the road and into her eyes with such an expression of shock that she almost laughs. "Who?"

"She's my resident. Did you honestly not expect me to find out? I saw you two, at the restaurant."

Beau's jaw is clenched. "She had to interview someone in my field, for a class project. She looked me up online. It was completely innocent."

"And I'm sure you were the only person she could possibly think of. If it was so innocent, why didn't you tell me about it?"

Beau is silent, his eyes back on the road.

"She tried to kill her last boyfriend, so might want to be careful with her."

"Claudia. I'm not her goddamned boyfriend."

"It's fine. I guess I shouldn't have felt so bad about almost kissing Graham."

Beau slams on his brakes just in time to avoid smashing into the car in front of them. "About *what?*"

"I guess we both have secrets."

At a red light, he turns to her again and she's surprised, and confused, to see the hurt in his eyes behind his silver-rimmed glasses. "Damnit, Claudia. Why are you *like this?*"

"Like what?"

"I didn't do anything with that college girl," he says. "She wanted to interview me. It made me feel important, I guess. But you, you and that guy from work...what does this even mean for us?"

"It means we can stop pretending."

"I was never pretending."

"Right." Claudia takes a deep breath. "Let's say you're telling the truth about Amberly. Maybe you are. But you're *still* not invested in our relationship. I can't get your attention, and I sure as hell can't keep it. Sometimes I feel like I live in our house alone."

"Claudia," he says quietly. "I have loved you since the moment I met you. But I can't get close to you. You won't let me. You keep me at arm's length, you always have. I used to think once we were married, it would be different. But we've been married for years now, and nothing has changed. You don't want anyone to know you. You don't want anyone to *see* you. Not your family, not your friends. Not me. I don't know why, and you'd never tell me. But it's hard, you know? It's fucking hard. So yeah, I retreat. It's the only way I know how to handle not having the kind of connection I want to have with my *wife*."

She looks at him, stunned. His words sink in. Is this how he sees her, really?

"We're here," he says. "Let's go celebrate the happy couple."

***

The Wyatt mansion is like something out of an old Southern movie, and it's all dressed up for this special occasion. Clusters of camellias, sourced from Ruby's favorite flower market in Atlanta, are arranged in vases of various sizes throughout the grand foyer and on the cocktail tables set up in the sunroom. A man takes their coats and directs them to a receiving line in the parlor, where Ingrid, Thomas, Mr. Wyatt, and an older couple greet guests. Mr. Wyatt is beaming from his seated position and laughing with each person as they pass. Classical music plays from somewhere inside.

Claudia smooths her hair self-consciously as she waits to get to Ingrid. Beau's words run through her mind on a loop. Could it be true, the things that he said? She's spent their entire relationship trying not to let her true reckless nature show, trying to be what she thought he wanted. And yet...could it possibly be that he wanted to know her, fully, scars and all, and he knew all along that she was holding back? The thought lodges in her chest, and she rubs her hand over the spot to try to ease the pain. Beau looks sharp and clean-shaven beside her in his suit and tie. It's rare to see him dressed up like this and she can easily see how someone else, someone like Amberly, might want him.

When they reach Ingrid, Beau attempts to change his tense expression to one of excitement. It doesn't quite work, and he ends up wearing the look of a deer in headlights. "Congrats, you two," Beau says, leaning in to kiss Ingrid on the cheek. Claudia does the same to Thomas, thinking all the while that she's *this close* to a killer. Then they switch, and Beau shakes hands heartily with Thomas while Claudia leans in to give Ingrid a hug. "I have to talk to you," Claudia says, into Ingrid's ear. "It can't wait. I have the video."

"You were supposed to let me know that earlier. Now it *has* to wait," Ingrid says, with a smile on her face. She looks as composed as if Claudia had just complimented her outfit. "I think I saw Ruby talking to the bartender a few minutes ago, if you want to find her." Claudia can feel the man and woman behind them, eager to get their hands on the engaged couple. Ingrid *is* stunning in her gold knee-length dress with the big rock twinkling on her finger.

"Find me," Claudia mouths to her as Beau pulls Claudia away and into the crowded ballroom. Ingrid is already smiling at the next person in the line.

There is nothing to do but wait. She and Beau head to the bar and Claudia orders white wine. She doesn't see Ruby. "We obviously need to have a serious discussion," Beau says, in a low voice. "But this is not the time, and it's certainly not the place."

"Agreed," Claudia murmurs, and takes a sip of her wine. And another. "We'll save it for later."

"Claudia!" Ruby comes out from the kitchen, dressed in a shimmery black jumpsuit. "What do you think of everything? Hey, Beau," she says. "You cleaned up nice."

He smiles, like he and Claudia aren't in the middle of a marital crisis. "Thank you, Ruby. You look lovely, yourself. I think I'll leave you two ladies to catch up."

They smile after him as he walks away, and then Ruby grabs Claudia's arm. "Did Thomas do it? Did you get the proof? We've been trying to reach you all day. Are we doing this, or what?"

"He did it. He was at Paxton's apartment that night."

Ruby's eyes grow wide. "Damn. I really thought we'd be wrong. Shows how little I know about the man of the hour."

"Yeah, I know. And Ingrid still wants to go through with this?"

Ruby nods. "I've asked her about a thousand times today. She's sure. I'll get all the audio connected. And then we wait, I guess."

"Ingrid doesn't know yet. That he's on camera, I mean. That she was right."

"You talk to her and let her know the plan is a go. I'll work on set-up."

"Got it."

But it's another half hour before she can get a one-on-one with Ingrid. Claudia is standing in a small group with Beau and his coworkers; they are laughing about some client and his quirks and Claudia has mostly tuned the whole thing out when she sees Ingrid finally headed her way. The group turns toward her as she approaches.

"Everyone enjoying themselves?" she asks. "There's dancing in the garden after dessert. I expect to see you all on the dance floor." She laughs and they do too, and then she takes Claudia by the elbow. "If you'll excuse us ladies for a quick moment..." she trails off and leads Claudia away.

"What did you find?" Ingrid asks.

Claudia glances around, instinctively wanting to gauge Thomas's whereabouts, lest he hear her spilling his secret.

"I watched the rest of the security camera footage. You were right." She hands over the thumb drive she's had clutched in her palm since she left her coat and purse at the entry when they arrived. "It was Thomas. He killed Paxton. I'm sure of it."

Ingrid may have put together an intricate plan to bring down Thomas McIntyre, but Claudia can tell that Ingrid hadn't *really* wanted to believe she would need to follow through with it. The color drains from her face, the red of her lipstick shining like blood on white linen. She's ready though, her shoulders squared and those red lips a determined line.

"He was at Paxton's apartment that night. He must have followed you, like you thought. The only thing I can think of is that he caught sight of the text messages from Amberly while he was there, and set the scene accordingly. It's too big of a coincidence for him not to have seen Paxton's phone."

"Does the footage show it? The...murder?" Ingrid asks.

"No. Just Thomas arriving, and then leaving. He does some weird things with the door key. It's all suspicious. Incriminating. But the rest is up to you. If this is still what you want to do. Are you sure you're sure?

We could take the camera footage to the police, keep it quiet. It doesn't have to go down like this, here."

"It does," Ingrid says quietly. "Everyone has to know. Thomas McIntyre needs to be ruined."

They're interrupted by a man walking up behind Ingrid and putting a hand on her shoulder, paying no mind to the fact that she's clearly in the middle of a conversation. "I'll handle it," Ingrid says to her, before she turns her attention to the man.

Claudia slips to the bar for a fresh glass of wine. The French doors are propped open near the bar and she can see outside into the lush, opulent garden. It's a mild and lovely September night. A pebbled path opens up into a round green lawn, and there's a checkerboard dance floor set up there beneath a white tent, surrounded by heat lamps that aren't turned on.

Her marriage is over. She knows it, she feels it. There's no coming back from her confession about Graham, from *whatever* Beau has been doing with Amberly, from the trauma Claudia has carried around all these years but never been able to share.

Her job is likely over as well. Margo wouldn't ignore the kind of conduct she witnessed today.

It's all over. It's a terrifying realization, the finality of it.

The relief of it.

She thinks of Killian. Her Killian, who may have been the love of her life but who was also a goddamned liar.

His death had been devastating enough, but then Claudia had walked into the Southern Baptist church in Dallas for his funeral and met his mother and father and brother...and Killian's *girlfriend*. A pretty brunette in a preppy dress, dabbing her eyes and talking about Killian like he'd belonged to her. *High school sweethearts*, his mother said.

All the time Killian had been curled around Claudia, all of those nights he'd told her his dreams, his secrets, all of that time there had been someone else waiting for him back home. For some godforsaken reason Killian's parents had chosen an open casket and so Killian was just *lying there*, doing nothing, while this shiny girl stood in front of the casket next to a giant photo of Killian and spoke about how she was supposed to have married him one day.

And Claudia sat there, and listened. The brown roots of her hair were pushing into the faded blue. Her dagger tattoo peeked out from the neckline of her black dress. She tried to ignore the looks. No one besides Killian's roommate knew her or what she was doing there (*a friend of Killian's* was how she'd introduced herself) but there were whispers. There were looks. *I'm sorry*, Killian's roommate mouthed to her during the service. She and the roommate had formed a kind of kinship, based on what they'd seen together. Claudia just shrugged because what else could she do? She didn't know if he had known about the girlfriend, but even if he had and even if he'd told Claudia all about it, there's no way she would have believed it until she sat here and saw it all unfold before her eyes.

It turned out that Killian had been living with bipolar disorder. Killian's roommate had told her, the morning they stood together and watched paramedics try, and fail, to revive Killian. He'd been diagnosed in high school. But he'd been okay. He had medication and a long-distance *girlfriend* and a stable college life. And then one random day, he'd met Claudia in a coffee shop. Claudia, the passionate, destructive girl who'd leaned right over the counter and kissed him on the mouth and tilted his world off its axis. He'd stopped taking his meds shortly after that. The signs were there that something was off, but Claudia had missed them.

She understood, there, at the funeral, that she was the reason Killian was dead. She'd killed him. Not the way that Thomas McIntyre had killed Paxton; not even the way that Amberly had tried to kill Paxton. Claudia had killed Killian just by being herself. Her wild, carefree, careless self. She'd dragged him down a road that had taken him away from the safe life he'd created and right into his own doom.

Killian was gone. But Claudia would make sure she never had another opportunity to ruin someone's life so thoroughly. She'd change herself so she'd never be driven by that passion again, so no one else could get swept up in it.

And that's exactly what she'd done.

Even in this fresh air and in her strappy dress, Claudia feels clammy. She's got to get away from here, even if it's only for a moment. She opens the wrought iron gate and makes her way to the sidewalk on the other side of the mansion.

She walks around the block of the historic neighborhood, glancing in the windows of the old stately manors and ignoring the pain of her shoes rubbing at her heels. She'd like to walk farther, right out of the neighborhood and into the forest and up to the top of Ellen Point, even. The moonlight and the streetlamps keep her from feeling suffocated by the darkness or the looming mountains; it's peaceful out here. But she knows she's got to get back to the party. Things have been set in motion, and she's got to be there for Ingrid when it all comes together. Or falls apart, depending on how you look at it. So she walks back up the path, through the iron gate, into the Wyatt's garden, and through the French doors. She can see the expansive dining room from here, can see everyone seated in preparation for dinner. Beau's been looking for her, she can tell by the way he catches her eye immediately, gesturing to the empty seat beside him. She heads in his direction, but just then there's a record-scratch sound, and everyone glances to the large speakers near the band's set-up. The jazz band has gone on break, and there's no music drifting from those speakers now.

Only the sound of Thomas McIntyre's voice.

CHAPTER 36

I ngrid has to admit, it's a beautiful engagement party. Twinkling lights, jazz band playing, delicious food. It's exactly the party Ingrid's father wanted. Even Harley had made the trip, though he'd pulled her aside again and asked why she hadn't broken off the engagement yet. *I know what I'm doing*, she'd insisted, and she hopes it's the truth. At least she and Willard have finally gotten to meet Mia, Harley's elusive girlfriend. Ingrid can see that her father is happy, and she hates to ruin his night.

But she's going to.

Every bit of this party is meaningless, absurd, *disgusting* in light of her grief. She understands the part she needs to play, but it's nearly impossible to force a smile—real or not—when Paxton is dead. And the man who killed him is right beside her.

She and Thomas McIntyre know this night is a sham. And yet, here they are chatting up family friends, their hands clasped together. It's a performance, and she has to fight the urge to recoil. When she looks at him, she sees a monster. Tonight is the night that everyone else will see it too.

Good.

The only thing that comes close to matching the magnitude of her grief is her thirst for vengeance. It's not enough for Thomas to be arrested. She needs him *ruined*, seen by everyone—Willard Wyatt, the

McIntyre family, the entire Ellen Point social scene—for what he is. That's why she'd chosen tonight, this celebration, this moment when he thinks he's winning.

"I need to talk to you," she murmurs, as they mingle around the room.

"Then let's talk, darling," he says, with a charming smile.

"I was thinking of a more...private conversation."

When the song ends, Ingrid leads him to her father's downstairs office, a room with a door. She closes it, even though she's about to confront a killer. Her phone is on a shelf nearby, where she'd intentionally left it atop a stack of books. She turns her back and discreetly presses the "Record" button before spinning to face Thomas.

They stare at each other. "Well?" he says finally.

"I know what you did," she says, trying to sound casual even though she feels like lashing out. She'd like to pull him limb from limb with her bare hands. But, it's important that she stay calm if she wants his confession. Ruby has made sure that Ingrid's phone is connected to the speakers outside, and the band has been instructed to take a break in five minutes. Everything is in place. Now it's up to Thomas to tell the truth.

"I'm sure I don't know what you mean," he says.

Don't let him deny it, she thinks. Everything rides on her bet that he'll make a smug confession. "You do. I have to hand it to you. I didn't think you wanted your money so badly that you'd actually kill for it."

He smiles. "Ah. That. That had nothing to do with the money. That was just for fun. It was all part of our little game."

The acknowledgment is too much. She steps close to him, looks him in the eye. She doesn't realize she's slapped him until she feels the stinging in her hand. So much for calm and casual. "You're a murderer. You killed Paxton Gale."

There's a gleam in his eye, even as he rubs his cheek. He strolls around her father's desk, studying the bookshelves. She prays he doesn't see her phone lying among the books. "So? You think you can control every-thing, Ingrid Wyatt, but you can't control *me*. You took away something I wanted, and in return, I took away something you wanted."

Like it's that simple, and Paxton was nothing more than a plaything. Like a pile of money is equivalent to a human life.

"How did you even know about him?"

He tells her everything, and he does it gleefully. It's more than she wants to know, and more than enough for a confession. He tells her about seeing a racy text message on her phone, and about the first time he followed her to The Prestige to see what she was up to. On the night of the murder, he followed her again, pretending to be a grocery delivery driver to get a resident to let him into the building, and tracked her right up to the apartment. How easy it was. He waited in the stairwell until she left. When Paxton heard the knock on the door, he thought it was Ingrid returning. Thomas stuck him with a needle the minute he opened the door.

It was the same drug cocktail he'd used on his business partner, back in Portland.

"I cared for his wife," he says, of his business partner. "She was too good for him. I *thought* she loved me too." So he *was* stupid enough to fall in love, after all. Talking about this mystery woman is the only time he sneers. Thomas thought he would get all of the money from the joint business venture, and that he'd have the woman's full attention once her husband was out of the way. But he didn't get the money, and the woman took out a restraining order when he tried to make a pass at her.

"My business partner tried to fight back, and I had to stage an entire car crash to cover the injuries," Thomas says. "I did what had to be done, but it was a learning experience. Your young lover was too surprised by my appearance to try anything at all. He was dead in minutes. Now, now. There's no need to cry. He didn't suffer. I'd planned to frame you for his murder, you know. Wouldn't *that* have been a story? Business mogul turned sugar mama turned killer. I love the sound of that. Maybe it would have been more fun to go that route. But fate intervened. Turns out I'm not the only one who wanted the boy dead." He pulls out a cigar and twirls it between his fingers. "It was easy. And Ingrid, knowing it would hurt you made it feel *so* good."

"Why are you telling me this?" Ingrid asks, pretending to pace back and forth until her steps bring her to the bookshelf. She leans against, as if standing is too much. It's not far from the truth, but her proximity to the shelf gives her the chance to stop her recording, and then to press play. It's the riskiest part; so much could go wrong now. If the Bluetooth connection doesn't work and his voice plays back here, in her father's office, Thomas will know he's been recorded. But no sound comes from the phone, which means Thomas's confession *should* be playing outside of the room, over the speakers as she'd intended.

"Because you're not going to do anything about it," Thomas says, and she can tell that he actually believes it. The same overconfidence that led him to believe he could go after WMB if he really wanted to is what makes him think she'd never challenge him. "You hate me," he continues, "but here we are. You care so much about what your father thinks that you'll keep this going for as long as you can. Hell, we might actually end up at the altar before it's all said and done, right *darling*? Admit it, Ingrid, this game between us thrills you too. You're just upset that this time, I got the upper hand."

She shouldn't be surprised that he's misread her. He doesn't know that she'd already made peace with sacrificing her reputation and her father's approval to be with Paxton. So she smiles, tightly. "I can't wait to get you back for this. And you know I will."

"I look forward to it. For now, why don't we go back to enjoying our engagement party?" But when he opens the door to Willard Wyatt's office and makes his way to the dining room, his own voice is booming over the speakers and there are a roomful of stunned faces staring at him.

"I think I'll take my revenge sooner rather than later," Ingrid says, quietly.

Carter McIntyre stands. "What is this, son?"

"*Your young lover, on the other hand...*"

Ingrid looks to her father, holding a breath. "Is this some sort of game?" Willard asks. "Or is this...is this the truth?"

Ingrid nods. "It's all true."

Her father slams down a fist on the dinner table. "This man is a...a...killer. Get him out of here!" Elodie Rose's police officer husband stands and strides toward Thomas.

From there, everything turns to chaos.

Thomas looks around at the sea of faces, then he turns and pushes past Ingrid so forcefully that she falls to the ground. He takes off running, with Elodie Rose's husband chasing after him and Carter McIntyre following behind. Eugenia McIntyre drops her martini glass and it shatters on the floor. Harley helps Willard out of his chair and to a standing position. "What on earth is going on?" June Pressman keeps asking to no one in particular and everyone all at once, probably because she wants to be sure she gets the details straight. Ruby and Claudia are at Ingrid's side before she knows it, each of them grasping an elbow and helping her off the floor.

"Are you okay, sweetie?" Ruby asks.

"It worked," says Claudia. "You fucking did it."

Ingrid doesn't answer, not yet. She's waiting. Thomas has made his way out the French doors. He's probably in the garden by now. He probably thinks he'll get away.

Then she hears it, the loud, sharp groan of pain.
That's how she knows the mushrooms have kicked in.

CHAPTER 37

"Well good morning," Claudia says, when she opens her front door for Ingrid the next day.

"It's official. I'm *un*engaged," Ingrid says.

"Well yeah, since your fiancé is dead and all."

"He's not dead, you know that. It's a coma."

"I could have sworn the plan was to out him as a killer and then have him arrested."

"I never specifically *said* that was the entire plan."

"Want to tell me why he collapsed in the garden?" Thomas McIntyre may have tried to run away last night, but he hadn't gotten far before he'd fallen to the ground, clutching his chest. An ambulance had arrived shortly after the police cruisers, and Thomas had been carted off to the hospital, leaving a yard full of confused guests gossiping amongst themselves.

"Depends. I don't want you two to get into trouble." Ingrid follows Claudia to the kitchen, where Ruby is sitting on a barstool with a cup of coffee. Beau had slept on the sofa last night after the party and had decided to spend his Saturday at work. The dramatic events of the party hadn't been enough to overshadow everything that had gone wrong between them. "You know, this really is such a pretty house."

"I know. It's a shame I'll be leaving it soon," Claudia says.

"What? What do you mean?" Ingrid asks.

"Beau and I..." Claudia says. "Let's just say we don't have what you think we have." She has more questions for Ingrid about what happened last night, but she doesn't want to hold back her own truth from her friends any longer. So she lets it all out: How she'd intentionally buried part of herself when she buried her first love, how she'd kept Beau at arm's length, how she'd become obsessed with Paxton and his death because it reminded her so much of Killian, how she'd come so close to kissing her work colleague in a drunken moment, how she'd followed Beau and caught him with Paxton's ex-girlfriend, how Beau swore it was nothing but everything is broken between them now, and how she is starting to see that it is mostly her own damned fault.

"Jesus," Ingrid says. "That's...kind of messed up."

"Well, I didn't try to kill Beau yet so I think your situation still tops mine," Claudia says drily.

Ruby bursts out laughing. "I'm sorry, none of this is funny. It's just..." She gestures to them both. "so, so messed up. Unhinged, really, the both of you." Despite the mood, Ruby's laughter is infectious and for a moment the three of them get caught up in a fit of hysterics, laughter and tears mixing together before it tapers off and the quiet settles around them again.

"Will you really leave?" Ingrid asks. "Is that the decision?"

"We haven't talked about it in detail yet, but I think I will."

"I'm sorry." Ingrid sits down on a barstool and Claudia pours her a mug of coffee.

"So? Last night? Cream and sugar?"

"Both please. You know most of it. That monster admitted to everything, like we hoped he would. I didn't even have to tell him about the camera footage."

"So, all that time I spent getting it was a waste?"

"No, it will be helpful one day, if he ever wakes up."

"Back to that."

"You did great with the Bluetooth setup, Ruby. I still can't believe Thomas spilled all of those details. I'm glad the guests heard every word." Claudia grabs a box of tissues from the counter and passes it to Ingrid when she sees the tears in her eyes.

"I can't help thinking, if I'd never taken Thomas's call in the first place or agreed to his stupid fake engagement..." Ingrid shakes her head. "Hell, if I'd stayed over at Paxton's apartment that night..."

"It doesn't help to think like that," Ruby says. "But I must say, your fiancé is a real piece of work."

Ingrid holds up the naked ring finger of her left hand. "Ex-fiancé, I thought we cleared that up."

"Ingrid," Claudia interrupts. "Why is Thomas in the hospital?"

"You saw it," Ingrid says, her eyes wide and innocent. "Everyone did. He just lost consciousness and dropped to the ground."

"Right then, at that exact moment?" Ruby says.

Ingrid raises her eyebrows. "Guess it was all the action. Strange, isn't it?"

Claudia sips her coffee. "What *really* happened?"

"You could be considered accomplices, if you knew."

"Ingrid Wyatt, tell us the truth!" Ruby says.

Ingrid wipes at her eyes with a tissue, looks back and forth between them, and shrugs. "Mushrooms happened."

"I'm sorry, what?"

"Heart of Death mushrooms. Amanita Cormeuma. No idea if I'm pronouncing it right. The poisoning symptoms present like a heart attack. They're supposed to be undetectable, at least that's what the newsletter said. We'll see what happens. It's not like I had any way to test them first."

"I'm sorry, *mushrooms*?"

"Remember the Friends of the Stream, and how they fought me on that land last year?"

Ruby and Claudia nod.

"Well, one of the reasons they wanted to protect that land is because a rare, toxic mushroom grows there."

"And?"

"And I went out there, okay? At night. It wasn't a glamorous experience. I picked the mushrooms and I prepared them according to the instructions I found online. I switched Thomas's hors d'oeuvres plate when he set it down, and *his* wild mushroom tarts were, well, extra-wild."

"Ingrid!" Ruby exclaims. "That could have gone wrong in so many ways. My team prepped that food. I could have been blamed."

"But it didn't. And you weren't."

"You poisoned him."

"I'm not proud of myself," Ingrid says. "Actually, I am. Can you believe all of that worked? Or, worked well enough, I guess. I *meant* to kill the bastard."

"You poisoned a man," Claudia repeats.

"I did what I had to do. I didn't know he'd be so eager to confess, and a part of me thought that even if he did, he would still end up talking his way out of it...and he had to be punished. This was...a failsafe. I didn't even *know* about what he did to his business partner. Thomas got what he deserved."

"Wow." Claudia looks, wide-eyed, at Ingrid. "I'm impressed. And a little afraid. You could get into serious trouble if anyone finds out about this. What about your company, and everything?"

"He *killed* Paxton. I've thought a lot about this, and about how my role in Thomas's stupid game led to Paxton's death. I'll take responsibility for whatever comes next." Claudia and Ruby know as well as Ingrid does that there's a good chance nothing *will* come next. With a family as connected as Ingrid's, there would have to be pretty damning evidence to turn suspicion to Ingrid.

"You were careful, covering your tracks?" Claudia asks. Ingrid nods.

"And what about your family?" says Ruby. "Your dad, and Harley? How'd they take it all?"

"Obviously, they don't know about the mushrooms. The rest? Harley never trusted Thomas, but even he was shocked to find out what Thomas was capable of. My father is upset. I told him everything, except, you know, the poison part. I told him about Paxton and me. Dad agrees that Thomas McIntyre got what he deserved, but he still wishes I hadn't chosen such a public way of bringing it to light. Reputation, and all that. But I'm done with caring about my reputation. Let them talk."

Claudia is amazed by how collected Ingrid appears, even after all of this. "Are you okay, honestly? You know all of this will be in the paper."

"Screw the paper. And I'm not sure I'll ever be okay. I have so many regrets. If Paxton had never met me, he'd still be alive."

"Don't do that to yourself," Ruby says.

"The police. Did they report all of this to Paxton's family?" Claudia thinks of Marilyn and TessAnne.

"They said they would."

"At least they'll have some answers."

"Yes, at least there's that."

The silence takes over again as they each try to process their own thoughts. As they try to pretend they feel better about it all than they really do.

***

It's almost too easy for Claudia and Beau to separate. There's no going back, now that everything is out in the open. There's too much hurt, too much mistrust. All that is left is the paperwork, dividing their money and assets and making it official. Claudia doesn't care much how it all shakes out. She'd been the one to offer to leave. Beau loves this house and their neighborhood more than she does. She doesn't know what will become of Beau and Amberly, but she'd told him everything she knew about Amberly's role in Paxton's demise. Let him make his own choices from here.

Claudia pulls clothes from her closet, stuffing them into a black garbage bag. The things she'll need immediately are already packed in her suitcase and loaded into the trunk of her car, but it all has to be moved sometime. Beau has been avoiding the house while she's been packing up, so she might as well get as many of her things as she can.

She's renting Ingrid's condo. The former tenants had moved out with short notice due to a job transfer, and Ingrid had promised not to charge her an arm and a leg since Claudia is now both unemployed and in the middle of a divorce.

Claudia could have actually managed to hold onto her job, if she'd wanted. Graham had thrown vague excuses at Margo after Claudia had fled the building: that what Margo had heard was a misunderstanding and something about The Prestige employees having a difficult time with the recent resident death. He wasn't wrong about that. Claudia can see, now, how unhealthy it had been to burrow so deeply into Paxton's life. Into his death. Since she'd ultimately gotten to the truth, though, she finds that she doesn't regret it.

Unbelievably, Margo had been willing to forget all she'd overheard, in light of the situation. But Claudia put in her two weeks' notice anyway. Too much is ruined for her at The Prestige. She doesn't trust herself to be in charge of anyone right now, least of all Graham. She can't deny that she'd felt a spark with him, that night all those weeks ago, and that she'd been jealous when she saw him with Liza. But she doesn't need another man on her mind right now.

She has an appointment with a therapist next week. Maybe, with some help, she can work through her guilt related to Killian's death. Who knows who she really is, underneath the weight of it all?

She'd filled out a job application at The Gilded Mug and she has an interview scheduled there next week. She's got some money saved up, and the coffee shop seems like a nice place to be while she figures out her next steps. She's got the experience, after all. She's also promised to help Ruby spruce up Kennamer Farms for wedding season.

Yesterday afternoon, Ingrid and TessAnne Gale had met her at The Prestige. It was an awkward meeting, Paxton's sister and his lover, but they had one last mission before Claudia was done there for good. They'd gone right up to Amberly's apartment and confronted her about the text messages. In exchange for not turning Amberly in to the police, they'd asked for one thing: Paxton's dog. None of them—Claudia, Ingrid, TessAnne, or Marilyn—knew if Amberly could actually be prosecuted for her role in Paxton's murder. The Gale family wasn't pursuing it once they learned there was an *actual* murderer who'd killed Paxton with his own hands. But the threat was effective, and Claudia suspected that Amberly didn't want the dog anyway. Ingrid did, and she left The Prestige with a delighted Charlie in her arms.

Nothing they did could bring Paxton back. But they didn't feel quite as hopeless as before.

Claudia turns her attention back to packing her things. In the back of the closet, her fingers brush against the familiar fabric of her old military jacket, the one she'd worn all the time back in college. She'd never been able to get rid of it because of how much Killian had liked it on her, but she hasn't worn it since his death. With a deep breath, she pulls it off the wire hanger. It's time to let it go, she realizes. She stares at the old thing, at the worn sleeves, the small coffee stain above the left side pocket. She sits down there, on the closet floor with the jacket in her lap.

Everything is ending.

But in a way, it's beginning too.

The weight of the jacket is familiar and comforting. Hesitantly, she slides in one arm and then the other. It's still big on her.

Sometimes the *why* is missing. Sometimes the *why* doesn't exist. She's trying to make peace with unanswered questions.

Claudia stuffs her hands into the pockets of the jacket. Her fingers graze something stiff inside the right pocket, but she can't get at it. It's hidden somehow. She holds the right side of the jacket away from her body with one hand and runs the other hand along the inside, to the interior pockets. When she slides her hand in, she feels paper. She pulls it out, holds it in her palm, stares at it in horror.

In wonder.

It's a piece of notebook paper, yellowed with age and folded into a small square. She carefully unfolds the edges to see that it's a letter, written in Killian's precise scrawl. She's never seen this before. She drops the letter to the carpet, but it's face-up and too much to ignore.

It's dated the night Killian died.

And it has Claudia's name at the top.

ACKNOWLEDGMENTS

Gather round, friends. Time to give hugs and flowers to the people who helped make this book happen.

Writing a book feels impossible and inevitable all at once. I'm proud of *myself*, this time, for pushing on past the impossible part to get to the good stuff. I'm so proud of this book, and I hope you feel it on the page.

The biggest, biggest thanks to my precious family—especially my sweet mama, whose belief in me is unshakeable nearly to the point of delusion.

And to Jason and Ryan, besties who *feel* like family, for all of the love and support (and margaritas and laughter and gossip.)

To the late great Freddy Jones, whose wild stories gave me inspiration. You'd have been the biggest champion of this book.

To Jenna, who was kind enough to read an early draft of this story and *not* tell me the whole thing was garbage (even when it was).

To my cover artist, Rachel Christley at The Author Buddy. Thanks for creating a cover that made everything else fall into place. And to my final beta reader, Perrin Brunson, also at The Author Buddy, whose feedback gave me just what I needed.

Thank you to Sarra Cannon, whose courses and encouragement and Heart Breathings community have given me so much this past year and to Amie McNee, a beacon of rebellious light for creatives everywhere.

So much love for the book bloggers, Bookstagrammers, and Booktokers out there who have changed the game (and changed authors' lives) by hyping up the books they care about.

Finally, to the readers. Thank you so much for supporting my Southern sad girl fiction. I hope this book makes you feel all the feelings. If you enjoyed Her Younger Self, it would mean so much to me if you would take a few moments to leave a review on your book site(s) of choice.

I've tackled some heavy topics in this work, and I hope I've handled them with care and compassion. Any missteps are my own.

ABOUT THE AUTHOR

Haley Harrigan writes stories about flawed Southern women and the messes they find themselves in. A flawed and messy Southern woman herself, she feels especially qualified to do this. Haley is the author of *Secrets of Southern Girls* and *Her Younger Self*. She graduated from the University of Georgia with a degree in Creative Writing, and she lives in Georgia with her family. She is a member of the Women's Fiction Writers Association. When she's not writing, you can find Haley reading books, buying books, happily buried underneath a stack of books, binge-watching TV shows from the early 2000s, organizing her planner in hopes of eventually organizing her life, or dutifully taking orders from the tiny rulers of her household (one adventurous daughter and one very sassy dog).

If you enjoyed Her Younger Self, get ready for more of Haley Harrigan's moody Southern style—this time with a dash of magic.

Just down the road from Ellen Point lies a small Southern town where whispers of magic fill the air...

The folks in Wildflower Glen adore a good rumor, and rumor has it that the Early Shop of Everything will give you what you need, whether you know you need it or not. But shop proprietor Cadence Early needs money, and the shop sure isn't giving her enough of that.

Rumor has it that the Early women are witches, but that's ridiculous. Sure, Cadence can *see* emotions, but that's hardly witchcraft. She's not even good at it.

Rumor has it that Early women don't need men. But there's a fine line between "don't need" and "can't keep," and Cadence has a story about a musician who trampled her heart.

Rumor has it the Early women keep to themselves, but as for Cadence, life with a chronic illness means she's not antisocial, she's just resting. (Okay, she might be just a *little* antisocial.)

When a true crime podcast host arrives in Wildflower Glen investigating a long-shuttered local nightclub and the suspicious disappearance of the club's owner, his findings threaten to upend the Early family's quirky reputation and twist it into something downright dangerous.

Because rumor has it one of the Early women is a murderer.

Lies and Lavender at the Early Shop of Everything coming soon! For release news and other updates, sign up for Haley's newsletter at www.haleyharrigan.com.